Nyagra's Falls

Nyagra's Falls

MICHELLE VALENTINE

A
SBI
PUBLICATION
A STREBOR BOOKS INTERNATIONAL LLC PUBLICATION
DISTRIBUTED BY SIMON & SCHUSTER, INC.

Published by

SBI

Strebor Books International LLC
P.O. Box 10127
Silver Spring, MD 20914
http://www.streborbooks.com

ISBN 0-9711953-4-X
LCCN 2002100265

Distributed by Simon & Schuster, Inc.
1230 Avenue of the Americas
New York, NY 10020
1-800-223-2336

Cover Illustration: Andre Harris
Typesetting and Interior Design: Kris Tobiassen

First Printing November 2002
Manufactured and Printed in the United States
10   9   8   7   6   5   4   3   2   1

This book is dedicated to—

My Mother, Dorothea McKenney, for her unconditional love, loyalty & support; for carrying me physically, emotionally, or financially when I was unable to carry myself; for loving & liking me when I couldn't bring myself to; & for always being proud of me no matter what roads I travel. I will always be a "Momma's Girl."

My one & only baby girl, Morgan Dorothea, for maturing my spirit & for motivating me to do & to be better; for making me take notice of & appreciate all that I might otherwise ignore; for showing me the elation & passion of the special love between a mother & her daughter. Just as I am, you too will always be a "Momma's Girl" & this is for your future, Cooki . . .

Every intelligent, beautiful woman out there who sometimes feels defeated in life and in love. "Mr. Right" is not just a concept. Happiness is not merely a theory. They do exist. Just hold your head high, don't change who you are, & never lower your standards or settle. God will send you all you need when you're able to handle it. Just be ready . . .

Acknowledgments

In bringing this project to fruition, I must acknowledge the following loving & supportive individuals who have made a major difference in my world and to whom I am eternally grateful:

God, thank You for bringing these words through my hands onto the paper, for giving me the patience & courage to pursue my dream & for giving others the ability to see & believe in my vision. Without You, I can do nothing but with You I can do it all.

The special men in my life who I know will always be there when or if I need them: My Dad, Larry McKenney, Sr.; Calvin Jones; Michael Bragg, & Haji Dixon.

My true sister-friends, who understand the real meaning of friendship & who have shown me nothing but support & love: Shonda Cheekes, my sister, to whom I am forever grateful to for introducing me to my publisher—without you, this may not have happened. We have a lot ahead of us—are you ready?—Jeanine Baez, Dalia Rodriguez, Kenyatta Toler, Taurina Carpenter & Diane Sampson.

The children who keep my spirit young & to whose village I belong: My brother, Larry, Jr.; Popi; Calina; Ramzey; Tasia; Mathew; Gabby; Heather & Halle.

The strong & powerful maternal figures that I am blessed to have in my life: Toni Stephens; Tori Green; Joyce Hendricks & Barbara Alberty.

My publisher, Zane, for believing in me.

My friends at Seligman.

My friends at XRN & The Coast to Coast Hip Hop Count Down.

Douglas Walrond, who in a very short amount of time has become a wonderful confidant, supporter and dear friend. I think you are the missing piece to my puzzle. Thank you for all that you are and for all that you inspire me to be. I love you more than words can say.

I thank you all for completing my universe & I hope I make you very proud.

One

As the second child in a family of six, I'm used to sharing things, but my man? I don't think so. Some women might say, "Just look the other way and reap the financial benefits—or better yet, get a little plaything of your own." But I just can't seem to get down with that program. We're well into the 21st century and AIDS is far too prevalent. I'm not about to let all the shit I've worked for during the past thirty-two years of my life get snuffed out just because I decided to receive the wrong penis. As they say, "I'm not going out like that!"

So as I look around the bedroom at all the crap he has, I ask myself, "Should I do like Angela Bassett in Waiting to Exhale and torch all his shit? Or should I be the nice Catholic girl my mamma raised me to be and neatly pack his bags?"

As acid boiled through my veins, I looked around the room and simply could not decide.

Michael and I lived in a townhouse we purchased two years before I caught his ass screwing around on me with some little hoochie chicken. We'd been dating off and on for almost four years and despite outside pressures, neither of us was really ready to get married. We were both still working on securing our careers. He'd just opened his own dental practice and I'd recently secured a vice presidency at an extremely successful advertising agency. Needless to say, neither of us was hurting for money.

To be honest, our relationship hadn't been all that great for a while—at least seven or eight months. I continued to stay because I'd already invested a great deal of time into it and I didn't feel like starting all over. Since I was already used to Michael's games and bullshit, I wasn't in a hurry to find, train, and get used to someone else. Plus, being the crazed security freak that I am, I knew I'd always be financially secure with Michael. At 33, he was at the beginning of an extremely promising dental career. I was financially secure myself but subconsciously, or maybe not so subconsciously, I needed a successful and financially stable man in my life—even if he did treat me like shit at times.

On several occasions, I really did want to leave Michael. There were times when he could be incredibly demanding and insensitive, almost to the point of emotional and verbal abuse. But I was strong and could handle that. I knew who and what I was, so his words just rolled off my spine like drops of water. I didn't get to where I was by being sensitive and weak. As long as he never laid a hand on me, I could pretty much deal with anything he had to dish out. Except for cheating, that is. I would not and could not tolerate cheating for one second. We're talking about my health now and I had to be healthy to make the kind of money I was used to making.

Still, I couldn't believe my eyes when I strolled in a day early from a business trip. I remember being so happy and really wanting to share a major deal I had just secured with Nabisco to do its TV and radio advertisements for the next two years. My series of meetings ended on Friday instead of Monday so I decided to catch an early morning flight home from Pittsburgh and surprise my man. I planned to take him out for a fabulous brunch at our favorite restaurant to celebrate my win.

Well, actually, I'm not telling the whole truth. I did want to surprise Michael. However, to be honest, I was a little suspicious. I'd been getting a lot of hang up calls at the house, which had raised my antennas a bit. Even though I had some idea that he was being a dog, I was still shocked when I walked into my kitchen to find "Little Miss Thang" cooking my so-called man breakfast with my powder-puff blue terrycloth Calvin Klein bathrobe wrapped around her scandalous body. I knew Michael could be bold and brazen, but I never dreamed that he'd actually have the audacity to bring another woman into my house. Go over to hers or take her to a hotel? Yes. Bring her to mine? Hell, no!

When I stumbled upon his nasty little secret, I knew right then and there that he'd have to pay dearly for his actions. And to top it off, the girl couldn't have been more than nineteen or twenty.

Not that it would've made a difference if she'd been my age, but I had shoes older than her.

Seeing her through the double-glass doors made my heart sink into my Gucci pumps. After I went into a silent cardiac arrest, I tried to walk quietly into the kitchen to catch her off guard. It only took a moment for her to realize I was there. She was petrified when she noticed me; damn near knocking over whatever the hell it was she was cooking. It smelled like bacon—a food Michael never wanted to touch my lips. We didn't even have a pack of bacon in the house when I'd left four days ago. She'd obviously brought it with her.

It was certainly a funny sight—swine cooking swine. She had to know a woman lived there because it was obvious. The townhouse had FEMALE OCCUPANT written all over it. Hell, all she needed to do was peek into my mirrored walk-in closet. Evidently, she had since her grubby little ass was in one of my favorite robes. I have no respect for a woman that would knowingly screw somebody else's man. She'd have to be dealt with.

I didn't even say a word. My eyes apparently said it all because she ran right out of the house, barefoot and all—in my robe. Personally, I didn't know where she thought she was going so I didn't bother to chase her. I knew she'd be back since there was absolutely nowhere for her to run and certainly no place for her to hide. We lived in the middle of No Man's Land and the only car in my driveway was Mike's BMW.

I walked through the living room toward the bedroom. My heart was pounding so hard, I thought my entire chest was about to explode. The bedroom door was cracked and I could see his trifling ass lying there fast asleep. Aw, how sweet! She was making him breakfast in bed.

I contemplated shooting him but I didn't have a gun. Stabbing him or throwing boiling water on his ass were also options, but he wasn't even worth it. I couldn't make any money from a jail cell. I decided to go inside and punch him so hard my fist would go right through his eye and end up on the pillow beneath his head. And that's exactly what I did.

Completely stunned and bewildered, Mike immediately jumped up from the bed screaming. The only thing I could do was scream back, cursing him all the way and calling him every profane name I could think of.

"Baby, baby, wait! Let me explain!" he yelled, trying to shield his naked body from my forceful blows. His shrunken dick and balls were swinging in the air like the Confederate flag flying over a redneck's doorstep. Oh, how I wanted to do a Lorena Bobbitt on his triflin' ass!

"I want you out of here! And you'd better go find your little bitch before I do!" I hollered at the top of my lungs.

Seeing that he could do nothing to calm me down, he grabbed his jogging suit from the chaise beside the bay window and clumsily attempted to dress himself, all the while ducking and dodging everything I was throwing at him.

After he was dressed, he headed for the door, the driveway and ultimately, his car. I hysterically ran outside behind him, still throwing all of his suits, shoes and belongings at him. I don't even remember what I was saying. I was just so enraged. Despite my frantic state, my aim was pretty good—if I do say so myself. A couple of his shoes connected right to the back of his neck. I felt like a pitcher for the Yankees.

"We'll talk when you calm down! You're making a complete spectacle of yourself!" he hollered from the car. At that moment, I saw his little whore run out from nowhere (still in my robe) and hop into the passenger side of the vehicle. I started to run after her and rip her ass to shreds, but decided against it when I saw all the neighbors out on their lawns observing our fiasco. Probably just as embarrassed as I was, Michael sped down the road at what must have been one hundred miles an hour.

So that's how it happened.

It really didn't surprise me. Michael wasn't any good and I pretty much knew that. But I just thought he was an arrogant, conceited and pompous jerk. I didn't really think he was a lying cheat. Once the smoke had cleared, I wondered how long it had been going on. I wondered if she'd been in my bed before. But I guess it really didn't matter. He and I were definitely over now. She could have him.

My very best friend, Trish, was happy—not for my pain, but for my final exit from the relationship. "Now are you finally going to leave him?" was all she asked.

The funny thing was that after that entire ordeal, once I got inside the house, I noticed that I hadn't even shed a tear. I actually felt as though the Empire State Building had been lifted off my back. I guess all I really needed was a solid excuse.

After such commotion, the house was empty and eerily quiet. I walked into the kitchen to the stench of burning pork and quickly dumped the frying pan into the sink. After I calmed myself a bit, I sat my aggravated bones down at the breakfast bar and dialed M-A-T-T-R-E-S. I requested that a new mattress be delivered immediately. I surely wasn't about to lie down in the same place where he'd fucked his whore. And first thing Monday morning, I planned to call my doctor to get an HIV test. If it came back anything other than negative, I'd certainly die in jail—my punishment for being a murderer.

To be honest, I was really OK with the entire Michael thing. I actually handled it a whole lot better than I would've thought. The only things I was concerned about were the test results and whether or not Michael would let me buy out his half of the townhouse. The nails on our relationship's coffin had been tightly hammered shut, but I certainly wasn't going to be the one to leave my home. I'd found the house and I was the one who'd decorated it. I definitely didn't want some judge forcing us to sell it and split the profits. I couldn't imagine living anywhere else. It was my home.

For the first time ever, I suddenly realized that I regretted not marrying him. Without a marriage certificate, I knew I'd have to buy Michael out if I wanted to keep the house. If I'd married him, I would've been able to cite adultery and not only get sole possession of the townhouse but probably also take him to the cleaners for years to come. Hell, I would've owned half of a dental practice without spending one day in dental school. Somewhere in the back of my mind, I knew there would come a time when I'd regret not getting that piece of paper. I could hear my mamma's voice in the back of my head saying, "I told you so!" But at least I wasn't stupid enough to have any kids by him. "No children out of wedlock" was a rule I never intended to break.

The good thing was that I could afford to buy him out—if he'd sell his half to me. I'd kill him if he didn't. I definitely feared that he'd want to make up and continue living as we were. Or worse, he'd want to buy me out. I'd never sell to him in a million years. I'd kill him first.

I've never had good taste in men. The episode with Michael definitely confirmed that. They say you're either lucky in love or you're lucky in business. My successful career definitely demonstrated excellence in the latter. As far as love was concerned, I was O for O and I wasn't getting any younger. At 32, I hadn't found one decent black man that I could actually picture myself growing old with. I didn't want to cross the color line, but some days I wondered if I'd have to. Enough bombs will eventually send a girl looking elsewhere.

Now Trish, on the other hand, is so lucky in love that I think she carries a solid gold cupid in her Prada purse. But she can't keep a job to save her life. She barely even finished college. It took her over six years to get through a four-year institution and she took no breaks. Schoolwork and a career are the last things on her mind. A couple of years ago, she claimed she was going to change her ways, buckle down and get serious. Her husband gave her a heap of money to start her own catering business. She really is an exquisite cook, but she doesn't have an ounce of business skill or professionalism.

Needless to say, it failed miserably. She couldn't meet deadlines or appointments and the rich Jewish ladies who hired her services irked her last nerve. She swears eventually she's going to try it again. But it really doesn't matter because a career means absolutely nothing to her. And why should it? Her husband's a professional baseball player and they have money piled on top of money. Shit, their money has money.

Trish and I have been best friends our whole lives and she always got the best guys. You know, the rich, smart, handsome ones. Not to mention the fact that she was always the one to break up with them. I mean, this is a woman who doesn't even know how it feels to be dumped or cheated on. And they always come back to her begging. She claims they bore her after a while and she needs what she calls "fresh meat." But I say her Creole mamma put some kind of mojo in her sweat glands that attracts good men. Whatever it is, the girl's definitely got it.

I was actually pretty surprised when she told me she was going to marry Rodney. To be honest, Trish can be so flaky when it comes to men that I didn't think it was going to last. But it's been going strong for five years now and they have two beautiful children—twins—a boy and a girl. Now could you ask for a more perfect life? As much as I love my career, something inside me really envies Trish. But, hey, I guess I'm not doing so bad . . .

"Girl, you've got to let me introduce you to some of Rodney's friends," Trish told me over the telephone as I tossed some leftover Chinese food in the microwave.

It had been fast food and take-out for the past four evenings. My firm was working on closing another big deal and it had been late nights at the office all week. However, I did promise myself that I'd visit my mamma over the weekend and get a home-cooked meal for the first time in ages.

"I don't know, Trish," I replied, setting the timer on three minutes. "I'm not really into professional athletes. You know me. Even in high school I wasn't into the jocks. I prefer doctors, lawyers, congressmen even. Men that stimulate my mind, no offense to Rodney."

"Oh, I'm not offended. I know Rodney's no brain surgeon. But that's the very reason why your ass is alone. You keep going for the same types. Anybody that spends that damn much time in school—how long are they in school? Like eight or nine years, huh?"

"It depends," I replied, knowing she was about to start up with her freakazoid sense of logic.

"Well, whatever. It's a lot of damn years in school, studying and studying, minimal partying, minimal sex. Girls probably weren't into them 'cause they were bookworms and nerds. By the time they graduate from med school, grad school or whatever post-secondary education and start to finally practice, they've got all this suppressed sexual and social frustration pinned up inside of them and they go fuckin' crazy!"

"You're the one who's fuckin' crazy!" I laughed.

"Really, Nyagra. The athletes have always had the females. They've always partied. You've been to the parties they throw after the games, so you know they're used to it. Sure, they may not be able to hold a conversation for a long period of time, but so what? Their bodies are fabulous and they're usually so good in bed that after you have sex, you don't need to talk; you're too damn exhausted. Take it from me,

Girl. You can't trust a man over thirty who's just now getting his first piece of real ass."

"You're sick," I said, shaking my head and shoving a fork full of lo mein into my mouth.

"And believe it or not, they're not all dumb. Most of them have college degrees and business ventures they've invested in outside of their sport, you know," she explained like a knowledgeable professor who'd studied the topic for many years.

In the background, I heard one of the babies crying.

"Is that Darnell or Danielle?" I asked.

"It's Danielle. She's been driving me crazy all day. She's coming down with a cold and she's been really cranky."

"Well, let me let you tend to her. I need to go over my final proposal for tomorrow anyway."

"You guys still working on getting that deal?"

"Yeah, and they're trying to play hardball with us on a couple of issues. I think we're going to get a commitment though—hopefully tomorrow."

"That's great. Listen, think about what I said. I know this guy who plays for the Knicks and he's really nice. He's also looking for a wife. Don't knock it 'til you try it, OK? You don't want to spend Christmas by yourself, do you?"

"I'm going to my mamma's for Christmas. Plus, a basketball player, Trish? I'm only five-three! And besides, how do you know he's looking for a wife?"

"First of all, everybody's the same height when you're lying down, and secondly, come on . . . Who are you talking to? You know I know things like who's married, who's divorced, who cheats. Just trust me."

"You're crazy! And besides who says I'm looking to be somebody's wife?"

"After what happened with that asshole, Michael, you'd think you'd learn. Ny, you're too easy on men. You need to make a man bust his ass for you—and I don't mean sexually. Sex is one thing; your heart and cooperation is another. Then once he gets you—emotionally, that is—he works harder at keeping you. You make shit too easy for them. Demand that that son of a bitch sell you his half of that house! It's yours! You found it! You decorated it! Every piece of artwork and sculpture in that place you found, bought, and mounted! It's your goddamn house, Ny! Stop being Mr. or should I say Ms. Nice Guy or Girl or whatever! You know what the hell I mean! Men love a difficult woman! Trust me!"

"I'll talk to you tomorrow, Trish," I replied, not in the mood for her antics.

"By the way, speaking of that fool, what's going on? Is he going to sell his half of the townhouse or what? Have you heard any more from him? What's going on? That could be his Christmas gift to you. Tell him that. What's happening? Since you've been trying to get this account, you barely talk about anything but work."

"Wasn't Danielle crying? Don't you have to go?" I questioned, not wanting to get into the drama about Michael.

"OK, OK. When you're ready to talk, you know where I am." She laughed, taking the hint. "I'll call you tomorrow."

I hung up the phone and walked into the bedroom. It looked pretty empty without Michael's stuff everywhere. He wasn't the neatest guy in the world and I was kind of used to his things being around. Without his stuff there to take up space, the room looked larger than usual—airy and a little lonely. In fact, I missed his stuff more than I missed him. He'd come to pick up the rest of his things last week, including everything I'd cut up and put cigarette holes in. I don't even smoke, but I bought three packs of Newports just to burn his shit.

I wasn't there when he came. I wanted it that way. I didn't want to hear any explanations or be exposed to any additional drama as the final hour arose. I wanted him out of my house and out of my life. During the one conversation we did have nearly two weeks after the incident, he attempted to proclaim his undying love for me, telling me the girl meant nothing and that they hadn't even had sex.

"She's an intern and I was helping her study for the boards. It got late and I let her sleep in the guest room," he lied.

Yeah, right. I must've looked like Bozo the Clown to him. But I said nothing about it. I didn't kick. I didn't scream. Most importantly, I didn't cry. I hate to cry, which is why I never do. Crying is for babies who don't wear makeup. Women who cry just end up looking like weak little girls who lost control. And it never solves anything. I can handle anything without shedding a tear. I'm not about to risk ruining my Chanel mascara and looking like a wimpy raccoon just to let some emotional drops of water stream down my cheeks. Nope, not me.

In our conversation, all I wanted to know was if he would sell me his half of the townhouse. There was no drama. I was in complete control of the situation. The truth of the matter was that I simply didn't love him. I realized that the very moment I saw that chick in my kitchen. I knew deep down Michael and I weren't going anywhere. I'd known it for ages. As I think about it now, I'm not sure if I'd ever really loved him. In fact, I don't even think I liked him. I think he just represented security to me. Well, financial, at least. But after witnessing his deceit, fortunately, I realized that I had my own financial security and I wasn't going to compromise myself just to have a man by my side.

Even though the HIV test came back negative, I knew I could never trust him again and I wasn't going to live in paranoia. Who cared if I spent Christmas without a man on my arm? Thanksgiving hadn't been so bad. I'd gone over to Trish's and it was actually really nice. She and her housekeeper cooked a magnificent dinner. Her family is great to be around, unlike mine, who I can only take in moderation. I adore my mamma, but when all of my brothers and sisters come together under one roof for any occasion, it usually turns into a fiasco. Mamma told me that everyone was coming to her house for the holidays this year. I opted to pass on Thanksgiving and join them for Christmas. I certainly couldn't take their company two holidays in a row. Needless to say, Mamma wasn't too happy with my decision but I knew in my heart that I was doing the right thing for me. With the exception of my older sister, Juanita, I didn't even really communicate with my siblings. And I only kept in touch with her because she called me damn near every day.

Anyway, as time passed, Michael constantly refused to talk to me about the house, which really pissed me off. Damn, that was the least he could do! He knew that it hadn't been all that great for a while. I guess that's why he'd gone out and gotten a toy. I knew he'd never end up with her—as a couple, I mean. Yeah, he'd probably sex her as often as he could, but knowing Michael that would be it. He'd never take her around his colleagues or his family. I knew that for a fact. He had an image and I didn't think she quite fit into it. But that wasn't my problem or my concern.

After all the drama and hoopla, I must admit that I was a little scared to get back into the dating scene. Even though Michael had been a true shithead, I had remained faithful to him. So I knew I needed to brush up on my skills. I wondered if I still had it. Yeah, yeah, I still got some attention from men on the street whenever I walked around in Manhattan on my lunch hour or going to and from the garage. But I never really took that seriously. Those messengers try to talk to everything in a skirt. However, I hadn't been on a real date since Michael and I moved in together two years ago. Lucky for me, work was taking up most of my time anyway. I probably wouldn't have a spare moment for a date for quite a while. What a relief!

"Nyagra?" Judy, my assistant, buzzed my office.

"Yes, Judy?"

"Victor Reece and Marcia Keller are here from StarzSports Apparel for your nine o'clock meeting."

"Is the small conference room ready for the continental breakfast?"

"Yes, I set it up about fifteen minutes ago."

"OK, take them in there. Let everyone who's supposed to attend know that they've arrived."

"Nyagra?"

"Yeah?"

"Wait until you see Mr. Reece."

"What? What's the matter with him?" I asked, a little concerned by her tone of voice.

She laughed. "What's the matter with him? Not a thing!"

I heard the other assistants giggling, but I didn't have a clue what they found so humorous.

I looked at myself in the cherrywood-framed wall mirror. I hadn't slept too well the night before and hoped I looked all right. I'd gotten up extra early to do some last-minute preparation for the meeting. I'm really not a morning person and wanted to meet later in the day, but the people from StarzSports insisted on 9 A.M. I think they were trying to test us. I'd been told by my superiors that the two StarzSports representatives were their toughest marketing reps, but they didn't know what or whom they were up against.

I was used to clients trying to get more for less. But I truly believed that our company offered the best expertise in the entire advertisement industry. We possessed some of the most talented slogan creators in the country. Several of our clients' profits had doubled—even tripled— after hiring us. They made their money back and then some. I sure hoped Mr. Reece wasn't some old-fashioned, bald-headed guy who couldn't understand my contemporary style of advertising. Our presentation was definitely geared toward a youthfully-minded audience.

As I marched down the long corridor in my Yves St. Laurent tweed suit, I adjusted my ribbed stockings. Mr. Reece and Ms. Keller were in the west side conference room sitting behind the silverfish-black table. Also present were my top slogan creator, Carol Phillips; a director we'd hired, Miles Lupone, and three other associates. As I approached, they both rose to greet me. I was surprised to see that Mr. Reece was a very handsome black man, seemingly in his early forties. He stood well over six feet tall with a reddish-brown complexion, low-cut hair and a beard with a hint of gray. He obviously worked out regularly because a muscular build was evident even beneath his Armani suit. In a word, he was fine! I guess that was what Judy was talking about.

He extended his well-manicured hand to me and I eagerly shook it. "Nyagra Ensley?" he asked, with a voice as eloquent as his appearance.

"Indeed. You must be Victor Reece."

"Yes, and this is my associate, Marcia Keller."

So caught up in his amazing presence, I almost didn't see the homely little blonde-haired woman standing beside him.

"Nice to meet you," I said to her.

"Likewise," she said.

I looked around the room at my staff.

"I assume you've met everyone?"

"Absolutely," he replied.

I glanced toward the table of refreshments. "Have you helped yourselves to some coffee, a Danish, a bagel or something?"

"No, no thank you. Our flight arrived early so Marcia and I stopped for breakfast on the way from the airport."

"How was your flight in from Atlanta?"

"The flight was fine. We landed early so that's always a pleasure. I'm not too keen on flying."

"Oh, I don't think anyone is these days. I was just in Atlanta not too long ago. It's a beautiful city."

He flashed a set of perfect teeth. "We love it."

I smiled as I sat in my chair at the head of the table. "Maybe in a little while you'll help yourself to some refreshments. Let us begin."

As Carol prepared the overhead slides for viewing, I explained the ad campaign my staff had devised, as well as the reasons why I believed our company could definitely take StarzSports Apparel to its next level. Not surprisingly, after two-and-a-half hours of convincing, Mr. Reece and Ms. Keller seemed pleased with our presentation.

"I definitely think we have a deal," Mr. Reece stated. "I'm impressed and I believe that Newman & Stein Enterprises has what it takes to take StarzSports to its highest level."

"Wonderful! The next step would be for us to draw up a proposal listing all the particulars. Basically everything we've discussed here this morning," I informed him.

"Sounds good," he stated, rising from the table.

"Thank you so very much, Mr. Reece. It was definitely a pleasure."

I confirmed the deal with my firmest corporate handshake. A fifteen-page detailed booklet on the capabilities of Newman & Stein Enterprises was handed to him and once he'd neatly tucked it away in his alligator briefcase, he grinned.

"Please call me Victor."

"OK, Victor." Our eyes met for a split second, but once I realized it, I immediately released his hand and turned to Ms. Keller. "It was a pleasure meeting you both and we hope to hear from you soon."

Everyone shook hands and began to disperse. It was close to noon and all that pitching had worked up quite an appetite.

"Let me show you to the elevator," I offered as I walked them down the corridor. After a brief moment of silence, I asked, "How long are you going to be in town?"

"I'm catching a three o'clock flight back to Atlanta this afternoon," Ms. Keller said.

"Oh, that's too bad. New York is such a great place to visit; especially at this time of year with Christmas a little less than three weeks away."

"I know, but I have two little ones at home."

"Oh, I definitely understand!"

Turning to me, Victor jumped in. "I'm staying until Sunday. My sister lives on Long Island. I decided to take a couple of days off and visit with her and her family."

"Oh, that's great! So, you know New York?"

"Quite well. I grew up in Queens."

"Wow, I had no idea! Well, you have a wonderful stay," I said as the elevator door opened.

We all shook hands once again. As we bid our final farewells, they entered the elevator and I headed back to my office. I felt great. As usual my mission had been accomplished. Another deal (and another bonus) made!

Against my better judgment, I decided to meet Trish and Rodney for dinner at Benihana, a very trendy New York Japanese Hibachi steakhouse. Somewhere in the back of my mind, I knew they were going to invite the guy Trish had been telling me about, but I went anyway. If he did come, it wouldn't be that bad because we wouldn't be alone. If he didn't, it still would be all right because I was tired of eating fast food and take out every night. Now that the StarzSports deal was secured, I figured I could try to live a little again.

I met them at the restaurant straight from the office about six o'clock. When I arrived, they weren't there yet, so I decided to have a Pina Colada at the bar while I waited. I hate sitting at bars alone. I think it makes a woman look too desperate. But there was nothing else for me to do. And for the first time in ages, I really needed a drink to relax. The week had been such a long one. With the final preparation of the StarzSports presentation, I'd been at the office every night until after ten. I was so glad that it was Thursday—only one more day before I'd see a couple of days off. I was definitely going to visit my mamma this weekend. I'd been trying to get there for the past month, but it seemed as though I never made it. Well, this weekend I wasn't going to let anything stop me. A team of wild horses couldn't keep me from heading to the peace and serenity of my mamma's house. I was determined to finally get some rest and relaxation.

"You here alone?" I heard someone ask. I was so deep into my thoughts, I didn't even realize the guy was speaking to me. "My sistah?"

I turned my head to see a very large man sitting at the bar beside me in leather pants, cowboy boots and a leather jacket with no shirt under it. He looked utterly ridiculous. Not only was it the first week in December with freezing temperatures, but he looked like a straight-up pimp. The hair on his chunky chest looked like small balls of rolled-up, jet-black lint. He had a mouth full of gold teeth and a gold medallion the size of my fist around his neck. That's another reason why I hate sitting at bars alone. You attract all kinds of shit. I really didn't want to be seen talking to him.

I glared at him. "Excuse me?"

"I asked you if you're here alone."

I looked around, hoping to see Trish and Rodney walk through the door. No such luck.

"No, um, no. I'm actually waiting for some friends."

"But you're here alone for now, huh?"

"Technically, I guess I am," I snapped as I repeatedly stared at the door as if the energy from my eyeballs would quicken their arrival.

"Ivan. Ivan King," he said, extending his hand that had a huge diamond pinkie ring on it. His nails were longer than mine, which really grossed me out. I looked down at his bony fingers and opted against shaking his hand, although I did give him a half-smile.

He retracted his paw and rubbed his chest. "So, what's your name, lovely lady? You know mine."

"Nyagra," I reluctantly answered.

"Oh, like in the water up by Canada? Niagara Falls?" he asked loudly, embarrassing the hell out of me.

I halfway chuckled. "Yeah."

"Get outta town!! Well, I'll tell ya, if you meeting your man, Ms. Niagara Falls, you should kick his ass to the curb, 'cause he shouldn't have your fine ass out here waitin' on him like this. If you was my woman wit' a beautiful name and face like 'dat, I'da picked you up from yo' front door. Didn't yo' mamma ever tell you never to wait on no man? That's what I tell my own daughters. I got four ov' 'em, ya know—an' one dey say is mine but I ain't too sure—but dat's anotha story. But all ov 'em—even da one in question—is jus as pretty as you is! They mammas ain't, but they is. Guess dey got dey daddy's genes!" He laughed, took a sip of whatever it was he was drinking and continued, "I'm in the music business, ya know, so that keeps me kinda busy, but I'd make time for a woman like you. Definitely . . . Shooooot, fine as you is. Know what I'm sayin'?"

I gave him the same phony half-smile I'd given him earlier, but said nothing. I'd actually stopped listening to him but, in the back of my mind, I heard him talking about how Black queens shouldn't let men dog them and this and that. He was so loud that everybody in the place was staring at us. I wanted to disappear into the red leather barstool.

When I finally saw Trish and Rodney walk through the door, I was so relieved!

I got up from the bar and left Romey Rome sitting alone. "Excuse me, my friends are here."

"OK, OK, Miss Niagara Falls! You enjoy your dinner, ya hear? Maybe we'll meet again. If it's fate, we will, Girl!" he called from behind me. I never even turned around.

"Who's that?" Trish asked, laughing.

"I don't know! What took you guys so long? You know how I hate to sit at bars alone!" I snapped as I hugged Rodney.

"Sorry. Danielle cried every time I walked toward the door, so I had to put her to sleep before we left."

As the maitre d' led us to our seats, I realized that Trish and Rodney were alone. Trish wasn't trying to make a "love connection" for me. I was glad I was wrong. We ordered our drinks, and I began to tell them about the day's events when all of a sudden, Trish called out, "Shawn! Over here!"

I turned to the door to see an exceptionally tall man walking toward our table. I knew I couldn't give Trish the benefit of the doubt! As he approached us, both Rodney and Trish stood up to greet him. He gave Trish a kiss on the cheek and Rodney a manly hug.

"Shawn, what a pleasant surprise!" Trish's phony ass grinned from ear to ear. "Shawn Franklin, this is my very best girlfriend I told you so much about, Nyagra Ensley."

We shook hands as he sat beside me. "Nyagra. What a beautiful name."

"Thank you."

He wasn't very handsome, but he was well-dressed. His Hugo Boss sports jacket flowed with ease as he strutted to our table. Despite his expensive attire, he was actually kind of awkward-looking. I guess most people that tall usually are. He had to be at least seven feet tall and everybody in the restaurant was looking at him. I didn't know who he was, I mean professionally, that is. He certainly wasn't one of the Knicks' superstars. I only followed the big names in sports, if I had time to follow them at all. Since I didn't recognize him, I figured he had to be one of the bench warmers. "Even the bench warmers make over three hundred a year, ya know," I could hear Trish's voice say in the back of my head.

As soon as this Shawn character fixated himself at our table, Trish suddenly transformed herself into my publicist. "Nyagra's the vice president of Newman & Stein Enterprises, an advertising firm that has a lot of high-profile clients such as Nabisco, Pizza Hut, and StarzSports to name only a few."

"Wow, Nyagra. That's pretty impressive," Shawn said.

I really wasn't in the mood for this. I wanted to talk about Victor Reece, but under the circumstances, I guess that would've been inappropriate. I tried to make the best of it and see where Shawn's head was since there was no getting out of it anyway.

"Trish tells me that you play for the Knicks?" I asked. "Aren't they playing tonight?"

"No, we're playing tomorrow. Would you guys like to come to the game? We're playing Chicago."

"We'd love to!!" Trish quickly answered. I felt like tossing her up on the grill beside my shrimp.

"Well, shouldn't you be practicing or something? I understand the Knicks haven't been doing that great this season," I said, testing him.

"Actually, I'm coming from practice now. I do have to be in by eleven, though."

He seemed like a gentleman. That was good, I guess.

I gave Trish the eye. "Thanks for the offer, but I promised my mamma I'd visit for the weekend. I'll be out of town until Sunday. Maybe next time."

Shawn grinned. "Absolutely."

Dinner went smoothly. The teriyaki shrimp and vegetables were absolutely delicious, much tastier than the food I'd been eating all week. After our initial conversation, I pretty much sat quietly as I listened to Rodney and Shawn talk about sports and Trish talk about the twins. I was barely listening to any of their conversations. Victor Reece occupied most of my thoughts.

At a quarter to nine, I excused myself to the ladies' room, hoping Trish would stay at the table. I knew if she cornered me alone, she'd ask me why I was being antisocial. No such luck.

"I'll join you," Trish said as she headed behind me. No sooner had we exited the dining room than she started in. "Ny, what's the matter with you?"

"I'm just not in the mood tonight. You know how hard I've been working on this StarzSports account. I just wanted to chill out with you guys. I'm not in the mood to be on my best behavior to charm a man."

"OK, but I think he's really into you. Why don't you just give him a chance?"

"I am. What do you want me to do? Sit on his lap?"

"That would be nice . . . " She laughed.

"Come on, Trish. I wanted to tell you about this guy I met today."

"Really! Where? Not another one of those Wall Street losers you meet on your lunch break? He's not a messenger, is he?"

"No, he works for StarzSports," I said as I entered the stall.

"What? Get out of here! So you got the account? Did he ask you out?"

"Yeah, I think we got the account. I mean we shook on it. But no, he didn't exactly ask me out. Well, not at all, actually. I don't even know anything about him. All I know is that his name is Victor Reece, he's the president of marketing at StarzSports Apparel and he's absolutely gorgeous."

"Is he black?"

"Yes. I haven't had to cross the line yet," I informed her.

"Well, I don't know. One of the last times we spoke, you said you were thinking about it so that's why I asked. He sounds like your type. What's the next step? Are you going to ask him out?"

I came out the stall to wash my hands. "Hell, no! You know that's not my style!"

"Nyagra, you're thirty-two and single with no prospects. I'd say your style hasn't exactly been working for you. You obviously need to get a new style, Girlfriend."

"Gee, thanks, Trish," I stated sarcastically.

"Well, still be nice to Shawn. You never know. You can never have too many prospects. Shit, you might spark a bidding war!"

"Whatever. By the way, my meeting was early this morning and I was so tired from last night that I didn't drive in. I'm going to ride back with you guys. Cool?"

"That's no problem."

We arrived back at the table to find that it had been cleared and the guys were pretty much ready to go.

"Nyagra's riding back with us, Honey," Trish said.

"OK," Rodney said.

"I'd be glad to drop you," Shawn interjected.

"Oh, no, it's all right. I only live ten minutes from their house," I assured him.

"Really, I don't mind. Trish told me that you live in Elmsford. I'm in Scarsdale. I've got to go in that direction anyway. I'm sure they want to get home to the twins. Besides, I want to."

I glanced at Trish, who I really could've killed.

"Well, OK then," I said reluctantly. Since he was one of Rodney's friends, I assumed he would be on his best behavior.

It was a brisk December night in New York City as we walked to the parking lot together. The merchants had begun to capitalize on the Christmas holiday with decorations and all kinds of holiday attractions. The Salvation Army Santas were out shaking their bells and Christmas carols echoed throughout the air. There's nothing like Christmas in New York City. It's certainly one of my favorite times of the year.

I wasn't surprised to see that Shawn drove a flashy, candy-apple red Lexus. Most professional athletes like to drive flamboyant cars and Shawn Franklin was no exception. It was nice, although I'm more into four-by-fours. I wouldn't trade my Range Rover for anything in the world.

Like a gentleman, Shawn opened the passenger side door for me. But he also drove like a bat out of hell and we lost sight of Trish and Rodney within a minute.

"So you must really like commercials, Nyagra?" Shawn asked, nearly screaming over the music blasting from the radio.

"Can we turn this down a bit?" I requested before taking it upon myself to reach over and lower the volume.

"Oh, no doubt. So, I was saying, you must really like commercials."

"My firm is responsible for creating a lot of them."

"Yeah? Which one might I have seen?"

"I don't know. Do you watch much television?"

"Whenever possible."

"We do all of the Toys 'R Us and Kids 'R Us holiday spots. We only have their holiday account, but I'm working on obtaining the whole thing."

"You must be a very busy woman. Do you have time for fun?"

"My job is fun to me."

"Yeah, basketball is fun to me, too. But I do other things."

I shrugged. "Yeah, so do I."

"How could you? Trish told me that you work all the time."

"Trish's mouth has been working overtime. If I worked all the time, I couldn't be here, now could I?" I snapped.

"Yeah, I guess you're right." He looked me up and down and licked his lips. "I don't know. I could be wrong, but you seem like you have a party animal under that designer suit somewhere that's just dying to get out."

"I'm glad you think you could be wrong because you are."

"Oh, am I?" Shawn asked with a gleam in his eye.

Where the hell is he going with this?

"Yeah, you sure are," I said.

The next couple of minutes were pretty quiet except for the sound of Lil' Kim's profanity blaring through the CD player. I'm all for girl power, but some of these female rappers are a bit much. As we rode along the highway, I couldn't wait to pull into my driveway. This guy was weird and giving off a strange vibe. I would've hated to have to kick his ass in his own car.

"You get off at Exit 8," I informed him.

"Hmmm . . . I could think of a few things I could 'get off' on." He smirked. I guess he was trying to be funny, which he wasn't. He seemed to have left the gentleman in the restaurant. Seeing that I obviously wasn't the least bit enthused, he continued, "I'm just kidding. I used to live in Elmsford myself."

"Oh . . . "

"You must be awfully lonely in that big townhouse all by yourself."

"Excuse me?" I stated, wondering how this guy knew I lived in a townhouse.

"Oh, Trish told me that you live in this fabulous townhouse all by your lonesome."

"What didn't Trish tell you?"

"Well, she didn't tell me what you like in bed."

Thinking he couldn't have possibly said what I thought he said, I asked, "Excuse me?!"

"Oh, was that too forward for you?"

"I think you're definitely out of line."

"I apologize. You just seem like a very open type of person. Even though we just met, I feel so comfortable with you."

"Well, you really shouldn't."

As we pulled off the exit and entered into a new thruway, I wondered what kind of weirdo this guy was and if he was interested in losing at least one of his testicles that night. Trish obviously didn't tell him a thing about my personality or about the switch blade and pepper spray I had neatly tucked away in my Coach signature bag. Trish knew I never left home without my weapons. The late hours I kept demanded certain precautions and I wouldn't hesitate to treat him like any ordinary perpetrator if I had to. I guess my best friend forgot to tell him about that.

"Now we take Exit 4, or were you also aware of that?" I impatiently asked.

"No, as a matter of fact, I wasn't."

Thank goodness the rest of the ride was quiet except for the CD player and me giving him specific instructions to my house. He should've been embarrassed. That's one of the reasons I hated going out with professional athletes. In my experience, most of them seemed to think that every female is anxious to jump into bed with them. If he thought he was about to get lucky, he was sadly mistaken.

When we finally pulled into my driveway, I turned to him. "Thank you for dinner and the ride home."

As I went to open the car door, Shawn grabbed my arm. "Nyagra, you don't have to play high post with me. You can be yourself. You may live in Elmsford now, but Trish told me you grew up in Harlem just like me. You know you wanna show me your panties."

I turned and looked into his beady little eyes. He had the face of a rat and needed to use some of his earnings to get his teeth fixed. If I'd had one of Michael's cards on me, I would have handed it to him with a quickness. And aside from his uncanny resemblance to a member of the rodent family, I simply couldn't believe the nerve of this guy. I was definitely going to kill Trish.

"If you don't let go of my arm you will wish you had," I said sternly, as I prepared myself to do a DMX on his ass and "lose my mind up in here."

I guess I was convincing because he raised both hands as if I was a cop. "It's been real."

"Real what?" I tossed open the car door and anxiously removed myself from his presence.

As I walked toward my front door, I could hear him calling from behind me, "I'll call you!!"

He didn't even have my number.

I was pissed off. I could barely get the key into the lock. Even before I put down my purse, I ran to the phone to call Trish. She definitely had a cursing-out coming to her.

Like the movie says, "Thank God It's Friday!" That's all I could think about. I was so anxious to get out of my office and take that drive up to my mamma's that I could barely concentrate. Luckily, my work-load was pretty light that day and I had a couple of unusual moments of free time. Just the thought of seeing all the homes garnished in beautiful Christmas decorations in Mamma's serene neighborhood of Hopewell Junction put me at ease. I loved my mamma's house. I always felt a sense of relaxation when I visited (unless any of my brothers or sisters were there). Even though she only lived a little more than an hour away from me, it felt like I was in Virginia or something. I was so happy that Mamma was finally able to enjoy her life in an atmosphere she could be proud of. She'd only had the home for three years but she truly seemed happier than I'd ever known her to be.

My parents had lived in the hustle and bustle of New York City for nearly thirty years—always in lower-income neighborhoods. All my life, I wanted my parents to reside in a calm and pleasant atmosphere—one without the constant sounds of police sirens and gunshots where I didn't have to worry about their well-being. I got out of the neighborhood as soon as I could, but I was often concerned about them.

At the time of my father's death, I was living alone in a spacious two-bedroom apartment in Riverdale. When he passed, I asked Mamma if she wanted to come live with me. Being such an independent person, Mamma quickly declined. She felt she'd be a burden on me even though she definitely wouldn't have been. Plus, the invitation was extended to her and only her. I suppose she didn't want to leave Cheryl, my younger sister who was living with her at the time. Mamma knew Cheryl couldn't pay the rent by herself and Mamma did receive a little money from Daddy's insurance company. She had no idea that he'd been saving for years so he could leave her a few thousand dollars when he died. The money Mamma got after my father's death allowed her to have almost enough for a down payment on a home of her own. When my accountant informed me of an area in upstate New York with great homes and lots of land for reasonable prices, I instantly thought of her.

I remember it as if it were yesterday. Daddy had been ill for nearly ten years. He'd had three strokes and the final one landed him in the hospital for quite a while. Eventually, we all began to realize that the end was near. I stayed by Mamma's side every step of the way—through all of the constant fights and arguments with my "ever so cooperative" brothers and sisters. Daddy stayed in the hospital for nearly seven weeks before he passed. During the funeral preparations, my brothers and sisters fought over everything from what kind of casket he should be buried in to who should sit next to Mamma in the limo. It was a terrible, drama-filled event.

There were many arguments, but the icing on the cake was when my oldest sister, Juanita, tried to force Mamma to buy a $500 designer suit to wear to the funeral. That wasn't Mamma's style at all, but Juanita was relentless and insisted that Ma make a good impression at the funeral. She pressured Mamma so much that she practically brought her to tears. Even though I tried to overlook as much as possible in an attempt to make things easier for Mamma, I eventually got into violent arguments with my brothers and sisters. You see the more you ignore my siblings, the more they push you. That's how I feel, but I'm sure they probably have their own set of negative comments to make about me.

Many times I've wondered if I was delivered to the right family at birth. I've always felt so very different from my siblings. I'm number two in a family of six—Juanita, David, Nathan, Monica and Cheryl make up the rest. Juanita is four years older than I am. I communicate with her more than any of the others, but that's probably only because she has no real life of her own and I sometimes feel sorry for her. Juanita can't seem to keep a job, a decent man, or make friends that are really friends. As far as jobs go, I think it's because she talks a lot. She lets people know too much about her personal life and eventually they end up using it against her. Juanita also puts up a lot of facades, letting people think she has more material possessions than she actually does. While she really does have a lot of stuff, she has used questionable methods to obtain it.

Juanita's the only person I know who's more superficial than Trish. But at least Trish has a rich husband who can afford her expensive tastes. As far as men are concerned, the men Juanita seems to choose use and abuse her. Maybe not physically—even though she has had a couple of physical altercations—but definitely mentally. She's been in countless destructive relationships and even dealt with a couple of married men.

Juanita also has this extremely bad habit of purchasing things with bad checks and then runs around like a chicken without a head trying to scrape up the money to put in the bank. It's a really stressful and nerve-racking thing for her, but she can't seem to stop. She's been doing it for so long that I don't think she could end it now if she wanted to. I think she has a slight mental disorder, not to mention a compulsive and impulsive personality. She's been going to therapy for almost a decade but her behavior has yet to change. She's also on public assistance. Even though I've tried time and time again to help her get off, she just can't seem to get her life together—not emotionally and not financially. I've helped her get jobs; she's lost them. I've lent her money; she's never paid me back. I've even given her money. But it only holds her momentarily. After a while, she's right back in the same predicament.

It seems as though Juanita's a big negativity magnet. Bad situations and people always seem to find their way to her. She's been through three bad marriages and her only daughter doesn't want to have anything to do with her. She was basically raised by Mamma and now lives with her father in California. Almost everything Juanita does or tries to do seems to sour for some reason. I've tried to help her so many times, but to no avail. Some days I really feel sorry for her. Some days I feel like a lot of her problems are self inflicted. She has done many messed-up things to me over the years and you know what they say: "What goes around comes around." But there's no sense in getting mad with her because she's suffered enough already. When she does things that are wrong to me, I just look at the source and try not to get offended. I think Juanita often tries to hurt others so that she doesn't have to concentrate on her own pain. I've learned through my own experiences that hurt people hurt people. Still I try to be there for her as much as possible because she has no one else. And she's not always that bad. She does have a sensitive and sweet side. And despite all her problems, I love her. In my heart, she's still my sister.

Knowing that Mamma was in that big house all alone made me want to leave work early to get a jump on the traffic. Looking at my butter soft leather overnight bag in the corner, I couldn't remember whether or not I'd packed a dressy outfit. Even though I'd only planned to stay the weekend, I really wanted to take Ma to The Chart House, her favorite restaurant in Dobbs Ferry. As I got up to look through my bag, Judy buzzed me.

"Yeah, Judy?" I called from the other side of my office.

"You have a call on line three."

"Who is it?" Judy always gave me the name of anyone holding on a line for me and her evasiveness annoyed me.

"Victor Reece."

I could picture her smiling through the phone.

"Victor Reece?"

Oh, my goodness, I thought. Did he change his mind about our account? But he couldn't have. He hadn't even gotten back to Atlanta.

"How did he sound, Judy?" I asked anxiously.

"As fine as he is!"

"Judy, seriously! Did he sound like he was . . . well, never mind. Tell him to hold."

I walked over to my desk, looked in the mirror and fluffed my hair. Then I remembered that he couldn't see me through the telephone receiver.

"Mr. Reece, how are you?" I nonchalantly said as if I had just been sitting there waiting for his call.

"Victor," he replied. I could see his pearly whites sparkling in my mind.

"I'm sorry, Victor. What can I do for you? Is there something you need me to clarify regarding yesterday's presentation?"

"This actually isn't a business call, Nyagra. I can call you Nyagra, can't I?"

"Absolutely."

"Well, as I told you yesterday, I'm going to be in town visiting my sister and her family for a couple of days. I was wondering if you'd like to join me for dinner tonight."

"Oh!" I exclaimed. I couldn't believe that of all weekends, this was the weekend he would be here, and this was the weekend I planned to visit Mamma. This could've been the opportunity of a lifetime. I could marry this man. But how could I disappoint Ma? I knew she'd be preparing a big dinner for me. She always did whenever I came to visit. How could I disappoint myself? Maybe I could drive up after dinner. Or maybe Victor and I would make passionate love after dinner and I could drive up tomorrow. Yeah, right, who was I kidding? I'm too much of a punk to ever do anything like that! Still I just couldn't pass up dinner with this guy. I just couldn't.

"Well, I'll be leaving the office around five today. What do you like to eat?" I finally responded.

"Anything. I hope you don't think that I'm being too forward but my mamma always told me to go for what I want," he replied. He was really surprising me with his directness.

I laughed and questioned, "What exactly is it that you want, Mr. Reece? Oh, pardon me, Victor?"

"Right now I want you to meet me for dinner at, let's say, six. How's that?"

"I suppose that's fine. Where shall we meet?"

"Would you like me to come into Manhattan or should we meet somewhere else? I'm on Long Island right now."

Remembering what Trish told me about making things too easy for men, I opted to have Victor come to me.

"I know of a wonderful soul food restaurant on Houston Street. It's called Mecca. Do you like soul food?" I questioned, figuring I should find out how "black" this man still was. So many of the brothers I meet in corporate America are just black on the outside; true Oreo cookies, if yaknowhatImean.

"Do I like soul food?" He chuckled. "Listen, I live in the soul food capital of the world."

"So, it's a date!"

"Yes, it's a date! Uh, you're not going to bring your husband, are you?"

"I wouldn't be meeting you for dinner if I had a husband, now would I? What kind of woman do you think I am?" I replied in jest.

"Oh, I was just checking! You never know these days! I just can't imagine a woman as beautiful as you not being married or attached."

"I just haven't found the right guy."

"Houston Street—6 p.m.?"

"Houston Street—6 p.m."

I hung up the phone and my knees felt so weak, I nearly fainted. I couldn't believe what had just happened. I was going to dinner with Victor Reece! I quickly called Ma to let her know that I'd be arriving a little later than originally planned. I still really wanted to go for that visit, but I had to tell her a little white lie. I explained that I had an unexpected dinner meeting with a prospective client in order to secure a deal I'd been working on for weeks, but I'd definitely drive up right after the meeting. In essence, it was true. Well, partially, at least. Victor Reece was still technically a prospective client until his company signed that proposal. I worded it that way because Mamma never would've understood if I told her I was going on a date. I adore Mamma but she knows my history with men and would've been hurt to think I was delaying my visit for some silly date that wouldn't amount to anything—again. But to me, Victor Reece was not some silly date. Little did she know that in my mind, he actually could be her future son-in-law. It sure was a good thing I'd worn something flattering to work that day!

Two

I stood on the corner of Houston Street freezing my ass off. People were packed into the foyer of the restaurant like sardines in a tin can, so I was forced to wait outside in the frigid weather. It was one of the hottest soul food places in the city and they didn't take reservations. I gave the hostess my name and walked back outside where Victor would be able to easily spot me. If I had attempted to squeeze into the crowd, he never would've found me.

I've always hated the cold and it must've been well below zero. I think in a past life I was an Island girl who spent every day on the beach bikini clad and barefoot. But in this life, the December wind chilled every bone in my body. I should've waited in the car until he arrived and then parked. But I didn't want to wait too long to give the maître d' my name.

Everybody seemed to be in the holiday spirit. The restaurant was definitely more crowded than usual and after what had happened to me at Benihana, I certainly wasn't about to wait by the bar alone. I decided to take a walk across the street to buy a pack of gum. I hoped he'd be there when I returned. I really didn't want Victor to know that I was waiting on him and I certainly did not want to look desperate. But I surely wasn't about to wait for him forever either. A man that arrives more than ten minutes late, especially for a first date, gives me a very bad impression. If I'm not important enough to him to be on time, then he's definitely not important enough for me to wait for. It also indicates that he has the potential to be an inconsiderate, selfish son of a bitch. I think Michael was late on our first date. I should have taken that as a hint of what was to come.

When I arrived back from the newsstand with a pack of Cinnamon Trident in hand, sure enough, Victor was standing in front of Mecca looking even more handsome than he had that day in my office. He was wearing a pair of nicely fitted deep-blue Levi's and a very expensive-looking brown leather jacket—probably Andrew Marc. I was glad he hadn't arrived in a suit. I wanted him to be able to be a "real" person, to be able to step out of "business mode." It was 6:07 so he'd just made my ten-minute deadline.

When I approached him, I was surprised by his friendly kiss on my cheek. Although I didn't attempt to kiss him in return, I certainly didn't shy away from his gesture. His lips were soft and gave me a tingling sensation.

"Were you waiting long?" I asked, knowing I only went into the store for five minutes. I figured I'd test him and see how honest he was.

"No, I just walked up. I borrowed my sister's car and traffic was terrible. I guess the holiday shoppers are out in full effect. I parked in the lot up the block. I'm glad you're just getting here. I would've hated to keep you waiting. I noticed the crowd in there and wondered if I'd be able to find you. I took a quick glance and didn't see you so I decided to wait out here."

Good, I thought. He's honest and considerate!

"Well, I guess we just have perfect timing."

We made our way through the crowd of buppies and wannabes to the small oak bar. I ordered a Perrier with a twist of lime and he ordered cranberry juice, which I found to be an interesting choice.

Obviously noticing that I had observed his request, he said, "I'm not really a drinker."

I was quite glad to hear that because I used to date a guy named Xavier who was a borderline alcoholic. He couldn't go anywhere without downing at least four Long Island Iced Teas. Thus his breath always reeked of alcohol and that was such a turn-off.

"Oh, neither am I. Every once in a while, I'll have a Pina Colada but I don't get to work out as much as I'd like and they say that alcohol is very high in calories."

"Well, you'd never be able to tell."

"Huh?"

"That you don't work out. You have a fabulous figure."

"Thank you." I blushed, a little flattered that he was inconspicuously checking me out.

"Oh, come on, Nyagra. I'm sure you hear that all the time. In fact, I'm really quite surprised that you were free tonight. I thought surely you'd be involved with someone, or at least have a date. I must confess that I wanted to ask you to dinner right after our meeting the other day, but I didn't have the courage. That's why I called you so last-minute. I had to get up the nerve."

"Well, thanks for the compliment, Victor, but my job keeps me pretty busy. Unfortunately, I don't get out too much. However, I did just get out of a long relationship."

"Oh, I see. How long were you involved?"

"We dated off and on for four years, but lived together nearly two."

"Wow. That's quite a while. Are you over it?"

"I think I was over it before it ended, but you know how it can be when you're used to something."

"Yes, I do." He paused as if he were thinking about his own life for a moment before he smiled. "Well, you seem to be handling it just fine. And as I always say, one man's trash is another man's treasure. His loss is my gain."

"Well, you're just full of compliments. But what about you, Mr. Reece? What do you have going on in Atlanta? A wife? A couple of kids? A dog even?"

He laughed, showing me that fabulous smile, took a deep breath and replied, "No wife. I'm divorced with one daughter, Mya. She's six and lives with my ex-wife in Birmingham, Alabama. And, as a matter of fact, I don't really like animals."

We definitely had that in common. I wasn't into anything that could shed all over my cashmere sweaters. Not to mention the fact that if it can't cry or give me grandchildren, I can't remember to feed it.

As the maître d' finally showed us to our table, I quickly thought about the information Victor had just shared. His history sounded OK. I wasn't too keen on divorcees, but I didn't want to jump to any conclusions. For all I knew, it may have been all her fault. The fact that he had a daughter didn't make me jump for joy either but at my age, it was pretty difficult to find someone childless and unattached like myself. Speaking of age, I decided I should ask Victor how old he was just to be certain that I wasn't way out of my league. I guessed he was about 38 or 39. A man of his accomplishments must've been working at it for quite some time. And although he did look extraordinarily educated and distinguished, not to mention handsome, Victor really didn't look a day over 30.

I took a deep breath and a sip of my water and decided to use a roundabout approach.

"So how many years have you worked for StarzSports Apparel?"

"I'll be with the company eight years come February. I began working for them right out of grad school."

"Oh, that's pretty much how it happened for me at Newman & Stein."

"But you're an incredibly young vice president, Nyagra. Were you one of those child prodigies or do you just look fantastic for your age?"

"Well, I did graduate from high school at 16 and I finished my undergraduate studies in three years. But that's only because I took classes in the summer. So, I was actually done with grad school at 24. I started at Newman & Stein during the summer of my first year of grad school as an administrative assistant for Mortimer Stein. He's the 'Stein.' When I got my degree they offered me an associate's position and fortunately, over the past nine years, they've allowed me to grow considerably." I hoped I didn't sound like a chatterbox, rambling on and on about myself.

"That's impressive. Newman & Stein is very lucky to have you. Now, if you finished grad school at 24, that must make you, um . . . "

"I'll be 33 in July." I grinned, not the least bit insecure about my age.

"Oh, most women don't like to discuss their age."

"Well, I figure you either get older or you die. Personally, I prefer to get older. By the way, we are in the same age bracket, aren't we?"

"Pretty much. I'm 39."

"Just checking. I'd hate to be dating someone my mamma's age. After a while, we wouldn't have too much in common, ya know." I laughed.

Thank God, he wasn't 50. I'm usually fairly good at guessing people's ages and I practically hit Victor's right on the nose. But there was that time when I was about 24 and I thought this guy I was dating was about 27. He turned out to be 44, but how was I supposed to know? He looked really young and I met him at an LL Cool J concert.

The food was especially good at Mecca that night and we both truly enjoyed our meals. As I sat across from Victor, I couldn't help but remember an article I'd read once that stressed the importance of observing what your date orders at a restaurant—especially on the first date. It went on to indicate that what a person orders can tell you whether or not you're well suited for each other and if the relationship will last. I don't know how true it was, but if I'd known that when I first went out with Mike, I probably would've excused myself to go to the ladies room and exited through the restaurant's back door.

On our first date, Mike and I went to the Shark Bar, another soul food restaurant. I just love African-American cuisine. He ordered the vegetable plate and while I was absolutely dying to order the ribs, I ordered a grilled Cajun chicken breast on a bed of spinach. That vegetable plate probably should've shown me ahead of time what a pompous, boring, unconventional idiot he was going to be. What kind of person orders a vegetable plate at a rib joint? Oh, if I'd only known then what I know now. Between the first date lateness and the veggie plate, I could have saved myself a whole lot of time and aggravation. So, keeping that article (and those incidents) in mind, I planned to carefully observe Victor's order.

I really wanted him to order before I did so I could check out his choices. No such luck. He was too much of a gentleman to let that happen. I decided to order the roasted lemon chicken breast with macaroni and cheese and collard greens. To me, that was a pretty safe meal. It couldn't get caught in my teeth, it wouldn't splash, and I didn't have to use my fingers. I didn't want to order the catfish (even though it was my favorite) because my breath would smell fishy for the rest of the evening. I didn't want to order the pork chops, another one of my favorites, because I wasn't sure how Victor felt about pork. It seems that for some reason a lot of black men seem to have this adamant dislike for pork and its connoisseurs. I say they've all been brainwashed by the media—probably the beef and chicken people. Pork has just as much shit in it as all the other kinds of meat processed in the Western world. People just don't know it. They think chicken and beef are safe. Have you ever been to a slaughterhouse? Well, I have! We had a chicken company as a client a couple years back and I visited their farm. Man, they pump those birds with all kinds of chemicals to make them plump and tasty. Don't be fooled, yawl. Don't be fooled. I remember this guy I kind of liked once telling me, "Lips that touch swine will never touch mine!" Well, needless to say that was a short-lived romance.

Michael had that same pork hang-up. That's why I was so surprised to see "Miss Thang" frying bacon in my house. Since Michael and I had broken up, I promised myself that I'd never let any man come between me and a BLT ever again. Not that I should've really cared how Victor felt, but it was our first date and if he felt that way, I preferred to find out sooner instead of later. However, I didn't want to risk ruining the current vibe. If this date continued to go well, there was definitely time for me to find out how he felt about pork chops and bacon—and even to convert him, if necessary!

Then there was the filet mignon, which was expensive. He knew I made a good salary, but I didn't want him to think I was a gold digger. So, I figured I couldn't go wrong with the bird. After I'd ordered, Victor ordered the smoked turkey wings with mashed potatoes and steamed squash, probably having the same reservations as I had. And I was quite comfortable with his order. I thought back to the article and realized that the request for poultry let me know that he was a little health-conscious. At the same time, the gravy and mashed potatoes told me that he wasn't a fanatic and could have a little fun sometimes. That was a very, very good thing.

I was careful to observe Victor's every move without looking like I was staring. The way a man eats can really make it or break it for me. Victor ate as eloquently as I'd expected. He didn't chew with his mouth open or smack his lips, nor did he speak with his mouth full. No food got caught in his teeth and he didn't get anything on his shirt or around the edges of his lips. Again, this man passed another one of my tests. I only hoped I looked as good as he did as I was eating.

As we neared the end of the meal, the conversation took a turn into the relationship area. I didn't really want to talk about Michael, but Victor seemed determined to discuss his ex-wife, Mallory, and their daughter.

I could see the pain in his eyes as he spoke, which forced me to wonder if he was really over this Mallory. "Mallory and I had a pretty bad relationship. I never really wanted to marry. I guess I did because she was pregnant with Mya. I really love Mya even though I don't get to see her as much as I'd like."

"Well, how is your relationship now?" I questioned, acting like the resident psychiatrist I would've been if I hadn't gone into marketing.

"It's better than it was, but far from perfect." He gazed into my eyes. "And why don't you have any kids? Don't you want to hear the pitter-patter of little feet around the house one day? Of course, you'll have to give up that big-time job, but it would be worth it."

I've always resented questions and statements of that nature. Why is it that a man can remain childless his entire lifetime if he so chooses, but women are always reminded that their biological clock is ticking or that their career must be placed on the back burner somewhere once they become a mamma?

I tried not to demonstrate that he'd actually annoyed me, so I quickly answered, "I've never been married and I don't believe in having children out of wedlock. I don't have any plans of even thinking about children until I'm in a solid relationship with someone I love a whole lot."

And what made him think that I would give up my job, anyway? Maybe my husband could be a stay at home dad. This is the new millennium, ya know.

"That's a good rule to stick by. If more females felt as you do, the black community would be a whole lot better off."

I felt like saying, "And if more men felt as I do and kept their dicks in their pants, the black community would be even better off." I was halfway ready to get into a debate with him about placing the entire burden of child rearing on women, but opted not to correct him. To save face, perhaps the entire evening, I clamped my teeth down on my tongue and simply replied, "I agree."

Trish would've been so proud of me. She'd always say, "Don't always have a debate with men. We know we're smarter than they are and deep down inside, they know we're smarter than they are. But they like to feel more intelligent, so let them. You can be smarter all the way to Tiffany's and Saks!"

"But you do plan to have children someday, don't you?" Victor asked.

"If I find the right man."

"Mallory's not the kind of woman you are, Nyagra. She has no sense of accomplishment or responsibility. She just wants to be taken care of, so I can really appreciate a woman of your stature. A woman with a great career like yours is a real turn-on for me. If Mallory would've been more like you, maybe we'd still be in love. But we try to get along for Mya's sake, though."

Didn't you just imply that mammas shouldn't have careers? I said to myself. Oh, if this brother only knew! Still, I wasn't about to get into my feelings regarding children with Victor on our first date. I liked him and didn't want to show my strong-willed and opinionated side. I also didn't feel like telling him that he'd just contradicted himself. So I acted as if I hadn't noticed and smiled. In the quest to be non-confrontational, I suddenly felt like a dark-haired dumb blonde.

"Well, as long as the two of you can be cordial, I'm sure your daughter will be just fine. It's not healthy for a child to see their parents fighting all the time."

As I looked down at the table, all I saw were empty plates and glasses. We must've really been hungry. The dryness of the leftover bones made it look like a couple of starving crackheads had just consumed the meal of their lives at our table. Our waiter grabbed our empty dishes and proceeded to ask about our interest in dessert.

"Just a Cappuccino for me, thanks," I said.

"Decaf, please," Victor said.

For the first time that night, there was actually a moment of silence. As I looked at him, he certainly was one of the most handsome men I'd seen in a long time. He even looked elegant in his casual attire. His skin was flawless and over our table's illuminating candlelight, he looked like a beautiful chocolate angel. The platinum strands of hair in his otherwise thick dark beard contributed to the glow that added to the unusual magnetic attraction I felt in the air. With the exception of the children question, he'd said and done everything right the entire evening. I must admit, I wanted to sip that cup of Cappuccino for at least two more hours just to be in his presence. I wanted to get into his brain and experience his every thought. My desire to get to know him better increased with every passing moment and I didn't want the night to end.

"Nyagra—that sure is a beautiful name and it definitely suits you. Where did your mamma get the idea to give you something so rare and lovely?" Victor asked, finally breaking the silence.

"Thank you for the compliment, Victor." I blushed. "To be honest, my parents actually conceived me on a vacation they took to Niagara Falls."

"Well, then it is one-hundred percent fitting." He smiled, showing me all his pearly whites. I really have a thing for nice teeth and this guy must've had a dentist somewhere in his family. Michael would've been so jealous.

"I've come to like it. I hated it as a child. You know how kids can make fun. But now it's definitely a part of me. I've never met another person with my name. Then again, I can never get personalized things unless I have them made."

"Have you ever been to Niagara Falls?"

"No, actually, I never have."

"Me either. You should definitely consider it. I mean, it's your namesake!"

"Oh, I plan to go one day."

"I've heard it's beautiful. Just like you."

This man had obviously been to charm school.

As I took the final sip of my cappuccino, our eyes stayed locked on each other. The chemistry between us was strong and we both realized it. I glanced at my watch and realized it was nearly nine o'clock. The time had seemed to fly by so quickly. I knew the date was ending and that I'd be thinking of Victor all the way up to Hopewell Junction.

Victor broke the momentary silence as well as our hypnotizing daze. "I'd really like to see the Christmas tree at Rockefeller Center if you wouldn't mind spending a little more time with me tonight."

I hoped I didn't appear overzealous when I replied, "I'd love to!"

Without looking at the tab, Victor dropped a $50 bill on the table and asked if I was ready to go. I certainly was. It felt so good to be with a man who simply paid the bill. Michael would always scrutinize the bill down to the last penny and find twenty things wrong with it—usually causing a scene and forcing us to leave most dining establishments angry. It got so bad that I eventually refused to eat out with him. That was just fine with Michael, since he was so incredibly cheap.

"Shall we take my car or yours?" Victor asked.

"I don't know. Maybe we should take a taxi. It's Gridlock City over there and we'll never find a place to park. The last time I went, all the parking lots were full. It shouldn't be more than about eight dollars in a cab."

"Sounds good!"

He was so agreeable—not a difficult personality at all. When Michael and I were together, everything was a hassle. If I said "yes," he said "no." If I said "black," he said "white." Always a conflict. Victor, on the other hand, almost seemed way too good to be true. I just couldn't understand how anyone could ever want to divorce him.

Victor helped me with my coat and we walked out into the same chilled December wind that had frozen my nose earlier that evening. Both of us were aware of the subtle racism that exists in New York City, so we decided that I should hail the cab. Within moments, we were experiencing our first New York City taxi ride together. As I sat shivering from the cold, Victor gently placed his arm around my shoulder and squeezed my body close to his. Even beneath my heavy wool coat, I felt a tingle and as our bodies touched, I wondered what it must feel like to kiss his lips.

"These cabbies drive crazy. Some things never change." Victor laughed.

"Yeah, they sure are something."

"Yellow cabs are one thing I don't miss living in Atlanta. They can definitely stress you out."

The ride to Rockefeller Center was basically quiet with the exception of our initial conversation. I didn't mind because I really didn't know what to say. In fact, I was pretty nervous. I felt like a giggly teenager and I didn't want to put my foot in my mouth. Victor also remained quiet. My intuition told me that he was feeling the same way.

When we pulled up to Rockefeller Center, the taximeter read $8.75. I was right. I was about to pay for it, being that he had paid for dinner and it was my suggestion that we take a taxi. Then a picture of Trish popped into my mind. But before I had a chance to make a decision one way or the other, Victor quickly reached into his pocket and handed the driver a $10 bill.

Through the large crowd, we made our way toward the Christmas tree that hovered over the picture-perfect skating rink. We couldn't get close enough to view the skaters, but we could clearly hear the festive Yuletide carols chiming through the air. Even though there were children and adults at every side of us, I still felt quite intimate with Victor who had now gone from having his arm around my shoulder to tightly holding my hand. He made me feel like a schoolgirl. We had to stay close to remain together in a crowd so large, but I think he still would've held my hand had there not been a soul in sight. We were really clicking. I don't know if it was the fact that there were so many people around, the bright lights, or what, but I suddenly began to feel very warm. Although the atmosphere was extremely crowded, I think it was his presence that was making my temperature rise.

"I sure do love to come over here to see this tree. It's my favorite New York thing. We don't have anything like this in Atlanta. My mamma used to bring us here every year when we were kids."

"Really? Wow. How many brothers and sisters do you have?"

"Just one sister. Elaine. We're pretty close. She's the one I'm staying with. She's married to a police chief and they have three kids."

"Is she the oldest?"

"No, she's my baby sister. How about you, Nyagra? Do you have any siblings?"

"Yeah, more than I'd like." I chuckled.

"You're not close to them?"

"No, not really. There are six of us, but I think I was switched at birth." I laughed.

"Yeah, I've heard stories about some families. But I just don't understand how you can grow up with someone your whole life and not be close."

"It's definitely possible."

"Yeah, I guess so."

Oh, God, I thought. Does he think something is wrong with me because I'm not close with my family? "It should be wonderful to have a big family, if everyone gets along. Unfortunately, my mamma's children cannot seem to agree on anything; let alone agree to disagree. Everything always turns into a big fiasco; from the smallest issue to the largest."

"That's sad. Big families can be a wonderful thing, especially around the holidays. One of my childhood friends came from a family of eight and I was always jealous. They didn't have a lot of money, but they sure had a lot of love. I've always wanted a big family. Money can't buy everything, you know. Well, maybe next time around."

We stood there snuggled in the cold. I could smell the scent of his cologne, which I pegged to be Armani. I couldn't help but think of what he said about "next time around." Although I surely didn't want to jump the gun, I momentarily hoped that I'd be a part of his next time.

The Rockefeller Christmas tree decorations were so beautiful. Not only did the tree hover so brilliantly over us as it illuminated the winter sky, but it was impossible to ignore all of the surrounding shops that were festively decorated. The brightness was absolutely magnificent and at the risk of sounding cliquish, it was indeed the most wonderful time of the year! Furthermore, my date with Victor was one of the most fabulous I'd ever experienced. I truly didn't feel as though we'd just met. I felt like I'd known him for years and I wanted to know him a lot better.

Around 10:30 we decided we should head back downtown to our cars. As much as I didn't want the evening to end, I still had that drive to Mamma's. The later it got, the more I wanted to take his fine ass home with me, but I wasn't about to get caught up in anything I wouldn't be able to handle in the morning. Thus, the best thing for us to do right about then was to part ways.

The ride to the parking garage was relatively quiet. I felt awkward as the evening neared its end, wondering exactly what the finale would be.

Would he kiss me softly on my cheek? Or would he kiss me passionately on my lips? Would he go even further than that and try to extend the night? I didn't know.

When we pulled up at the garage, Victor again paid the fare and we exited the taxi. Trish would've been so proud that I hadn't come out of my pocket for anything. In fact, Victor even paid for my parking.

As we walked toward the attendant and handed him our ticket stubs, Victor said, "Nyagra, I had one of the best evenings I've had in a very long time. Thank you."

"So did I. Thank you." I was glad he wasn't going to put me on the spot by making me an offer I'd have had to force myself to refuse. "When are you going back to Atlanta?"

"Sunday afternoon. Will I be able to see you again before I go?"

"Well, I've been planning to spend the weekend at Mamma's house for quite a while. I didn't plan on returning until Sunday evening sometime. I need to get away for some badly needed R&R. In fact, I'm driving up there when I leave here. The truth is that some people at this company called StarzSports Apparel have been giving me a pretty hard time over the past couple of weeks and I desperately need some rest," I teased.

Victor joked right along with me. "Really? Well, you just tell me who they are and I'll put them in their place. Where does your mamma live?"

"In Hopewell Junction. It's about 45 minutes above Westchester County."

"That's some drive. It's pretty late. Are you going to be all right?" Victor seemed quite concerned and I liked that.

"Yeah, I'll be fine. I'm used to it. I live in Elmsford so I'm no stranger to driving upstate."

"It must be really nice up there. Especially at this time of the year."

"Victor, you're really into the holidays, aren't you?"

"Yeah. It's my favorite time of the year."

"Well, why don't I give you the number to my mamma's so at least we'll speak before you leave." I didn't want to seem desperate by rushing back to see him before he returned to Atlanta. For once, I wanted to set a better tone at the beginning of a relationship.

Victor reached into his pocket and pulled out his Palm Pilot. He quickly opened it and typed in Mamma's phone number as I recited it, after which he typed in my cell phone number and then my number at home. As the attendant pulled up with my midnight blue Range Rover, I thought he was going to offer his sister's number to me, but he didn't. I hoped he'd feel comfortable enough to call me at Mamma's. After such a fantastic night, I didn't want Victor to just disappear from my life with me only being able to reach him at StarzSports. But it was just as well, for had he decided to never call me, I'm sure I wouldn't have called him—no matter how much I might've wanted to.

As I began to walk toward my four-by-four, Victor grabbed my arm and I knew it was about to happen. Just as I held my breath like some ditzy teenage girl, Victor planted a nice big juicy kiss right on my lips. Though it happened fast, I could feel the ultra-soft tenderness of his full lips and a sensation shot through my body unlike any I'd ever felt.

I must've looked totally dazed because somewhere in the back of my mind I heard him ask, "Nyagra, are you all right?"

"Oh, yeah, yeah, I'm fine."

"I'll call you." Victor smiled as he walked toward his sister's money green Toyota Camry. I could've melted in my Donna Karan pumps.

I jumped into my jeep feeling higher than a kite, turned the CD player to disc three and drove off into the New York City streets with Musiq Soulchild pumping loudly in my ears. I couldn't believe the evening I'd just experienced!

It was a little after eleven so I decided to phone Mamma from my cell phone and let her know that I was on my way.

"You should've called sooner. I was worried," she scolded.

I assured her that I'd be there shortly and though I sensed a bit of an attitude in her voice, I was so happy, nothing could ruin my mood.

The city streets were really packed. There was so much traffic that if I hadn't known any better, I would've thought it was 11:15 in the morning rather than damn near midnight. But for a change, I felt completely at ease. The traffic wasn't stressing me out. I just absorbed Musiq's voice and lyrics as he crooned about loving his woman until the end of time, no matter what—as long as her heart stayed the same. I wanted to know what it felt like to have a man love me so ultimately, so unconditionally—so eternally. I hoped that Victor would be the one to take me there.

Once I got onto the highway, traffic moved quickly. All the way up to Mamma's, I couldn't help but think about that phenomenal man. I really wanted to get to know him better. There was something mysterious about him and I liked that. I was a little interested in his relationship with his ex-wife, but figured I'd find out all of those details soon enough. My senses had been a little piqued at the mention of her name, but I figured that I was just being paranoid.

The incident with Michael and his tramp had really compromised my trust in men. But logic reminded me that Michael and Victor were two totally different people.

I decided that I wouldn't tell Trish anything about my weird vibe concerning his ex-wife. Surely she'd want to play Sherlock Holmes and investigate the issue to the fullest. I didn't want to think of anything that might make me question the reality of the date I'd just experienced. As I drove and listened to my CD player, which now filtered the beautiful sounds of Kenny G's sax, I just wanted to bask in the pollution-free upstate air, think of Victor's soft full lips, and relax, and relax, and relax . . .

I slept until nearly noon, which was late for me. Mamma didn't bother me, seeing how tired I was when I woke her momentarily to let her know I'd arrived. Thanks to the wonderful mamma that she is, I arose to the fabulous aroma of cinnamon French toast, scrambled eggs, bacon and sausage. She knew it was my favorite and since I'd kicked Michael out, it was no secret that I was making up for the two years I'd been pork-free.

I washed up in the adjoining bathroom before going downstairs. When I entered the kitchen, I was quite surprised to see my brother, David, sitting at the kitchen table. I knew he had to be there because of something negative. He never visited when things were good. I truly wasn't in the mood for any drama during what was supposed to be my weekend of rest and relaxation with Mamma.

"Good morning, Sleepy Head!" Mamma gave me her biggest Kool-Aid smile. I knew she was being overly enthusiastic because she was well aware of the fact that I would be ultra pissed to see my low life of a brother.

"What up, Sis?" David said, barely looking up from his food.

"What's up?" I said in a "What the hell are you doing here?" tone of voice. I kissed Mamma on the cheek and sat down at the other end of the table.

"What brings you up here?" I asked my brother.

"Needed some peace," he answered.

"I made your favorite, Ny. Cinnamon French toast, scrambled eggs, slab bacon and Park's sausage. I even heated the syrup. I figured you'd be getting up around this time," Mamma quickly interjected.

"You needed some peace? Since when?" I asked David, without acknowledging Mamma's comment. David faked a smile and opened his mouth only to shove another piece of bacon in it. He didn't say a word.

As I looked into my brother's eyes, I wondered how Mamma must've felt to see what kind of adults both of her male children turned out to be. David is one year younger than me. He and my other brother, Nathan, are supposedly ex-drug users. If you ask me, I say they're both current drug users. They've also both been in and out of jail a couple of times. I know that people who have been in jail can turn their lives around if they want to. But as far as I'm concerned, neither of them has even tried to change. They're always trying to get something for nothing, and both of them simply refuse to clean up their acts. In fact, David's a master manipulator. I call him the User King. If you don't suit his purpose, he has no use for you and he'll do whatever he has to do, say whatever he has to say to get whatever he wants to get out of you. Luckily, I'm hip to his bullshit so we barely interact. He's definitely got a lot of issues, though.

For one thing, he's married to two women. That's right. My brother's a bigamist. They know about each other and everything. And he spends time with whoever is doing the most for him at the moment. They even have similar names—Mona and Marva. He married Mona first. They met while he was in jail and have three kids together, the youngest being just a year old.

Personally, I've always wondered how anyone could have sex with Mona. When he met her she was a petite size five. Today she's well over three-hundred pounds. She's sickly, too. She suffers from severe asthma and is in and out of the hospital all the time. She says the weight gain is a result of the steroids her doctors prescribed to control her asthmatic condition. I could deal with the weight—everybody's not meant to be thin—but this chick also smells like a truckload of donkeys. The obesity is one thing, but there is simply no excuse for the funk. I happen to think that she's just so busy trying to keep track of my brother and doing her best to keep him away from Marva, that she doesn't tend to her own needs; not to mention those of my nephews and niece. Or maybe the rolls of fat prevent her from cleaning all the nooks and crannies properly—I mean, there are so many. But whatever the case, ol' girl needs to do something about that.

Then there's Marva who's been messing around with David since the tenth grade. We all grew up together. But David didn't marry her; he married Mona. Still all the while he was married to Mona—and in and out jail—he messed around with Marva until he just eventually married her, too. Somewhere in my family I once heard that he told Marva he'd divorced Mona but he didn't. He's also known as the The Lying King. Needless to say, my brother wears many crowns—but none that have any stones. In any event, I think that by now she should know that he never got a divorce. They all still deal with each other. And despite all of Mona's efforts to keep David and Marva apart, they had a baby who was born just one month after David and Mona's second child, Daniel. I think Marva named the child David, Jr. just to spite Mona. In my opinion, they're all a bunch of wackos.

It's really sad. But as far as I'm concerned, the ones who are truly suffering are the children because none of the adults are fit parents. Marva has about five kids of her own including David Jr. David claims all of her kids and they all call him Dad, which is actually no slack off his back. He can claim all of them because he doesn't actually support any of them. What I cannot seem to understand is why these two women would constantly fight over this piece of man who refuses to work, has a drug habit, periodically goes to jail, has several major health problems, and ultimately doesn't treat either of them well. I guess he must have some kind of other talents I'll never know about!

"How'd your meeting go last night, Hon?" Ma questioned, snapping me out of my train of thought.

"Pretty good. I'll tell you more about it later."

"Oh, you don't wanna talk in front of me?" David questioned defensively.

"Why wouldn't I want to talk in front of you?" I said, rolling my eyes.

"Whatever," David snapped as he picked up his plate and went into the living room. I was glad to see him go. As usual, he looked scruffy and unkempt. He desperately needed a haircut and looked like he hadn't slept in weeks. Knowing his lifestyle, he probably hadn't.

"What's that about?" I asked Mamma.

Mamma placed my plate in front of me. "He came up here last night on the train. I picked him up from the station. He needed somewhere to stay. I knew you were coming and how you'd feel about it, but how could I say no?"

"What about his women? Why couldn't he go stay with one of them? How can a man have two wives and still be homeless?"

"I don't know. He said something about Mona changing the locks and I think his ulcer's bleeding again."

"Really," I said sarcastically. "What about the other one? Why couldn't he go there?"

"I don't know, Ny. I didn't ask. When he asked me if he could come here, I just couldn't say no. He is my child too, you know."

My mamma the martyr!

I shoved a fork full of food into my mouth and quietly hoped David hadn't planned to stay the whole weekend. If he did, I certainly wouldn't. There was no way I would've been able to rest and relax with him around. I knew it was only a matter of time before he tried to hit me up for a loan, which we both knew he would never repay.

"Well, on a better topic, sit down and eat with me," I said to Mamma.

She sat across from me with her infamous cup of tea. Mamma had been drinking a cup of tea every morning for as long as I could remember. As a little girl I would see her at the kitchen table sipping from the same white porcelain cup with little blue flowers on the side. For some strange reason, I enjoyed watching her daily ritual. It was a part of her.

"No breakfast for you?"

"Naw, my tea is all the breakfast I need."

"Oh, don't tell me you're watching your figure, Ma."

"No, no, not at all. I leave that to other people!" She laughed. "No, I'm just really not in the mood to eat right now. Maybe a little later."

"I know you're not letting anything or anyone stress you out, are you, Ma?" I inquired, glaring my eyes toward the living room where David was sitting in front of the television.

"I'm fine, but I can't help but worry. Your brother doesn't look well at all," she said in a whisper.

"Well, when you do the kinds of things he does, you can't look good, Ma. But those are the choices that he's made and he can't blame anyone but himself—and you can't blame yourself either."

"I don't blame myself. It's just that when you have kids, you always want them to want the best for themselves. It saddens a parent when a child doesn't make wise decisions and choices. I guess you'll understand when you have children of your own."

"Believe it or not, Ma, I do understand. They are my brothers and sisters and it upsets me when they do stupid things, so I can just about imagine how you must feel. But they're all adults now, and you can't raise grown folks. You've already done your job. I know one thing. He'd better not ask me for any money. And how long does he expect to stay here?"

"I don't know. He hasn't said."

"Well, don't you think you should ask him?"

Mamma didn't answer. She just got up from the table with my empty plate and went to the sink. That meant she wasn't about to ask him. And that meant my weekend of relaxation wouldn't happen. I decided to change the subject and ask her if she was up for going to the mall with me. They had the greatest mall up there and the sales tax was a little lower, too. I hadn't even started my Christmas shopping and I really wanted to get into the holiday spirit, now that I knew I had that StarzSports deal sealed.

Speaking of StarzSports, I was trying really hard not to think about Victor, but I kept seeing his perfect smile in my mind.

"Yeah, I'd like to go with you, but I don't really want to leave your brother here all alone."

Now that really pissed me off. Mamma knew I'd come there for fun and relaxation, and she was going to spend the whole time worrying about him? I might as well have just turned around and gone back home.

"Ma, come on. I know you're not going to spend my whole weekend worrying about him, are you? What is it? Are you afraid to leave him in the house 'cause you think it won't be here when we get back?" I sarcastically questioned.

She looked at me with that "Shhhhhh, he might hear you!" look.

"Listen, I came up here to have a good time, not to watch you worry about folks who aren't even worried about themselves!"

I hated to snap at Mamma, but she was starting to aggravate me. I'd been looking forward to this weekend for a long time, and I wasn't about to let anyone mess it up for me. My mamma didn't say a word, which made me feel even worse. I couldn't believe this!

"Do you mind if he comes with us?" Mamma finally asked.

"Yes. As a matter of fact, I do! The last time he came shopping with us was when he stole a T-bone steak from the supermarket! Remember? I'm not going into a mall with him! He'll get us all arrested!"

There was a moment of silence before Mamma turned to me and said, "Nyagra, would you be too disappointed if I opted to stay here with David? Someone needs to keep an eye on him. He's not well and with ulcers, you never know. What if it starts to bleed and he needs to go to the hospital?"

"Then he'll call an ambulance! You know what, Ma? Forget it! If you're going to stay up here and baby-sit your son all weekend, I'm just going to go back home."

I got up from my seat and walked out of the kitchen. I could hear Mamma call my name as I climbed the stairs, but I kept going. I passed my brother who was nodding off. His now-empty plate was on the floor and I nearly stepped right in it. He disgusted me. As I made my way up the stairs to the bedroom, I wished I had some way to contact Victor. I started thinking that if he called we could perhaps spend another day together. I decided to take a shower and not even unpack.

If I leave within the hour, I'll be able to make it home before four, I thought. I knew Mamma would be upset if I left, but I couldn't stay there with David. He looked and acted like a drug addict, which made me real uncomfortable. If I couldn't stand being in his presence for one weekend, I sure didn't know how I was going to survive Christmas dinner.

Despite the circumstances, I was totally determined to enjoy a nice hot shower before I made my exit. Ma had this therapeutic showerhead and as the warm water ran down the crevices of my body, I stood completely still, just so I could feel each drop of water seeping its way into my pores. I felt like I was on cloud nine. As I closed my eyes and drifted into the steam-filled atmosphere, I couldn't keep Victor out of my thoughts. I wondered if he'd call, if he was thinking of me in the same way, if I'd see him before he returned to Atlanta, and when or if I'd see him again after he returned. I closed my eyes and imagined that he was in the shower with me, kissing my body and caressing each and every molecule of my moist skin. Then I snapped back to reality.

"I should slow down. I'm behaving like a schoolgirl with a crush," I thought out loud. It wasn't too wise to daydream like that. Besides, I didn't even know if he'd call.

I turned off the shower and found my way through the fog to the towel rack. I wiped off the mirror and took a good look at my face—something I hadn't done in a while. It was amazing. Lately, I'd been so busy that I hadn't even had a chance to check myself out. It looked all right, but I started to see signs of age.

All those late nights and early mornings at the office were starting to show. My light, almond-colored complexion didn't look as young and vibrant as it used to. I could now see laugh lines and signs of crow's feet by my eyes—something I'd never noticed before. I even saw what appeared to be the beginning of dark circles underneath my eyes. There was also a coarse gray hair smack in the middle of the front of my head, which I felt compelled to pull with a pair or tweezers I found in the medicine cabinet. They say that if you pull out a gray hair, ten will come back in its place. But that one hair looked so out of place in the center of my head, I simply decided to take my chances.

"Nyagra, you've got to start taking better care of yourself, Girlfriend," I said aloud. "Maybe weekly facials will do it. I think I'll call Naomi Sims' spa on Monday. Maybe I'll even break out my dusty old gym membership card and try to take some sort of class a couple of times a week."

After I completed my thoughts about my new health and beauty regimen, I smeared some moisturizer on my face, grabbed the cocoa butter lotion and headed for the door. As I quietly entered the bedroom on my tiptoes to ensure that I wouldn't drip too much on the carpet, I could see David by the window, digging inside my overnight bag searching for only God knows what (my wallet, no doubt). If I'd had a gun, I surely would've shot him.

"Do you mind telling me what the hell you're doing?" I practically yelled, obviously startling him. He jumped up and stood beside my bag with the guilty grin of Alice in Wonderland's Cheshire Cat.

"Answer me, David! What the fuck are you doing going through my bag?"

"I wasn't going through your fuckin' bag! I was looking out the window! I like the view from this side of the house!"

"Oh, you were looking out the window?! You're going to stand there and lie right in my face?"

I stepped closer to him, ready to slap the shit out of his ass, until I remembered that I still only had a towel wrapped around my body.

"I don't have to lie to you! Who the hell are you?" he yelled back.

At that moment, Ma appeared in the doorway. "What's all this yelling about? What's going on here?"

"This crackhead was trying to steal from me!" I told her.

"Who you calling a crackhead? I ain't gotta steal from you! I told you I was lookin' out the fuckin' window, you stuck-up bitch! You think you better than everybody but you ain't shit! You came from the same place I came from!"

"Yeah, well, if I ain't shit, you must be less than shit! 'Cause you're nothing but a common low-life junkie thief!"

"Fuck you, bitch!"

I could see the drugs in his eyes. He was over the edge and I couldn't understand how Ma couldn't see or admit it.

"Stop it! Stop this right now, both of you!" Ma finally yelled, stepping between us. She was shaking and I could see that her face was red with anxiety and anger.

"Stop what? Stop him from trying to steal from me?! I guess he wasn't bold enough to ask for a loan this time—so he just decided to take what he wanted! But you know what? You want me to stop, Ma? Well, I'll do even better than that!" I stormed over to my bag. As I struggled to hold the towel in place, I tossed the bag over my shoulder and went into the steamy bathroom, slamming the door so hard that paint fell down from the ceiling onto the top of my head. I quickly threw on my nylon Nike sweatsuit and shoved my feet into my sneakers. Not even bothering to lace them, I re-entered the now-empty bedroom, gathered the rest of my belongings and headed down the stairs toward the front door.

"Nyagra!" Mamma called from the kitchen.

"Ma, I'm going. I really wanted a stress-free and relaxing weekend. Instead I've got to watch my stuff and hope that it'll all be here when I leave," I said as I walked toward her.

"Honey, I don't want you to leave," she said. I could see that she was really upset and I hated upsetting my mother, but I had to do what was best for me.

"I know, Ma, but I can't stay here with him. Your son is a thief, Ma. He has a drug problem and you refuse to admit it. Drug addicts will do whatever they have to do to get high. Don't you understand that? Letting David stay here is not helping him, Ma, and it's also putting you and your home in danger. David needs help. If you want to help him, don't let him stay here. Get him some professional help."

"You're right. I'm going to suggest it, Nyagra. But I still don't want you to leave. You're here to visit me," she stated, almost in a childlike manner.

"Yes, but you've got to understand my position. I'm not up for this drama. I came up here to get away from the drama. But obviously, it's followed me. At least at home or even at my office, I don't have to worry about anybody stealing from me."

"Nyagra, he says he was just looking out the window," Mamma said, slipping back into the unrealistic state that seems so common throughout my family.

My family has this strong trait of being unable to face reality. I've noticed it in every single one of my siblings. You know how some families all share the same nose or eye color? Well, the Ensleys all share the trait of unrealistic thinking—a fear of facing what is true and real. Everyone except for me, that is. I swear, I was switched at birth.

"Ma, I'll call you later," I replied, shaking my head and knowing I was fighting a losing battle. I turned and walked out of the kitchen, grabbed my bags, and headed toward the front door.

"What a waste!" I mumbled, as the door slammed behind me.

I drove all the way back to Elmsford, totally pissed that I'd even wasted my time going there in the first place. I couldn't believe Mamma's blindness, and I really didn't think I'd be able to keep my word about spending Christmas with them.

I wasn't on the highway more than five minutes before my phone rang. I figured it was Mamma and although I truly didn't want to answer it, I knew I had to. I didn't have the heart to turn my back on my mamma. Deep down inside I understood that she was simply being the only way she knew how to be.

"Hello?" I asked, without looking at the caller ID.

"Ny?" the voice said. To my surprise, it was my sister, Juanita.

"Yeah?" I stated, knowing she was about to get into dialogue about the incident. I was in no mood.

"Mamma is really upset that you left. You should go back."

"Juanita, please! Don't get involved. I'm going home."

"Did you hear what I just said? I said our mamma is really upset!" Juanita tried to use the voice that used to scare me into doing whatever she wanted me to do when I was ten years old. Unfortunately for her, that shit stopped working twenty years ago.

"Did you hear what I said? I said I'm going home and for you not to get involved! In other words, mind you own business, Juanita. This does not concern you and you shouldn't get involved."

"What do you mean this does not concern me? My mamma is back there crying her eyes out because you left her house all in a huff and you say 'this does not concern me'? Of course, it concerns me! I'm her first-born!"

"Well, did your mamma tell you that that I caught your crackhead brother digging inside my bag trying to steal from me?"

"Are you sure he was trying to steal?"

"Oh, brother! They got to you, too? Well, big sister of mine—my mother's first born, I don't exactly remember your ass being so eager to give him the benefit of the doubt when he stole your fur coat and threw it out the seventh-floor window to Hector Martinez so you wouldn't see him take it out the front door. If I remember correctly, which I do, you wanted to cut his throat, and tried! So, get off my back and like I said— mind your own business!"

She knew what I said was factual. "Listen, all I'm saying is fuck David! Ma's totally upset! She's been waiting for weeks for you to come up there to stay with her! She was really looking forward to it."

"Well, if she was really looking forward to it, then she would've told his ass to leave when I caught him inside my bag. How is she just going to let him steal from me? Obviously, my being there wasn't that important!"

"Ny, you know Ma's not aggressive enough to ask one of her children to leave her house. You're being unreasonable and unrealistic."

I couldn't believe my ears.

"You know what, Juanita? This isn't a situation that warrants reason—although I think being robbed is a good enough reason to leave the scene in my book. Now, if you don't have anything else to talk about, I'll have to let you go."

"You know, you always have been contrary!"

"Yeah, yeah. I know, whatever."

Juanita continued rattling on about how I shouldn't have left Ma's house and how Ma doesn't need to be left alone with David. But her voice just became miscellaneous chatter in the back of my head. Finally, I decided to tell her a little white lie just to get rid of her. I just couldn't bear any more of the dramatics.

"Listen, I'm going through the mountains. Our connection is really bad . . . Juanita? . . . What was that? . . . What did you say? . . . I can't hear you . . . Hello? . . . Helloooo? . . . " Then I simply disconnected her ass and turned the phone off. Enough was enough!

To add to my aggravation, there was an accident on the highway and traffic was backed up for miles, causing me to arrive home at nearly 5:30. I approached the house and grabbed the day's mail from the box.

As I pushed open the front door, I heard the telephone ringing but chose not to answer it, doubting that it could be anybody other than Mamma or one of my "wonderful" siblings.

I dropped what proved to be my unnecessary overnight bag onto the imported forest green, Ethan Allen butter-soft, Italian-leather love seat, glanced through the mail and tossed it onto the coffee table.

"I'm so sorry I'm unavailable, but you know what to do, and I'll do my best to get back to you if you leave a name and a number. Have a nice day!" I heard my own voice say over the speaker of my so-called state-of-the-art answering machine.

Every time I thought about that machine, I was reminded of the Service Merchandise salesgirl who'd sold it to me. "An electronic personal receptionist" was what she'd called it. But it was really nothing more that an overpriced phone gadget. She obviously saw a sucker coming 'cause I'd paid well over $100 for that silly machine. Believe me, it was no better than the $39 one I'd had for damned near five years. It was supposed to have all these great advanced electronic features, but they were of no use to me because I didn't know how to work anything on it other than the on/off switch, the play button, and the greeting recorder. I guess I could eventually read the owner's manual—if I could find it-but, in the meantime, I surely felt ripped off.

Beeeeeeep!!!!

"Uh, Hello, Nyagra. This is Victor Reece . . . ," I heard through the speaker.

"Oh, my God!!! Victor Reece!" I said out loud. Should I pick it up? Should I call him back?

"I tried you at your mamma's but she said you'd already left. Maybe you're on your way back home. I was hoping we could get together again tonight. I'm leaving tomorrow and . . . "

That was all I needed to hear. Like a love-stricken teenager, I made a mad dash for the telephone and within a half a millisecond, regained my composure enough to manage to sound calm, cool and collected.

"Victor?"

"Ms. Ensley, how are you?"

"I'm fine, thank you," I lied. "I just walked through the door. You have perfect timing!"

"You decided not to stay with your mamma?"

"Well, she had an unexpected house guest and I felt it really wasn't a good time for me to be there."

"Well, I'd be lying if I told you that I'm sorry you had to cut your visit short. But I'm hoping that this means we'll be able to spend another evening together. I had a great time last night."

I blushed. "So did I and I'm sure another delightful evening can be arranged."

"Great! Where should we go? Why don't I come and pick you up?"

Oh, God! I thought. Should I let him come to my house so soon? I barely know him! My first instinct was to tell him that I'd meet him at our chosen restaurant, but then I heard Trish's annoying voice in the back of my mind: "Don't make life so easy for a man. Let him go out of his way and come to you. Once you start him out on the 'easy, I only have to do minimal for this woman' road, it'll be virtually impossible to get him to eat out of your hands later!" I heard her nagging voice say.

So, after a moment of thought, I figured it would be all right. If he turned out to be a psychopath or something, my company had all his information at StarzSports. He'd be pretty easy to trace. Plus, I'd surely let Trish know that I was going out with him. Not that I really thought he would risk his entire career by attempting to violate little ol' me.

"I guess that'll be fine," I finally replied.

"You guess?" He laughed. "What do you think? I'm a psycho or something? You don't trust me, Nyagra?!"

I giggled. "Well, I don't know, Victor . . . I'm really not a trusting person and I don't really know you yet."

"Fair enough," he chuckled. "Well, would you feel more comfortable meeting me someplace?" he asked, now a little more serious.

"No, I'm just joking. I'd be delighted to have you in my home. Let's see. It's going on six now so around eight or so?"

"That's perfect."

I gave him directions from Long Island to Elmsford and hung up the phone. I looked around the house. With the exception of my overnight bag and the mail I'd just tossed on the table, it was spotless.

"Thank God I had the cleaning lady in here yesterday morning," I said aloud with my hands on my hips.

Realizing that I didn't have much time, I pulled off my sweats as I headed into the bedroom. I turned on the shower and used the remote to click on the stereo. Although I felt like I'd just taken a shower, being angry with David, coupled with sitting in traffic, had surely caused me to work up a sweat. And I really wanted to be fresh and clean for Victor. After all, a shower that's taken for a day out with your mamma can be quite different from a shower for a hopefully romantic evening with a man of Victor Reece's caliber.

Once the bathroom had steamed up, I stepped into the glass stall. I momentarily stood beneath the water and let the steaming hot drops beat down on my neck as I absorbed the sounds of Toni Braxton (her debut album, of course). The music echoed crisply as it penetrated the Bose micro speakers Michael had strategically mounted on the burgundy and cream tiled walls—one of the only good things he ever did around this place (although I had to nag him for two months to get him to comply). As I smoothed Tiffany's silky shower gel on my body and hummed along with Toni as she "Breathed Again," I hoped that the moment would eventually come for me to breathe. Shit, lately I'd felt like I was about to die of asphyxiation.

As I showered, I really enjoyed the massage from the showerhead. The sensation of the warm water pounding swiftly onto my shoulders placed me into a much-needed deep state of relaxation. I didn't realize how stressed I'd been, but I had to prepare for Victor's arrival, so I got out and wrapped my body in a burgundy monogrammed towel.

As I entered my bedroom, the phone rang. I glanced at the clock, which read 6:38. "Hello?"

"What's up, Girl?"

It was Trish.

I sat down on the bed and began to apply Tiffany body lotion to my legs and feet. "What's going on? I was just about to call you."

"I just called your mamma's. She told me you'd left. What happened?"

"Sibling bullshit."

"Which one?"

"David."

"He was up there?"

"Yeah. Ma said his ass stumbled in there late last night. You know if I'd known he was going to be there, I wouldn't have gone."

"What was he doing there?"

"He claims Mona changed the locks on him or some old craziness. He's probably lying."

"So, what happened? You left just because he was there?"

"No. I caught his ass trying to steal something out of my bag while I was in the shower!"

"What?"

"You heard me. The nigga was trying to steal out my bag—probably looking for my wallet. Then when I busted his trifling ass, he said that he was looking out the window. Can you believe that?"

"What'd your mamma say?"

"She basically tried to side with him!"

"What?"

"Well, not outright. I guess she was trying to stay neutral. But how can you in a situation like that? Right is right and wrong is wrong. I know she doesn't want anyone to think she's playing favorites or anything, but goddamn—the nigga was stealing from me! There's got to be some sort of line you don't cross; wouldn't you say?"

"Drug addicts don't have any lines."

"You got that right." I sighed, getting up from my bed and walking over to the armoire to find the perfect pair of thongs.

"Wow, so what happened? You just left?"

"Hell, yeah, I left! I went up there to get away from the bullshit and stress and walked right into a whole 'nuther heap! I actually haven't been home long. Just long enough to take a shower."

"Damn, Girl. I'm sorry your weekend didn't go as planned. I know you'd been looking forward to it for a while."

"Then I'm in the car and Juanita calls me like I've done something wrong, telling me how upset Ma is and to go back to her house. But she shut the hell up when I reminded her of that time he tried to steal her fur coat."

"Oh, yeah, I remember that. He threw it out the window to Hector Martinez, didn't he?"

"He sure did. Anyway, after a couple of minutes I couldn't take it anymore so I faked a bad connection and cut her ass off."

Trish laughed. "Just like you do to me when I'm talking about something you don't want to hear." "I do not! I never do that to you!" I giggled as I lied.

"Yeah, yeah . . . Anyway, so what's up? What are you going to do now? It's Saturday night and Shawn Franklin's been asking about you."

"Shawn Franklin can go to hell and so can you for even bringing up his name," I said jokingly.

Trish giggled. "All right, all right. Why don't you come over here? Rodney's away for the weekend looking into a new business venture. The kids are at his sister's since she's taking them to a birthday party tomorrow. And I felt like making some straight-up Southern cuisine. I've got some beef spare ribs on the indoor barbecue grill and I'm about to fry up some chicken. I'm even making a little macaroni and cheese and collard greens."

"Damn, Trish. What's the occasion?" I asked as I slipped into my silk thong.

"No occasion. Just felt like cooking. You know how I get sometimes."

"You're not depressed about anything, are you? The last time you went all out like this, you and Rodney had that big fight."

"No, everything is fine. I actually wanted to try out a new recipe for peach cobbler and you can't make dessert without dinner. So, what's up? You coming over?"

Trish's cooking was hard to pass up, even for Victor Reece but, I replied, "I'd absolutely love to, but I have a date."

"A date? You little sneak! You have a date and you didn't tell me as soon as you picked up the phone?"

"Damn, Trish! You act like I haven't had a date in ten years!"

She giggled. "Well, have you? I mean have you really?"

"Oh, shut up!"

"Do I know him? It better not be that asshole, Michael!"

"Come on. Do I look like a goddamn fool to you? I'm trying to go forward, not backward!"

"All right . . . come on, come on, tell me. Who's the mystery fellow?"

"Victor Reece."

"Victor Reece? Mr. StarzSports?"

"Um, hmm."

I stood in the middle of my bedroom floor in my bra and panties and told Trish everything about Victor's call to my office and the details of our wonderful date. With the cordless phone on my shoulder, I told her about our fabulous dinner at Mecca and the visit to Rockefeller Center. As I walked inside my closet and began to search for the perfect outfit, I even told her about his ex-wife and daughter.

"It sounds like there could actually be something to this," she said.

"I'm not going to lie. I kind of hope there is."

"Wait a minute. I know you don't sound as anxious when you talk to him as you do right now, do you?"

"No, no. Don't worry. I hear your little nagging voice in the back of my mind every step of the way. I assure you, I'm following all of your directions."

"Good and don't you stop. I know you're an educated woman and know all about marketing and business. And when I decide to try my catering business again, I promise this time I'll listen to everything you say. You're the expert on that subject, but leave the men thing to me. On that, I'm the expert. This guy sounds like he has a great deal of potential. My only problem is that you don't have any of his phone numbers and he has three for you. I'll tell you this much. If he leaves New York without giving you a home telephone number, he's trouble. Trust me."

"I know. I've been thinking about that."

"Well, don't worry about it. Just keep it in mind. For now, it seems like he's done everything right," Trish said, sounding like a business-woman and strategist. To her, relationships are sort of a business.

I decided to wear my chocolate-colored angora mock-neck sweater with matching leggings. On my feet I donned a pair of brown suede Charles David boots that complemented the leggings quite well and accentuated my lean but shapely calves. I figured the outfit would be comfortable and could probably fit into any atmosphere. I laid it on the bed and began perfuming every inch of my body with Tiffany—of course.

"Why don't you stop by the house and let me meet Mr. Wonderful?" Trish suggested.

"Oh, Trish. I don't know. It's kind of early. It's only our second date and I'm already introducing him to my friends? Wouldn't that be kind of pushy?"

"Now would I suggest for you to do something pushy? Come on, Ny. I'm not suggesting that you come over and stay. All you have to do is tell him that you've got to drop something off. You come in first, leave him in the car, and when you go back, tell him you want him to meet your oldest and dearest friend. He'll come to the door, we'll shake hands, I'll give him the once-over without him even knowing it, and you guys will be on your way. It's as simple as that."

"Yeah, well, you do make it sound pretty simple."

"It is, Silly! I just want to feel his vibe. You know I'm good at that kind of stuff. It'll take two minutes tops."

"I guess it can't hurt."

"It certainly can't!" she assured me.

"I'd better go so I can be ready when he gets here. He's pretty punctual."

"All right. What are you wearing?"

"A mock-neck with matching leggings and suede boots."

"Sounds good. What color?"

"Chocolate."

"I don't have to worry about you and fashion. You always look good, Girl."

"Well, what'd you ask for then?" I jokingly snapped.

"Just curious! Go ahead. I'll see you guys in a little bit."

"OK."

I hung up and quickly jumped into my clothes. I had a little more than a half-hour before Victor was scheduled to arrive, and it would take me that long to do my hair and makeup. I sat at the vanity and began to apply my custom-blended foundation. As I stared into my reflection, I realized that I had not had a man in my house since Michael had moved out. I was a bit nervous about it, too. I don't know why, but every time I bring a new guy into my house for the first time, I always feel anxious and uneasy about it. However, once my date arrives, I feel fine. The anxiety vanishes and I usually end up being quite a good hostess, if I do say so myself. I think it's just some sort of mental thing.

By 7:45, I was ready. My face was completely made up the natural-looking way, which is the only way I wear makeup. I decided to do my hair in a simple ponytail with a part on the right side. As I waited for Victor, I wondered if I should call Ma to make sure that she was all right. I decided against it, not wanting to start up a big thing again. I certainly didn't want to be in the middle of a conversation about David when Victor arrived. That issue could wait until the morning.

The sounds of Mint Condition flowed through my speakers. I'm an avid listener of good music and always keep the best in my disc player. It relaxes me and sets my mood. I hoped it would do the same for Victor. To further enhance the atmosphere, I went into the bathroom cabinet and retrieved a can of air freshener to make the house smell fresh and clean. A few drops came out, but it was almost empty. I went into the kitchen and lit a vanilla incense stick I found in the drawer Michael had left behind. He was appalled by aerosol cans and their contribution to the corrosion of the ozone layer. Whatever! As soon as I kicked his ass out, one of the first things I did was buy five cans of Wizard air freshener in five different scents. But they were downstairs in the basement supply closet and I didn't feel like going down there. The incense quickly started to kick in and the house smelt really good. I was nervous but more than ready for him to arrive.

The clock read 8:02 when I heard Victor's car pull into the driveway.

I didn't want it to look like I was just standing around waiting for him so I ran into the den and pulled out a copy of Zane's Addicted. I opened it to a miscellaneous page and strategically placed it on the living room table to make it look like I had been chilling out reading.

Why am I fronting? I asked myself. The doorbell rang and I opened the door to find Victor looking as handsome as ever.

"Victor!"

He reached down to hug me tight. "Nyagra, you're even more gorgeous than you were last night. I didn't think that was possible!"

"Thank you. Please, come in."

Victor stepped across my threshold. He reminded me of a black version of Greek God Zeus. He was beautiful! This time he wore dark brown wool slacks and a cream-colored cashmere mock-neck beneath a long brown, double-breasted wool coat. His brown lace-up Gucci oxfords matched impeccably. The man definitely had good taste. That was plain to see. Then again, Victor probably would've looked good in a brown paper bag.

"Let me take your coat," I offered.

"You have a lovely home, just as I expected." Victor smiled as he looked around and handed me his overcoat.

"You did?" I questioned, walking to the closet and placing his coat inside.

"Definitely. I can tell that you're a woman with good taste and a knowledge of fine things."

"Oh, really?" I smirked, as if I believed he was trying to run a line.

"Really. I'm being very honest! You and this lovely home certainly go hand in hand."

"Thank you. Have a seat. Can I offer you something to drink? I know you're not big on alcohol, but I've got some cranberry juice and soda."

"Cranberry juice would be great," he said, sitting on the sofa.

I headed to the kitchen hoping (praying even) that I actually had some juice. Luckily, there was a bottle in the cabinet.

"Where do you want to eat? I'm in your territory now, so you'll have to lead me," Victor called from the living room.

"Well, what are you in the mood for?" I asked as I reentered the living room with his juice.

"Hmmm . . . " Victor eyed me lustfully. This was the first time he'd made a sexual gesture and I liked it. "I'm open to whatever. I'm not all that picky."

"Well, there's a lovely little Italian restaurant not too far from here. It's not fancy, but the food is wonderful and the atmosphere is definitely charming."

"I love Italian food."

I smiled. "So, we'll go there." I turned off the music and grabbed our coats from the closet.

As I handed him his coat, he eyed my mink and calmly stated, "Nyagra, I'm an anti-fur activist. Would you mind if I asked you to wear something else?"

"Oh, oh, OK . . . um, not at all. What about shearlings?" I jokingly questioned.

"I guess they're OK. They don't kill the sheep to make shearlings, do they?" he replied quite seriously. I was actually attempting to make light of the situation, but he obviously found nothing humorous. So I just grabbed my shearling from the same closet and like the gentleman that he was, he helped me put it on.

He's one of those animal rights fanatics, I thought to myself. Man, I paid over $10,000 for that mink!

"If you don't mind, Victor, I need to make a quick stop at my best friend's house to drop something off for my godchildren. It'll only take a moment and it's on the way," I said as I closed the front door behind us.

"Not a problem."

"Shall we take your car or mine?"

"We should probably take yours since you know exactly where we're going."

"Fine."

The ten-minute ride to Trish's was quiet and a little uncomfortable. I think the fur coat issue threw a bit of a curve ball into the mood. I hoped it would get back on track, but I also couldn't help but think about those fanatical personalities that I'd seen on the news boycotting fashion shows and furriers, throwing paint on people's clothes and screaming obscenities—as if this wasn't a free country. In any event, I was absolutely convinced that if this relationship was to go any further, I'd surely have to change his mind about my mink. I'd be damned if I was going to treat my mink like it was some pork chop sandwich. I'm sorry—he'd just have to get the hell over it.

I pulled into Trish's circular driveway and stopped my Range Rover in front of the door.

"I'm going to leave the jeep running 'cause I'll be back in a flash!" I smiled.

"I'll be here," he replied. I rang the doorbell of her exquisite French Tudor mini mansion and Trish opened the door so quickly that I knew she must've been standing at the window waiting. I stepped into the foyer and she asked in a whisper, "So, how's it going?"

"You don't have to whisper, Trish. He's in the jeep. He can't hear us!" I laughed.

"Oh, oh . . . " She giggled. "Anyway, is it going well?" she continued at a more normal voice level.

"Yeah, it's going OK. He's against fur coats, though."

"What? One of those paint throwing fanatics? Oh, please!"

"I know, right. But I figure I could probably change his mind on that eventually."

"Yeah, well, one good fuck and he won't give a damn what you wear!" She laughed.

"Oh, shut up! Girl, you're crazy!"

"Well, you look great as usual. Where are you going for dinner?"

"Bella Roma's."

"Umm, romantic. Are you ready for that?"

"Oh, it's not all that romantic. I'm just in the mood for fettuccini."

"Yeah, right."

"Really! But I must admit, your food smells damn good, Girl," I said as I took a good whiff of the aroma that flowed throughout the air.

"I told you!"

"Save me a plate."

"Come over tomorrow for lunch. There'll be plenty left and I don't expect Rodney or the kids to be back until the evening."

"I'll be here."

"Well, go get Lover Boy!"

"OK."

I ran out to the jeep and tapped on the window. As he rolled it down, I said, "Victor, since you're here, I'd really like you to meet my best friend in the world."

"Well, all right." He shrugged. He stepped out of the jeep and walked up the steps to Trish's door where she was standing.

"Victor Reece, I'd like you to meet my oldest and dearest friend, Trish Hill."

"Very nice to meet you." He reached out to shake her hand.

"Likewise." Trish grinned as she did the same.

"The holiday decorations on your home are beautiful," he said, complimenting her with that infamous charm. It was true, though.

Every year Rodney would decorate their house to make it look like a fabulous miniature Christmas castle. This year was no exception. It was lovely.

"Thank you. It's my husband's tradition," Trish replied. "Well, you guys enjoy your evening."

"OK, Girl," I said as I gave her a hug.

"Pleasure meeting you," Victor said.

"Same here," Trish responded.

"I'll call you tomorrow. We're on for lunch, right?" I confirmed, walking down the steps toward the jeep.

"Absolutely!" she called from the doorway.

As we drove off, I felt something was weird about Trish. She must've sensed something. I didn't know what, but I figured I'd deal with it the next day. Tonight was for me and Victor. And I wanted him, even if one day it would only be a memory.

Three

"Check, please," Victor called to the waiter.

Dinner was magnificent. Bella Roma's never let me down. The conversation was stimulating and intriguing once again. This time I learned all about his childhood in Queens. He grew up living with his mamma and sister, Elaine. His mamma had passed away two years earlier from ovarian cancer and he and his sister were very close. We shared all kinds of stories, but given my background, my topics of conversation focused more on my academic accomplishments than my family life.

On the other hand, Victor spoke almost exclusively of his family and even showed me several pictures of his daughter at different stages in her life. It was evident that he was really into his child. I could tell he truly adored her. She was a beautiful cocoa-colored little thing with thick black ponytails and her Daddy's twinkling eyes. Over dinner we both opened up to each other a great deal. Surprisingly, I felt very comfortable with him even after the mink coat issue—comfortable enough to tell him about my situation with Michael and the townhouse—an issue I rarely discussed.

The mood in Bella Roma's was a lot more romantic than I remembered. Then again, the last time I'd been there was with Michael, and there was nothing romantic about him. With Michael, everything was scheduled, planned, and ultimately sterile and stiff—just like his office. Whenever we did anything together, I always felt like he was about to perform a root canal on me.

Victor and I were much more relaxed and even got bold enough to have two glasses of red wine, which helped the conversation flow like water. Neither of us was drunk, but we were certainly loose. Again I did not want the night to end. As I looked into his dark brown eyes above the candlelight, I wasn't so sure if I was going to let it.

Victor paid the check, and the ride back to the house was filled with laughter and flirtatiousness—quite different from the ride to Trish's house. It was obvious that there was a strong attraction between us. I can't deny that I truly wanted Victor to make love to me and hold me tightly. Even before Michael and I had broken up, it had been a long time since we'd made love. We'd periodically have sex but we hadn't made love in over a year. Not that I was actually "in love" with Victor, but he definitely had a tenderness about him that I knew could translate into a lot more than just quick sex.

"Nyagra, thank you for making this visit to New York so memorable," he began as we pulled into my driveway.

I blushed. "Well, I enjoyed your presence as well."

"You're as beautiful on the inside as you are on the out."

"Thank you and you are a very fine gentleman, Victor Reece." In the back of my mind, I said to myself, Nyagra, cut the bullshit. Are you going to give up the goods or what?

Just then, Victor reached over and placed his cushiony soft lips on top of mine. I eagerly returned the motion and before I knew it, Victor's tongue was half-way down my throat and his masculine, well-manicured hands were all around my body. As I lost myself in his arms, I wanted to melt and allow him to sweep me away. It didn't matter that we'd only known each other for a few days. It didn't matter to me that he held the strings to a multimillion-dollar account for my firm. All that mattered to me at that moment was whether or not he had a condom in his pocket.

"Wait a minute. Wait a minute," I stated, pushing him away a bit.

"Oh, I'm sorry. Is there something wrong, Nyagra? Am I moving too fast for you?" he questioned as he rose up off me.

"Hell, yeah!" said my brain.

"Hell, no!" said my body.

"No. No. Maybe we should just take this inside," said my lips.

I couldn't believe I said that. The behavior was totally unlike me. We'd just met. What was I doing?

"Are you sure? I really don't want to rush you. I can wait as long as you want me to," he assured me.

His compassion and understanding made me want him that much more. Maybe that was part of his charm or maybe that was part of his con. Whatever it was, it was working because I nervously smiled.

"I'm sure, Victor. I'm sure."

I opened up my front door and couldn't switch on the light before his full, luscious lips were all over my body, sending sensations throughout my cells that I hadn't felt in years. Unable to resist each other, we fell inside the house. If it had been up to him, we probably would've made love (or rather "had sex") right in the middle of my living room floor. This may sound funny, but I actually didn't want to cheapen the experience any more than it already was. So, I opted to lead our hot and heavy behavior upstairs to the bedroom. Most of our clothes dropped off along the way. I was so glad that I'd put on a matching bra and panties set. Usually I didn't because no one is looking but it wouldn't have mattered anyway. I wanted this man. In my heart I knew I really didn't know anything about him, but my desire to be physically intimate with him was too great for me to control. It was like an animal had come out of me that had been caged up for centuries. I barely recognized myself.

Even though the room was dark, I could clearly see the shadow of Victor's manhood stiffly standing at attention like a highly decorated U.S. soldier. I nearly fainted with excitement as I watched him remove a condom from its wrapper and put it on. Once he was ready and completely "armed" for lovemaking, I sensuously led him over to the bed where I guided his muscular hands through the motions of removing my undergarments. I laid my body down in the center of the goose-down comforter that covered my king-sized bed. Within seconds Victor's body was on top of me and finally inside of me. The thrust of his fabulously muscular physique in and out of my flesh took me to a place that I'd never been before in my entire life.

I wasn't a virgin and I'd experienced my share of sexual partners, but this man was totally out of this world. He was gentle and rugged at the same time; hard yet soft. It was the best sexual experience of my life. Victor kissed places on my body that I never knew existed. He wasn't afraid to explore my crevices as his baby-soft flesh melted on top of mine. The rhythmic motion of Victor's lovemaking was like a graceful ballet, sending me into a frenzied passion, yearning for more and more with every stroke of his love. And the brother could hang, too. This was no five- or ten-minute event. I don't know how long it lasted or how many times we repeated the union of our flesh, but like the S.O.S. Band, he certainly took his time and did it right!

I'm definitely going to church on Sunday, I thought.

The sun shone brightly through the bedroom window, so brilliantly that I could barely read the digital numbers on the clock on the night-stand. As I squinted and blocked the sun with my hand, I realized that the clock read 8:45 A.M. I also discovered that Victor was gone.

I pulled myself up from the bed and grabbed my robe from the chaise. I hadn't even heard him leave. I went downstairs into the living room. Looking around, I realized that he was gone. I walked into the kitchen to see if he'd left a note. To my surprise, there was one on the counter.

Dear Nyagra,

I didn't want to wake you—you were sleeping so peacefully and looked so beautiful. I had a 9 A.M. flight back to Atlanta but I will call you as soon as I arrive.

PS. You were fabulous!

Victor

"Hmm, sweet note but still no phone number," I said out loud. It was early so I decided to try to get a couple more hours of sleep before I went to Trish's. I wished he would've awakened me before leaving, but there was nothing I could do about that. So I jumped back underneath my fluffy comforter and thought about how good Victor had made me feel as I drifted back off to sleep.

"So he really had it going on in the sex department, huh?" Trish asked after I'd finished telling her all about my escapade.

We sat in the middle of her den floor totally pigging out. All the leftovers from the previous night were sprawled on a blanket. I couldn't help but stuff myself. For some reason I was starving, and Trish is one of the best cooks in the world.

"Yeah, he definitely had skills, but then he left in the middle of the night. I don't even know what time. That really wasn't cool to me," I said, sucking on a barbecued chicken wing.

"You didn't wake up? You usually sleep so softly."

"Yeah, I know."

"He must've really rocked your world!" She cackled. "But seriously, Girl. That's some shady shit. And still no phone number, right?"

"No, but it doesn't necessarily mean he's shady. Maybe he just didn't want to wake me. He said he'd call when he got to Atlanta," I stated, a little on the defensive. I didn't really want to think that Victor was full of shit.

"Ny, a 9 A.M. flight to Atlanta would've touched down by eleven. He could've called you at least by noon. You didn't leave your house until after one," Trish reminded me. But I didn't want to be reminded. I wanted to be ignorant and blissful for once—at least for a little while before I was forced to face reality. Every once in a while I fall into the Ensley motif and decide to ignore reality. This was one of those occasions.

"Trish, can't you just let me bask in the sunshine for a minute? Why can't you just let me savor the moment? Why do you have to ruin it?"

"I'm sorry, Girl. I won't say another word."

"No. No. It's not that." I sighed. "It's just been a while since I've been excited about something, or should I say someone. You know that. I just kind of want to enjoy it for a few minutes; even if it ends tomorrow. I know you're looking out for my best interest. I know . . . "

"You know I am . . . ," she replied, taking a sip of her lemonade. "Listen, I just want you to be careful. I don't want you getting all caught up in this guy and he turns out to be a fantasy. I just don't want you to get hurt."

"I know, but I'm a big girl. I can handle whatever negative things result from me giving it up so quickly. I mean, I really only did know him a few days. But we're both consenting adults and I wanted him, Girl."

"Is that what you're thinking? Child, please. I don't think that's the reason for his behavior at all. I sexed Rodney the first night I met his ass. And look, we've been happily married for years. If it's meant to be, it will be. It doesn't matter if you wait one night or a thousand. Victor does seem like he has a lot to offer. He's fine and all that and he's got a lot of charm going on and his position at StarzSports doesn't hurt. But, Girl, personally, I think this man has TAKEN written all over him. What about this ex-wife?"

"I don't know. What about her?"

"Well, I'm just not so sure that she's an 'ex.' Whatever the case may be, there's definitely another woman stashed somewhere."

"You really think so?"

"Yeah, I know these things, Girl. I could tell by the look in his eye when I shook his hand."

"Come on, Trish. How the hell could you tell that by shaking the man's hand?"

"Trust me. You know I have a sixth sense about these kinds of things. That little boy in that movie with Bruce Willis doesn't have shit on me." She laughed. "All I'm saying is be careful. If you just want to have a little bit of fun, especially since he's that good in bed, go ahead. Just make sure the brotha wears a condom and don't go falling in love or anything crazy like that. You have nothing to lose so enjoy yourself. But be careful."

"But I don't want to be sexin' somebody else's man. I do have morals, you know."

"So do you want me to do a Sherlock Holmes and investigate this guy?"

"Oh, Trish, I don't know. I don't want to be stalkin' the man or anything like that."

"You won't be. But how the hell do you expect to find out anything if you don't do some investigation?"

"Maybe I should just ask him."

"Oh, yeah, Ny. Why don't you just ask him? He'll tell you the truth. He'll say, 'Oh, yeah. I wined you and dined you two nights in a row. We made passionate love on the second night, but that ex-wife I have. Well, she's not so ex. But you don't mind, do you?' Yeah, that's what he'll say.

Don't forget that he already told you that she's his ex-wife. What do you think? He's going to come clean now? After the sex was so good?" She smirked.

"Yeah, maybe you're right."

"Listen, like I said, have fun with it. He'll call you eventually. Feel it out. Anyway, it would be a long distance relationship and those usually don't last too long. So just enjoy it while it lasts. Who knows? In a couple more weeks, you might not even want to be bothered."

"Let me get more ice for the lemonade," I said as I got up with the empty bucket in my hand and headed toward Trish's magnificent gourmet kitchen.

"Grab a couple more rolls from the warmer, too," she called.

I filled the bucket from the ice machine and snatched a linen napkin from the drawer for the rolls. All the while I was thinking of last night's experience with Victor.

No matter what, I still should've waited longer to become intimate with him. Maybe he was still married. After all, what woman in her right mind would divorce a man like him? As I sat back down on the floor with Trish, she must have noticed the look on my face.

"Listen, don't go getting all dismal and concerned on me," she said. "You should be up and joyous! Hear you tell it, you just had the best piece of ass you've ever had!"

"Yeah, but now you've got me thinking."

"And you should always be thinking! That's how we women lose control. We get all wrapped up in a man and then stop thinking! Women run this world. Where we mess up is when we stop thinking. Men will always play their little games. The way we stay in control is to let them play their games and play along with them. But never let them know that we're hip to the bullshit. You and I both know that I've had my share of OPM."

"Opium? The drug? What the hell are you talking about?"

"O-P-M, not opium. O-P-M. Other people's men, Girl. Other people's men. The ones that are married, living with somebody, the ones that try to run that bullshit by saying 'Oh, I've never had a girlfriend' and every chick they've been with feels differently. Well, all of them are other people's men. But the thing about me is when I'm tired of them, it's over. They think that I think they're all mine. But I know the deal. It's like I can spot them a mile away. So I use them for whatever purpose. Whether it's money, gifts, trips, fun, excitement, whatever. Until I get bored or the excitement dies down, whichever happens first, and then on to the next one. Of course, that was all before I married Rodney."

I laughed. "Of course!"

"Seriously, you know I haven't cheated on Rodney. Lucky for him, he hasn't given me a reason to. But you're single. You're financially secure and independent, you're beautiful. The world is yours, Girl!"

"Yeah, well I don't know about all that."

"It's true, girl. Now listen, if you want to find out about Lover Boy, just let me know. I have a couple of friends in Atlanta who I'm sure could give me the scoop on his ass," Trish assured me.

"Yeah, OK. I'll let you know. And don't you go finding out anything until I do!"

"OK. OK."

"I'm serious, Trish!"

"I said OK, didn't I?"

Sunday passed with no word from Victor. It was Monday morning and I was on my way back to the office for another diligent week. The next account I was going after was Wendy's Hamburgers. I'd heard through the advertising grapevine that it was severing ties with its advertising firm and I was confident we could come up with some great campaigns for the company.

My agenda was quite busy: meetings on how to go after the Wendy's account; a brainstorming, new-business pitch session; a commercial shoot for a cookie Nabisco was introducing; and a follow-up conversation with StarzSports Apparel requesting signatures on our proposal. That was the call I dreaded most.

I wasn't about to start calling Victor at the office, even if it was for business. I hoped my little romp in the sack with him didn't cost Newman & Stein this account.

In any event, I certainly wasn't going to tell anyone at the office what had happened over the weekend. And even though I felt that my assistant, Judy, knew something, I surely wasn't going to confirm a thing. I didn't have any friends at my office although I conversed with Judy more than anyone. She was a 24-year-old black woman, just out of college who I actually liked very much. Her ambition, drive and personality reminded me so much of myself at her age. So when I interviewed her, I knew immediately that she should be hired. She was a graduate student at NYU, and she'd only been working for me since I'd become vice president. Although I hadn't known her very long, I felt quite comfortable with her but not enough to let her know about my escapade with Victor Reece.

Generally speaking, I really had nothing in common with my co-workers since ninety-five percent of them were older white men. I could somewhat identify with a couple of the other female executives, but most of them were older Caucasians as well. Basically, the relationships I had with them were purely professional. I felt like they weren't interested in my personal life nor did I care about theirs. Overall, the office climate was pleasant and everyone seemed to respect one another—at least on the outside—although a couple of people had gotten a little huffy when I was named VP. But that was their problem, not mine. And since no one had ever said anything to me about it, it was easy to ignore.

I got to the office about nine and as I exited the elevator, I saw Will, the Federal Express guy, standing at the reception desk. All the young women in the office had a crush on Will. I'll admit he was cute. A looked a bit young, though. Whenever he'd drop off the morning packages, all the women in the office would make up any excuse to come out into the reception area, and I could tell that he definitely noticed. Whenever I saw him, he'd always try to flirt with me, but I'd never pay him any real attention. I mean, he was the Federal Express guy, for heaven's sake!

"Hi, Nyagra! You're looking beautiful today as usual." He smiled as I exited the elevator.

"Thank you, Will." I blushed as I passed him.

I could hear all the women giggling behind me. I walked into my office and tossed my briefcase onto the leather love seat. For some reason, I suddenly felt like turning around and going back home. The winter sun was beaming through the shaded window and bouncing off the framed mirror on the wall. The glare was so intense that I could barely see. Before I could sit down in my chair or lower my blinds, Judy was already buzzing me.

"Yeah?" I called as I walked toward the intercom.

"Victor Reece on line one," she replied. My heart started pounding so hard I swore I could see it through my blouse.

"Nyagra Ensley," I stated with composure as I lifted the receiver from its cradle.

"Nyagra."

"Oh, I see you made it home all right."

"Yes. As a matter of fact I did." He laughed. Personally, I didn't see anything funny.

"Is this a business call or a personal call, Mr. Reece?"

"Both."

"OK, business first. What's going on with the execution of my proposal? Is this a done deal or what? My people would really like to get started on this," I stated, using my authoritarian voice to mask my discomfort.

"Well, it's definitely a done deal, as you put it. We were most impressed with your company and we certainly want to give you our business. In fact, my assistant is getting the necessary signatures as we speak."

I smiled. "Well, that's what I like to hear."

"So, can we get to the personal aspect of this call now that you know your deal is closed?"

"I suppose so." I smirked. I found it difficult to be angry with him as we spoke. It was almost as if he had some sort of spell over me that prevented me from being pissed. Not only did he leave my bed in the middle of the night, but it also had taken him two days to call.

"I absolutely loved our evening together," he continued.

"I enjoyed myself, too."

"You were fabulous!" he whispered.

"Oh, I was, was I? Well, you weren't so bad yourself. However, I'm not too keen on disappearing acts."

"I'm sorry about that, but I did have an early flight."

"You could've still said goodbye."

"You were sleeping so perfectly. I didn't want to disturb you."

"I would've preferred that you disturbed me."

"OK, it won't happen again."

"Thank you."

There was a moment of silence before he finally asked, "So when can I see you again?"

"Why don't you tell me?"

"Hmm, how about this weekend? I'll fly up. That is, if you don't have plans."

"It's only Monday, but I suppose I'm free." I replied nonchalantly.

"Well, then, I'd say it's settled. I'll take a 6:30 P.M. flight Friday and I'll be there before nine. You will be at the airport to pick me up, won't you?" he inquired.

"Yeah, I guess I can be there."

"You better!" he joked.

"Just e-mail me all of the information."

"I can hardly wait!"

"I'll be looking forward to it, too!" I confessed.

"Do you have a busy week planned?"

"Yes, very."

"Yeah, so do I."

"Well, we'll be in touch toward the end of the week."

"We certainly will."

"OK."

"And Nyagra?"

"Yes?"

"You'll have your proposal in your hands no later than Wednesday morning."

"I'll be waiting for it." I smirked, hanging up the telephone receiver. I could've done a triple somersault. If I knew how to moon walk, I would've done that, too. I felt so happy and proud of myself, I just didn't know what to do. I got the guy and the deal and had I been a cigar smoker, I surely would've lit one up to celebrate. Life is good.

I wanted to call Trish to let her know that he wasn't just going to disappear from my life—"hit it and quit it" as she called it. But it was nearly time for my staff meeting. I had so much to do—new issues to address, the commercial shoot, among other things. Looking over my planner, I realized once again how busy the week was going to be. It was going to be even longer now that I was awaiting Victor's arrival.

"You know Ma checked David into the hospital again, right?" Juanita informed me as I prepared our Lean Cuisine meals. I hadn't seen my sister in a couple of weeks and she really wanted to visit. She'd paged me earlier that day in one of her depressed modes. Although I wasn't really in the mood for company, I suggested that she meet me at the office and stay overnight at my house. Since it wasn't planned and I really don't cook during the week, I hadn't taken anything out of the freezer. So I figured Lean Cuisines would be just fine.

I love my sister dearly, but probably only because she is my sister. Most likely I wouldn't have been her friend had we met under any other circumstances. She really has way too many issues, and generally, I like to stay problem-free. I don't exactly know what her problems stem from. It's pretty difficult to pinpoint. I mean, we were raised under the exact same roof and I didn't seem to suffer from the emotional ailments she possessed—never mind the financial. Then again, I seemed to be the only one out of six children that appeared to be half-way productive. Or should I simply say that I am the only one who pretty much has it together socially, emotionally and financially—depending on one's definition of the word "together." I guess productivity is in the eye of the beholder and to them, I might be the one who's abnormal.

Anyway, out of all my brothers and sisters, Juanita is the only one I have any regular communication with and thus, she's my only biological connection to my childhood.

I've known Trish all my life and she is truly like a sister to me. But, of course, she wasn't raised in our household and thus, did not experience the true feeling of being one of my parents' children, raised as an Ensley in a three-bedroom apartment with five other siblings.

As I pulled the steaming Lean Cuisine meals from the oven, Juanita began, "All this modern technology in this kitchen and you put those things in the oven? What's wrong with the microwave? We could've been finished eating already!"

I grabbed a couple of forks from the drawer. "Yeah, well, I'm old-fashioned and to me, the microwave is purely for reheating things—and for popcorn. I don't believe in cooking in the microwave. Things taste so much better when you put them in the oven."

"If you say so . . . " She laughed.

We took our meals to the breakfast bar. Her visit was unplanned and informal and I truly didn't feel like setting the dining room table. Of course, knowing my dear sister's personality, it was a bit of a risky act for she tends to be quite petty and a bit of a nitpicker. In the back of my mind I knew one day I'd hear, "You would've set the table for anyone else, but not for me!" However, that particular day I really couldn't have cared less. I was tired and the fact that I even invited her over on a Tuesday night was something she should've appreciated.

My sister suffers from chronic depression, the disease. She had sounded pretty terrible on the phone earlier that day and I didn't want her to be alone that night. Although I had an early breakfast meeting with Wendy's, I knew that Victor would be coming, so I wouldn't have been able to see her over the weekend. Therefore, I asked her to stay over. Not to mention that if I hadn't invited her, I knew she would've asked me to come anyway. If I had told her "no," she would've wanted to know why and I wasn't ready to tell her.

"Did you hear me when I said that David's in the hospital again?" she questioned as she cut her chicken marsala. It actually looked pretty good for a frozen entree. I decided to have the spaghetti with meatballs.

"Yeah, I heard you."

"No comment, huh?"

I stuffed a meatball down my throat. "Nope."

"Well, have you even spoken to Ma since you left on Saturday?"

"Nope."

"Why not?"

"Been busy. I do work, you know."

"What's that supposed to mean?" she asked, obviously offended. Insecure people tend to get defensive quickly and although I wasn't actually making reference to her unemployed ass, I could sense confrontation, which I was not in the mood to deal with.

"What that's supposed to mean is that I have busy days and work long hours and when I get a moment of free time, I'm not in the mood for bullshit. And as long as your brother is staying up there with Ma, there will always be bullshit," I snapped.

"Oh . . . ," she said, seemingly relieved that I wasn't making reference to her.

"Well, I called on Sunday and Cheryl was there. I think she's staying there now, 'cause I called up Monday morning around nine and she answered the phone."

"Oh, really?" I replied, totally uninterested.

"Yeah, and as usual, she pissed me the hell off. Sometimes I really feel like going up there and smacking her head clear off her neck."

"So what else is new?"

"Well, it's just not called for. I thought that when Ma moved without her, I wouldn't have to go through that crap anymore. Now it's starting all over again."

"Yeah, well, what happened?" I asked. I wasn't really interested but knew that she'd tell me anyway.

"She answered the phone when I called and when I asked for Ma, she said, 'She's at the store,' and slammed the phone down in my ear."

"Yeah, well, like I said, what else is new? That's the very reason why she and I always used to get into it when they lived on St. Nicholas Avenue."

"Yeah, I know. But I get real sick and tired of her rudeness. I told Ma and, as usual, she said nothing."

"But, of course," I said sarcastically.

"Anyway, if it happens one time or a million, I'm never gonna get used to it."

"You might as well. She's always been like that and she always will be. She must be one miserable heffa to be that damn nasty all the time, 'cause anybody who's genuinely happy and content just isn't that mean every single day. I just can't take the personalities. That's why I only deal with those people in moderation. I don't even think I'm going up there for Christmas."

"You're not going for Christmas? You have to! Ma will be heartbroken! I want you there, too. I was planning to ride with you."

"Yeah, well, when your siblings start acting like the assholes that they are—which you know that they will—she won't say a word. I can't take that shit! It's like they have all the rights and we have none. But it's always been like that. I guess I've just outgrown the drama. The last holiday we tried to spend together was damn near five years ago and there was conflict then. I just don't feel like ruining my holiday. And it truly pisses me off that no matter what they do, Ma seems to just look the other way."

"Well, that's her way of staying neutral."

"Neutral, my ass! The way I see it is if you don't help to stop a problem, you're making a contribution to it. Her silence condones their behavior! That's the reason I just don't deal. We all know that I'm the only one who helps Ma out financially and I will continue to do so. That's my way of showing that I care. But I really don't feel that I'm obligated to spend time with her children. They may be my siblings and you can quote family this and family that. But to me, family is as family does and people in the street have treated me better than they have. Shit, Trish has been more of a sister to me than Monica and Cheryl and both of them have actually lived in my house at one point or another."

"Well, I'm in the process of trying to find a job now so that I can help Ma, too."

Yeah, right, I thought, but didn't dare say. Juanita had been in the process of finding a job for five years.

"In fact, I need you to do another resume for me and maybe lend me 20 or 30 dollars—just 'til the first of the month," she continued. Every dollar I'd ever lent that woman has turned into a gift. I wasn't about to help her any more financially until she showed me that she was trying to help herself. But I wasn't about to get into that right then. I was just too damn tired.

"What's going on with you doing manicures and pedicures?"

"Well, I'm still doing 'em, but it's not paying the bills. My clients have been too unreliable. They've been canceling at the last minute and somebody even gave me a rubber check."

"Oh," I replied, not really believing her. "Well, what happened to the resume I did for you a couple of months ago? Nothing has changed on it. Why can't you use that?"

"Oh, it's in my house somewhere. But don't you still have it on your computer?"

"Yeah, I guess I do."

I glanced at the clock and noticed that it was after nine. I really wanted to get a good night's rest. I'm way sharper when I have at least eight hours of sleep.

"Sorry I'm not going to be much company tonight, but I have a breakfast meeting."

"Oh, that's OK. I just appreciate getting out of my house."

"Yeah, I hear ya."

"So who are you meeting with? Anybody good?"

"Well, I hope so. I'm trying to get Wendy's as a client," I replied as I grabbed our empty plastic dishes and tossed them in the trash.

"Oh, that's cool! Your life is so exciting!" Juanita smiled, obviously impressed.

"I don't know about all that, but it's not so cool yet. Tomorrow's only our first meeting."

"You'll get it. You're good at what you do."

"Thanks for the vote of confidence."

"So, will that mean that you'll get free hamburgers every time you go into a Wendy's? Or maybe they'll send you a year's supply." She laughed.

"No, I don't think so. Besides, who the hell would want to eat all those damn burgers?" I joked.

"So, how's the love life? Any word from that knucklehead, Michael?" Juanita asked as she brought our glasses to the sink. I was really hoping she wouldn't go there.

"I haven't heard from Michael in a while—thank God—but otherwise, it's pretty non-existent," I lied. I wasn't about to tell her anything about Victor. I wasn't ready for that.

"You really shouldn't work so hard, Ny. Don't you think it's time you start dating again? I mean, you wouldn't wanna end up like me, would you?"

"There's nothing wrong with not being in a relationship, Juanita. That's the problem with us women. We always define our success by whether or not we have a man—any man, good or bad—just as long as he's male and has the proper body parts," I replied, surprising myself at how much I was beginning to sound like Trish.

Juanita giggled. "I'm not saying that. I'm just saying all work and no play makes Ny a dull girl! But then again, I don't have a job and I don't have a man either, so I wonder what that makes me!"

"Crazy." I laughed. "We've got to leave by 6:45 so set the clock in the guest room for six, OK?" I told her as I snapped off the kitchen light.

"OK. Goodnight, Little Sis." She smiled and headed toward the guest room.

"Sleep well, Juanita . . . "

As I watched her walk down the hallway, a faint memory of us as children popped into my mind. I couldn't seem to understand why or how her life had taken such a negative turn. The unemployment, the enormous debt, the therapy sessions, the depressing atmosphere in which she lived all really bothered me from time to time. Sometimes I believed that her life troubled me more than it did her. But what could I do? I mean, she wasn't a bad person. In fact, she actually had a very good side to her. Still for some reason, bad things seemed to follow her. It hadn't always been like that. I could remember a time when it wasn't.

Juanita and I were our parents' first two babies. I could remember us at the ages of 14 and 10 as if it were yesterday. Juanita was older and I looked up to her for everything. At that age, I wanted to be just like her. Man, I wanted to be her! I wanted her clothes, her friends, her life! I wanted her approval and acceptance on everything I did. In my mind she was the prettiest, smartest and toughest big sister anyone could ever have.

We were a team. Sometimes against our parents, sometimes against David and Nathan, and sometimes against the world. Cheryl and Monica were little babies back then so we didn't think too much about them. But at school Juanita always had my back. She was my big sister and everyone knew that if they messed with me, they messed with her. It's so funny how much things can change in twenty-five years. Or maybe it's not so funny at all.

Four

What an exasperating week! The Wendy's Corporation decided it wanted to hire us but on a trial basis only. I was a little disappointed, but at least a trial basis was better than nothing. In any event, I was quite confident that after seeing what my staff could do, the senior execs at Wendy's would be just as impressed as those from StarzSports. However, this time, I'd definitely keep this deal purely professional.

The Nabisco commercial shoot had also gone well, although it looked a bit grim at the beginning. We went for what I like to refer to as the "kid approach." No one can resist the smile and sales pitch of an adorable little kid. But as we all know, children tend to misbehave and have mood swings. Our adorable actor was no exception. Thank goodness he eventually came around and by the end, I believed the commercial would not only be a smash among viewers, but I was sure that it would definitely send the sales for Nabisco's new cookie straight through the roof. Damn, I'm good!

It was now Friday afternoon and still no word from Victor. I wasn't about to call him at StarzSports and make myself look desperate. However, as he had assured me, I did receive the signed proposal Wednesday morning. At least he proved honest on that issue.

The next step on the StarzSports project was to forward the actual contracts and secure a professional athlete who wouldn't try to break our pockets. Hah! That was a long shot. It had been my experience that professional athletes—famous or not—have egos the size of Europe and like to play plenty of hardball. And their agents—man, we won't even talk about their agents. However, I had lots of faith in myself and was pretty confident that I'd eventually get the best spokesperson for the money.

As I sat at my desk going through a stack of papers and contracts that required my signature, I couldn't help but think about Victor. Was he in fact married, like Trish had speculated? That would've been pretty messed-up.

I looked over at the clock and it was nearly three. I didn't even know whether or not he was still coming. He hadn't e-mailed me any information, nor had I spoken with him since our last conversation. Yeah, he might've been fine, educated, charming, and really good in bed, but he sure was unreliable. I decided to try to take our little rendezvous for what it was and refused to think about any future plans regarding the two of us. It took a bit of concentration, but I forced myself to take my mind off of that man and get into the work that was before me. If he called, he called, right? I knew one thing for sure. I definitely wasn't going to go running to any airport without hearing from him.

Finally, as I signed the last document and took a deep breath of relief, I figured that I could probably get out of the office a bit early. I'd earned it. It had been another grueling week and I deserved to get a jump on a little rest and relaxation. Since I hadn't heard from "Lover Boy"—as Trish had called him—I planned to stop by the bookstore and buy a novel. Or maybe I'd finish that Zane book over the weekend.

It was a couple of minutes after four when I started packing up my stuff to go home. Obviously, Victor wasn't going to keep his word. There was absolutely no sense in hanging around the office waiting for him to call. Those days were over.

I grabbed my coat and headed out of my office past Judy's desk.

"Judy, I'm heading home. I'm tired and need a little rest."

"Yeah, you've had a really busy week. All those breakfast meetings. Whatever happened to lunch meetings?"

"I know, right?" I laughed. "Anyway, have a great weekend. I'll be in the car. As usual, my cell is on if you need to reach me."

"OK. Have a good one!" I walked toward the elevators and saw Nancy, the receptionist, signing for a package. Will was standing at her desk.

"Wow, it's a little late for FedEx, isn't it?" I asked.

"We got something in late for you guys." Will smiled.

He really was cute, but not my type.

He looked like a jock and I was more into intellectuals. But he was still cute nonetheless.

"Are you the only Federal Express guy that delivers to us?"

"As a matter of fact, I am. Why? Were you looking for someone else?" he jokingly questioned.

"No, no. Not at all. I just figured you guys had specific routes and times," I assured him.

"We do, and you guys are on my route. This firm just rarely gets late afternoon deliveries. I guess all your clients mark your packages for early morning delivery."

"Oh." I grinned. The elevator finally came and I said, "Well, have a good weekend," to both of them.

"Wait, I'm coming, too!" Will said.

Surprisingly, the elevator was empty. Will pushed the lobby button, turned to me and said, "Getting outta here early, huh, Nyagra?"

"Yeah," I replied with a sigh.

"Anything good planned for the weekend?"

"No, not really. Just a little much-needed R&R." I was surprised that I wasn't stressing that Victor had pretty much stood me up.

"I'm sure your husband will be happy to see your face home early."

"Not married," I stated, trying hard not to make eye contact with him.

"Oh. Well, your boyfriend, then."

The elevator doors opened on the ground floor and I quickly exited and smiled. "No husband, no boyfriend, no dogs, cats or goldfish. Just me."

Will did his best to catch up and finally made his way beside me. "Well, since you're unattached, do you think I could take you out for lunch or something one day?"

"I don't think so, but thanks for the offer," I replied, going through the revolving doors.

"Why not? I'm a nice guy." He laughed from the revolving section behind me.

"I'm sure you are but I'm still not interested," I stated, trying to be as nice as possible.

"OK, well, have a nice weekend!"

"You, too!" I replied, trying hard to disappear into the crowd.

"You should go to lunch with him. He really is cute!" I heard someone beside me say. I turned to see an older sophisticated-looking Caucasian lady standing beside me waiting for the light. You never know who's watching.

"Not my type."

"Well, then you need to change your taste! Do you see those dimples? I'd go to lunch with him. He comes to our office, too. All the young girls love him!"

"Have a good weekend." I smiled politely as I slightly raised my eyebrow and picked up my speed to ensure that I left her behind.

Even though I left the office early, I didn't make it home until almost seven. Traffic crept all the way up the interstate and it was frustrating. I didn't get to stop at Barnes & Noble and by the time I walked through my front door, I certainly didn't feel like cooking. I was in the mood for Japanese so I decided to order shrimp and vegetable tempura with rice from one of my favorite restaurants. While I was waiting for the food to be delivered, I decided to jump in the shower so that I could be in full relaxation mode by the time my meal arrived. I didn't want to miss the delivery guy, so I didn't wait for the bathroom to steam up before I got in.

As I stepped into the shower, I heard my cell phone ringing. The caller ID indicated that it was Trish. Eager to hit the shower, I let her go to voicemail but called her back on the speaker phone in the bathroom right before I jumped into the stall.

"I'm home," I said when she picked up.

"Oh, I thought your ass might be out with Lover Boy. You in the shower, Girl? You know I hate it when you call me on that damn speaker phone! Especially when that busybody Michael was there listening to our every word."

"Well, he's gone now and it's only me so chill out. I want to get clean before the delivery guy rings the bell with my food!" I yelled from the stall.

"You ordered out? Where's Lover Boy?"

"Who knows? He never called me back with any details or anything."

"What? See, I told you."

"Yeah, yeah, I know. Whatdaya want? A biscuit?"

"Oh, shut up! Aren't you pissed?"

"I'm not even thinking about it."

"Why didn't you call me? I would've come over. What'd you order?"

"Shrimp and vegetable tempura from White Pearl."

"Man, I haven't had that in ages! Why didn't you call me?"

"'Cause I just want to chill out. I'm going to eat my food and watch a little TV, which I rarely get to do. Does Urkel still come on?"

"Girl, Urkel hasn't been on in years."

"Damn, well, I guess I'll see what's on cable and try to finish that book by Zane. It's good but I've been so busy I just can't get a moment to read more than two chapters at a time."

"Oh, so you're just chillin' tonight."

"Yep, tonight and tomorrow."

"Oh, well, that's one of the reasons why I'm calling. Tomorrow I wanted you to do some Christmas shopping with me. Are you up for it? There's only two weeks 'til Christmas, Girl, and I still haven't gotten that damn motorcycle for Rodney."

"You want me to go motorcycle shopping with you? Trish, I don't know shit about motorcycles."

"Neither do I! But you look and sound really smart so they won't be so eager to jerk us."

"If you say so. Yeah, all right. I'll go with you, but not early."

"No, it won't be early. The sitter isn't coming until noon, so I'll come over and get you after she gets here. See, you won't even have to drive. I'll be your chauffeur. Plus, I need to get some more stuff for the kids. Have you bought any gifts yet?"

"No, actually I haven't." I laughed as I turned off the shower.

"Damn, then you should be the one asking me to go shopping! What are you waiting for?"

I grabbed the towel and wrapped it around my dripping body. "I don't know. But I don't exactly have that many people to buy gifts for, you know. Just Ma, Juanita, you and your family, my nieces and nephews and Judy. That's about it."

"Oh, so I assume you decided not to go up to your mamma's for the holiday?"

"Nope. David's in rehab again and I'm not up for the drama that's associated with those people."

"I hear ya. So what's up? You're coming over here then, right?"

"To be honest, I haven't really thought about it yet."

"Well, you're not spending it alone, so I don't see what there is to think about."

"I can't spend every holiday with your family. Rodney will begin to think I don't have a life of my own. Besides, I was just there for Thanksgiving."

"So what? So was the rest of my family. Are you crazy? First of all, Rodney and the kids love you. You're their godmamma, for heaven's sake! I can't believe you! Ny, you're my sister! You are family, Girl. I can't believe your ass doesn't know that by now—after twenty years. You know, as smart as you are, you sure are dumb sometimes!"

"OK. OK." I laughed as I threw on my purple terrycloth sweat suit.

"We're actually having a good amount of people over for Christmas this year. Some of Rodney's family is coming up from Richmond, so you won't feel like it's just us—if that's any consolation."

I shrugged. "It doesn't matter."

Trish really was like my sister and I loved her dearly. Just as I tossed my bra and panties into the hamper, the chime of the doorbell resonated through the air. I was beginning to wonder what was taking my food so long. I was starving!

"Trish, my food is here. Let me go."

"OK, 'Miss I don't wanna be bothered with my best friend tonight.'"

"Don't take it personally, Girl. You know how I get sometimes."

"Lucky for you, I'm not." She chuckled. "Call me later if you're up to it. I'll be here. Otherwise, I'll see you tomorrow."

"All right," I said, hanging up the phone and anxious to get my food.

I ran to the door and opened it, not even looking through the peephole, which is something I almost never do. But I was just so hungry and I knew it had to be the delivery guy. However, to my surprise, standing there with a huge smile on his face, holding my bag from White Pearl restaurant was none other than the infamous, unreliable Mr. Victor Reece.

I was quite shocked to see Victor. I was also flattered. I couldn't believe that this man actually had come in from Atlanta and to my house without calling in advance. He really was so unpredictable!

"I wanted to surprise you!" He grinned as he sat at the breakfast bar gazing at me with stars in his dark brown eyes. I stood by the sink and began removing my food from the brown paper bag.

"You really should've called. What if I wasn't here?" I questioned, almost reprimanding him.

"Well, I decided to take my chances. Now come over here and show me some love."

I reluctantly walked over to where he was sitting and put my arms around his body. He gently kissed my neck and I felt like I was surely going to melt like an ice cream sandwich sitting on top of a preheated oven.

"I missed you," he whispered softly in my ear.

"Oh, you did, did you?" I asked sarcastically. I pulled myself out of his strong and masculine embrace. "Well, I obviously didn't order any food for you. You are an unexpected visitor, you know."

"That's OK. Can't we share your tempura?"

"I suppose so." I smiled. Suddenly, I wasn't as hungry as I had been twenty minutes earlier. This man had the strangest effect on me.

He eyed me seductively. "But then again, maybe I should just have you for dinner!"

"Oh, I don't think so. You'd probably get an acute case of indigestion and I'm out of Pepto Bismol." I laughed. "Hey, how'd you know I got tempura, anyway?"

"I had to find out what I was paying for, didn't I?" Victor pulled me close to his body. I could smell his cologne—Boucheron for men—I knew it well. The warmth of his body made my own temperature rise and once again, I began to feel stuck on stupid. "Can I have some more of what you gave me last weekend? I've been thinking about it ever since I returned to Atlanta." He breathed heavily in my ear.

I desperately wanted to pull away from his embrace and yell at the top of my lungs, "Hell, no! I want to talk! Tell me why you didn't call when you got back to Atlanta! Tell me why you just showed up on my doorstep tonight without letting me know that you were coming! Why don't I have a home phone number for you? Goddamn it, Victor! Are you still married?!!!"

But my lips were paralyzed and I said nothing. In fact, I could barely move. It was actually as if this man had some sort of wicked spell over me. He was in control and it irked the hell out of me. I hated not being in control. I was starting not to recognize myself and I really didn't like it. I absolutely hated it!

I found myself leading this man, whom I barely knew, to my bedroom. And again, I felt my clothes dropping onto the floor beneath our feet along the way.

I looked over at the clock on the nightstand. It was 4:13 A.M. I don't know how or why I woke up. I just did. The moonlight was shining brightly through the window and I could see the silhouette of Victor's beautiful body lying beneath my down comforter. His magnificent, strong-looking back faced me. I wanted to touch him but decided not to disturb his peaceful rest.

Well, at least this time he's still here, I thought. We had made love all night, if you want to call it that. Whatever it was we did, we did it over and over again. I could still smell the scent of our perspiration in the air. It had been a passionate evening but for some reason, I wanted to wake him with a good swift kick. Perhaps I really wanted to kick myself for allowing this man to have so much damn control over me. I used to be very good at holding out. With Michael, I could go without it for weeks, months even. But I couldn't resist Victor. Yeah, he was a great lover. Probably the best I'd ever had. Definitely the best I'd had in a long time. But it was so much more than that.

It wasn't only his bedroom skills. It was him. His mystery. His evasiveness. His charm. In fact, the things I hated about him were the same things I loved. I'm not even sure if I really wanted to know whether or not he was married. Part of me liked things just the way they were, but my sensible and logical side hated it. That's the part of me I was battling with that morning before the sun rose.

I guess Victor could feel my presence over him because he groggily turned over on his stomach and faced me. As he slowly opened his eyes, he smiled and softly whispered, "Hello, beautiful."

"Hi." I blushed as I uncomfortably ran my hand over my rustled hair.

"What's the matter?" he questioned as he gently stroked my cheek.

"Oh, nothing. I just couldn't sleep. I thought I heard something outside," I lied.

"Oh." He smiled as he yawned and stretched.

"Let's talk, Victor," I boldly suggested.

"Let's talk?" He laughed. "It's the crack of dawn!"

"That's OK. We're both awake, aren't we?"

"Well, I don't know," he joked. "Maybe you're just a part of my dream."

I smiled, acknowledging his joke, but I was still serious.

"If you really want to talk, shoot. Personally, I could think of a few better things to do. But what do you want to talk about? Work? Love? Life? Whatever?"

"How about all of the above, but why don't we start with life?" I suggested.

"Fine. What's up? How's life treating you, Nyagra Ensley, you beautiful black woman, you?" he questioned, still in a joking tone.

"Victor, I'm serious," I firmly stated. I didn't want to ruin the light-heartedness of our mood, but Trish had me thinking and I had to protect myself from him. I was actually falling for him and I needed to know some things sooner rather than later.

"Oh, well, this sounds important, Nyagra. What's on your mind?" he asked as he sat up in the bed.

His bare chest looked so scrumptious that it was so difficult for me not to be distracted. I looked at him perched in my bed with only his lower torso covered by the comforter. But I was smart enough to know that although he appeared to be quite enticing and delightful, he could also be potentially very dangerous. Sort of like a black widow spider. Or should I say widower? I tried hard not to focus on his physical male beauty and took a big swallow.

"I need to know more about you, Victor. I probably should've asked these questions before we became intimate, but what's done is done."

"Well, what do you want to know?"

"I want to know about you. About your life, your past, your present, your hopes for the future."

"Nyagra, I thought we talked about all this over dinner last week. What have I left out?"

"That's what I want to know. Have you left anything out?"

"No. There's really not that much to know about me. I'm a regular guy!"

"Victor, you're the president of marketing at a major international sports apparel corporation. You are not just a regular guy."

"Well, my job is not a regular job. But me, I really am just a regular guy."

I was a bit impressed by his modesty but continued full force with my interrogation.

"Victor, what's life for you like in Atlanta?" No need to beat around the bush, right?

"What's life for me like in Atlanta?" he repeated. "Well, Nyagra, life for me in Atlanta is very, um, very, should I say eventful."

"Elaborate."

He shrugged, obviously not seeing the relevance of my questions and thus a little annoyed. "Well, I spend a great deal of time at the office or at work-related meetings and events."

"What do you do for fun?"

"Wait a minute, Nyagra." He laughed agitatedly. "I'm not so sure I'm comfortable with this early-morning interrogation. I feel like I'm in a precinct."

"Do you?" I stated as if I were completely innocent. "No, really, Victor. I'm not trying to make you uncomfortable. I truly just want to know what your personal life is like. Like I said, I should've probably asked you these questions before, but . . . "

"Are you trying to ask me if I'm seeing anybody else?"

"Yeah, I suppose I am." Now I was uncomfortable and starting to stutter. Maybe I was blowing things all out of proportion. It wasn't like we were headed for the altar or anything.

"Well, Nyagra. The answer to that question is that when I'm in Atlanta, all I have time for is work. Socializing comes very low on my priority list, unless it's a work-related party or event."

"When you go to these so-called 'work-related' parties or events, do you go alone?"

"Nyagra, why are you asking me all these questions? Aren't you enjoying the time we're spending together?"

Hearing that response, I decided to sit up in the bed and stare Victor straight in the eyes. His answer, not having a phone number where to reach him, and his other strange behavior forced me to believe that Trish was right. Victor Reece had something to hide.

"Whether or not I am enjoying our time together is not the issue, Victor. I want to know if you are sleeping with anyone else or dating anyone else, for that matter. I want to know exactly what I'm dealing with so I know how to proceed. I want to make sure we're on the same page," I firmly stated, finally getting my nerve back.

"OK. OK. No, Nyagra. I'm not dating or sleeping with anyone else besides you. As a matter of fact, I haven't dated or slept with anyone since we've been seeing each other. I'm completely unattached."

"Is that so?" I inquired with a raised brow, still unsure if he was being honest. I could usually spot a liar or a con artist a mile away, but for some reason, with him I simply couldn't tell. That's why he was so potentially dangerous. If he was lying, he was really good at it. Maybe I had finally met my match.

"Yes, that's so. We're having a great time together, Nyagra, but you can't expect to find out everything about me in just a couple of weeks. As time passes, you'll learn all you need to know. I promise you that. However, I assure you that I haven't been intimate with anyone since I've been with you."

He beamed as he put his arms around me. I guessed he was telling the truth. At least I wanted to believe that he was. I had no proof that he wasn't being honest, but I still wasn't sure.

After that conversation we made love again and then we watched the sun rise. I must admit, it was beautiful. I hoped this man was truly upstanding and honest. I wanted to believe him. But it seemed a bit too good to be true. There still was the strangeness regarding his behavior.

But I knew one thing for sure. I certainly wasn't going to let him leave New York again without obtaining a home phone number. I wasn't about to let that happen.

As I awoke to the smell of breakfast, I looked around and realized I was in the bed alone. With sleep still in my eyes, I focused in on the clock, which read 9:47.

"His ass had better be in that kitchen," I said out loud to myself as I got up and put on my robe. I would've been so upset if he'd slipped out while I was sleeping for the second time. I never would've forgiven him—or myself. As I walked toward the door to exit the room, Victor entered carrying a tray loaded with goodies for breakfast. I was amazed.

"Get back in that bed!" he jokingly ordered.

"Victor! You've been up cooking?"

"Yes, I have. Did I tell you that I have exquisite culinary skills? See, that's just one of those things you're going to have to learn about me as time goes on. Now get back over there 'cause I was making you breakfast in bed! And take that robe off!"

I knew that Victor actually had a sensitive and romantic side but serving me breakfast in bed? That was the ultimate! Maybe this guy was really the one. It was high time for me to have some personal happiness, finally.

I quickly slipped out of my robe as he had instructed and crawled back into the comforts of my king-sized bed. I was anxious to enjoy the fabulous treats set before me. My plate was piled high with French toast and bacon (I guess he was OK with pork after all.) There was a saucer with scrambled eggs and another adorned with fresh fruit. He'd obviously gone to the market before I woke up, because I didn't have half the things on the tray in the kitchen. This guy was absolutely amazing!

I beamed. "I can't believe you!"

"I'm sure you'll enjoy everything. I am a pretty good cook, so I've been told," he bragged.

"If it tastes half as good as it smells, it'll be fabulous!" I bit a piece of bacon. "Where's yours?"

"Still in the kitchen. Let me get it," he replied as he exited the room.

He returned a few minutes later carrying a tray of his own, piled with the same goodies he had prepared for me. He really was a good cook. Everything was delicious! I couldn't believe this. I hadn't felt this good in ages and I truly wanted the feeling to last. At that particular moment, I didn't even care what the hell his life was like in Atlanta. All I cared about was our time together. However, I did believe what he'd told me earlier that morning about being unattached. I wanted to believe him. I think there was a part of me that needed to believe him. I wanted to relax with the idea that Victor and I were an item. But I also didn't want to think too hard about it. I wanted our relationship to progress naturally and I truly believed that it would.

"Girl, where are you? I've been calling your ass all weekend!" I heard Trish's voice say over the answering machine. It was Sunday evening and I'd just returned from taking Victor to the airport. I tossed my coat and purse onto the couch and quickly grabbed the phone, hoping to catch her before she hung up.

"Hello?" I asked, hoping she was still there.

"What's up? Where have you been? You stood me up yesterday! I thought you were going shopping with me!"

I laughed. "Girl, don't kill me. I am so sorry, Girl! I totally forgot!"

"What's so funny? I had to go out there motorcycle shopping all by myself and I didn't buy a thing. I left two messages on your machine last night. And you weren't answering your cell phone."

"I forgot to charge my phone so it went dead. And I turned off the house phone."

"Damn, you really wanted to be missing in action this weekend."

"I was with Victor," I replied softly, almost a little ashamed for choosing the company of a man over that of my best girlfriend.

"Oh, so that explains why you stood up your best friend! A man or should I say a penis?" she huffed, trying to throw a serious guilt trip on me.

"I'm so sorry, Trish. You know I don't usually do shit like that."

"Yeah, yeah." She chuckled, indicating that she wasn't really angry. "So tell me what happened. You were with Victor? Hold up! What do you mean you were with Victor? When I spoke to you last, you were waiting for tempura and getting ready to read about some addicted nympho!"

"Yeah, I know. He surprised me! Wasn't that sweet?"

"Oh, yeah. Sweet as a sugar cube. In fact it was so sweet, I'm about to go into a diabetic coma," she stated sarcastically.

"Oh, come on, Trish. See, that's why I didn't call your ass!"

"OK. OK. Well, did you have a good time?"

"Very. Girl, Victor is too sweet to be married. I haven't had that much fun in years!"

"Oh, yeah, only morons and obnoxious jerks get married. Sweet men don't marry," she snapped.

"You know, Trish, I'm not in the mood for your sarcasm. I just had a really good weekend, and I don't want to let your ass get me to thinking about all types of negative shit. Then the whole thing gets ruined for me."

"I'm not trying to ruin anything for you!" she said in her most innocent voice.

"Yeah, yeah. I think there's a little bit too much hateration in the air these days. You need to take a lesson from Mary J. Blige, bitch!" I snapped as I grabbed my coat and hung it up in the closet.

"Whatever, trick—well, spill the details—what'd you guys do that was so fantabulous that you couldn't at least call me and cancel?"

"Are you asking because you want to know or are you asking because you want to pick it apart and get me all paranoid again?"

"Both." She laughed. "No, seriously. Of course, I want to know about your wonderful weekend, Girl!"

"Well," I began as I tossed myself onto the sofa. "I was waiting for White Pearl to bring the food, right? And Victor just shows up here holding my tempura. He'd obviously caught the delivery guy, paid for the food, and rang the bell. Girl, I was so surprised! We made love all night. He made me breakfast Saturday morning, then we went shopping for Christmas gifts. I finished my Christmas shopping, by the way. Then we went ice skating . . . "

"Ice skating?"

"Yep. Isn't that something? He's amazing! He's so much fun, Girl. We went to the movies, too. Then we went out to eat and came home and made some more fantastic love."

"Damn, Girl, you been fuckin' all weekend! Can you walk?"

"I'm walking just fine, thank you!" I giggled.

"You did use condoms, didn't you?"

"Of course, I did! Whatdaya think, I'm crazy?"

"Just checking."

"Well, anyway, I just came back from dropping him at the airport."

"Now, tell me, Ny. Did you get the home phone number?"

"As a matter of fact, not only did I get his home and cell phone numbers, but I also got his exact home address. So there!" I tried to rub in her face that she had been all wrong about him.

"Well, good. You should've been had it all along." She sighed.

"Trish, I think he's a good man. I actually questioned him about his personal life. He told me that he's unattached and that he hasn't dated or slept with anybody since we started seeing each other. It's only been two weeks but I guess it's a start. And I didn't get the sense that he was lying."

"Not for nothing, Girl, but you didn't think that asshole Michael was cheating on you either."

"Well, I had my suspicions about that."

"Yeah, right. Well, in any event, I'm glad you had a great weekend. You still could've returned my calls, though."

"I'm sorry. The weekend just went so fast."

"So, when are you going to see him again?"

"Hopefully for Christmas. We're supposed to be planning a weekend to go skiing."

"Christmas is less than two weeks away."

"I know and I absolutely cannot wait!"

"You're going to spend Christmas in a hotel?"

"Well, not really, but I'm tired of bombarding myself on your family and I'm surely not going up to Mamma's."

"Why do you feel like you're bombarding yourself? You know you're family."

"I know, I know, but still. I'm always the only one without an escort. You know Michael never liked to do shit and if Victor really wants to spend Christmas with me, I'm not going to say no."

"OK, if you say so. But you'd better be back for New Year's. Rodney and I just decided to throw a little party here at the house and I'm not bringing in the New Year without you. We always spend New Year's together and I don't want this year to be an exception. I'm also going to cook a big smorgasbord and invite some potential clients, 'cause you know I'm starting my catering business again, right? Bring Lover Boy if you want to, but you'd better come."

"I'll be there. I won't break tradition."

I felt so good inside but I could still hear Trish's reservations about Victor in her voice. But nothing could remove the smile from my face. Victor's visit had instilled a bit of hope for my personal happiness. I finally had something other than work to think about and actually look forward to. His presence had made me feel good about myself and my future. I believed that he was a good man. I suddenly found myself thinking of marriage and children. I'd never even thought about having children of my own. I wondered if I would be a good stepmamma to his daughter. I could tell that he was a decent father. If we decided to have children, I knew we'd be a great team. As my thoughts rattled one after the other, I realized that I may have been going too far. Take it one step at a time. One step at a time, I told myself.

One step at a time . . .

Five

It was four days before Christmas and the snow was coming down harder than ever. The weatherman had predicted a white Christmas. But as beautiful at it was, I was hoping the snow would stop. Victor and I had opted not to go skiing, but he had promised that we'd spend Christmas day together. The last thing I wanted to hear was that the airports were closed.

I hadn't seen him since our fabulous weekend, but we'd spoken every day. Sometimes I called him (at home even) and sometimes he'd call me. I was growing more fond of him with each conversation we shared and was looking forward to spending the holiday in his presence. With a little persuasion and a lot of luck, I was even hoping to get him to stay until New Year's. I didn't know how possible that was going to be, but I was surely going to try.

The holidays were a funny thing for me. Depending on what was going on in my life at the time, I was either totally into them or totally not. I'd always enjoyed the season as a kid, but the years that I was with Michael had put a little bit of Ebenezer Scrooge into my personality.

"The white man has commercialized the holidays!" I could hear his voice saying in the back of my mind. The truth of the matter was that he was just a cheap ass, selfish Grinch who simply didn't want to spend the time or the money warranted to go out and select gifts for anyone except for his fat, snobby mamma. One year we didn't even buy a Christmas tree. He refused and stubborn me decided not to get one to decorate by myself. We argued so much about it that Christmas day came and went almost unnoticed. In fact, we'd usually split up on Christmas—me stopping by Trish's and Mamma's and him going by his family's (or so he said). His family never really liked me so I always opted not to join him. After all the accomplishments I'd made during my life, to them I was still from Harlem—a ghetto monger, as his mamma once called me.

Michael had been born and raised in Scarsdale to a brain surgeon father and a black socialite mamma. In their eyes, no matter what, I was beneath him. Whatever! Black people who are prejudiced against other blacks should be ashamed of themselves. The KKK would kill us all in a heartbeat; no matter what the family history or social status.

Anyway, Michael and I never exchanged gifts, which was actually fine with me because I totally wasn't into shopping for his picky, critical ass anyway. He complained so much about the one birthday gift I'd bought him in the very beginning of our relationship that not only did I take it back to the store, I decided right then that I'd never purchase anything for him again. I never did and he never bought me any gifts either. I should've known then that he was an idiot. As I think back to the details of our life, I wonder why I was stupid enough to stay in that relationship as long as I did. Oh, well, live and learn.

When I was a kid, my father used to go in the woods with my Uncle Paul and chop down our Christmas tree. Every year for as long as I could remember, we'd have a family tree-trimming party. It was so much fun. The six of us kids all got along then. Christmas simply isn't the same without a tree in the house and I never intended to let another year pass without getting one. The smell of the fresh pine makes me feel wonderful inside and out. It reminds me of those childhood days when my family interactions were pleasant and peaceful. So, over the weekend I got Rodney to help me bring the eight-foot pine tree home, and they all came for a small tree trimming party. It was actually really nice. Mamma and Juanita joined us, too, and I'm happy to say that it was "drama free!"

There was no talk of my other siblings or the incident a couple of weeks earlier. For once, Juanita didn't start her crocodile tears about her past pains and no one got on anyone's nerves. I wished things could always run that smoothly. I guess Juanita's medication was starting to kick in and that could've been the reason for her mild temperament. Thank God for Prozac!

The drive down to Manhattan was slow and hazardous, even in my Range Rover. The snow was falling quickly and the roads were extremely slick. I actually saw a couple of little cars skid across the highway and wondered if I should turn around and take the day off. I surely would've gone back home if our office Christmas party wasn't that night. I had no real desire to attend, especially alone. However, this would be my first Christmas party as a senior exec, so I figured that I should obey company protocol and participate in the politics.

It was nearly eleven by the time I made it to the office because of the weather and the disastrous traffic. The snow continued to fall but the streets were still filled with people—last-minute shoppers, I suspected. That was the thing about New York City; nothing could stop people from getting out and about. Not even a severe snowstorm.

I arrived at my office to find everyone in the holiday spirit, enjoying music and Christmas goodies. I even caught Mr. Stein out of his office—a rare occurrence! Everyone was dressed up in party gear and work wasn't on anyone's mind. For the first time in a long while, I was even cheerful. Was it because after the party, I had a week off for vacation? Was it because it was Christmas and everyone else's joy was rubbing off on me? Or was it because I was looking forward to spending more time with Victor? Perhaps it was a combination of everything. Whatever the reasons for my sudden jolly mood, I didn't know. I didn't even care. All I knew was that I wanted to feel like this forever.

"I'm so sorry I'm not going to be able to make it," Victor told me over my cell phone. I walked into the lobby of the Four Seasons Hotel, trying to muffle the music and party conversations of my colleagues. "I've just been notified that I've got to be on the set of a commercial that's going to be shot with this year's Dream Team at 5:45 Monday morning. The marketing rep who was originally supposed to handle this suddenly went into the hospital to have gallstones removed." He sighed.

"Well, couldn't you come for Christmas Eve and maybe fly back early Christmas Day?" I asked, extremely displeased.

"I thought of that but this guy also left me with an unfinished commercial treatment and marketing plan. So, I'm probably going to be working on that until 5:45 Monday morning." I'm sure he sensed my disappointment from the silence that resonated through the receiver. "I'm sorry, Nyagra."

"Well, I know how demanding work can be," I finally said with a humongous lump in my throat.

"But I want you to go over to Trish's and have a great time for the both of us, OK?"

"I'll try."

"We'll talk, though. And I promise I'll come up next weekend. Maybe we'll even go on that ski trip we talked about. It'll be New Year's and I'd love to bring it in with you. Besides, I've got to see you. I've got to give you your Christmas gift."

"Oh, Victor, you didn't have to buy me a Christmas gift," I stated even though I was happy that he had. I'd stood in line at Neiman Marcus for nearly an hour and bought him a Ralph Lauren green and white plush terrycloth bathrobe. The line for monogramming was even longer, but he was worth it. Needless to say, after all the trouble I had gone through, I surely deserved something.

"I wanted to. Where are you, anyway? I hear a lot of noise in the background."

"My office Christmas party at the Four Seasons Hotel."

"Oh, fancy, fancy."

"Well, a little."

"Yeah, you guys can throw big parties, thanks to all the money you're getting from StarzSports!" he joked.

"Excuse me, Mr. Reece, but we throw our Christmas party here every year!" I snapped.

"I'm sure you look absolutely beautiful," he replied, now with a more serious tone.

"Well, thank you. But I wish you could've been my escort."

"Yeah, me, too."

"Well, let me get back inside. I'm sure they're all wondering where I've disappeared to."

"OK, I'll call you tomorrow."

"All right." I flipped the receiver and walked back into the ballroom. My disappointments never seemed to cease.

Snow had fallen all night, but the sun was shining brightly through my window early Saturday morning. It was Christmas Eve and even though I'd left the tree lights on all night, something about it just didn't feel like it was the day before such an enormous holiday.

During the night, I had a dream. I was in the apartment where I grew up in Grant projects in Harlem. Everything looked exactly the way it did when I was little. The television and sofa both sat in the same places. Even Dad's chair stood right where it had for twenty years of my life. I was a little girl again, except that I was in the same body that I possess today. In my dream, I was looking up at the Christmas tree, which appeared tall and bright with thousands of festive decorations. Beneath it lay hundreds of beautifully-wrapped gifts. As I stood staring in awe of this mammoth tree, I decided to reach down and open one of the boxes. I was quite surprised to see a framed photograph of Victor Reece. It must've been an 8-by-10 and in the picture with him were two other individuals whose faces I couldn't seem to remember. I think one of them was a child, but for the life of me I couldn't recall the other.

I woke up still wondering about my dream. Maybe the child was his daughter, Mya. Maybe the other person in the photo was me. I couldn't tell. But I knew one thing for sure. I had to see Victor for Christmas. I couldn't bear to spend another Christmas all alone or as a third wheel.

As I quickly collected my thoughts, I jumped out of bed and grabbed the cordless phone from its base. I dialed information for American Airlines. I inquired about flights leaving for Atlanta. I knew my chances were slim to none. I mean, it was Christmas Eve. Not to mention that with the snow, all flights might be cancelled. But I had to try. I figured if I was able to get a flight out, I could be at Victor's house before sundown. I'd surprise him, just as he had shown up on my doorstep unannounced. We wouldn't have a big family dinner, but we'd be together.

Despite the snow, the airlines were operating, but American was totally booked. After 45 minutes and conversations with ticket agents who graciously informed me that they couldn't fit me on any flights, I was finally able to get a seat on Continental Airlines Flight #629. It would leave JFK Airport and arrive in Atlanta by 9:42 p.m., provided that there were no complications or delays from the weather.

I immediately gave the agent my credit card number, paid a hefty $732 and happily began to throw a couple of things into my overnight bag. The airline was robbing me blind, but I was on my way to visit Victor!

Thank God, the Heavens decided that they'd delivered enough snow in New York City! I sat in my window seat plucking my eyebrows and anxiously awaiting our landing in Atlanta. All I could think of was seeing the surprised look on Victor's face when he opened his front door. I only hoped that he'd be as elated as I'd been that night he stood on my porch holding my shrimp tempura. I also hoped he'd like his robe. I'd purchased an extra large to ensure a comfortable fit on his statuesque frame.

As I sat in my seat trying not to concentrate on the turbulence, I thought back to my conversation with Ma earlier that morning. She'd called me bright and early to convince me to change my mind about not coming for Christmas dinner. I apologetically informed her that I was going to have to stick to my original decision and sit this year out. I knew she was upset as she tried her best to make me feel guilty for disappointing her, but I tried hard to ignore her sad tone of voice. I hated disappointing my mamma, but I despised being around my siblings even more. Besides, the way I saw it, I'd already given Ma and Juanita their Christmas presents at my little tree-trimming party. Therefore, I didn't owe anyone a thing; especially not my presence.

Actually, I couldn't have gone even if she'd been able to persuade me. I'd already purchased my ticket to Atlanta. Of course, I conveniently avoided telling her this little fact. My mamma never would've forgiven me if she knew that I was spending Christmas in another state with a man I'd only known for a couple of weeks rather than join her and my so-called family for her fabulous Christmas dinner with all its delicious trimmings. As much as I wanted to see Victor, I did regret not being able to enjoy Mamma's cooking.

Victor was working so hard that I knew we'd most likely go to some sort of restaurant to eat Christmas dinner. I considered that to be so sterile. It was also something I'd never thought I'd do. However, even though I'd miss Ma's food, the pros definitely outweighed the cons. I figured I'd drive up to see her sometime during the week and have some leftovers. After all, I was off for the week and I didn't plan to stay with Victor any later than Sunday. He needed to concentrate on his work and with me there, he'd surely be distracted.

Against my better judgment, I called Trish from the airport and told her that I'd decided to head to Atlanta and surprise Victor. I figured that if I called her and I was already at the airport, she couldn't say anything that would talk me out of going. In so many words, she pretty much said that I was stupid. Not really because I was going, but because I was paying for my own ticket. She was obviously mad that I wasn't going to be having dinner with her, Rodney and the kids, but I acted oblivious to the attitude in her voice.

Until that day, I never realized how popular I was or how many people wanted to be in my company. I guess that made me pretty lucky. Some people don't have anyone and here I was with two invitations where I knew there would be a simply delicious meal. Unfortunately for them (and maybe even for me), I felt the need to do my own thing. I loved them, but I thought I was in love with Victor. At that point, he was just a wee bit more important. In any event, I wished her Merry Christmas and told her I loved her and that I would stop by on Monday when I returned.

"I hope you're not the one who gets surprised," she snapped before we hung up. I felt like telling her to go straight to hell, but since it was Christmas Eve, I held my tongue.

What was actually a two-and-a-half-hour flight felt like twelve because of my anticipation. When we finally touched down in Atlanta, I quickly exited the airport and hailed a cab. The weather was brisk in Atlanta, too. However, it was definitely better than the damp freezing cold that I'd just left behind in New York.

It was after ten as I looked through my Palm Pilot to find Victor's address. I could feel my heart pounding beneath my red cashmere sweater. As I told the address to the driver, I felt what seemed like an entire family of butterflies fluttering around in my stomach. I was nervous.

"Visiting?" the cabby asked, trying to make small talk.

"Yeah." I smiled.

"Where you coming from?"

"New York City."

"Oh, I like New York. Heard you guys got a lot of snow there recently."

"Yeah, we did."

"Lucky you got a flight out, huh?"

"Yes, very."

After about twenty minutes, we drove down a long, dimly lit, tree-lined block with several beautiful mini-mansions and estates sparsely positioned on spacious lawns. Each home elegantly boasted of Christmas spirit, making the streets resemble a little winter wonderland. Victor's home was no exception. When we finally turned onto a dead-end street and pulled in front of an exquisite brick French Tudor home, the cabby said, "That'll be $26.80, Ma'am."

I handed him thirty-two bucks, told him to keep the change, and wished him happy holidays.

"Thank you and same to you, Ma'am!"

As I walked up the steps to Victor's gorgeous home, I could see an enormous Christmas tree in front of the window. Wow, it's rare for a single man to have such a nicely decorated tree, I thought. There were two cars in the driveway—a Benz and a Jeep Cherokee—and I could see movement inside the house. I was glad he was home. I took a deep breath and rang the bell. At first no one came to the door but I stood there, certain I'd seen someone through the window. After a few moments, someone opened the door. It was a woman—attractive, petite with short dark hair and wearing only a long red silk robe.

"Can I help you?" she questioned.

I was certain that I had the wrong house. "Oh, I'm sorry. I must have the wrong home. I'm looking for . . . "

"Mommy! Mommy! Is that Santa Claus?" a child yelled as she ran toward her mamma. She halted as she saw me instead of a jolly old man with a snow-white beard in a red suit. The girl, dressed in a robe identical to her mamma's, looked familiar, but I couldn't place her.

"Mya, didn't I tell you to go to bed? When Santa does get here, I'm going to tell him to go to another little girl's house, one who listens to her Mommy when she says, 'lights out!'" the woman jokingly said.

"I'm going! I'm going!" The girl pouted as she walked away from the door with her ponytails swinging.

"I'm sorry. Who were you looking for?" the woman continued.

Mya? That was Victor's daughter from the picture he showed me when we went to Bella Roma's! I knew I'd recognized her. As I stood there practically speechless, looking in the face of this woman, I felt like disappearing from the face of the earth. If I could've melted into the pavement, I surely would have. Just as I was about to thank her and run to the nearest hotel where I could throw myself across a bed and scream out in pain from this heartache, I heard a man's voice call, "Mallory?! Maal, who's that at the door?"

Suddenly, Victor's handsome, conniving, lying ass appeared in the doorway beside his wife. He was wearing a robe that almost matched the bedroom attire of the rest of his family. Isn't that sweet?

Upon seeing my face, Victor looked as though he was about to pass out. I, on the other hand, wanted to jump around his neck with all four of my limbs and puncture his jugular. If it hadn't been for the look on his poor innocent wife's face, and the happiness in the eyes of his daughter who was eagerly awaiting Santa, I probably would've raised holy hell in his little picturesque and serene neighborhood. Obviously, I felt like a huge pile of shit. But in my case, misery doesn't love company. I just didn't want to ruin that beautiful child's Christmas by causing a nasty scene and exposing Victor's family to his infidelity. Perhaps on Groundhog Day. Perhaps on the Fourth of July. Maybe even on Easter. But definitely not on Christmas Eve. Christmas is the single most important holiday to a kid. And that child never would've been able to get that fiasco out of her mind.

"I'm sorry. I was looking for 72 Willow Circle," I stated with a huge lump in my throat and tears in my eyes just waiting to drop.

"Oh, this is 78 Willow Circle. 72 is the Gilberts' home. They're just a few houses down!" Mallory called, trying to be ever so helpful.

With a crooked smile, I turned and walked down the stairs. By now my eyes were burning so terribly that I felt as if someone had rubbed a whole box of salt in them. I think tears wanted to fall, but I absolutely refused to let them. I'm not weak and I don't cry, I told myself. I may get mad; I may get even; I may punch, kick and scream. But I do not cry. Not even over the likes of Victor Reece.

"Thank you!" I called back, without even turning around.

"Merry Christmas!" she continued.

Trembling, I continued down the sidewalk. In my heart, I wished that Victor would've called my name and tried to run and stop me from walking away. I wanted him to tell me that I wasn't seeing what I thought and that this polite and helpful woman was actually his sister. But he didn't. He didn't say one word. He just stood there watching me as I disappeared down the dark street into the night. I walked straight ahead. I couldn't turn around. I couldn't say a word. I think I lost my voice so I just continued to walk. I had no idea where I was or where I was going but I wanted to walk until I physically fell off the edge of the earth. Emotionally, I think I already had.

Six

It was the worst Christmas of my entire life. It was more dreadful than going to Trish's unescorted or going to Mamma's and fighting with my brothers and sisters. If I had been a magician and skipped over Christmas Day, I certainly would've made the calendar flip from December 24th to December 26th. If only I could've known what lay behind the beautiful French oak doors of 78 Willow Circle, I surely would've saved myself the anguish of looking into the deep brown eyeballs of Mrs. Victor Reece and having her cheating husband act as though he'd never seen me before in his life. If I would've had it my way, I would've been the Grinch who stole Christmas.

I spent Christmas all alone in Hartsfield International Airport. Well, technically not all alone. There were plenty of other frustrated travelers trying to make it to their destinations. However, what probably separated me from them was that they most likely were trying to go someplace to enjoy the holiday while I was simply attempting to return to an empty townhouse.

When I left Victor's front door, I walked to the corner and attempted to call a taxi company. Luckily, I'd taken the receipt from the cab that dropped me off and there was a number on the back. Still, I stood on the corner of Willow Circle for over forty minutes before the stupid cab finally arrived. Contrary to popular belief, it does get cold in Atlanta, and I was a human ice cube by the time I was able to climb into the warm car.

I opted not to spend the night in a hotel. That only would've made me feel more depressed. Not that I was suicidal but people kill themselves alone in hotel rooms on holidays. The depression might have been too much for me to bear, so I figured I'd go right back to the airport and try to get the hell out of dodge before I exploded with anger. But I knew I'd be able to keep it all in its proper perspective in a public arena.

It was damn near midnight by the time I got to the airport and it was hell trying to get a flight out. The next available was leaving at 8 A.M. I had no choice but to purchase a first-class ticket and camp out on one of those uncomfortable rock-hard seats at the gate while I waited for the plane to board—over six-and-a-half hours later.

Obviously, while sitting in the airport for hours, it was difficult not to concentrate on the night's events. I tried desperately to take my mind off Victor and his bullshit, but it really was difficult. All I kept seeing in my mind was the picturesque little "happy" family that he'd lied about in my face. I wondered if "Dear ol' Mallory" knew that her man was a lying cheat or if she, like most women who love cheating men, thought she had the perfect family—or chose to create that scenario in her mind. I couldn't believe Victor had actually lied about his entire personal life. It wasn't the first time something like this had happened to me and I couldn't believe how stupid I'd been—again.

"But he gave me his phone number and address. What on earth was he thinking?" I asked myself as my head pounded with pain.

I must've dozed off in my seat because the next thing I knew I felt the hustle and bustle of people around me. When I opened my eyes, I saw at least thirty people in line waiting to board the flight. I jumped up and went to the agent on duty.

"Do I have to get checked in?"

"Do you have a boarding pass?" the young woman asked, seemingly in a bad mood that she had to work on Christmas Day. I quickly showed her my boarding pass. "Well, board," she snapped.

Obviously, she didn't realize that she was speaking to a borderline lunatic who was about to crack at any moment. After the evening I'd just experienced, she didn't know how close I was to turning into Linda Blair from The Exorcist. I figured it was best for me and for her if I ignored her behavior. I really didn't want to end up spending Christmas Day in jail after everything else that I'd already endured.

Even though I usually don't drink alcohol (and generally don't even enjoy the taste), I ordered a Bloody Mary from the flight attendant as soon as I was seated. It tasted terrible, but I wanted something that would pretty much knock my ass out. I didn't want to spend three hours in the air thinking about Victor Reece and his fictional "happy" family.

All I can say is that I felt like pure-d-shit! I took out my compact in an attempt to make myself look a little bit more human. Not surprisingly, the reflection that stared back at me was horrendous! My eyes were red and my skin was pale. Even though I hadn't shed a tear, I sure looked like I'd been crying all night. My hair looked a mess, thanks to the wind and cold I withstood as I waited for a taxi on the corner of that dreadful Willow Circle.

There it was, Christmas Day and I was sitting on a flight that I practically had to beg to get a seat on, having a nasty ass Bloody Mary for breakfast. And the drink didn't work as fast as I would've liked. For about a half-hour, all I could see in my head were Victor and his family. As I continued to envision them, my psyche took me back to the dream I'd had the other night. Now that I'd thought about it, I realized that the woman in the photograph was Victor's wife—not me. In fact, I realized that I'd seen Victor's entire family before I actually saw them in real life. It was weird. I guess a higher force was trying to warn me, but as usual, I didn't listen.

I suddenly realized I'd fallen asleep again. We were touching down on the runway of LaGuardia Airport. Although it was Christmas Day, believe it or not, there were still a lot of people in the airport. I guess New York really is the city that never sleeps!

As I made my way to the taxi stand, I felt the return of that menacing migraine coming on. It was probably the result of the "very nutritious" Bloody Mary that I'd guzzled down for breakfast. There was still snow on the ground and it was frigid, but the cab was warm and even quite comfortable. I groggily told the cabby my address, leaned on the headrest and closed my eyes.

We pulled up to my driveway shortly after ten. I still had the full day ahead of me if I chose to do any holiday socializing. But I didn't.

All I wanted to do was go inside and toss myself onto my bed. I wanted the day to go away. I didn't want it to be Christmas, but I obviously didn't have any control over that. I figured that if I slept the day away, I could wake up on December 26th and in essence, I could miss Christmas Day.

When I walked into the house, I noticed that the red light was furiously flashing on my answering machine. I figured it was probably Ma, Juanita or maybe even that asshole, Victor Reece. Once I dropped my belongings on the sofa, I pressed the "play" button, quite curious to know if he had the audacity to dial my number after humiliating me on what was probably the most important holiday of the entire year.

"Beep!" I heard through the machine's speaker.

"Hey, Girl. It's Trish. I guess you really decided to go! You're crazy! Well, anyway, hope you're having a great time! Merry Christmas! We love you and wish you were here with us! Call as soon as you get back. And hey, you better not stand us up for New Year's!"

Beeeeeeeeeeep!

"Nyagra, it's your mamma. I hope you change your mind and come on up for Christmas dinner. Call me."

Beeeeeeeeeeeeeep!

"Ny, it's Juanita. You know Mamma wants your butt up here for Christmas dinner, so come on. Drive up! We'll all be waiting for you. Call us, OK?"

Beeeeeeeeeeeep!

Damn, I thought. I don't get this many messages when I'm home!

"Um, Nyagra? It's Mike. "Um, I just wanted to wish you a Merry Christmas and a Happy New Year. I miss you, Ny. Call me, OK? I'm staying at the Regal Royal. Room 1701."

"Fuck you!" I said out loud at Mike's voice.

Beeeeeeeeeeeeeeeeep!

"Nyagra, it's Victor. I know you probably don't want to hear an explanation for what happened yesterday, but I certainly feel the need to explain. I doubt you'll call me back, so I'll call you."

I couldn't believe the nerve of that mutherfucker! How dare he call me with that bullshit? How dare he try to ruin what was left of the Christmas holiday? He sure had a lot of shit with him!

Victor's message was the last one. I erased everything, but left the machine on and turned the ringer off. I wasn't taking any calls. I couldn't bear to speak to anyone and especially not Trish. I surely didn't feel like hearing her "I told you so." Oh, she'd never say it—in those words, anyway. But she'd definitely have the "I told you so" attitude, and I'd never be able to live it down. Not to mention that she'd never let me choose another man again. If I told her what happened with Victor, she'd be trying to hook me up with every unmarried athlete in the tri-state area! Again I felt that I'd made a bad decision and to be honest, I was ashamed. I felt so stupid! I had to keep what happened between me and Victor a secret. I couldn't tell a soul. Not even Trish. Especially not Trish!

Feeling as badly as I did, I decided to do something I never do. I went into the bathroom and got a Valium that I had left over from when Michael pulled my wisdom teeth out. I took one and hoped that it would help me sleep right into Tuesday morning. It did . . .

Christmas was over. Thank God! The Valium really knocked me out. When I woke up the next day, it was nearly noon. There were several messages on my machine from Ma, Juanita and Victor. With the ringer off, I never even knew they'd called—not that I would have answered it anyway.

I went into the bathroom to wash my face and brush my teeth. I couldn't imagine what Victor could possibly have to say that would justify the scene I'd just witnessed. There was nothing he could tell me that would've made me feel any better. They all looked so happy together so I knew that he wasn't having problems with his wife. All he could do for me was explain why he had so blatantly lied in my face, other than wanting to get me into bed. In any event, I couldn't deal with him until I was ready and I didn't know when that would be—if ever. I was still too emotional about the subject and the last thing I wanted to do was wimp up during our conversation.

Sleeping so late had obviously drained my stomach because when I finally crawled out of bed, I was absolutely famished. I think I had a hangover, too. I don't really drink, so I think I might've overdone it on the Bloody Marys. As I began to scramble some eggs, the phone rang again. I figured it would be best to allow the machine to answer, just in case it was that trifling Victor. But to my surprise, it was Juanita.

"Hey," I said, picking up the receiver after I heard her voice through the answering machine.

"And where the hell have you been?" she asked.

"Around. I told you guys I wasn't coming," I said as I added a dash of salt to my eggs.

"I cannot believe you didn't come and you didn't call your mamma on Christmas Day."

My temples were throbbing and I was suddenly in no mood to talk to her.

"I did call, but I didn't get an answer," I lied.

"Well, she was probably on the phone long distance with Aunt Rita and didn't want to click over. You know you should've kept calling until you got her."

"Listen, I have a headache and I'm not in the mood for this."

"Oh, you're not in the mood for this? OK, Nyagra. Well, then why don't we change the subject? Did you have a nice Christmas?" she asked sarcastically.

"It was fine," I lied again.

"Well, what'd you do?"

"Cut the sarcasm, Juanita. Did you guys enjoy your family dinner?" I asked, trying to get her attention off me and onto her own holiday experience, which wasn't very difficult. She was quite easily distracted.

"Well, it was nice."

"I hear a 'but' in there somewhere. What happened?" I asked, almost not wanting to know.

"Well, Cheryl and I got into a pretty heated argument. I guess we'll never get along."

"Yeah, probably not. I'm glad I didn't come. I really wanted peace," I said, as I shook my head thinking about my incident with Victor. How peaceful was that? I asked myself.

"Well, I still say you should've come. For Mamma, at least."

"I'll see Ma sometime this week."

"It's not the same."

"Did David come? Is he out of the rehab?"

"Yeah, he came and he brought that smelly bitch with him and the kids."

"He brought Mona? I'm surprised. He usually brings Marva to family things. She bathes."

"I know but Mona has a car now so no matter how funky she is, you know his mind is scheming on getting it. It's a used car, but it's a car nonetheless. I think her brother gave it to her or something."

"Oh. Well, is she still big and fat?"

"Oh, of course. And she smells like shit. I don't know if she doesn't wash her ass or what, but there's no damn reason for her to smell like that. It's just disgraceful. And she can't blame it on being heavy 'cause I'm a big girl and I always smell good."

I laughed. "What I want to know is what the hell he sees in her. They're still having sex 'cause the baby is only a year old. I don't see how he could have sex with her."

"Me either, Girl."

"By the way, how are the kids?"

"They seem all right. The two boys seem fine, but they dress Dayna the same way they dress the boys. I told David that she's matured and should be wearing young ladies' clothing. But what do I know?"

"How old is she now—like 13 or 14?"

"Yeah, something like that."

"Maybe I should have her work in my office over the summer, to get a positive female role model in her life."

"That would be a good idea. She loves your ass. She asked for you about a hundred times. But Mona practically has her raising those two boys, so I don't know."

"That's terrible. At that age, she doesn't need to have the constant responsibility of a 7- and a 1-year-old."

"I told David that, too. But again, what do I know? Mona is so busy chasing David all around the town, she's barely raising those kids. All she's concerned about is keeping David away from Marva."

"Pretty sad, huh?" I stated as I now prepared my plate of scrambled eggs, turkey bacon, and an English muffin.

"I'd say," Juanita replied.

"Where are you? At home?"

"Yeah, I just got in. I have a client in a half-hour."

"OK, well, I'm about to eat. I'll call you later," I said. Then the phone clicked and I wasn't sure if I should answer, figuring it might be Victor.

"You have another call. Go ahead. Answer it. Call me later," my sister instructed.

"OK," I hesitantly replied.

I really didn't want to but I decided to click over. However, I didn't say anything.

"Hello?" the voice on the other end said in an uncertain tone. It was that lying bastard. I immediately hung up the phone. I still wasn't ready to deal with him.

I lounged around the house that day. After the initial shock, I actually didn't feel as depressed as I thought I would. I guess I was kind of used to shitheads. However, I still wasn't ready to talk to Victor and decided to keep the answering machine on. He called two more times only to be greeted by my mechanical secretary. Each time, he pleaded for me to pick up the phone. It was almost like he knew I was sitting there listening. Of course, I refused and laughed each time he was disconnected after exceeding the time limit.

At about three o'clock, I called Trish. Before I dialed, I had contemplated on what story I'd tell regarding the prior day's events. For the first time in over twenty years of friendship, I actually deliberately lied to my best friend. I couldn't bear to tell her the truth and hear the lecture that I knew would accompany the situation at hand. No. This was something I felt I couldn't share with anyone.

Trish was really glad to hear from me. She informed me that they'd had a wonderful Christmas and Rodney had absolutely loved his new motorcycle. She in turn had received a new six-carat wedding band—as if that woman needed more diamonds. Some girls have all the luck!

"So what was his house like? Expensive? Does he have good taste?" she questioned, giving me the third degree. It was difficult to lie to her but under the circumstances I felt as though I had to.

"Yeah, pretty good."

"Was he surprised to see you?"

"Yeah, he was definitely surprised."

"Did you see any signs of any female? You know, perfume bottles or an extra towel or toothbrush in the bathroom?"

"Um, no. Not at all."

"Well, Girl, I'm glad to say that this time I was all wrong. I'm happy that you had a good time." I felt like blurting everything out, but I just couldn't.

"So when are you going to see him again?" she asked.

"I'm not sure. Both of us are about to get real busy at work, so there won't be much time for visiting."

"You are coming over New Year's Eve, aren't you? I told you that I'm launching my new catering service that night, too, didn't I? I'm going to do all the cooking and hopefully some of my guests will hire me to cater some of their functions. You can't miss it. You promised!"

"I'm coming."

"Are you sure?"

"Yes! What are you going to call your company this time?"

"Trish's Delights. How's that sound?"

"It sounds fine—if you follow my business plan this time."

"I will! I will! So you have to be there. You have to see the people's reactions to my cuisine."

"Trish, your cuisine has never been the problem. Everybody loves your cooking. It's your professionalism that sucks."

"Used to suck. Not anymore. This is going to be my year. You just watch. But you'd better be there. You'll be impressed."

"I will, will I?"

"Well, what about Lover Boy? Is he going to be your date?"

"Oh, I don't know about him. I'll know toward the end of the week." I lied, knowing Victor definitely wouldn't be going anywhere with me.

"You're definitely hiding something."

"What?" I replied. She knew me.

"Come on. Come out with it. Something happened and you're not saying."

"You're crazy."

"After twenty years, you think I can't tell if you're hiding something? Come on. Spill it!"

"Trish, I am not hiding anything. I told you everything!"

"You told me nothing! And what is it with these one-word answers?"

"I don't know what you're talking about." Just then the phone beeped. Thank God, I had another call. "Hold on." I clicked over without thinking. "Hello?"

"Nyagra, please don't hang up . . . " It was Victor. I was silent. "Please let me talk to you," he pleaded.

"Hold on," I snapped. Changing my tone of voice, I clicked over to Trish and said, "Speak of the devil. Let me call you back."

"Oh, OK. Well, make sure you do."

"What do you want, Victor?" I asked once I had him on the line again.

"I just want to explain."

"Explain what? That you've been married the whole time you were screwin' me!" I yelled.

"Nyagra."

"Why don't you explain why you lied out of your ass about every detail of your personal life? Or why you're a fuckin' idiot!"

"Nyagra, if you'd be quiet for one second, I want to let you know a few things."

"Why do you want to let me know now, Victor? Don't you think it's a bit late to be letting me know these things?"

"Yes, and I want to apologize. But it's not what it seemed."

"Oh, I see. I walk up to your beautiful picture-perfect house on Christmas Eve and I see you, your wife and your daughter—all dressed alike—just like a happy family, enjoying the holiday spirit, waiting for Santa. And you act like you've never laid eyes on me, even though you were just in my bed a couple of days before. But it wasn't what it seemed! Huh! So what the fuck was it, Victor? A figment of my goddamn imagination? Or did it never really happen at all. Maybe it was all a fuckin' dream!" I screamed, shaking with anger.

"I know that you're angry and you have every right to be."

"Oh, gee, thanks. I'm so glad that you've validated my emotions. I feel so much better now."

"Listen, Mya wanted her parents together for Christmas. She begged me, Nyagra. I couldn't disappoint her. But they don't live with me. Like I told you, they live in Alabama. We are divorced."

I didn't believe one word he said. "Oh, yeah, you guys looked real divorced, all dressed up in matching pajamas. You looked so bitterly sweet, so unhappily happy," I sarcastically replied.

"Nyagra, I'm telling the truth."

"Yeah, well, so am I. I have never been more humiliated than when I was standing in your doorway on Christmas Eve. If there was nothing going on with your so-called ex-wife—which I'm not too sure that she's your ex, anyway—why did you act as though you'd never seen me before in your life?!"

"She's really emotional and she can be unreasonable, hysterical and erratic. I didn't want to start a big thing on Christmas Eve. I didn't want to ruin it for Mya!"

"You've got to be the biggest bullshit artist I've ever met! Either that or you must think I have Bozo the Clown written on my forehead!"

"I am not bullshitting you, Nyagra!"

"Don't call this house again!" I screamed as I slammed the telephone down. I couldn't believe the nerve and audacity of that man! I surely hoped I didn't have to deal with him ever again for business or otherwise. For that moment, I thought about turning the StarzSports account over to someone else. I couldn't believe what I had gotten myself into!

I really wanted to enjoy the time off from work. I was long overdue for a vacation and the recent turn of events in my life had made me even more exhausted. I had a great desire to really get away. I felt like just taking a trip by myself to the Caribbean and chilling out on some beach with white sand. It was ever so tempting, but I'd promised Trish I would bring in the New Year with her and I couldn't disappoint her. After all, I already felt guilty about lying to her.

As I looked out the window, I could see frozen patches of snow on the front lawn. It was still cold, but the weatherman had depicted that we'd seen the worst of the snowfall. I hoped for an early spring and a better year than the previous. I continued to stare out, with my mind blank. The sun was bright and for some reason, I started praying for Michael to agree to sell me his half of the house. I really wanted to go into the New Year as the single owner of my home. I couldn't believe how ridiculous he was being. I mean, he hadn't lived there in months. The logical thing would've been for him to just surrender his 50 percent. We surely weren't getting back together. I guess it was just his way of holding on to a part of our relationship. My mind told me to walk away from the window and call him at his office, demanding that he sell it to me. Then I thought that maybe I should just take his ass to court. However, I simply stood there gazing out of the window. I couldn't move. It was as if I had mentally drifted off into the Twilight Zone. In fact I think I even saw a faint silhouette of Rod Sterling until the phone began to ring and snapped me out of my mode.

Initially, I didn't want to answer. At this point in my life, there were too many people I truly had no desire to converse with. But the machine didn't pick up and the caller was persistent. On the ninth ring, I answered.

"Hello?"

It was Mamma. "So how was your holiday?" she asked in her familiar Mamma-like "I'm pissed that you chose not to do what I asked you to do" voice.

"Oh, hi, Ma. Merry Christmas." I tried to sound jovial. Sadly to say, she was actually one of the people I could've lived without talking to at that moment.

"Why haven't you called me?"

"I called you on Christmas Day, Ma. I didn't get an answer. Juanita said you might've been on the phone with Aunt Rita."

"Oh, well, why didn't you call until you got me? You knew I was there."

"Well, I had a couple of things to do."

"On Christmas Day?"

"Mamma, did you have a good holiday? I heard the meal was fabulous," I said, trying to change the subject a bit.

"Well, you know it was good. And there are plenty of leftovers."

"Great, I'll be up there sometime this week."

"How about spending the night on New Year's Eve? Like usual, I'm cooking another big meal for New Year's Day."

"No. I'm going to a party at Trish's on New Year's Eve."

"I can't believe you! You were there for Christmas and now you're going there for New Year's, too?"

"Mamma . . . "

"Nyagra, fine," she huffed. "How about coming New Year's Day? Everyone's gonna be here and I really want you here, too. Ya know, David's been in treatment and he's better than he was the last time you saw him."

"Good for him and his."

"Well, if you'll come on New Year's Day, I'll take what I can get," she replied, obviously trying to make me feel guilty.

"Mamma . . . "

"What?"

"I'll definitely be there New Year's Day," I assured her.

"Well, OK, then. I'll be expecting you no later than noon."

"OK."

Oh, God. Now I had to go!

I couldn't believe how fast the week had gone by. By choice, I had done little but lie around the house and relax. I finally finished the book I was reading and tried to catch up on the soap operas that I hadn't seen in years. Ironically, although they'd changed a couple of characters, as well as added and killed off a few others, I still knew a lot about what was going on. That's the funny thing about the soaps.

I spoke to Trish nearly every day, but opted not to visit. I was fighting a state of depression and if I'd seen her, she would've known right away. Over the telephone, I was able to hide my feelings. But I knew that if she'd taken one look in my eyes, she would've realized that I was dealing with something. And I really wanted to prove to myself that I could handle what I was going through alone.

The weatherman had been wrong like usual, and we ended up getting another four inches of snow. I was kind of glad, though, because it was the perfect weather for staying inside, which is exactly what I wanted to do. Plus, with the snow falling, no one was trying to come and visit me. I lived on the top of a hill that was very difficult to climb in lousy weather. That was the major reason I had purchased my 4-by-4.

The snow and the cold didn't make me feel the least bit guilty about staying inside every day. I slept well, ate well, and just began feeling good about myself again. I cooked all the good things I loved to eat that you couldn't get from the Chinese or take-out restaurants—something I rarely got a chance to do. I must've gained five pounds, but I felt damn good about it!

Determined not to have my bliss rudely interrupted, I kept the answering machine on to shield myself from the shady individuals I didn't want to speak to. Victor was still calling at least once a day. But overall, I really enjoyed my time off with no work, no "pain in the ass getting on my nerves" male companion, no nothing. Just me with me, loving me—totally into me! When I felt like eating, I did. When I felt like sleeping, I did. If I felt like sitting on the toilet and reading five or six chapters straight, I did. If I felt like soaking in a bubble bath for two or three hours, I did that, too. There was nobody there to bang on the door complaining that I was taking too long or saying that they needed to get in there. In fact, I didn't even close the bathroom door. Hey, a girl could really get used to this!

New Year's Eve finally snuck up on me and interrupted my routine of laziness. Trish's party was starting at ten and I figured I'd make my entrance around 11:30. Since I hadn't felt like going shopping for anything to wear, I opted to wear a little red Gucci dress that I'd bought for the Essence Awards the previous year.

I don't know why but I was feeling particularly sexy that night, and the red dress fit my mood perfectly. It was short, low-cut with spaghetti straps, and totally seductive—yet completely classy, which is how I always like to be and which Gucci only knows how to be!

Although I knew it was below zero outside, I was determined to be sexy so I figured that in the name of Victor, I'd throw on my Maurice Valenci mink to keep me warm! I was sure that I'd be able to attract a couple of Rodney's dizzy jock friends.

I could've used the comfort of a good strong man with little or no conversation right about then—just something nice to look at and touch with no strings attached. Man, half of Rodney's friends couldn't even spell the word "attached!" But obviously the intellectual ones weren't right for me because they seemed to only know how to play childish games of deception. I figured that perhaps I should take the advice of that little old white lady and attempt to change my taste for the New Year! Whatever the case, I was bound to attract someone in that dress. I was determined to make this New Year's Eve a night I'd never forget.

Seven

It was a freezing cold New Year's Eve. Even though the snow had stopped, it must've been twenty below and the roads were extremely slick. I had to drive ten miles per hour all the way over to Trish's, forcing me to arrive later than I had wanted.

In any event, I made my grand entrance at nearly midnight. If I do say so myself, I was looking quite fabulous; especially compared to how I'd looked when I first arrived back from catching that trifling Victor. I was proud of the way I'd bounced back from yet another romantic disappointment. Despite the recent events, I was doing just fine. I knew my Mr. Right was out there somewhere just waiting for me in his Gucci shoes and Hugo Boss suit. Somewhere . . .

As usual, Trish and Rodney's home looked spectacular. Their colossal Christmas tree was still up, and the entire main entertaining room sparkled with gold trimmings along the borders of the walls and doorways. There were tuxedo clad servers walking around with trays of delicious hot and cold hors d'oeuvres. Needless to say, the place was packed and filled with a festive spirit and everyone seemed to be having the time of their lives. Trish had even hired a live band and the place was jumping.

It was no surprise that Trish had been eagerly waiting for me. No sooner had I crossed the threshold of the parlor than she rushed up to me in a reprimanding tone and questioned, "Girl, where have you been? It's damn near midnight! But I knew you weren't gonna let me down!" We hugged as she took my coat. "You look fabulous!" she continued.

"So do you," I stated, observing her classy black strapless long slip dress. She was as elegant as the surroundings. Trish really knew how to do it up. She was the hostess of the year. Man, as I looked around, I realized that she was the hostess of the decade!

"I see you're here solo. Where's Lover Boy?" she questioned, observing the fact that I had arrived alone.

"He couldn't make it." I shrugged.

"Well, not to worry. You and I are the best looking things in here and tonight I'm happily married, so they're all yours." She chuckled. "And don't sleep on these brothas, Girl. There's a lot of eligible, fine, rich men in here, Girlfriend," she whispered in my ear as we walked into the main room.

"Thank you," I sarcastically responded.

As we entered, Rodney greeted me with a massive hug and kiss. As usual, he looked handsome. I was instantly reminded of how great he and Trish looked together. They were one of the few couples that I could honestly say were truly made for each other.

Trish was right. There were a lot of fine men in that room. I didn't know if they were rich or not but they certainly looked like it. They were probably all athlete friends of Rodney's, but who cared? Certainly not me. Not that night. I wasn't exactly looking for my soul mate. But contrary to what Trish had said, there were a lot of beautiful women in that room as well. In fact, there was nothing but good-looking people in the whole room.

Along the grand window at the far end of the room was an elongated rectangular table covered with an elaborately embroidered gold cloth. It was simply gorgeous. From where I stood, I could see a delectable spread of tantalizing foods including a turkey that must have weighed at least forty pounds, two ice sculptures at each end as well as a lobster boat strategically placed right in the center. She'd really outdone herself this time.

For some reason I drifted off into mental space as Trish described all the eligible men in the room. Her voice became a mere whisper in my psyche. For one brief second, I actually wished that Victor had been able to join me. I even wished that I'd busted him after New Year's. Although it only would've prolonged my ignorance and ultimately my pain, I would've enjoyed going home with him after celebrating such a wonderful holiday. To make love to him until the sun rose would've been quite a nice way to start off the New Year. However, the shock of finding out his actual marital status wouldn't have been a nice surprise. Although I could've still used the physical pleasure, I guess a higher force wanted to spare me the additional mental anguish.

"William Peterson, this is my best girlfriend, Nyagra Ensley," I heard Trish say as I snapped back into reality.

"Pleased to meet you." He smiled as he extended his large well-manicured hand toward mine.

"Likewise," I replied. He was a handsome, older gentleman with thick salt and pepper hair and a matching beard and mustache. He reminded me of the legendary Dr. J and looked like he'd experienced many successful endeavors. He must have, for Trish would've never introduced me to a slouch. She wouldn't have even invited any to her home.

He must've had about fifteen years on me, as handsome and distinguished as he appeared. But what the heck? Like I said, I wasn't trying to meet my soul mate. Maybe I could've used someone a little older; wiser even. Maybe I was due for a man too mature for childish games. He'd probably played them already in his twenties, thirties or even in his forties. Maybe this was what I needed. He was probably rich as hell, too. But whatever age he was, he sure was fine!

"Nyagra, what a pretty and unusual name." When he grinned, he reminded me of a slightly older version of Victor.

"Thank you." I blushed.

"Bill is one of the few black men on the Athletics Board of Directors for a Division 1 College. He's one of three in the country, I think. He used to be Rodney's coach in high school." Trish laughed in her ever-so-fake "take notice of this guy" laugh. Little did she know, I already had.

"That must be quite interesting." I smiled.

"I enjoy it. How about you, Nyagra? What do you do?"

"Well, let me go make sure all my guests have champagne. It's nearly ten minutes to. I'll be right back!" Trish interjected. She rushed off and I reached for a glass of champagne from the passing waiter's tray.

As I took a tiny sip from the crystal flute, feeling a bit talkative, I matter of factly stated, "It's a wonderful thing when you can do something you love and get paid for it, isn't it?"

"Yes, it is. What was it that you said you did?" he asked.

"Oh, I'm the vice president of an advertising agency, Newman & Stein Enterprises. Have you ever heard of it?"

"Have I ever heard of it? Of course, I have! Didn't you guys just take on the StarzSports Apparel account?"

"As a matter of fact, we did," I said proudly, surprised that word had traveled so quickly throughout the industry.

"Every rookie I know is dying for that StarzSports endorsement. Have you guys chosen anybody?"

"Not yet, but we're in the process of narrowing it down."

"OK, everybody!" Trish yelled from the center of the room as she turned everyone's attention to a big screen television (that I hadn't even noticed prior to this moment) which now showed the enormous silver ball from Times Square slowly descending toward the ground.

"The countdown is on!" she continued in her festive voice.

In the final moment, everybody animatedly chorused together, anxiously awaiting the arrival of a new year. "Ten, nine, eight, seven, six, five, four, three, two, one! HAPPY NEW YEAR!"

Music furiously echoed from the speakers, from the television, from outside and from everywhere.

Everyone was jumping up and down screaming, "Happy New Year!" and hugging and kissing each other. They clearly were elated to embark upon a new year and even more anxious to leave the previous one behind.

Even my new friend, William Peterson, extended open arms to me for a hug, which I graciously reciprocated. A person couldn't help but to be happy in a room filled with so much joy. Whatever problems anyone had when they walked through the front door of Trish's beautiful home, they clearly had forgotten after that ball had dropped.

Trish came over to me and embraced me tightly.

"Happy New Year, Girl." She warmly smiled.

So the party was on. The band played good music—the kind Trish and I really loved. The servers walked around with great things to offer.

Everything that was on that elaborately-set table was being carved, dished out and served. I was hungry and picked something from probably every tray. Of course, everything was absolutely delicious! To work off the food I was tossing down my throat, I danced a little with William and with Rodney. I recognized a couple of faces, but knew no names. I was really having a ball.

After a little while of eating and dancing, William pulled me to the side. "You want to get some air?"

"Sure."

I was burning up from dancing, even though Trish had plenty of cool air coming through the vents. William and I walked toward the front entrance of the house, gave the coat-check girl our tickets and waited as she retrieved our outerwear.

The cool air felt particularly good on my face. My coat warmed me just enough to still be able to enjoy the crispness and pollution-free air surrounding Trish's house. Through the enormous bay window behind us, I could see the silhouettes of people still dancing and having a good old time. After a moment of standing silently, William said, "They sure do have a beautiful home."

"Yes, they do."

"So tell me all about yourself, Nyagra."

Oh, here goes the first personal conversation filled with a million questions and a million lies. The bullshit stage, I thought.

"What do you want to know?" I asked as I seductively smiled.

"First of all I want to know why a beautiful, smart woman like you isn't married or even attached? Why on earth are you at a New Year's Eve party unescorted?"

"How do you know I'm not?" I slyly questioned. I decided to make this fun.

"Well, Trish mentioned that you're single and I couldn't help but notice you when you arrived—all alone."

"Oh, good 'ol Trish . . . always trying to make a love connection. She means well."

"Yes, she does. I think she just wants to see you happy."

"But I am happy. Very happy."

"That's good to know since I firmly believe that happiness starts within."

"It most certainly does."

"Yes, but you still haven't answered my question."

"Oh, why I'm not married?"

"Yes."

"Well, I guess I just haven't found the right guy." I felt like I was having my first date with Victor all over again.

"I'm surprised. I'd think a woman like you would have a million suitors just lined up to take you out."

"Well, I'm looking for someone special and I'm quite picky."

"Oh, I see . . ."

"So what about you, William? Why is a distinguished gentleman like you flying solo? Where is Mrs. Peterson and baby Peterson?"

"Well, Mrs. Peterson is deceased. Well, let me be a little more honest, the third Mrs. Peterson—the one I adored and firmly believed was my soul mate—is deceased. The other two; who knows where the hell they are? And as for baby Peterson, I have no children." He laughed.

I felt bad that his last wife had died, but three wives?! But at least he seemed pretty honest. After all, he was already divulging information that he didn't have to. I would've never known about his wives if he hadn't told me. That seemed like a pretty good sign. But anyone who's been married three times has got to be flaky. There was obviously something wrong with him. But isn't there always?

"My condolences with respect to your last wife," I stated.

"I still miss her," he said sadly.

"How long has it been?"

"Four-and-a-half years. And it's still particularly difficult during the holidays."

"I would imagine so. When you really love someone, you can't just forget about them, no matter how much time passes."

"You're right." An awkward moment of silence lapsed. "I know you want to ask about the others," William said.

"Excuse me?"

"My other two wives. I know you want to ask about them. Women always do."

I had to laugh. He kind of read my mind, but I wouldn't have dared pursue the issue on my own. At least not during our first meeting and definitely not on New Year's Eve. But since he'd opened the can of worms, why not get the information?

"Well, yeah," I said bluntly. "Why did you marry so many times?"

"My first wife, Vivienne—I married her when I was 18 because she told me she was pregnant and I wanted to do the right thing . . . "

"I thought you said no children."

"She had a miscarriage, I think. To be honest, I'm not a hundred percent sure she was ever really pregnant, but the past is the past."

I felt stupid. I figured that before I put my foot in my mouth again, I'd better just shut up and listen.

"Her father never wanted us to marry anyway, so he pressured her relentlessly and we got an annulment eleven months later."

"I'm sorry."

"Don't be. I didn't love her. At 18, how can you really love anybody? I just wanted to do the honorable thing."

"That's good."

"My second wife, Suzanne, slept with my brother. I never got over that. We divorced after three years."

"Gosh," I said. Did this guy have really bad luck or was he just trying to get sympathy? "How old were you when you married her?"

"Twenty-nine."

"Wow."

"Then there was Julia—the love of my life. I married her when I was 36. We were happily married eight years before she was diagnosed with breast cancer. She survived two mastectomies, but the cancer had already spread to her brain. She passed away two years after her diagnosis. Like I said, that was four-and-a-half years ago. I don't think I'll ever marry again."

Man, either this guy was an open book or he had his stories down pat.

"So, now you know. I like to let all the skeletons out of my closet from the beginning. I'm 51 years old and too old for games."

Damn, I knew he had at least fifteen years on me, but it was eighteen to be exact.

But in the scheme of things, did it really matter? The guys I'd been with previously were all pretty much in my age group and all of them were sorry. Maybe an older man would do me some good. After all, I wasn't looking for anything serious.

"Are you guys gonna stand out here holding the house up all night?" Trish suddenly poked her head out of the front door. "Come back inside. The DJ took over from where the band left off and everybody's getting down on the dance floor!"

As we entered the house, I could feel the vibration of the music in my chest. The band was taking a break and the DJ was playing one of my favorite songs. As we glided to the beat of the music, William and I just moved onto the crowded floor.

Hmm, he can dance, too, I thought. I tried not to concentrate on him, but I couldn't help wondering what he was thinking. He had spoken candidly with me so soon that I had to figure why he'd be that open. In past experiences, I'd found most men chose not to disclose too much personal information until questioned. Even then they tended to avoid the nitty-gritty, hard-core facts. Only when backed up against a wall-or busted-do they usually come clean. And that's only if they have absolutely no other choice. Trifling ass Victor Reece would've probably carried on the facade forever if I'd let him! But William seemed different. He had a touch of innocence in his eyes. He reminded me of a puppy yearning for a sweet and gentle master.

As perspiration trickled down my forehead and I could feel the little drops of sweat slowly rolling down the crease of my spine, I opted to make my exit from the incredibly crowded dance floor. I decided to cool off in the dining area with a plate full of Trish's delicious goodies. I desperately wanted to get down and dirty and really enjoy the exceptionally tasty but quite messy cuisine. But despite the temptation, I was on good behavior. There were other guests in the dining area and I didn't want to embarrass myself. So I didn't suck the broiled chicken wing dry like I would've done at home nor did I go back for a second helping of the gooey macaroni and cheese. I was a "perfect" lady and William didn't slurp or smack either. I knew we were both trying hard not to be obvious about watching the other. At the same time, we were trying to enjoy our food without being sloppy. It was actually quite humorous. I'm sure that any outsider looking at us from afar would've found it downright hilarious.

William and I chatted comfortably, like we'd known each other for years. I told him all about my career and he seemed to be impressed and interested. In turn, I also eagerly listened to all of his stories about the blatant racism he'd experienced coming up in a field where there were very few people of color.

"Of course, most of the athletes are all black, but I rarely see a face at my occupational level that in any way resembles mine," he explained.

He was indeed an interesting man. However, I noticed that he was finishing off quite a few drinks. I think that was what was really making him talk. Even prior to our conversation in front of Trish's house, I think he had devoured at least four. I wondered if he was that communicative or if he would've told me of his wives without those six or seven Long Island Iced Teas. Oh, don't get me wrong. It wasn't like he was sloppy drunk stumbling all over and blowing alcohol breath in my face. He was just extremely chatty, and I didn't know how well he could actually hold his liquor. For all I knew, he might've drank like that all the time. I still couldn't help wondering whether he could safely drive home. To be honest, part of me kind of hoped he wouldn't.

William talked my ear off in that grand dining room. By the time I'd finished my plate of food, I think I knew probably all there was to know about him. I'm not complaining. After all, I am in the field of communications. It's my career, but damn! I'd never met such an open man and although it was unusual, it was refreshing.

As William eagerly told me more about his life, I felt a pressure-filled tap on my shoulder. I spontaneously turned around only to see Shawn Franklin—the buffoon from Benihana—looking just as goofy and awkward as he had the night we'd met.

Oh, brother! I thought as I rolled my eyes toward the ceiling.

"Happy New Year, Nyagra!" He smiled as he rudely interrupted my conversation with William.

"Happy New Year to you, too," I unenthusiastically replied.

"Are you enjoying yourself tonight?"

"I am and this is my friend William Peterson. William, this is, what was your name again?" I asked, knowing damn well I could never forget the name of such an obnoxious asshole.

"Shawn. Shawn Franklin," he abruptly replied as he forcefully shook hands with William. "Long time, no see, Nyagra, and you're looking beautiful. Are you gonna save me a dance?"

"No, I don't think so. But thanks for the offer," I snapped, turning my head.

"Oh, I'm sure your dad won't mind. I mean, after all, it is New Year's Eve."

"The lady said she doesn't think so," William firmly stated, obviously offended by the "dad" referral.

"OK. OK. I'm not trying to raise your blood pressure, man. I just wanted to dance with an old friend," Shawn said as he showed that same obnoxious smile that almost made me mace him in his Lexus. I chuckled falsely and shook my head.

We are not "old friends," I thought. Shawn raised his hands, again reminding me of that night in his car and strolled away like the moron he knew so well how to be.

"Hey, Nyagra, how's the commercial business?" he sagaciously asked as he strolled his ignorant ass out of sight.

"You'll have to excuse him. He's very obnoxious," I explained to William.

"Old boyfriend?"

"Not hardly," I replied. There were a few moments of silence, which gave me a chance to think about how William had responded to Shawn's ignorance. He seemed offended by Shawn's reference to him as my dad, which was kind of funny to me. I wondered if it was the liquor talking for him again, but I really didn't care.

Trish had been the perfect hostess—pretty, fun and full of so much life. It was easy to see that every single guest was having an absolutely magnificent time. There was plenty of good food, drink and music. But at 2:57 a.m., I was more than ready to get out of there. William must've felt the same way because after completing what I believed was his eighth Long Island Iced Tea, he said to me, "Nyagra, why don't we leave and go someplace a little bit more intimate?"

I truly wanted to. I really did. But I just wasn't sure if I should.

"More intimate?" I questioned. "Well, what do you have in mind?"

"How about my place? It's not too far from here. We could have some cappuccino, if you like, and maybe listen to a little George Howard or Kenny G. Do you like jazz?"

"Absolutely." I smiled, impressed by his choice of music.

"So what do you say?"

"Well, OK," I hesitantly replied. I got up to walk back into the main room. "Let me say goodbye to Trish and Rodney."

"Give them my best. I'll get your coat and meet you at the valet."

As I entered the room, I saw my closest friends still getting down on the dance floor in a crowd of people. The funk classic, "Flashlight," was playing loudly and I felt myself sliding toward them to the beat of the music.

"I had a wonderful time!" I shouted over the music into Trish's ear.

"You're leaving?" Trish shouted back.

"Yeah!"

"Already?"

"Already? It's three in the morning!"

"I know but the party's still jumpin'!" She laughed as she gave me a big hug. I gave Rodney a kiss on the cheek and Trish stopped dancing to walk me to the foyer.

"So what do you think of William?" she asked as she leaned in my ear.

"He's very sweet."

"Sweet, single and fine and distinguished and loaded!" She laughed.

"And old!" I chuckled.

"I know, I know." She laughed. "He may be old but the Bentley is new!"

Trish and I slapped a forceful high-five and burst out laughing.

"Yeah, well, despite his age, I think he's cool people. In fact, we're leaving together."

"Get outta here! Really?"

"Yeah. So tell me. Is he safe?"

"Of course, he's safe! I told you he used to be Rodney's coach in high school—a wholesome man. Girl, you couldn't get much safer!" she assured me.

"Are you sure? Let's not forget that you're the one who introduced me to that Shawn character and his ass was anything but safe. In fact, he was a fuckin' pervert!"

"Yeah, I know, I know. I didn't know he was like that. I haven't known Shawn for longer than six or seven months. But Rodney's known William for over ten years. By the way, did you see Shawn? He was asking for you."

"Yes, unfortunately I did." We giggled together. "But really, Trish, is this guy a decent guy? I mean, really?"

"Ny, he's a good guy. Despite the fact that he's been married three times, he's a good guy. He just chose lousy women—although his last wife was good, but she kicked the bucket."

"Yeah, I know. He told me all about it."

"See, that's a couple of points for him right there. Most men wouldn't tell you shit!"

"Yeah, I know."

"And he's older, wiser. Maybe you need that."

"That's what I was thinking. I just wanted to make sure he's all right because I'm going to his place."

"Aw, sookie, sookie now . . . yes, Girl. He's all right. Better than all right."

"Well, I had a great time. You really outdid yourself."

"Thanks, Ny. I'm so happy you came. But hey, wait a minute! You're going to William's house? What about Lover Boy—Mr. StarzSports?"

"Lover Boy?" I asked, knowing exactly who she was referring to.

"Yeah, Lover Boy. What's his face—Victor?"

"Oh, Victor's in Atlanta, Georgia and I'm in Hartsdale, New York," I nonchalantly stated.

"You sure are, Girl. You sure are! Have fun!" We hugged once more and I exited out the front door. William was waiting patiently at the valet stand holding my coat. As I approached him, I couldn't help but notice how stunningly handsome he was and figured that ten years ago he must've had women crawling at his feet. In fact, even at his age, I'm sure he still had his share of female suitors.

"Now are you good enough to drive?" I asked.

"Absolutely," he replied.

I was not one hundred percent convinced but decided to take his word for it. I gave my ticket to the parking attendant and before I knew it, both of our vehicles were pulling up in front of us. I was a little curious to see exactly what kind of car he was driving. I was interested in his taste. I know Trish said he owned a Bentley but I was sure that was not his only vehicle. Needless to say, I wasn't surprised to see the attendant pull up in a navy blue Mercedes Benz 600 SL. A car like that totally fit him. Classy and timeless, yet sort of subdued. Not flashy—but extremely classy. In fact, it would've surprised me to see him get into anything less. A moment after checking him out, I was climbing into my Range Rover.

I smiled through my window. "You lead. I'll follow."

The ride to William's house was quick. The highway was nearly empty at that hour, so what was likely a twenty-five-minute ride was now a mere fifteen. The roads were still a bit slick, so I used a little extra precaution. I barely had an opportunity to think of conversation pieces nor did I have time to really decide whether or not I was going to sleep with him. I wanted to. All evening I had been in a sexy mood, but I didn't want to seem like a whore or like I always went to bed with men I'd only known a few hours. Truthfully, I felt that by having sex with William, I was getting even with Victor. On the other hand, I really just wanted to be touched and held, and William seemed like the perfect man to do it.

As I drove, of course I thought of all the reasons why I should have just turned around and driven my black ass home. But at the same time I figured that at least this time I'd have a first-hand opportunity to visit his house and see if there were any "womanly" things around. He hadn't expected me to come so he didn't have time to hide anything, I thought as I made a left into his driveway.

His home was indeed lovely. Looking at yet another French-style Tudor split-level home from the outside made me wonder what a single man such as William did with all that space. From the looks of it, he must've had at least four or five bedrooms.

I got out of the jeep and walked swiftly toward the front entrance. The air was still frigid and I was anxious to step into the warmth of his living room.

"You'll have to excuse the mess. I didn't exactly know you were coming." He laughed as he stuck the key in the lock and opened the door for me to step across.

"That's quite all right. Now I get to see how you are on an everyday basis," I replied as I stepped into the main room. It was incredibly large with a shiny hardwood floor and cream-colored walls. It was filled with all types of natural colors-lots of browns and forest greens. It looked rich yet comfortable. At a glance I noticed that there were two custom-made bookshelves carved into the wall filled with sports-related books. And to be honest, the room wasn't the least bit messy.

He took my coat. "Make yourself at home."

"You have a lovely home." I smiled, strategically placing myself at the far-left corner of the extremely plush sectional. I didn't leave him any room to sit to my left, thus forcing him to sit close on my right if he wanted to be near me.

"Thank you. Julia and I bought it together. It was her dream home. We were planning to have a lot of children. But now it's just me and sometimes it feels too big. Looking at four unused bedrooms can get depressing. But I didn't want to sell it after she died. I feel like her spirit is still here."

I nodded as I listened. I could see he still missed his wife and for one quick moment wondered if this was something I should really even get myself into.

"Stop looking down the road, you security freak! Enjoy the moment for a change!" I heard a voice say in my head—I don't know if it was mine or Trish's.

He broke the momentary silence. "Would you care for a cappuccino?"

"I'd love one!" I smiled. William exited the room and I could hear him hustling and bustling in the kitchen. As I waited, I observed the exquisite detailing around the ceiling and the doorway. It must've taken a long time (and a lot of money) to build and create the detailing on this room, I thought. I couldn't help but wonder whether or not it was William or his deceased spouse who was behind the home's personalization. But I supposed that it could've been like that when they moved in.

William returned quickly with a silver tray carrying our cappuccino in two little white porcelain cups. He placed the tray on the rectangular, glass-topped oak table in front of us and sat close to me on my right.

"It's hazelnut. I hope you like it."

"I'm sure I will."

The cappuccino was quite good, but surprisingly, there was little conversation. William had put on a George Howard CD and we both sat and listened quietly. Perhaps he had talked so much at the party that he had nothing else to say. Or maybe it had been the liquor talking and the cappuccino was sobering him up. Whatever the case, there was plenty of silence. We listened to nearly three songs until I decided to break the ice. "Trish and Rodney sure know how to throw a party, don't they?"

"Yes. They're quite a pair of socialites. He's done quite well for himself. He's come a long way." He laughed. The atmosphere felt kind of awkward. Just an hour ago, I had been completely comfortable with William. But now I realized that I had felt far more comfortable with him at the party than I did in his living room. Now I felt as if I truly didn't belong there. I actually wanted to think of an excuse to head for the door. And as far as making any kind of physical moves—that seemed almost out of the question.

As I was about to take the final sip from my cup, William said, "You've got to excuse me. I'm a little nervous."

I was surprised to hear him say that, although it was quite obvious. In fact, his nervousness was making me nervous!

"I think we both are." I smiled, trying to help him feel more at ease.

"You're a very beautiful woman, Nyagra, but I haven't been with a woman since my beloved Julia passed away four years ago."

William moved a bit closer to me on the couch and smiled innocently. The beautiful sounds of George Howard's sax flowing through the air with the dim and calming light from the crystal lamp set the mood perfectly. I almost forgot that it was now New Year's Day and that we'd just left a jumping party at Trish's house. As the caffeine from the cappuccino began to settle in my stomach, I suddenly began to feel calm and relaxed in William's living room, and once again I felt as if I'd known him forever instead of just a couple of hours.

We both sat on the sofa enjoying the atmosphere when suddenly William put his arm around me. I hadn't felt such a tingle in my skin since Andrew Stevens kissed me on my lips in the eighth grade. It was weird! As my mind wandered back to the hallway of PS 131, William quickly turned to me and kissed me right on my lips, gently placing his tongue onto mine. It was nice. It wasn't a sexual kiss like the ones I had shared with Victor. No. It was far more gentle and caring. My physical contact with Victor had been lustful and exciting. Maybe subconsciously I knew that he was forbidden fruit. But William's kiss was different. I could tell that he genuinely liked me. That one day he could even love me. And that I might want to love him. Oh, here I go thinking about the future again instead of just enjoying the moment, I thought.

"I'm not going to run any lines on you, Nyagra. I know men probably run lines on beautiful women like you all the time. But I feel like I've known you a hell of a lot longer than a few hours," William whispered in my ear between kisses. I could smell the mixture of Long Island Iced Tea and hazelnut cappuccino on his breath. Surprisingly, it didn't turn me off. It had the opposite effect. "I know we don't know each other well, but I'd really like to make love to you," he continued as he tightly embraced me.

"You're right. We don't know each other too well," I stated, still unsure about what I wanted to do. I wanted to see exactly where he was going with his dialogue. I had no objection to two consenting adults making the conscious decision to have intercourse during their first or their twentieth meeting. Trish had made me feel quite comfortable with that. I just needed to know where his head was so that I wouldn't have to deal with self-worth issues in the morning.

"If I am rushing this or making you feel the least bit uncomfortable, please let me know. That is definitely not my intention. I don't want to scare you off," he said, now sitting upright on the couch beside me.

"Well, William, I really need to know what's going on inside your head. I don't want us to misunderstand each other. We had a nice evening together—great conversation, great dancing. In fact, this probably has been the best New Year's Eve I've ever had. But I really want to go into this new year feeling positive. I've had an eventful year—to say the least—and I don't want to start a new year feeling badly because I brought it in having sex with some guy I'll never speak to again."

"I understand. I know I'd really like to see you again—to try to have a relationship, even. There's absolutely no way I could let you walk out of that door and out of my life. There's no way we could never see each other again without giving each other a chance. No way, and if you want to wait until we spend more time together to indulge in sex, I have no objection. Absolutely none," he assured me.

"I appreciate that, William. I know it's New Year's Eve and we're both feeling good and all, but I'm not trying to get used—nor do I want you to feel as though you've been. The truth of the matter is that I've had a difficult year relationship-wise, and I'm truly unsure if I even want to get involved for a while. I have to be honest. I don't want you to look for something I can't give to you and vice versa." I thought to myself that he was really the one about to get used because I was just out to have a good time.

"My using days are over, Nyagra. I'm too old for games. I can tell that you're a very special lady and I want to get to know you better starting right now. It's really late and being the gentleman that I am, I couldn't let you drive home at this hour anyway. But if you choose to sleep in the guest room, that's fine. I have four of them." He laughed.

There was a moment of silence before he began kissing the back of my neck in a way that sent more tingles down my spine than when our lips had touched. I had a serious weakness for kisses on my neck. Victor had capitalized on that weakness and that was one of the reasons he'd gotten so damn far with me.

"But if you want to sleep in the master bedroom, you're more than welcome," he whispered.

"I think it would be best for me to sleep in one of the guest rooms," I responded, surely to his surprise.

He suddenly stopped and lifted his mouth from the nape of my neck and smiled. "OK, well, whenever you're ready, you can retire for the evening. I'm actually gonna sit here and listen to a little bit more George."

I wasn't ready to go to sleep. I was actually ready to receive his mature muscular physique, but I wanted to test him. I planned to have sex with him that evening, but when I was ready. I wanted to be certain that he understood and respected the word "no" before I'd give him an admission ticket. In the back of my mind, I couldn't believe how much I was acting like Trish.

I've never treated sex with this much planning and thought. I suppose that's why I was always getting into trouble. Sex to me was one hundred percent emotional and zero percent logical. However, after my Victor incident, I needed to acquire some logic (and a little bit of game). I always gave in to men too easily. As Trish had told me, I always made things too simple for them. That's probably the reason I never had good luck. Well, starting that night—on the first day of a new year—with a man over ten years my senior—I adopted a new attitude toward my sexuality and my romantic relationships. And I wanted to see just how much William really wanted me.

We were both silent until I decided that it was time for me to exit the room and begin our little game of cat and mouse. I wanted him to follow me without being too aggressive, yet I wanted him to stay put without being too laid-back. Before I rose from the couch, with the sexiest body language I'd probably ever utilized, I wondered what his actions would be.

As I got up to leave, William gently grabbed my wrist. "I want you, Nyagra. Believe me, this won't be a one-night stand."

"Show me to my room," I softly stated as I held his hand and began to walk toward the living room door.

"No, let me show you to my room," he whispered sweeping me off of my feet and carrying me down the hall to a huge bedroom with an enormous king-sized, four-post cherrywood bed. It sat elegantly on a 12-inch elevated platform in the center of the floor. A dim crystal nightlight allowed me to barely see the decor of the room. As I focused in on my surroundings, I could see that there were built-in bookshelves filled with tons of reading materials, indicating to me again what an intellectual man I was dealing with.

As he placed my body on the bed and gently removed my shoes, slip and stockings, I felt sensuously erotic and quite ready to receive him. I lay motionless as I watched him unbuckle his belt and slip off his slacks. He stood as still as a statue just looking at me—almost as though he didn't know what to do next. I was silent as I observed his body in the dim light. He had a nice physique for a man

his age. However, his manhood didn't stand at attention the way Victor's had, forcing me to wonder if I was really turning him on. In addition, his frumpy white boxer shorts suddenly reminded me that this man was old enough to be my father.

After what began to feel like an eternity, I watched him as he walked to the dresser in the far-left corner of the room, opened the top drawer and pulled out a bottle of pills. He swiftly popped one into his mouth dry and swallowed hard.

What the hell is this man doing? I asked myself. Either he saw or sensed my confusion because he turned in my direction and shrugged.

"Viagra . . . Viagra for Nyagra." He chuckled. "Hey, I'm a rapper!"

I wanted to laugh and cry at the same time. I almost choked on my own saliva, realizing that this man needed a prescribed tablet to make his dick hard. Watching him awkwardly move about in his saggy Fruit of the Looms and swallow that pill without a drop of fluid stopped all of my sexual juices from flowing. Unable to make a move, I lay silently in the bed as I continued to observe him. He made his way back and clumsily climbed on top of me. He attempted to remove my panties. But for some reason, he couldn't seem to do it by himself. Not wanting to embarrass him, I remained quiet as I placed my hands on his to assist him. He slipped my panties below my thighs, my knees, my ankles, and ultimately onto the floor. Everything was taking so long and flowing so poorly that I began to feel like we were in class and I was the teacher. If I'd been thinking straight, I would've immediately locked my legs and ran out of there. But I figured I might as well go through with it. After all, I had no one to blame but myself.

After what seemed like an eternity, we were finally both naked with the exception of his dress socks and the condom he had fumbled to put on his falsely semi-hard dick. I looked into his eyes, which indicated that he was concentrating so hard that he totally forgot about any form of foreplay or kissing. He aggressively wedged himself between my legs and attempted to penetrate my body. As much as I wanted to, I could no longer stay quiet and allow him to participate in a sexual act in that manner. After all, I wasn't about to get anything out of this! I'd heard that those impotency pills weren't cheap either. I wanted him to at least get his money's worth.

In an attempt to slow him down a bit and perhaps get a little enjoyment out of this encounter, I tightened my body and whispered in his ear, "William, slow down . . . I'm not going anywhere . . . take your time."

"I know, I know, baby . . . it's just been so long," he hotly breathed in my face.

I could smell every ounce of liquor he'd consumed all night, and the stench of his breath almost knocked me out. Eye-to-eye, nose-to-nose, face-to-face—he suddenly wasn't as attractive or desirable as he'd been thirty minutes ago on his couch, as he attempted to poke his way inside of me in the name of so-called passion. As much as he seemed to be trying, he wasn't doing anything besides applying pressure to my body as he frantically searched for my doorway. All he was doing was squashing me. Although I barely felt a thing, he was finally inside of me. He panted frantically like a grizzly bear that had been shot and left for dead. I halfway couldn't tell if he was having sex with me or having convulsions. I tried to catch my breath, but I couldn't help feeling as though I was being squished by a big yellow school bus. Then before I could breathe—before I could make sense out of what exactly was happening, he reached his pinnacle and dropped his entire body weight on mine. Not only did I feel flatter than a pancake, I think I heard one of my ribs crack. I also wanted to disappear into thin air.

"I'm always better the second time around," he grumbled as if he had just participated in a decathlon.

If he thought I was going to put myself through that twice, he was sadly mistaken.

Forget it, buddy . . . you had your chance.

William then clumsily rolled off my body and almost instantaneously began snoring like a La Machine food processor as soon as his head hit the pillow. I laid there silently staring up at the ceiling. I looked over at William who was sleeping and snoring on top of all the covers like an old drunk in a junkyard. The condom was still on his keeled-over miniature penis. So much for Viagra.

I suddenly felt sick. My stomach seemed like it was about to explode. I ran to the bathroom where I buried my face in the toilet and puked out what felt like my entire brain. After I pulled my face out of the toilet, I sat on the side of the Jacuzzi, placed my head on the olive-colored tiled wall and let out a huge sigh. I was relieved that it was over and began to think of how I was going to make my exit without waking him. I didn't want to say that awkward middle-of-the-night goodbye, but I surely wasn't going to stay. I was far too embarrassed to face him in the morning light. It was almost as if I had been the one popping impotency pills and performing so terribly! Not to mention the fact that he seemed like the kind of guy who would ask, "How was it?" or "Was it good?" And I'm not the type to lie about something like that, so what on earth would my response be? Would I reply, "It was horrendous!" Or would I try to spare his feelings by responding, "Oh, it was heavy." After all, that was the only sensation I experienced while he crushed the shit out of me. He'd probably think that I was an ex-flower child or offspring of some 1960's hippie and assume that my use of the word "heavy" meant "it blew my mind" or something like that. In any event, I thought it might be simpler to just leave quietly and never speak to him again. I was going to flip the script on his ass and never call him, treating him like so many guys have treated females.

Although I must've stayed in the bathroom nearly twenty minutes, William never came to see if I was all right. I suppose his ass was so drunk that he didn't even realize that I'd left the bed. It was easy for me to get dressed and leave without waking him. As I quietly slipped on my clothes, William's loud snoring—open-mouthed and sounding like a food processor slicing carrots—echoed throughout the room.

Through a crack in the heavy burgundy velvet curtain, I could see the winter sky beginning to transform from black to a light shade of blue. By then, I wasn't being as quiet as I could have, but the man never even budged.

Slipping on my pumps, I cringed as I thought about his terrible performance and how wrong I'd been to think that an older man might have been what I needed. I should've hooked up with one of Rodney's young athlete pals. At least the chances of leaving unsatisfied and disgusted would've been extremely slim. But now I was just assed out—

with nothing! My little game and out-of-character behavior had me feeling like shit without a thing to show for it-no mate, no relationship, no dignity, and no fun. At least if I'd walked out of there after a passionate and satisfying sexual escapade, my slutty behavior might've been worth it. If I got lucky, William wouldn't remember a thing about what had happened between us. Perhaps he'd think it was all a dream. But just in case I wasn't so fortunate—and I usually wasn't in these kinds of cases—I'd have to tell Trish not to give out my phone number. Since I hadn't taken his, it would be quite easy never to communicate again.

I didn't give a damn how nice or "good" this guy was; it should've been illegal to perform that poorly in bed unless you're 16 years old! To be honest, William Peterson had sexually humiliated me so terribly that I never wanted to lay eyes on him again. I felt embarrassed, nauseous and drunk all at the same time. I was so emotionally and physically sick that I wanted to close my eyes and cry. But I dared not shed a tear—not even in my current state. Crying was something I just didn't do. However, if this experience was any indication of the kind of year I was going to have, I certainly didn't like where I was headed.

It absolutely has to get better! I sarcastically thought as I hastily sped away in my Range Rover.

Eight

Against my better judgment, I decided to keep my word to Mamma and join my family for New Year's dinner. After the way the previous evening had ended, I was in no mood to spend time with my siblings, but I just couldn't disappoint my mamma again. I was still a little woozy from the night before but I rose early. I dropped by Trish's to pick up two of her fantastic, delicious sweet potato pies and drove my 4-by-4 up to Hopewell Junction with hopes that the day would turn out better than I had anticipated. Of course, she tried to grill me about my night with William, but I refused to talk. I told her I wanted to leave all bad dating experiences behind me in the previous year. As I drove away, she vowed to get it out of me later.

An hour later, I was at Mamma's. To my surprise, the driveway was full, so I figured that I was the last to arrive. I let myself in with my key and walked smack into a foyer filled with absolutely wonderful aromas. Although the apartment that I'd grown up in was completely different from Mamma's new home, the scent of Mamma's food instantly gave me an intense feeling of nostalgia. I was suddenly reminded of all the holidays my family had spent together when I was growing up and how the food had been so magnificent and plentiful and the fights so few and far between. All of a sudden, I felt 12 years old again.

I softly shut the door behind me. I heard voices coming from the family room, but decided to enter the kitchen, knowing that was where Mamma surely would be. There was laughter on the other side of the swinging door, which I pushed open to see Mamma, Juanita and Cheryl diligently working over our New Year's Day dinner. For two people who generally couldn't stand each other, my sisters appeared to be getting along just fine, which pleased me a lot. I certainly didn't want to enter a house of feuding people.

"Nyagra!" Mamma smiled as her eyes lit up with joy.

"Hi!" I hugged her tightly. I placed the pies on the countertop, awkwardly hugged my sisters and quickly offered my assistance.

"We left the potato salad for you, since you make it the best. Everything is chopped. You just have to put it together," Juanita said.

"OK!" I happily stated. I washed my hands at the sink and eagerly began to search for a large mixing bowl. "I saw a lot of cars outside. Who's here?" I asked, beginning to combine my ingredients.

"Everybody. I'm so glad to have everyone together for the first time in so long," Mamma answered.

"Who's everybody?" I questioned, wanting specifics.

"David's here with Marva and all the kids."

"Which set?" I joked. We all laughed.

"Like I said—all of 'em!" she replied.

"I was glad to see them but a bit surprised that Mona let them come," Cheryl stated.

"Nathan and Terri," Mamma continued.

"Get outta here! Terri came out the house?" I exclaimed, shocked that this woman had decided to venture out into the world.

"Yep!" my sisters said in unison.

"I've got to go out there and say hi!" I said.

"Maurice is in there, and Monica and Paul went to visit his family in the Bronx last night, but they should be here any minute," Juanita informed me.

"Oh, when did they get here?" I asked.

"They flew in yesterday afternoon, and by the way, what did you do last night that was so important that you couldn't come up here?" Juanita asked in her "trying to pluck my nerves" tone of voice.

"Trish threw a big party that I'd known about for months. Didn't I tell you? Ma knew about it; thank you very much," I stated in a joking (but serious) manner.

She nodded her head as if to say a sarcastic "no" and turned to take the Virginia honey ham out of the oven.

"Guess who else is here?!" Mamma asked. "Billy and Greta!"

I hadn't seen Mamma's younger brother in over ten years. Uncle Billy was my very favorite relative but he lived in Montgomery, Alabama and I hadn't laid eyes on him since my college graduation. I loved him for all the reasons everybody hated him. He was so open, loud and honest. What was perceived as aggravating and invasive to my sisters was simply genuine and down-to-earth to me. Uncle Billy could call a person "fat," "chubby" or "ugly" in the kindest way—if that's possible. He never meant to hurt anybody's feelings. He simply came from the notion of "you are what you are—be proud!"

Uncle Billy was also one of the most generous people in the universe. If you asked him for anything, he'd go out of his way to make sure that he got it for you. I remember my second year in college, and although scholarships covered one hundred percent of my tuition, I still had to pay for my books. Mamma and Daddy were having a rough year financially and couldn't really help me. So Mamma put in a call to Uncle Billy and in the blink of an eye, I had all of my books no sooner than it had been requested. It was because of this that my sisters always said that I was his favorite. I don't think he ever outwardly showed favoritism toward me, although he'd always talk to me for long periods of time. I just think I was the only one interested in his wild stories.

I always knew that Uncle Billy and Greta had money. In fact, they were the only people I knew who actually made it big selling Amway. I never thought anybody ever made any real money off of that until I got older and realized that all their traveling was because of their Amway business. They called themselves "diamonds" and were always trying to get my parents to get into it, but Daddy thought it was a bunch of "hogshit." Mamma, on the other hand, was way too introverted to try to sell anything to anybody.

As a little girl, and even into my teens, I remember Uncle Billy and Greta coming for visits every couple of months and telling me about all the places they'd traveled. They always brought us gifts from those places. My brothers and sisters were never interested in their stories, but I was. I guess that's why they talked to me the most. To me, they were such an exciting pair and I wanted to hear all about their adventures. I guess that's why they always called me the most outgoing of my parents' children. I liked hearing about their travels. It was my way of learning about new places.

I always had dreams of having more than what my parents were able to give us. Since childhood, I wanted to travel and experience new people, places and things. That's probably why Uncle Billy and Greta intrigued me so. Whether I was their favorite or not, they were definitely mine. I loved them dearly. Greta, who Uncle Billy referred to as Ol' Boobie, had been his girlfriend ever since I could remember. They never married, and they didn't have any kids, but she was still a full-fledged member of the family. Upon hearing that they were in the house, I had no choice but to drop what I was doing and go say hello.

It was a rare occasion that so much love was displayed in Mamma's house. Uncle Billy and Greta were as happy to see me as I was them. My nieces and nephews were also excited to see me, the aunt they rarely saw but who always sent gifts. I sometimes wished that things could be different between me and my family but as we all grew up, my siblings and I grew pretty far apart. After a while, none of us really had anything in common, other than the fact that we shared the same mamma and daddy. At first the emotional distance between me and my brothers and sisters bothered me. But I later accepted that we simply belonged to different worlds.

My brother Nathan still lives in the housing project where we all grew up. In fact, he lives in the very same apartment. He kept it when my parents moved to 145th Street. To his credit, he does keep it nice and neat. He lives there with his girlfriend, Terri, who nobody ever sees. I used to say that she's a figment of his imagination. Before that New Year's Eve Day, I hadn't seen her since Cheryl's 21st birthday party (and we were all pretty surprised to see her then!) They are a strange pair. Every other month, Mamma tells me that Nathan says she's pregnant. However, we never hear of any baby being born. I say they're both crazy. Juanita swears that Terri is an elephant since her gestation period seems to be over three years. In addition to this craziness, neither of them work. They have boarders in their apartment who pay the rent so they live pretty much expense free. But believe it or not, sometimes they still don't have money for their rent. Personally, I think they sniff the rent money. Mamma's in denial, but I'm not. Nathan used to work, but a couple of years ago, he was injured on his job. He received a cash settlement of about $100,000. He never gave Mamma one red cent and he blew (and I mean literally) every penny. Today, he has nothing to show for it. I was so angry with him and I guess deep down I still am. I can't believe how someone could want to just waste their life away. Being the sucker for a sob story that I am, I even lent him $100 not too long ago. He was supposed to pay me back on the first of the month. I guess he got me on a technicality because he never actually said what month, although I automatically assumed he meant the next month. So I guess I shouldn't have been too surprised when four months later, he paid me back $50 of it—or should I say $45. When I went to pick it up, he told me he spent $5 on a sandwich and some beer while he was waiting for me on the corner. He still owes me the other $50 and has asked me to lend him more money since then. I refused and he cursed me out, telling me that I was selfish and not family-oriented. "That's what's wrong with this family!" he yelled in the phone. "Nobody ever wants to help anybody!" At that point, I told his ass that if "nobody" wanted to help "anybody," he wouldn't still owe me $50! I may have a good heart, but I'm no fool.

My two younger sisters, Monica and Cheryl, are quite an interesting pair. Monica is 27 and Cheryl is 25. They have a great deal of potential, but neither have any real goals or ambition. Cheryl used to say that she wanted to be a gynecologist. But that girl has the bedside manner of Adolph Hitler! She'd have lawsuits up the ying-yang for killing women during routine pap smears and pelvic examinations for being so damn rough.

Let me give you a little insight on how these people lived before my mother bought her house. You see, before Mamma moved to Hopewell Junction, my sisters and their boyfriends all lived with her. But a few years ago, Monica finally met her husband, Paul. He's from North Carolina. He asked her to move down there with him and she did— without any job prospects, money, or even the ability to drive a car. She just up and left. I think she was hoping that he'd save her from some- thing—namely herself. But anyone should know you can't run from yourself; you'll be wherever you go. So even though she claims to be happy, I know that deep down inside she's miserable. In my opinion, all broke people are miserable.

Paul works but can barely support them. They only have one car, so she's completely immobile. But she couldn't drive if they had another vehicle, anyway. In actuality, she has no life. She's always been overweight, but since she's been in North Carolina, she says she walks to the gym down the road from their apartment every day. She must walk there, but she must never go inside. The last time I saw her, she didn't look like she'd shed a pound. In fact, I think she put on a couple. Apparently, she just sits around the house and watches TV all day because every time I speak to her, she asks me if I've seen this show or that show.

Personally, I don't see how anyone could be happy living a life like that. But you never know. Maybe she's quite content, although her constantly crabby attitude says otherwise. She has great difficulty handling any kind of pressure so she calls Mamma constantly—creating an enormous telephone bill that she can't pay. She's been unemployed since she's been there (with the exception of working at Pizza Hut for three days). Sometimes she calls Mamma collect. That pisses me off because Mamma has no income other than Dad's pension and Social Security and I usually end up paying the bill.

I used to try to give Monica ideas about how to start her own business. She's an incredibly talented writer and chef. I told her she could write novels or start a catering business from home. I even offered to invest in her financially so she could get started—to no avail. I guess some people are happiest when they're unhappy.

Believe it or not, at one point, we were all pretty close. Monica has lived with me several times during her life. I used to let her stay with me for weeks at a time when I lived in Riverdale. But over the years we've all grown apart. However, even though Monica's ultra-critical, finds something wrong with almost everything and tends to be extremely defensive, she's actually the nicer of the two.

The baby of us all, Cheryl, has a nastiness about her that could put icicles on the tip of a flaming torch. When they both lived with my parents, they would verbally and physically fight—worse than any cat and dog. I'm not even sure if I've ever heard Cheryl say the word "sorry" to anyone—ever. She puts up this front like she's tough and strong, but in actuality, she's just an insecure spoiled little brat. She's the epitome of the youngest child—the "baby"—and my mamma never seems to find wrong with anything she does.

Even though my sisters both have a great deal of potential, they truly lack drive and determination. Cheryl was in college, but she dropped out to work a dead-end job. She says she hates it and wants to go back to school, but so far she hasn't made any attempts. When Mamma moved up to Hopewell Junction, Cheryl opted to move into her boyfriend's mamma's apartment with him instead of moving with Mamma. She doesn't have a car and she really wouldn't have been able to commute to and from work. To be honest, I was pretty glad when she decided not to move with Mamma. Her personality can be extremely difficult to deal with, and I was quite tired of always having to go through her to deal with Mamma. Although I didn't really want Mamma living alone, I wanted to deal with Cheryl on a regular basis even less. When she's is a good mood, she's OK. But when she's in a bad mood, she's a terror. This girl suffers from PMS, Post MS, and MS. To put it bluntly, she's usually a bitch.

Needless to say, when she decided to stay in the city and live on 112th Street with Maurice, I was pleased. She swears it's just temporary, until they can save enough money to get a place of their own. But it's already been quite a while.

Upon entering the family room, the greetings toward my brothers that New Year's Day—even David—and their companions were quite cordial, despite our frequent past differences. The day seemed as though it might actually have some promise. Maybe it would be a nice New Year's Day gathering after all.

Dinner was served at three o'clock and I must admit Mamma really outdid herself. Monica and Paul returned around two and unfortunately, the mood changed slightly. She seemed to walk in with a bit of an attitude, but everyone tried to ignore her and allow the festive mood to prevail.

After entering the dining room, I couldn't help but notice that the table looked positively stunning. Mamma's embroidered cream-colored tablecloth was so pretty beneath her best porcelain china that one couldn't help but be drawn to the fantastic display of savory choices. It included baked ham, collard greens, macaroni and cheese, roast beef, fried chicken, smoked turkey wings, black-eyed peas and rice, buttery corn on the cob, candied yams, and homemade buttermilk biscuits—to name only a few. The layout appeared so scrumptious that I probably gained ten pounds just looking at the spread.

Once we'd all found a place at the table, Uncle Billy said the blessing. Despite my hesitation about coming, seeing the smile on Mamma's face made it all seem so worth it. It was quite obvious how happy she was to have her family together in her dining room to enjoy her feast on New Year's Day.

For what must have been the first twenty minutes of the meal, the only sound that could be heard throughout the room was everyone's lips smacking and the faint echo of the food hitting our happy bellies. Finally, after biting down on a piece of holiday ham, Uncle Billy broke the silence.

"So, what ya'll waiting for? Where the babies?" he asked, looking at Monica and Paul.

"We'll have children when and if we decide," Monica snapped, being her usual defensive self.

"Well, ya betta get ta decidin'. What you now, Monica, almost 30?" Uncle Billy questioned as if he hadn't noticed her tone.

"And?" she snapped again.

"Don't go bein' like me an' Greta here. Every house needs some babies in it. In fact, I'm still tryin' to get Ol' Boobie here ta give me a couple."

"Yeah? Well, you shoulda been tryin' about twenty years ago!" Greta laughed. The whole table giggled at Greta's response, as well as at the thought of this couple who had to be almost out of their 50s having a baby. "I couldn't even do it if I wanted to—that shop went out of business years ago!"

"That's not true these days. I saw in the National Enquirer a woman 80 years old havin' a baby. Technology can let you do ANYTHANG . . ." Uncle Billy laughed while Greta sucked her teeth and rolled her eyes at him as if to say, "Yeah, right!"

It was funny, but I couldn't help but see the icy expression on Monica's face. She obviously wanted to be a grouch for whatever reason. In any event, her demeanor didn't faze Uncle Billy a bit and the rest of the meal was devoured as we all listened to him talk about his and Greta's recent trip to Greece. All was going quite well until Juanita decided to bring up that she felt they always brought me the best presents from their trips.

"And what about that beautiful little black doll you brought Nyagra from Egypt, when you only brought me some sort of silly rock?" she stated as she buttered her biscuit.

"Hey, that rock was from the bank of the Nile River! Your father told me you had a rock collection and what better addition to your collection than a rock from the bank of the Nile River?" Uncle Billy asked.

"A rock collection? I never had no rock collection. David had the rock collection. But then again, how would Daddy know that? He was never home."

At that moment I knew the happy, warm atmosphere was about to cease. It was almost as if I could see the gray cloud rising and the storm approaching.

"Damn, Juanita. Why are you crying about a rock that was given to you fifty million years ago? You should be glad the man brought your ass anything at all," Cheryl said sarcastically.

I agreed with her, but decided to remain silent. Still, I knew it was now about to be on. Juanita, who had venom in her eyes, then turned her attention toward our youngest sister.

"Who's crying? Do you see tears in my eyes? Do you hear me sniffling? I'm just asking my uncle a question. Besides, nobody's talking to you." Juanita snapped.

"All right, all right. Don't start this mess. We're having a perfectly good day," Mamma interjected.

"Well, Mamma, you should tell your daughter to mind her own business! She's always gotta have something to say!" Juanita said emotionally.

"She can't tell me anything. I'm grown. I say what I want, when I want. That's what happens when you become an adult. You should try it one day," Cheryl said.

"Ya'll crazy," Nathan said as he got up from the table.

"I'm tired of you disrespecting me, Cheryl! I am an adult! Maybe you should grow up and stop living off people! At least I have my own place to live! And stop fornicating in your Mamma's house," Juanita said.

"Well, if I'm living off people, what are you doing? You're living off my tax-paying dollars. Maybe if lazy people like you would work, I'd have more money in my pocket. Why don't you get a job or do you wanna be a welfare queen your whole freakin' life?—and as far as fornicating goes, at least I'm getting some!" Cheryl barked.

I knew it, I knew it, I knew it, I said to myself. I knew my family couldn't get through one holiday without declaring war on one another. I knew it was going too well! The festive atmosphere was too good to be true! All I could do was stare down at my plate and feel so embarrassed that Uncle Billy and Greta were witnessing the ignorant and uncouth behavior of my sisters.

"All right, bitch!" Juanita yelled, raising up from the table and heading toward Cheryl. Thank goodness David grabbed her before Juanita could reach her or else food and drink would have been all over the place.

"Now do you see why I didn't wanna come here?" Monica said to her husband before she ran from the dining room.

All of a sudden it seemed like everyone and everything was in an uproar. The kids were crying. Juanita was crying. Cheryl was cursing as Maurice escorted her from the room, and ultimately from the house.

By now, I had an excruciating headache. I was ready to jump in my jeep and head back down the highway to a more peaceful atmosphere. I should've known that my family couldn't enjoy one holiday without someone causing havoc. I should've followed my mind. But since I didn't, I had no one to blame but myself.

Most people are upset when their vacation is over. Not me. I was more than ready to get back to work and back to seeing accomplishments. My personal life had been so depressing and unsuccessful that had it not been for my career, I probably wouldn't have seen any fulfillment whatsoever. It's a pretty sad state of affairs when you actually look forward to going to the office, but that was my life. Unfortunately, my work was all that I seemed to have to enjoy.

The morning I arrived back in my office for the first time in the new year, I was ecstatic to see my fully-executed contracts from StarzSports Apparel. Obviously, they'd arrived while I was on vacation and because our office virtually closes down during the Christmas holidays, no one had touched them.

I thumbed through the agreement to see Victor Reece's signature on the final page. I wondered if he'd forwarded these to me before or after our encounter Christmas Eve. The date on the accompanying Federal Express envelope indicated that it had been sent on December 30th. I was quite surprised to see that he'd opted to still go through with our deal despite the recent turn of events. I guess he still had some sort of ethics. Not to mention that he certainly would've had to explain himself to his company had he decided at the last minute to back down after making a commitment and executing the proposal. He would surely need an extremely good reason and I'm sure that an affair gone bad wouldn't qualify. In addition, I knew that the folks at StarzSports Apparel realized that Newman & Stein was definitely the best company for the job. Still, I wasn't looking forward to doing business with him. I'd always known that it was generally bad to mix business with pleasure, and now I was going to have to pay for it with the awkwardness of dealing with him regarding the account. In any event, I figured I'd deal with that when and if I had to.

The office was quiet with the exception of a few senior associates mulling around. I guess a few people were still on vacation. Even Judy would be out until next week and I had a temp. However, I knew the week would go by quickly. Despite the unusual peacefulness, I had quite a bit on my agenda. I had to interview directors for the Wendy's commercial, meet with the new "Dave," and approve the final edit on the Nabisco ad. I also would be leaving Thursday to fly to Houston to meet with the Dallas Cowboys' Rookie of the Year, DaVon Garrett. Before I had gone on vacation, it had been discussed with the StarzSports representatives that upon execution of the agreements, DaVon was an athlete who should be investigated. The people at StarzSports were quite interested in DaVon and he was our top pick for the commercial. When I told Trish that I was going to Houston to meet him, she begged me to let her come. And although I surely could've used the company and realized she had an ultra-tight marriage, DaVon was just her type and I wasn't about to tempt her.

"I just wanna meet him!" she assured me.

"No, I don't trust you. And besides, he's only 21 years old!" I said.

"I like 'em young. That's when they're tender, moldable and in their prime! Plus, age like the late, great Aaliyah once said, 'Age ain't nothin' but a number!'"

As I sat in the stillness of my twenty-second-floor office facing the East River, I couldn't help but notice the heavy falling snow. There were still holiday decorations on the streets, which were unusually desolate. The few people who were walking around were being swooped in every direction by the wind and the snow that fell relentlessly. There had been a few flakes falling as I'd driven down the expressway, but now it seemed to be coming down in droves.

This is like the sixth snowfall this winter and it's only the first week of January, I thought aloud. I absolutely hated driving in bad weather and hoped that the snow would stop by rush hour.

"The lighting is way too dark," I stated, as I sat around the mahogany conference room table in the office of Tré Donquio. Tré was the Italian director we had used for the Nabisco commercial. Although there had been an obvious language barrier, Tré had been chosen for the commercial because of his usage of unique angles and his ability to capture a detailed script in a minute-and-a-half spot. My writers had come up with the perfect script for the advertisement during a last-minute, brainstorming conference call. The starring child actor and the rest of the cast had been hand-picked, and the mission to be humorous was surely accomplished. Needless to say, I was extremely aggravated by the fact that the lighting had been poor. Tré's translator relayed my message to the eccentric Italian upon which he responded—in Italian—in a seemingly irate manner. Even though I could not understand what the hell he was saying, I was sure that I didn't like his attitude. My associate, Rachel Altman, and I inconspicuously made eye contact.

"Is there anything you think should be changed, Rachel?" I asked, before the translator or the director could reply.

"No, actually I think the work is quite good. Although I do agree about the lighting," she answered.

"Ms. Ensley," began the translator, "Tré feels that he did his very best on the lighting instructions, but if you remember, it was a rainy day."

"I don't care if there was a blizzard outside and we were in the middle of it, you adjust the lighting accordingly. I know that. I don't want to offend Mr. Donquio but this commercial is absolutely perfect with the exception of the lighting. The child actor is an African-American and his complexion looks ten times darker than he actually is. He's blending into the background. We're right on target with respect to the budget and as much as I'd like to keep it that way, something must be done. I can't turn this in as a finished product. I will not turn this in as a finished product," I informed them. Again Rachel and I sat quietly as the translator repeated my words in Italian and listened to the director's reply.

"Tré doesn't believe there is anything he can do. The film could be lightened, but that process takes time and he'd have to send it out to be done. Unfortunately, he's leaving for Naples to shoot a documentary in the morning," the translator informed us.

"Well, then I suggest he send it wherever he has to ASAP if he wants his second-half payment. We're paying a lot of money for him to produce a satisfactory finished product and if he fails to do so, not only won't I pay him but I'll also sue the pants off of him and have him blacklisted. My company is the top advertising firm in the country, and I'm quite sure that he doesn't want to ruin his relationship with us just as we'd rather not ruin ours with him. However, we'll do what we have to in order to ensure that our product is the very best it can be. After all, as you recall, this meeting is supposed to be to correct any details before the commercial goes to final, not for him to show me what he thinks my final product should be."

Again we listened to the Italian dialogue between the two of them. Tré's tone of voice seemed a bit disturbed but after a few moments the translator smiled. "May he have forty-eight hours?"

I looked at Rachel, laughed a little, and stated, "Forty-eight hours tops."

We rose from our plush seats as we firmly shook hands with Tré, the translator and his assistant. I couldn't believe he was trying to stick me like that. The worst part of my job was that sometimes I had to show these men just who was going to authorize the cutting of their checks. Often they'd attempt to get away with things with me that they'd never try with a man—and certainly not a white man. But they didn't know who they were dealing with. I didn't give a damn what documentary he had to film in Naples. I had a deadline and I wasn't about to let Tré Donquio make me miss it. I was scheduled to meet with the Nabisco executives at 3 P.M. Tuesday afternoon and it was already Wednesday. I had less than a week. I had an 8 A.M. flight to Houston the next day, but would return that same evening. I was cutting it close, but if Tré Donquio had a copy of the commercial on my desk by nine Monday morning (hopefully with perfect lighting) I would be A-OK.

"You have four messages from a Mr. William Peterson," Meg, my temp, informed me as I passed her desk and headed toward my office.

The snow had lessened into just a few powdery flurries, so I decided to go back to the office to pick up my plane tickets and laptop computer before heading home. I felt my skin crawl as she mentioned William Peterson's name and wondered how he'd gotten my number at work. Then I remembered Trish had told him the name of my company and figured that he'd simply dialed information.

"Throw them out," I instructed her. I had nothing to say to William Peterson. In fact, I think I was more embarrassed than he should have been about our "incident" on New Year's Eve.

I walked into my office to see a dozen long-stemmed red roses sitting in the middle of my desk. Confused as to which recent loser had felt the need to send me such a gorgeous bouquet, I opened the card to see that they were from William.

Thank you for helping me bring in the new year right.
Call me (914) 655-0995

Love,
Bill

"That was bringing the new year in right?" I asked myself out loud. I wanted to toss the whole arrangement into the trash, but they were beautiful. I did rip up the card and toss it in the garbage. Part of me felt a little badly, since he did go out of his way to send roses and all. But I surely wasn't going to call him. It would've been too uncomfortable for me to talk to him; especially since he seemed to actually enjoy our encounter.

I grabbed my laptop from the desk and headed toward the door. As I took my round-trip airline tickets from Meg, I said, "I'll be in the car. The cell is on if there are any emergencies. But if Mr. Peterson calls again, tell him I'm out of town on business and that you're uncertain when I will return. Tell him you're a temp," I instructed the homely little secretary. I hoped that she could pull it off. She seemed so timid and shy that she looked like she might choke on her timid little tongue if she attempted to tell a lie. I couldn't wait for Judy to get back.

I heard the elevator door open and dashed to the reception area, nearly knocking over Will, the Federal Express guy.

"Oh, I'm so sorry!" I embarrassingly stated.

"No problem. You can knock me over anytime," he jokingly said.

"Happy New Year, Nyagra. How was your holiday?"

"It was nice, and yours?"

"Quiet."

"Oh, well you have a nice evening," I said as I stepped inside the elevator.

"I'd still love to take you out to lunch one day."

I shook my head. "No thanks."

"Well, I'll keep asking until you say yes. You'll change your mind— one day. I'm patient." He smiled. I couldn't help but to smile back. He was cute and always so friendly to me. Still not my type, though.

I overslept. I don't know how, but I did. The clock went off at 5:30 A.M. but I didn't jump out of bed until 6:15 when the driver called to say that he was waiting outside my house. The sound of the telephone ringing startled me and I jumped up from my bed. I had no time to shower, so I just washed up quickly, brushed my hair up into a bun and threw on a pair of jeans and a white button-down shirt that I'd just gotten out of the cleaners.

I'd been on the phone all night with Juanita. She was going through one of her manic-depressive phases. From the moment I walked in the door at seven o'clock, my phone was ringing off the hook with Ma hysterically telling me that Juanita had told her that she was contemplating suicide. I could barely get my coat off before I was dialing Juanita and questioning her as to why on earth she would tell our mamma something so disturbing. She was crying hysterically about things that had happened ten years ago. She told me that she hadn't meant to hurt Mamma by telling her about her suicidal thoughts. I think she simply wanted some attention, which made me so angry with her that I didn't know what to do. After several hours of drama, I was finally able to calm her down and get some rest myself. Unfortunately, it was damn near 3 A.M. by the time I crawled into bed. I suppose that would explain my lack of desire to rise at the appropriate time. In any event, I tossed a pantsuit into my overnight bag, grabbed toiletries and was out the door. Thank goodness, I got a driver who pushed that car like a bat out of hell. Luckily, I made the flight with fifteen minutes to spare.

I couldn't have asked for a more pleasant flight. Despite a few flurries falling, there was little turbulence and I was actually able to doze off for an hour, awaking refreshed and ready to deal with DaVon Garrett who I'd heard that he was quite a piece of work. I had briefly looked over his profile and could tell from the press photos that he was handsome. At 21, he was one of the highest-paid rookies in football history with a huge ego to go along with it. Although I wasn't really in the mood to deal with an overpaid, oversized brat, after all of Trish's ranting and raving, I was a little anxious to meet him.

I was greeted at the airport by a black Lincoln Town Car which took me to the Ritz Carlton hotel. My room was a beautiful suite with a poolside view, but all I really wanted to do was throw myself head-first into the king-sized bed in the center of the room. Unfortunately, I could do no such thing and proceeded to call DaVon's agent to reconfirm our meeting. He was more than cordial and informed me that everything was ready to go and that DaVon was looking forward to meeting with me at one o'clock. His demeanor sounded pretty good to me.

Maybe he won't be as bad as they say, I told myself with hopes that my encounter with DaVon Garrett would be more of a breeze than a tornado.

It was hot as hell in Houston—95 degrees, at least. It was an unusual heat wave and I hadn't exactly brought anything with me that was suitable for warm weather since it had been 10 below zero in New York. Lucky for me I'd brought an all-season crepe suit I felt I'd be able to get through the day in. By the time I got to my hotel room, my body was damp with perspiration and my jeans and white shirt were stuck to my flesh. In a word, I felt disgusting! Thank goodness I had just enough time to shower and change before meeting with DaVon and his agent, Henri Andersen, at the Golden Room restaurant. The Golden Room had been DaVon's request. He was an incredible fan of Thai cuisine. I, on the other hand, wasn't quite so fond of it, but a potential client's request is a potential client's request. I certainly wanted to make him happy with the hopes that he wouldn't attempt to break the pockets of Newman & Stein or StarzSports Apparel.

I arrived at the restaurant exactly at one. DaVon wasn't there yet and I hadn't expected him to be. He seemed like the type who liked to arrive late and make a grand entrance.

I decided to sit at our reserved table (rather than at the bar) and wait for "Mr. Rookie of the Year." I looked around the restaurant and was a bit surprised that the place was so crowded at that hour. I assumed that most people were there for business, just as I was. It was pretty trendy for a Thai restaurant—not traditional at all. I was glad about that, for the very last thing I wanted was to be in a stuffy restaurant talking about a multimillion-dollar deal. I wanted this guy to be as comfortable as possible when he agreed to my terms.

I ordered a Sprite with a twist of lime and just as it was being served, in walked DaVon Garrett—making the entrance I'm sure he wanted. Every head in the place turned and watched as he strutted his way over to where I sat. Six-foot-six in tight deep-blue Levi's, a white tee shirt and cowboy boots. Alongside him-almost unnoticed in his shadow-stood a short portly, gray-haired, brown-skinned man in a ten-gallon hat.

That must be Henri Andersen, I thought to myself. As they approached the table, I rose to greet them.

"Henri Andersen." The shorter man, seemingly in his mid-50s, smiled as he gripped my left hand with the appropriate amount of firmness.

"Nyagra Ensley," I replied as I reciprocated the handshake. Like a gentleman, DaVon shook my hand and waited for me to sit before he did. The waiter quickly came to us and took our orders. They had "the usual" and I simply had a sesame chicken salad.

"So, Ms. Ensley, this is the DaVon Garrett, the Dallas Cowboys' 2002 Rookie of the Year. DaVon is going to be a big star—a big star. I tell you, Ms. Ensley. Look at 'em. He's got star quality. He's going to be the biggest athletic personality since . . . since O.J. Simpson. At least, before O.J. killed that white girl—well, allegedly . . . .But what I'm tryin' ta tell ya is that this boy's going to be big! The boy's just in his first year and everybody loves him. Hey, what's not to love? Look at that face! Have you seen a better-lookin' kid in football? Shit, have you seen a better-lookin' face anywhere? This boy is loved by kids and adults all over the country. Forget tryin' ta be like Mike! In just about a minute, kids all over the world are going to wanna be like DaVon. I know it doesn't rhyme, but we'll think up sumthin' that does. I gotta tell you, Ms. Ensley, we're real interested in what you gotta say on behalf of your company and StarzSports, but we've been talking to Nike also and they like DaVon. I mean, who doesn't? So if you really want us to go with StarzSports, you really gotta make it worth our while." Henri Andersen was laying into me before I could even pull my chair close to the table.

When he finally came up for air, I had no choice but to begin my own long-winded pitch. The game of corporate ping-pong was on.

"Well, Mr. Andersen. I agree with everything you've said about DaVon. We also believe that he is going to be a great athlete. He already is! That's the very reason why he's StarzSports' first and only choice. I understand that Nike is interested in DaVon. You're right! Who wouldn't be? But take my word for it, Mr. Andersen. StarzSports is a much better company for DaVon. With the likes of Michael Jordan, Tiger Woods and all the other professional athlete heavyweights they have on their roster with proven shoe sales, DaVon will never be the "big cheese" over at Nike. However, at StarzSports, on the other hand, there's not as much competition. I can tell you're a brilliant sports agent so I'm sure you know that what a rising star athlete needs is someplace where he can truly shine. Someplace where his voice is really listened to.

Someplace that doesn't have ten other guys just like him. Someplace like StarzSports . . . " I bullshitted and threw my charm on his country-bumpkin ass with the hopes that in my own way, I could convince him that his athlete wasn't quite as good as he believed him to be—at least not yet anyway.

As the waiter placed our food before us, I realized that my tactic was obviously working because Henri Andersen looked at me with a bit of "maybe you're right" in his eye.

"Well, what kind of endorsement are we talking? Actually, since you're a sistah, I'm going to be honest with you, Ms. Ensley. Nike wasn't talking that much. Not exactly what we were looking for."

It was working.

"Well, Mr. Andersen," I said.

"Oh, call me Henri," he interrupted.

"OK, Henri." I smiled. "We at Newman & Stein, as well as every-one at StarzSports, really believe in DaVon. We're looking to do some-thing like a one-feature spot for DaVon—strictly concentrating on him and the shoe—most likely to run during prime time for no less than four months, possibly six. We'd also like to do a radio spot with DaVon pushing the shoe over the airwaves of mostly urban radio stations. We'll even throw in a year's supply of StarzSports' apparel—any thing he chooses, as many as he chooses. Oh, and one last thing: If StarzSports' sales increase considerably over the next six months, thanks to these advertisements, I think that perhaps toward the end of the year we'd be quite interested in talking about an actual DaVon Garrett shoe."

For the first time since we'd sat at the table, I actually saw an eye-brow rise on DaVon's face. Until that point, he hadn't made one sound or given any indication that he was even listening.

He actually lifted his head from his brown rice, put down his fork and mumbled, "Nike didn't say nuthin' 'bout givin' me my own sneaker."

"Um, huuum," Henri began as he cleared his throat. "So what kind of money are we talking about, Ms. Ensley?"

"Oh, Henri, I absolutely hate discussing actual dollar figures with my clients and/or people I'm going to do business with." I coyly smiled. This guy obviously didn't know this business if he was expecting me to outright tell him how much we'd be paying this kid. Something like that is always stated in a written proposal. Once the proposal is signed, then we forward actual contracts. I've been doing this stuff for a long time and that's just how it's done.

"However, I'm sure that you and DaVon will be quite pleased with the more than generous compensation for this endorsement. The way I see it, you guys certainly can't lose in any shape, form or fashion by going with StarzSports Apparel. Our policy is that after our meeting here today, if you and DaVon are interested in what I've just expressed, my company will draw up a proposal. Once you sign the proposal, we forward contracts. The proposal just loosely lists all we're going to do for you and all you're going to do for us. It's sort of a mini-contract. You aren't bound to us until you sign that proposal. If you get our paperwork and you are in some way unhappy with what we'd like to pay you or anything else indicated, we can negotiate. You don't have to sign it until you're completely satisfied with the deal. If you choose not to sign with us, it will simply be as if we never met—my company and StarzSports' loss. But if you are happy with it—as I'm very sure you will be—we'll have an exclusive deal and everyone will win. And of course the proposal will state in writing everything I've stated here to you today."

"Including the thing about my own shoe?" DaVon asked.

I smiled. "Including the thing about your own shoe."

After a moment of silence (I guess he didn't want to look too anxious), Henri Andersen enthusiastically said, "Draw up the proposal . . . "

"I most certainly will. In fact, I'll call my office this afternoon and ask that they get started."

We all shook on it and finally began to dig into our food. I was really hungry but didn't want to devour my salad in front of strangers. To my surprise, the food was actually quite good. DaVon had a nice personality and this was also a surprise. He was a bit cocky, but not half as bad as I'd expected. Henri Andersen, on the other hand, was pretty loud and rowdy. Perhaps he was just a typical fun-loving Texan. At moments, I couldn't help but think he was overdoing the whole "Southern hospitality" thing.

"So how long are you in Houston gracing us with your Northern beauty, Ms. Ensley?" Henri asked.

"Oh, I'm actually catching a seven o'clock flight back to New York tonight."

"Not tonight, you're not. Haven't you seen the news?"

I grew concerned. "No, actually I haven't. What's going on?"

"New York City is covered in snow. Both your airports are closed. That one in Jersey, too."

"What?! But I just left there!"

"Yeah, well, I saw the news right before I left the house to get DaVon here, and according to Channel 4 it started about 11 A.M. and they're getting an inch every five minutes. You better call the airport. They said it's the worst blizzard in twenty years!"

I couldn't believe this shit! I had to get back to the office. I had to speak to the folks at StarzSports Apparel and get all the details finalized on this deal. Not to mention that I simply didn't want to spend the weekend in Texas.

"Well, it's Thursday already, Ms. Ensley. Houston's a beautiful place. Why don't you just stay the weekend and tour the city?" Henri suggested.

Hell no! I said to myself. "Oh, no . . . I, I really wish I could, but I have to get back to the office. I have so many things to do." I forced a grin.

He laughed. "Well, you might not have a choice!"

What seemed so humorous to him seemed like an utterly distasteful joke to me. I didn't want to stay in Texas. I couldn't stay in Texas! I had a load of shit to do back in New York and I wouldn't be able to accomplish a thing sitting in a hotel room in Houston, Texas. It wasn't like my temp could handle things for me. After all, she could barely handle things with me there.

After the meal was finally done and paid for with my platinum American Express card, like two Southern gentlemen, Henri and DaVon walked me to my car, where the driver sat patiently in front of the restaurant. We shook hands (to say goodbye as well as to seal the deal) and the driver sped off. I couldn't help but to think about being stuck in Texas when I had so much to do back home, and I was completely consumed with that thought the entire ride to the hotel.

Once in my room at the Ritz, I quickly turned on the Weather Channel. They confirmed what Henri had told me about the conditions in New York City. I was stranded.

"Girl, they say it's the worst snowstorm in twenty years!" Trish stated through the phone receiver. I had called to tell her that I was stuck in Texas and to pass the time while I devoured the burger I had ordered from room service. I felt like being bad so I ordered a cheddar burger deluxe from room service, something that hadn't touched my lips in I didn't know how long. I was bored. What the hell was I going to do in Houston, Texas alone? I deserved some sort of reward for all the stuff I'd been through in the last couple of weeks, and the aroma of that greasy medium well-done cow on a lightly toasted Kaiser roll was just the thing to hit the spot. The shoestring French fries only added to the delight.

"Well, I'm stuck here until the airports open. At least this is a five-star hotel and at least I can expense everything, ya know," I said, as I shoved a fry into my mouth.

"Why don't you call DaVon and tell his fine ass to give you a tour of the city? Houston's really nice," she suggested.

"I don't think so."

"So, you haven't even told me. How was Mr. Garrett?"

"Oh, he was fine."

"I know that, silly. I mean, what was he like? How was his personality?"

"Well," I began, taking a sip of my Sprite, "he was actually pretty quiet. Not a big talker at all. In fact, his agent—this guy named Henri Andersen—did most of the talking. So much so that for a brief moment, I almost forgot his ass was there."

"How the hell could you forget his fine cocoa-brown, six-foot-six-inch ass was there? Ya know, sometimes I think you're really brain-dead, Ny."

"Seriously! I was in the process of sealing a multimillion-dollar deal. I didn't have time to pay attention to his ass. And besides, the only time he opened his mouth was when the issue of his getting his own sneaker came up. That was it!"

"Do you mean that he was quiet as in 'I'm the strong, silent type that only speaks when there's something significant to say' or he was quiet as in 'I'm really just a dumb jock and don't really understand this business stuff so I'll let my agent do the talking' quiet? There is a difference."

"Whatever. I didn't exactly have time to try to read his brain, Trish. Like I just said and in case you didn't realize by everything I've been saying, I was trying to cut a multimillion-dollar deal."

"Well, excuuuuuse the hell outta me!"

"You're excused." I huffed, kind of put off by her ignorance and one-track mind. Just as I was about to suggest that I call her back, there was a knock at the door.

"Let me go. Somebody's at the door."

"OK. Call me later."

I jumped up from the table and opened the door only to see the bellhop standing there with an unbelievably large vase of long-stemmed red velvet roses. I was quite surprised to see flowers and anxious to know who they were from.

"Just delivered, and they're as lovely as the lady receiving them." The bellhop smiled as he entered the room and placed them on the credenza. I handed him a $2 tip. I strolled back from seeing him out the door to the table with the mammoth roses. I figured they were probably from Henri Andersen but said aloud, "With my luck Bill Peterson tracked me down."

However, to my great surprise, the card read:

Sorry you're stranded. Call me if you want to get out of your room.

Hoping to hear from you,

DaVon Garrett
899-0988

I gently placed the card beside the crystal vase. For some reason, I had the weirdest feeling. DaVon was fine, but incredibly young and totally not my type. However, I hadn't any inkling that he was the least bit interested in me, and it made him seem a little mysterious. I truly hate to admit it, but it turned me on just a little bitty bit.

Nine

"I'm surprised you called." DaVon grinned as we sat in his chauffeur-driven Mercedes Benz limousine. The sun was just about to go down and the city looked wonderful; not as bright as the Big Apple, but nice for a Southern city. The weather was still mild, but there was now a slight breeze and it felt so good going through my body. I could've used a light jacket but I had limited clothing with me. I put on the jeans and white shirt I'd arrived in. Since the shirt had long sleeves, I figured I would be all right.

As I sat beside DaVon on the dark, plush, leather seats, I, too, was surprised I had called. But I was stranded and figured that I could either spend the evening in my hotel room on the phone listening to Trish or I could spend the evening being harmlessly wined and dined with DaVon Garrett. I guess I called because I felt no threat from him. We could never be a couple nor was I the least bit romantically interested in him. He seemed so young and innocent that I'd surely be able to out-smart him if I needed.

"The flowers you sent were beautiful and I figured that since I'm stuck here, I may as well see the city." I shrugged.

"So are you sayin' that you only called me 'cause I'm better than watchin' TV all night?"

"No, no . . . that's not what I mean at all!" I laughed, trying to make both of us feel at ease.

"What I meant was that I was quite glad to take you up on your offer since I'm forced to be a visitor of your city. I must admit, though.

I'm a bit surprised to see you without Henri. He seems like he tries to keep a very good eye on you."

"He tries, but after business is taken care of, I have no use for him."

"I see."

"Well, Nyagra, I'm not happy that you're stuck, but I am happy to get to know you a little better." He smiled in a unique way. He was handsome but not as distinguished as Victor. Still there was something about him that I liked. He had full lips and straight, white teeth with a slight gap between the front two. In a strange way, it was extremely sexy. In fact, in a strange way, he was extremely sexy. I was finally starting to see what Trish had been talking about.

I repositioned myself on the leather seat. "So where are you taking me?" I questioned.

"A friend of mine is having a cocktail party at Terrace on the World. Ever heard of it?"

"No."

"It's a great café one hundred stories up in the sky. They even have an outside deck and it's a perfect night for it. The sky is clear and you can see every star. I think it's your type of place. Very classy." It seemed a bit odd for me to hear DaVon talking about stars and the clarity of the sky. He simply hadn't struck me as the type of guy who noticed such things.

"How can you tell what kind of places I like?" I teasingly questioned.

"I'm pretty good at reading people—especially women."

"Oh, you are, are you?"

DaVon demonstrated an outgoing personality. In the restaurant with Henri Andersen he had appeared to be extremely reserved and almost shy. But now, he surely wasn't at a loss for words.

The car moved through the city at a swift pace and as we stopped at a light, DaVon's cell phone rang.

"Talk fast," he instructed the caller, as he flipped the phone to his ear. I was a bit put off by his abrasiveness, but reminded myself that he was a 21-year-old millionaire. How could he not have an ego?

"Not interested," DaVon said to the person on the other end of the receiver. "You heard what I said!" he snapped, closing the phone and focusing his attention on me. He grinned. "Excuse me. Henri's always trying to get me to do this benefit or that benefit. I think he tries to repay old debts with my services."

I was quite shocked to hear him talk to his agent in that manner when he'd been so silent over lunch. Perhaps he was trying to be a show-off, but I appeared not to notice, and didn't comment on his statement.

"So Nyagra, how old are you?" He took my hand as he inquired. He caught me off guard with his question, as well as his embrace of my hand. I couldn't deny that we definitely had some sort of chemistry going on and because of this, I wasn't certain if I should tell him the truth or not. However, I did feel a bit uncomfortable with the thought of where this was going. I'd learned my lesson about mixing business with pleasure from Victor. In no way did I want to further jeopardize this StarzSports account. I momentarily regretted accepting his invitation. I really wanted a simple evening with no strings attached. So not in the mood for games, and determined not to allow this encounter to go very far anyway, I opted to be honest.

"32."

"You coulda fooled me. You don't look a day over 25. But I'm into more mature women. Little girls do nothing for me. I'm way too mature for most girls my age. Are you into younger men?"

"Into? DaVon, I hope we're both clear on what's happening here. I don't know about you, but I don't really consider this to be a 'date.'"

"I'm not into labeling situations."

"You sure are into the word 'into,'" I sarcastically stated.

"Well, you know . . . I'm the type of guy who likes to find out things about people. I like to know where people are coming from. Where their heads are. What they're into." He laughed at himself as he used the word once again.

"OK . . . But you're questioning me like we're on a date."

"Well, what do you consider this to be?"

"I consider this to be, um . . . Well, you're doing a multimillion-dollar deal with my company and I'm stranded here thanks to a blizzard, and you're nice enough to keep me company," I awkwardly explained.

DaVon laughed hard and replied with great confidence, "Oh, OK. Whatever you say. When the night is over and you've had one of the

best times of your life, let me know what we should call it then." He
reached over and opened the mini-bar closet.

"Can I offer you a drink?" he asked, popping the cork on a bottle of
Crystal.

I waved my hand. "No, thanks. I'm not a drinker."

He poured himself a glass. "For some reason, I knew you were going
to say that. Do you feel uncomfortable with me being twelve years
younger than you?"

I shrugged. "Not at all. Like I said, DaVon, this isn't a date."

"Oh, right . . . " He laughed.

We pulled up in front of an exquisite skyscraper with huge dark-
tinted windows and a mammoth gold awning. The valet opened our
door and as I looked up at the building, I realized that I was dressed
inappropriately.

"DaVon, I can't go in there like this!" I exclaimed, looking down at
my jeans and white button-down shirt.

"Yes, you can. You're with me. Besides, don't let the outside fool you.
Look at me! I'm not dressed up. Nobody's gonna be dressed up. This is
Houston. Nobody dresses up."

I observed his tall, muscular physique in his black linen slacks and
tan collarless button-down shirt. He was casually dressed, but he still
looked more appropriate than I did. But he was DaVon Garrett! I guess
he didn't have to dress formally. I was sure that all eyes would be on him
regardless. I suddenly felt very uncomfortable. In fact, I just wanted to
disappear. I definitely wished I'd stayed in my hotel room.

We took the glass elevator up to the one-hundredth floor. Neither of
us said a word as we rose to the top. I'm sure he knew I was uncomfortable, so he remained silent until the door opened into a magnificently
crowded room, endowed with chandeliers and mirrors. Without hesitation, I visually skimmed the room and to my surprise, everyone was
casually dressed.

"See. What did I tell you? This is Texas, not New York." He was
charming. And it transcended into a seemingly fun-loving, spontaneous
personality. Despite his stern demeanor on the telephone and in the
limo, one-on-one he was quite soft-spoken and laid-back. I could tell
from our ride in the limo that he could hold a conversation, but he was

not necessarily talkative. Except for the fact that he had a lot of money, perhaps he was just an average 21-year-old. Still, something did seem a little different about him.

As I observed him, his mannerisms and his aura, I suddenly wondered what it would be like to get to know him better. Knowing that I shouldn't have been thinking like that, I shook the thought out of my mind and tried to focus on the atmosphere of the room.

Terrace on the World was indeed a magnificent place. At 100 stories in the sky, you could see every light, bridge and waterway in Houston. There were windows surrounding the entire room and the view was incredible. The sky was so clear, it almost looked like a painting. Brightly shining stars resembled priceless diamonds twinkling in the night. It was as lovely as a masterpiece created by Van Gogh. DaVon was right; it was my kind of place. However, a place of its beauty in New York City would never allow its patrons to wear jeans, and almost everyone in the room was dressed in jeans and/or a cowboy hat. There were at least two or three hundred people and it was incredibly lively. A jazz band played at the front of the room and jolly Texans stood around laughing, talking, smoking and just having a good old time.

"Mr. Garrett! Happy New Year!" the well-dressed maitre d' exclaimed as he firmly gripped DaVon's hand.

"Hey, Les, how's it going?"

"Who's your beautiful lady friend?"

"This is Ms. Nyagra Ensley. She's from New York."

"Well, Happy New Year to you, too, Ms. Ensley. And enjoy Houston." Les smiled as he kissed my hand. We walked deeper into the room, and as expected, all eyes were on DaVon. Men and women alike seemed to be in awe of his presence—just like earlier that day at the Golden Room. It was impossible not to notice DaVon Garrett as he stood tall with cockiness and an air about him that said, "Stop whatever you're doing. I've entered the room."

"What do you think?" DaVon asked, breaking my train of thought.

"It's a very lovely place."

"I want to introduce you to a couple of my friends." He grabbed my hand and led me through the crowd to the other side of the room. We approached a group of men with bodies similar to DaVon's—obviously teammates. Trish would've been in absolute heaven! As we walked up, they all shook hands with DaVon and exchanged manly hugs.

"Yo, you still recuperating from Puffy's New Year's Eve party in L.A.? I thought you were gonna drink yourself into a coma!" said one guy with an incredibly large gold rope chain around his neck. I thought those had gone out of style years ago, but obviously not.

"Hey, it was New Year's Eve! Everybody gets drunk on New Year's Eve!" Davon joked with them.

"Well, enough of that. No more excessive partying 'til after we bring home that Super Bowl trophy," another dark-skinned gentleman said with a laugh.

"Emmitt, this is a friend of mine from New York City, Nyagra Ensley," DaVon stated. Emmitt firmly shook my hand and smiled. "Nyagra. What a pretty and unusual name."

"Thank you." I blushed.

"Nyagra, these are a couple of my teammates—Emmitt, Marcus, Ray and Tony. Emmitt threw this party as sort of a post-New Year's celebration," DaVon continued.

One by one, they each shook my hand.

Emmitt laughed. "I hate throwing parties on New Year's Eve. People just don't know how to act. They get all drunk and crazy. But a week later they've all recuperated from their hangovers and calmed down. Plus, they probably drank so much on New Year's Eve, that they can't even drink too much a week later. So it actually saves me money, too."

"What brings you to Houston?" Tony questioned.

"Business, but Mother Nature decided to deliver a major snowstorm back home so I've become a tourist of your city unexpectedly." I didn't really want to indulge in any details or have anyone to think that I was being unprofessional by spending the evening with DaVon. After all, it really was innocent.

"Oh, I heard about that storm you guys are having. I think it's been falling for almost ten hours now," Marcus said.

"Yeah, so she'll be visiting longer than she anticipated." DaVon grinned and gently grabbed my wrist. "Come on. We're gonna go check out the view."

"Nice meeting you all," I said as we headed for the deck.

They were all gentlemen and cordial in their salutation. The average girl might've been in awe knowing that she was surrounded by such fame and fortune. But since I wasn't all that familiar with football, or its superstars, I really didn't know who the guys DaVon had just introduced me to were. Emmitt was a name I'd heard of before because he's like their biggest star. We'd actually looked into him for the StarzSports deal. But he would've cost us too much. I'd also heard rumors about his terribly arrogant demeanor, but that evening at Terrace on the World, he didn't seem arrogant at all. With the exception of Rodney, I had this pretty negative image of professional athletes. In my mind, they were all like Shawn Franklin—obnoxious and overconfident, believing their own hype. But DaVon's teammates seemed like really nice guys. They also seemed like regular people, not star-struck by their own fame. Like DaVon, they definitely had star qualities, but were ultimately charming.

The Houston air was mild and felt good blowing through my hair. The view from the deck was amazing, and there were a few people also enjoying the view. But as soon as we entered the deck, DaVon grabbed me around my waist. "You are a very beautiful woman, Nyagra."

"Thank you for the compliment." I smiled, pulling away from him.

"What's the matter? Is it me?" he questioned.

"DaVon, I really don't care to mix business with pleasure. You're a very nice young man, but I've learned that it's just not a good thing to do."

He huffed. "So that's it. I'm too young."

"Well . . . that is definitely a factor as well. But honestly, I've learned the hard way that mixing business with pleasure can be very bad for business. DaVon, please don't take it personally."

"Oh, so you've done the do with one of your co-workers before? Or was it a client?"

"Done the do? Whatever . . . " I huffed, turning my back to him and reminding myself just how young he actually was.

"Well, whatever happened in that situation, you can't deny the fact that there's chemistry between us. Is it just me or do you feel it, too?"

I hesitated before I responded, for I knew that I needed to handle this matter delicately. Yes, there was a certain amount of chemistry between me and this 21-year-old hunk. But he wasn't my type. I'd never get involved with a professional athlete—especially one a dozen years my junior. My name is Nyagra Ensley. Not Trish Hill.

"I appreciate you bringing me here to this lovely café in the sky, but . . ."

He interrupted me. "Answer my question. Is it just me or do we have really good chemistry?"

"DaVon, long time, no see," a very attractive mocha-colored woman in a tight purple mini-dress stated as she walked up to us and put her hand on his cheek. I was relieved that she'd diverted his attention, but simultaneously, I felt a wee bit disrespected. I knew we weren't on a date, but she didn't. "What's up, Veronica?" DaVon asked, a bit cold and distanced. I assumed she was an ex-girlfriend or some type of old fling.

"Happy New Year." She grinned at him like I wasn't even standing there with my hand in his palm.

"Thanks."

"Call me," she whispered in a sexy manner before seductively walking away from us.

I watched her sashay like the Queen of the Nile. "Girlfriend of yours?" I chuckled.

"Nah. Believe it or not, I haven't had many girlfriends."

Knowing that couldn't hardly be a true statement, I asked, "Really? Do they know that? After all, not too many women act that way with men they're just 'friends' with."

"Just because I take a girl out a couple times doesn't make her my girlfriend. Until I find the right woman, football is my girl."

I was not one-hundred percent certain I wanted to open this can of worms, but with nothing else better to talk about, against my better judgment, I questioned, "Oh, I see. And what is the 'right' woman in your eyes?"

"Well . . . " He thought a moment. "The right woman to me is one who has her own life, her own mind, her own career, just her own set of issues goin' on, ya know? Somebody educated and smart; not only book-wise, but she's gotta have common sense, too. In a lot of ways, that's more important than book smarts. She shouldn't be impressed by the fact that I play pro ball, like most of the women I meet. She should be impressed because I'm a deep, sensitive brotha."

He chuckled. I laughed a bit, too, quite impressed with his answer. I was so sure that he was going to say the right woman had to a have a big butt, long hair, and no less than a D cup. I was quite surprised to learn that DaVon had almost as many requirements for a mate as I did. I didn't think that any other human being was that picky.

"Oh, and she does have to be fine," he added, after a moment of thought.

I laughed. "I'm sure. Well, you've got quite a list of requirements. More than I thought you would, actually. A woman like that will be very difficult to find."

"Maybe not as difficult as I once thought." He gazed deeply into my eyes, with a million implications in his voice.

In an attempt to resist his tranquilizing gaze, I turned away and focused on the view over Houston. "The view up here is absolutely magnificent."

"I knew you'd like it."

"How do you think you know me so well in just a few hours?"

"I told you. We have chemistry. Even if you don't wanna admit it. Even if you wanna run from it, like you're doing."

"I beg your pardon?" I jokingly but seriously asked.

"I can tell you're uncomfortable being here with me like this. You know there's something between us, but you wanna stick to your 'no mixing business with pleasure rule,' so go ahead, for now, that is. I'm getting my DaVon Garrett sneaker no matter what, anyway." He chuckled.

"That's right. And I don't want to do anything that might jeopardize you getting that DaVon Garrett sneaker," I said in jest along with him.

"Seriously, Nyagra. How could us hooking up jeopardize the deal? StarzSports wants me. You know it. You guys came to me. So as long as I say 'yes,' it's a done deal. I said 'yes,' so what could we do to jeopardize that? Tell me. And if you give a good answer, I'll back off. I promise."

"First of all, I'm old enough to be your . . . your big sister."

DaVon huffed. "Oh, brother! I already have a big sister and I don't need another one."

"Seriously. Eleven years is a lot."

"My mamma had thirteen years on my pops and they were married more than twenty-five years before he passed away."

"Well, that's not the norm. "

"I'm not the norm."

"DaVon, those types of relationships rarely work out. Plus, it's really bad timing for me. I haven't been having very good luck in the relation-ship department lately. And if this goes sour, it might be uncomfortable for us to work on this project together. StarzSports really loves you and I happen to think you're good for the endorsement, as well. There's a lot of money riding on this deal with you, DaVon. For you and for me."

"Well, maybe it's time for your luck to change. Who says our friend-ship has to go sour? Aren't we two rare types of people? I've never met another woman like you. You're a very beautiful woman, Nyagra. And the way you handled Henri really turned me on. I've never seen him so taken by anyone before. After our meeting today, I knew I had to get to know you better."

"Really? You could've fooled me."

"Why? 'Cause I let Henri do all the talking? It was a business meet-ing and Henri is my business manager so I let him handle my business. That's what I pay him for. It would've been inappropriate for me to try and push up on you at that meeting. So contrary to what you might think, I do have couth. But when I realized that you were stranded, I figured that must've been a blessing from above. I had to take advantage of the opportunity presented before me."

DaVon was saying all the right things in all the right ways. His per-sonality caught me so off guard that I realized I had definitely underes-timated his intelligence and undermined his ability to be a gentleman. I had a prejudice against professional athletes—especially young ones. But DaVon Garrett spoke with the charm and experience of someone years his senior. Talking to him as the stars glistened and the breeze blew gently over our faces, if I had not known for a fact that this man was only 21 years old, I never would've believed it.

After a moment of silence between us and just the sound of the band playing in the background, DaVon cornered me against the rail-ing and whispered in my ear. "Give it a chance, Nyagra. If you don't like it, there's no strings attached. But don't not try it because you're scared you might like it."

"You're awfully sure of yourself for someone of your age."

"I have an old soul."

DaVon and I spent the rest of the evening dancing to the sounds of the fabulous jazz band. We had an absolutely wonderful time. I couldn't remember the last time I had laughed and danced that much. It wasn't like the stuffy parties I was used to in New York City, where everyone thought they were too cute to dance and break a sweat. The party at Terrace on the World was filled with people who wanted to have a good time just eating, drinking, dancing and being social. As the evening progressed, I realized that DaVon was an extremely fun-loving guy with a great sense of humor. He liked to innocently poke fun at people and make fun of their clothes and hair. He really was quite funny. His Texan accent was also appealing to me. It wasn't extremely heavy. In fact I didn't hear it in every word he spoke. But it was just enough to remind me that he was a Southern boy who knew how to have a good time and forced everyone in his presence to also enjoy themselves.

He was Mr. Popularity. Everyone seemed to know and adore him. And anyone who didn't know him wanted to. Everybody who came up to us was certain that the Cowboys were going to the Super Bowl and would become the champions. Of course, that would've been great for StarzSports and thus for Newman & Stein. It was hard not to feed into the hype of DaVon Garrett. I wasn't even into football but was truly impressed with the effect he had on people (business was always on my mind.) As I spent time with him, I was positive that he was the perfect man for our ad. Over the course of the night, several more beautiful women came up to him with the same demeanor as the young lady on the deck, only to be treated nonchalantly by DaVon. A couple even tried to be catty, but it was impossible for me to feel intimidated or jealous because he was totally into me that night. I couldn't help but to feel flattered. Even as he talked to others, he held my hand and never diverted his attention away from me. He introduced everyone to me as "his friend from New York." He was so outgoing, I began to feel outgoing—the introvert that I am. Because he was so popular, I suddenly felt popular. In fact, he was a superb ego booster for me after my last two lousy romantic incidents.

The party started winding down about one. The band still played, but the music was more mellow and tranquil than it had been hours earlier. I could tell it was Houston, because in New York, parties are still going strong at that time. As I sat with DaVon at the bar drinking a wine glass of pineapple juice while he sipped grapefruit juice, we continued to laugh and share our childhoods and experiences. He told me about his days at Florida State and how he grew up poor in Miami, one of five kids.

"We didn't have much money, but my parents adored us and each other," he informed me.

"How many brothers and sisters do you have?"

"Just two sisters. I love them a lot. We're very close. I'm the baby. Connie's 24 and Daphne's 30."

They're both younger than I am, I thought to myself. I was beginning to feel like I was the only one who couldn't stand my family. As we sat at the bar and watched everyone slowly leave, we continued exchanging interesting stories as our attraction to each other grew stronger. I was totally intrigued by his finesse and charm and impressed by the wisdom he possessed at such an early age. He didn't have the sophistication and worldliness of Victor, but I think that's what drew me to him. He had an innocence and vulnerability about him. In talking with him, I found out that despite the effect he had on the public, he was actually an insecure little boy who just wanted to be loved because he was DaVon Garrett—"only son of Madge and Charles Garrett, little brother of Connie and Daphne," as he put it.

"All my life I was babied and given preferential treatment by everyone—my parents, my teachers, other kids—just because I was good at football. Plus, being the only boy in the family and the youngest, of course, I was the favorite. So even when I was bad or mean, nobody ever got mad at me. I never got punished. Sometimes I'd do things just to see what would happen. But I never got more than a slap on the wrist. At one point I even wondered if my parents really loved me 'cause whenever they punished my sisters, they'd always say, 'We do this because we love you.' And I never heard that. In some ways it was cool to be liked by everybody. But a lot of times, I knew it wasn't real. To be honest, I really always just wanted to be liked 'cause I'm a nice guy with a cool personality." He grinned.

As much as I hated to admit it to myself, I was quite in awe of DaVon Garrett. The way his eyes twinkled when he spoke and the simple ray of charm that I'd failed to notice earlier that day in the Golden Room were in full bloom that evening.

"You ready to get outta here?" he asked.

"Yes," I replied.

DaVon grabbed my hand and led me toward the exit. Our ride down to the lobby was silent, but our eyes seemed to be engaged in deep conversation. The limo was right in front of the building and the chauffeur eagerly opened the door for us. At first neither of us said a word as the car moved through the deserted streets. Here I was again at that awkward time of the evening where I had to decide whether or not the night should end or if another dimension of the evening should begin. I hated this moment of a date; if this was really even a date. Plus, I never seemed to make the right decision. After my last two escapades, I knew that my judgment wasn't the best and therefore I certainly wasn't ready to get sexually involved with DaVon Garrett. I didn't even know if I wanted to date him. Sure, we'd had a great evening, and he was charming, sweet, fine, and incredibly young. But outside of the lovely atmosphere of Terrace on the World, and the elegant black limousine, could we really ever become a couple? I honestly didn't think so.

"Are you going to your hotel room and calling this a night, or would you be interested in having a nightcap at my house?" DaVon finally asked, breaking the silence.

He's so straightforward and to the point, I thought. I liked it but it also caught me off guard, thus making me apprehensive. If I agreed to extend the evening, I might've found myself swimming in waters a bit too deep for my liking. If I ended the evening and went to my hotel room alone, I probably would've been thinking of what might have happened all night long. Mostly because of my recent experiences, I was just hesitant overall about spending any additional time with DaVon. I didn't want to start liking him in a romantic way. I simply didn't want to subject myself to yet another disappointment. However, I was able to soothe my mind a bit by telling myself that at least he wasn't married. That was for sure. And as young and strong as he looked, I knew he wouldn't fall asleep on top of me!

"Well, I really need to get some information regarding flights to New York," I replied, not really answering his question.

"Why are you so anxious to leave? Aren't you having a good time?" he jokingly asked, reminding me immensely of a pouting little boy.

"Of course, I'm having a good time. But I do have work to do at the office and I surely can't do anything from a hotel room here in Texas. You do want that DaVon Garrett shoe, don't you?" I coyly smiled.

"Yeah, I do. But it's already Friday and you and I both know that ain't nothin' gonna happen 'til Monday. That's why you need to just relax and spend the weekend here with me in Houston. Come on. You can stay in one of my guest rooms or I'll pay for the rest of your stay at the Ritz; if that'll make you feel more comfortable. Besides, I'm sure the airports are still closed, so you might not have a choice."

"Well, I still have to find out."

"OK. You can find out at my house. I have a 64-inch, flat-screen, portrait-styled TV hooked up to a state-of-the-art satellite dish in my rec room. You could probably pick up your local news."

His offer sounded tempting. I was curious to see the kind of home he lived in. I wanted to be with him, but I didn't want to sleep with him. I hoped he was serious about allowing me to use one of his guest rooms because there was no way that I was about to share a bed with him. However, I would have preferred the accuracy of my local news to find out what was going on back in New York. I certainly didn't plan to stay the entire weekend, but it was going on 2 A.M. Friday morning. Even if I took a flight out later that afternoon, I'd be too exhausted and jet-lagged to go to the office. Not that anyone would be there anyway except for my temp, Meg.

"I'll take you up on that nightcap offer, but I do need to see what the weather is back in New York. I will sleep in your guest room."

He grinned. "I have three of them. Take your pick."

DaVon instructed the driver to go to his house, which I happened to think he was heading anyway. The rest of ride was quiet. I'm sure a million things were going through his head, just as they were going through mine. As we rode, I noticed that he lived a bit out of the city. Along the road were huge trees and hills that were picturesque even in the dark. I also realized that I was completely unprepared for an overnight stay. I figured I could borrow one of his T-shirts, but what would I do for a toothbrush?

We finally drove up what seemed to be a never-ending winding road that led to his home. We pulled around the oval driveway, which must've been at least fifteen feet high. There was a mini-house on the side of this mansion. Set at least one hundred yards back from a spectacular impeccably manicured lawn, the cream-colored house still displayed signs of Christmas decorations on the outside. It was illuminated by lights shining from the roof. I was astonished to see that a rookie had a home of this magnitude. After all, he was just in his first year as a pro. I assumed that he must've spent his entire signing advance as a down payment for this home. It must've been worth at least $3 million.

When we entered the house, I was startled by the incredibly high ceilings and magnificent marble floors. There were winding staircases to my right and to my left. On the same level were two huge and intricately detailed oak doors that I assumed led to the main rooms. There was an airy feeling in the foyer and a grand skylight directly above my head. It was indeed a beautiful place but I almost felt like I'd entered a museum.

I followed DaVon through the oak doors into another magnificent room with ivory leather furniture, ivory carpeting and spotless ivory detailing. There was an ivory marble fireplace with an eminent portrait hanging over it of DaVon with three attractive women. I assumed that the woman sitting in the chair who appeared to be older—but not that much—was his mamma, Madge, and his sisters, Daphne and Connie.

I looked around the room. "You have a very beautiful home," I complimented.

"Thanks. My sister, Daphne, is an interior decorator. She's basically the one who got all this stuff. I like it, but sometimes it feels like a museum in here."

"Is that you with your sisters and mamma?" I asked, referring to the portrait on the wall.

"Yeah. Ma's in the chair, as I'm sure you can tell. Connie's on the left and Daphne's on the right. Mamma lives in the guesthouse. Since my father died last year, I've been taking care of her."

I sat on the sectional as DaVon proceeded to press a few buttons on the wall. As he did, what had appeared to be an ivory oblong lacquer closet in the center of the wall opened to reveal a large color-television screen. I must admit, I was a bit impressed.

"Here," he said as he handed me a remote control the size of my shoe. "Flick around. I'm sure your local news is on there."

I laughed. "What a big remote control!"

"I have 450 channels! It's gotta be big!"

Sure enough, after a moment of channel surfing, I was able to find News 4 New York. Just as I'd suspected, the airports were still shut down. Still not wanting to believe it, I found the Weather Channel and waited for New York to pop up in the forecast. Much to my dismay, this channel indicated that the airports might reopen Saturday but with many delays. Against my will, I would be spending the weekend in Houston after all.

DaVon smiled. "So, do you want me to send someone to pick up your things from the Ritz?"

"DaVon, I just can't stay here in your house!"

"Why not? I told you that you could use one of the guest rooms. You don't have to sleep in my bed, unless you want to."

"Come on. What if my company or StarzSports got word of this? I could be risking my job."

"Well, I wouldn't want you to do that. But who'd tell 'em? I sure wouldn't!"

"I know, DaVon. But you know how things can get out. I don't want the folks at StarzSports Apparel to think that you and I have something 'going' on and feel as though there's a conflict of interest," I explained.

"Oh, so you let your job dictate who you can and can't be friends with?" he asked in a huff.

I shook my head. "DaVon, come on."

"The fact is that you can't catch a flight to New York anyhow. Whether you like it or not, whether StarzSports likes it or not, you're stuck here. It's not like I can spend the whole weekend wining and dining you, anyway. I have practice tomorrow at noon and a game on Sunday. I was just trying to be nice. So you can either stay at the stuffy old Ritz Carlton or you can enjoy the warmth and comfort of my home. It's totally up to you, Nyagra."

"It's totally up to you, Nyagra," I replied, mocking him.

We laughed together and laid our heads on the back of the sofa. It had been such a long day that I'd nearly forgotten that I'd just arrived in Houston that afternoon. It was late and after such a fun-filled evening, it was obvious that we were both tired.

"I had a real nice time tonight, Nyagra," DaVon said after a moment of silence, his head still resting on the back of the sectional.

"Yeah, me, too."

"Maybe after practice tomorrow I can show you around Houston."

"I don't want you to tire yourself out, DaVon. I want you to be ready for that game on Sunday. In fact, don't you think you should be going to bed about now? You've got to be rested for practice tomorrow."

"You sound like my mamma."

"Uuugggh!" I said, suddenly remembering the age difference between us and surely not wanting to be compared to his mamma.

"Oh, I mean it in a good way! Really! I definitely didn't mean it as a reminder of our ages. Come on, you know you're not my mamma's age! But the best wives do remind guys of their mammas! Come on!" He jokingly put his arm around me. "In fact," he continued, "I would only marry a woman that reminded me of my mamma."

I rolled my eyes up into my head. "Yeah, OK."

"Seriously! My mamma and I are very close." He laughed, squeezing me tightly.

"Are you close with your sisters also?"

"Not really, but I try to keep the peace for Ma's sake."

I was relieved about that. Not that I didn't want him to be close to his sisters, but I was beginning to think that I was the only one who didn't particularly care for my siblings. As he loosened his embrace, our faces turned toward each other and the tips of our noses touched. Suddenly, we were staring eye-to-eye, looking directly into each other's pupils.

"You have the most beautiful hazel eyes I have ever seen," he whispered.

I could feel the warmth of his breath on my face, and it felt nice. It was the weirdest thing but the air he breathed was cool and warm at the same time, which really turned me on. I couldn't smell every beverage he'd consumed all night long, as I had during my New Year's Eve episode with Bill Peterson. DaVon's breath was fresh—like he'd just sucked on a breath mint or something. I hadn't seen him put anything into his mouth and I liked that. Leaving nothing to chance, I had periodically ingested my one-and-a-half-calorie Tic Tacs throughout the evening. I never entered into a social situation without them and that evening was no exception. Because of this, I felt confident that my breath was in good condition and hoped that it was as pleasing to him as his was to me. It must've been, for after he expressed his sentiments, he firmly planted a tender kiss on my lips. Unable to resist the softness of his luscious lips, I eagerly reciprocated and before I knew it, we were all over the ivory leather and each other. His large, strong hands gently gripped my waist as we continued to kiss deeply and passionately, finally unveiling the chemistry that had been brewing between us all night. I wanted to push him away, knowing in my mind that I shouldn't be getting involved with him in this manner. However, for some reason, I couldn't.

Our physical contact felt so right, yet simultaneously, so wrong. I think that's part of what excited me so much. My brain twirled a mile a minute, making it difficult for me to concentrate on any one thing— including our passion. I'd been suppressing feelings of disappointment from my recent romantic experiences and secretly yearned to feel special. At that moment with DaVon, I surely felt like I was the only woman in the world. But I had to force myself to come to my senses. He probably made all the women he was with feel that way. And I knew this feeling with him could only be momentary. I mentally admitted how vulnerable I clearly was, thanks to my recent experiences, and as he fervently ran his robust hands up and down my back, I became uncomfortable with the physical attraction we shared. I also remembered the statement he'd made about football being his girlfriend. No matter how good I felt right then, I knew I was setting myself up for yet another disappointment. If I'd simply been looking for a good time, DaVon

Garrett was surely the guy to give it to me. But at 32, I was in search of a stable, long-term, fulfilling romantic experience. I could never receive that from this handsome 21-year-old, rich football star. Understanding this and acting with my mind instead of my heart (and my sexuality), I pulled myself away from DaVon's arms and mumbled, "I can't do this, DaVon."

DaVon immediately released me from his embrace. "You're right. We're probably moving too fast."

I was pretty shocked to hear him talk like that. I figured he was used to plenty of "wham bam, thank you, ma'am" experiences and that my name would be just another addition to his lengthy list of conquests. To hear him indicate that he actually felt we should slow down absolutely amazed me. DaVon was an unpredictable guy with an incredibly sensitive side that could really make a girl say, "Aw . . . " On the surface, and judging from our meeting at the Golden Room, his personality gave off misleading traits of arrogance and immense conceit. But after spending the evening with him, I knew there was a lot of depth to what lied behind his dreamy eyes, although I was extremely hesitant to attempt to find out just how deep his still waters ran.

"How about showing me to my room?" I suggested as the heat swelled beneath my collar. DaVon gently wrapped his hands around my wrist and silently led me out into the foyer, up the winding staircase. The top floor of his home was just as lovely and spacious as the ground level. It was obvious that the man adored the color ivory, for the plush carpet, the walls, and the entire decor was the color of untouched cream. We walked into a large room off to the left with a queen-sized canopy bed draped with sheer cream-colored scarves. The room hardly looked like a guestroom, except for the fact that it appeared to have been untouched. Everything sat perfectly in place, making the room look like a romantically enchanting photo straight out of Gracious Homes magazine. The antique armoire added class and sophistication to the atmosphere, displaying the impeccable taste of DaVon's sister. She was obviously good at what she did.

If this is a guest room, what must the master bedroom look like? I asked myself. But I knew I wasn't ready to know. And I didn't think DaVon was either, although I was certain that this young man would be quite easy to seduce. But I didn't want to play with the fire that lied within him. To my credit, I was intelligent enough to realize that my emotions were far too raw to dabble in a pot where I was sure I would eventually get burned.

"You should be pretty comfortable in here, but if you need any-thing, the master bedroom is in the west wing of the house. Just knock," DaVon instructed.

I continued to look around. "This is a very beautiful room."

"I'm glad you like it," he whispered. It sounded like he had a huge lump in his throat. It was obvious that it was an awkward moment for the both of us. Ten minutes ago we'd been tightly wrapped in each other's arms sharing passion and adoration. Now it seemed like neither of us knew what to say. I think we both wanted to fall onto the fluffy duvet-covered down comforter and pick up where we left off on the sectional downstairs. But we couldn't—we wouldn't—so we just stood at a standstill, both of us appearing to be extremely uncomfortable.

"If you sleep late, I'll probably be gone when you wake up. I leave at ten to get to the stadium," he said.

"I'll be up by eight. I have to call my office and make arrangements to take care of everything at the hotel. In fact, is there an alarm clock in here?" I asked, looking around.

"Yeah. The television can be set to come on at a specific time. As far as your things are concerned, I'll have my driver take you over there so you can handle all of that while I'm at practice." He walked over to the lovely brass-detailed, free-standing closet and opened its sliding door to reveal what must have been a twenty-five-inch Sony Trinitron TV set. He pressed a few buttons on the remote control pad. "You're all set for 8 A.M. So, will you stay for the weekend?" he continued.

"Well, I need to find out what's going on with the weather. I can't make you any promises, but I'm pretty sure that the weather won't per-mit me to leave tomorrow, so we'll at least have one more day together."

He sighed. "Oh."

I smiled awkwardly. "How about if we have breakfast together at let's say, um . . . 8:30?"

"I work out from seven to nine. How about if I have my mamma prepare breakfast for us at 9:30?"

"Your mamma cooks breakfast for you?"

"Every morning. I'm a really terrible cook. If it was up to me, I'd eat bagels and boiled eggs every day. But it's no thing. Ma likes cooking for me. I think it makes her feel needed. She's been complaining about being bored ever since she moved in. Cooking for me gives her something to do."

"His Mamma lives with him?" my voice echoed inside my head. I took a deep breath and asked, "Your Mamma lives here? I thought you said she lived in the guest house?"

"Yeah, she does, but I still consider that here. My sister Daphne lives here, too. But don't worry. It's not like you'll be bumping into them in the bathroom or anything like that."

"Well, OK. I guess I'll see you at breakfast," I said. What else could I say?

"Do you need a T-shirt or something to sleep in?"

"Yeah, that would be great." I smiled. Did he forget that I'd walked through the door with nothing but the clothes on my back?

DaVon disappeared, only to return a few moments later with a blue Dallas Cowboys' T-shirt. As he handed it to me, I graciously stated, "How very apropos."

"Well, what were you expecting—49ers jersey?" He smiled, breaking the tension that was evident in the atmosphere.

"That door over there in the corner is a bathroom. There's clean towels in there, as well as fresh toiletries."

"Almost as if you were expecting me," I suggested with a tone of laughter.

"No, not exactly. Mamma just keeps the room that way." He shrugged. "Sleep well, Nyagra. I'll see you at breakfast." DaVon walked toward the bedroom door waving his hand.

"Thanks."

DaVon closed the door behind himself and left me standing in the middle of the beautifully romantic room all alone. I felt so awkward and strange, wondering if he was standing on the other side debating about rushing back in and taking me in his arms as passionately as he'd done earlier that evening. But five minutes later, I was still standing alone, so I figured that he had gone on his merry way.

I undressed myself, laying my jeans and white shirt on a large oak rocking chair with a winter green and cream-striped padded seat in the far left corner of the room. Because the room was so large, there was an airiness about it as well as a bit of a draft. Feeling the cool air on my body as I slipped on the oversized T-shirt, I quickly shut off the overhead light and slid into the wonderfully soft canopy bed.

As I lay there feeling as if I was about to fall asleep on a bed of clouds, I could hardly believe that I was in DaVon Garrett's house. It was even more amazing that we were actually sleeping in separate beds and he hadn't tried to force the issue. Part of my attraction to him was his gentlemanly quality that turned me on immensely, making me quite tempted to go searching through the halls of his home for his room. But with my lousy luck, I'd bust in on his sister. So I ferociously fought the voice inside my head that justified such behavior and opted to stay right where I was.

What if my job finds out that I'm staying at his house? They'll surely remove me from this account, I thought to myself. I was putting my entire career at risk by taking our relationship outside of the "business only" category, and I wasn't about to lose this business that I had worked so hard for. Goddamn this StarzSports account! First, that trifling Victor Reece and now this guy. Although I knew that it was unlikely to get out, I was still quite concerned about what anyone would think if they knew that I was sleeping in DaVon's house; even if it wasn't in his bed. I was still under his roof, and the truth of the matter was that I really did want to make love to him. I knew I could not love him after only one night, but after that evening, there were indeed qualities about DaVon that I could eventually love if I decided to give it a chance. But did I want to give it a chance? Not really. I didn't think it would be a wise thing to do.

So many emotions stirred within me as I lay in that bed dressed in his T-shirt. My desire for him grew with every second. Yet, at the same time, I continued to become angrier and angrier with myself for being such an incredibly hopeless and unrealistic romantic. Again I permitted myself to be swooped in by someone I barely knew. It was just that his gentleness and charm forced me to feel extremely certain that sex with him would be passionate and beautiful versus just a good fuck. I honestly believed it would be "making love" because the chemistry between us demonstrated a love and appreciation for each other as people. We truly liked each other and our act of fornication surely would've been an unforgettable event. But I absolutely refused to act on my emotions. I wanted to be with him, but I was also very confused. Part of me actually questioned if what I felt for DaVon was reality or if I was just so in search of true love that I was now willing to look almost anywhere; even in the arms of a 21-year-old kid. Was I becoming that desperate? I surely didn't want to be, so I figured that the smart thing would be to stay in that room alone.

I stared at the ceiling in total darkness as my mind did somersaults with desires of sexual lust, but it was also as if I was paralyzed by God who, for my own good, was forcing me to lay in the middle of that down mattress like I'd been nailed to it. As I tried to fight the thought of DaVon's magnificent hands caressing me against his body, I closed my eyes tightly and finally drifted off to sleep. I had hopes of at least dreaming about making love to this incredibly tempting and seemingly delicious young man who I was sure could mean nothing but trouble for me.

Ten

Filled with anxiety, I tossed and turned most of the hours that I laid in DaVon's guest room. By the time I was able to get into a really good sleep, the television came on, telling me that my time for resting was indeed over. Groggily and quite disoriented, I focused my vision on the picture tube and the digital clock in the right corner, which read 8:01 A.M. With great effort, I pulled myself from the canopy bed and slowly walked into the bathroom. Knowing that I needed to rise in order to plot my next plan of action, I turned on the shower, allowing the room to become a steamy, foggy haven. While I waited for the atmosphere to succumb to my liking, I splashed cold water on my face from the brass pedestal. As to be expected, the bathroom was a lovely little sky-blue room with thick blue carpeting and a glass shower stall. The brilliance of the light from the Texas sun glared through the skylight, making it unnecessary for any artificial lighting.

The shower helped wake me and prepared me for the call I needed to make to my office. As I let the warm water pound forcefully on the nape of my neck, I felt quite proud of myself for exercising such restraint the night before. Despite my desires for DaVon, I had remained in the guest bed alone, the way a good girl with morals should have. My mamma would have been proud of me.

I spoke with Meg who informed me that the weather conditions were still poor and that the airports were still closed. "The office is basically empty. Mostly everyone called in or they're still on vacation," Meg said.

I sighed. "Well, it looks as though I'm stuck here until the airports open. Since everyone is out, no work can be done anyway. In fact, you should leave at noon."

"Thanks, Nyagra."

I hung up the phone and was tempted to call Trish, but I was certain she'd die of heart failure the moment I uttered anything about staying over at DaVon's house. I ultimately decided against it, figuring that the conversation we would share should take place when I was absolutely certain that no one was listening.

For the first time in ages, I didn't rush. When I was completely dressed, it was nearly 8:30 and time for me to meet DaVon downstairs for breakfast. I tiptoed out of the room, unsure of where the kitchen was located. I followed the aroma of food that led me to the first floor around the back. I entered a beautiful gourmet kitchen to see DaVon sitting at the table reading the morning paper and an older but seemingly hip woman pouring him a glass of orange juice. I immediately recognized her from the portrait in the entertainment room. A petite, maple-colored woman dressed in a red and blue DKNY sweatsuit with auburn shoulder-length, loosely curled hair, Madge Garrett didn't look a day over 40. She was very attractive but I felt an extremely dominating air in her presence, which forced me to feel nervous meeting her; especially under such conditions. I didn't want her to think I was some tramp that had spent the night with her son after only knowing him twenty-four hours. I truly hoped that she was aware that I had indeed slept in the guest room. And while it wasn't that I was afraid of her, it was just that I really liked DaVon and, for his sake, I didn't want to bump heads with Mamma.

"Good morning," I nervously said as I entered the room.

"Hey, there she is!" DaVon smiled, brighter than the Texas sun. His mamma, on the other hand, wasn't as friendly. She didn't even crack a smile.

"Ma, this is Nyagra Ensley," DaVon stated.

"Nice to meet you." I smiled, reaching out to shake her hand.

To my surprise, she didn't comply. Turning her back to me, she merely replied, "Have a seat. I've prepared poached eggs and oatmeal, my baby's favorite. As you can see, there's plenty of fresh fruit right there. But my baby boy needs his protein and iron. Isn't that right, Baby?" She grinned as she rubbed him on his head. He displayed a mile-long smile, shaking his head in agreement. I hated poached eggs, and oatmeal reminded me of regurgitated bread. But I didn't want to hurt her feelings so as she placed the plate of food in front of me, I smiled and helped myself to the fresh fruit on a rectangular platter in the center of the table.

"Ma, Nyagra's the vice president at the advertising agency that represents StarzSports. They really want me," he explained to her.

"Of course, they want you, Baby. Everybody wants my DayDay . . ." She turned and looked me up and down. "You plannin' 'ta give my DayDay a good deal?"

"Definitely," I assured her.

"They really want me, Ma," DaVon told her, sounding so much like a little boy and so unlike the man on the leather sectional the previous night.

Madge had fire in her eyes as she sat down at the table with us. "Well, don't go signin' nuthin' 'til Henri takes a good look at it, and make sure you take it to your lawyer. I don't want missy here ta be thinkin' that she can get over on you 'cause she's kinda cute and she spent the night here last night."

Did she just insult me? I asked myself. Or did she compliment me in a roundabout way? She did say I was cute, didn't she?

"Aw, Ma, I'm gonna make sure the logistics are right. Trust me."

I was still unsure of how to take her. It was very obvious that she wasn't too keen on her "baby boy" having a woman in his life. As I watched her gaze into his eyes and lovingly stroke his face with her every word, it seemed as though she believed that she should be the only woman in her son's life. Needless to say, sitting at that table with the two of them, I felt pretty uncomfortable.

"Well, ladies, gotta go to practice," DaVon finally said, rising from the table.

"OK, DayDay. Have a good practice, Baby," his mamma said.

"Nyagra, the airports are still closed," Davon informed me.

I sighed. "I know."

"So does that mean I'll have the pleasure of your company for at least another evening?"

Madge rolled her eyes with a huff, got up from the table, and walked over to the refrigerator. I acted like I didn't notice her behavior and dreaded that he was about to leave me with this woman.

"Yes, I guess you will."

"Great! My driver will be here to pick you up and take you to your hotel at noon. Is that all right with you?"

"That's fine," I replied, wishing that the pickup was earlier so I could escape the company and ill vibe of Madge Garrett.

"I'll be back around four. I wanna show you around Houston. In the meantime, make yourself comfortable around the house. The pool and the guy are out back." He grinned and kissed my hand.

"Why can't Ny—Ny . . . what is your name, young lady?" she asked in an irritated tone.

"Nyagra," I informed her.

"Whatever. Why doesn't the driver take you sightseeing while DayDay's at practice? He'll probably be tired when he comes back from practice. Plus he needs rest for his game tomorrow."

"No, Mamma. I wanna take her." DaVon pouted, suddenly reminding me of a spoiled 5-year-old.

She shrugged hesitantly. "Well, you know your mamma wants her baby boy happy so if that's what you wanna do, I guess it's all right. Go ahead. Show Natasha our beautiful city. I'm sure she's not used to such loveliness, coming from a city like New York with all its crime and pollution."

The name's Nyagra and she guesses it's all right? I thought. What kind of weird shit is going on here? Is this man 21 or 2?

"Thanks, Mommy. Gotta go." Mommy?

"Give Mommy some shuga," Madge demanded as she kissed DaVon on his lips.

"Ma, can you make sure that Nyagra's not bored while I'm gone?"

"Huuuum, Baby, I'm sorry but I do have things to do today. I'm sure Nirvana can amuse herself," she mumbled under her breath.

"Nyagra," I muttered under mine.

"See you beautiful ladies later." DaVon smiled as he exited the kitchen. I was a bit disturbed by the strange mamma and son interaction I'd just witnessed, but I chose not to concentrate on it. Trying to look busy so that I wouldn't have to engage in conversation with Madge, I quickly picked up the morning paper that DaVon had left behind. I didn't want her to say anything rude or obnoxious to me, because I knew I wouldn't sit by quietly in acceptance. I hadn't climbed up the corporate ladder by being passive and meek, and if pushed, I knew that as a reflex, I'd display the arrogant part of my personality without hesitation. Unfortunately, despite the false interest I attempted to show in the newspaper, I couldn't escape her wrath. No sooner did I hear the front door shut than she started in on me.

"Ya know, Nannette . . . ," she began with the same fire in her eyes as before—this time hotter.

"No disrespect, Ma'am, but my name is Nyagra," I interjected.

"Whatever . . . Listen up. My baby boy is a real ladies' man. He has women staying over here all the time. And I'm gonna tell you like I tell the rest of 'em: Don't go getting all strung out on my boy 'cause all you are to him is an easy lay. He's 21 years old and he's just sowin' his oats with your ass. And ya better use some sorta protection 'cause my DayDay ain't got no time for no babies. After all, football is his alpha and his omega."

Although I'd halfway seen it coming, I was still caught completely off guard by her blunt character assassination and ultimately felt utterly insulted. I truly felt like cursing her ass out and if I hadn't been in DaVon's house, I very well might have. However, I maintained my composure, took a deep breath, and with just as much fire in my own eyes, replied, "I understand that you are very protective of your son, Mrs. Garrett, as well you should be. I'm sure there are a lot of young women out there that would like to trap DaVon into being with them. Fortunately for you and for me, I am not one of them. With all due respect, Ma'am, for your information, I didn't sleep in your son's bed last night. I slept in a guest room. In fact, your son is in pursuit of me—not vice versa. So, it would be greatly appreciated if you wouldn't speak to me like I'm some common tramp. I'm the vice president of a very influential advertising agency in New York City and I came here to help your son's career. Don't you be the one to hurt it by making enemies with me."

I was bluffing, for I would never have allowed DaVon's mamma to lose the deal for him. He and I had way too much riding on it. But it felt really good to threaten her and put her controlling ass in her place at the same time.

"I'm not trying to make enemies, Nyagra. Oh, that's such a pretty name," she said with a totally different tone of voice and persona. "I love all my baby's girlfriends. You just seem like a nice girl and I don't want you to get hurt by falling for my baby boy."

"Thank you for the advice, Mrs. Garrett, and the breakfast." I falsely smiled as I got up from the table and left the kitchen. As I exited the room, I could've sworn I heard her swearing like a sailor, calling me all types of bitches. But I didn't care. I was quite sure that she'd treated other women her son dated in that manner, but her tactics could not and would not work on me. She was obviously a bully, but at 32 years old, I wasn't about to be intimidated by some controlling, domineering mamma in a DKNY sweatsuit who was afraid that one day her son might actually fall in love and she'd have to share him and his money with another woman. Her rough and tough mannerism didn't frighten me a bit because I saw right through her ass. This wasn't high school and I wasn't "clueless." Still, I knew that if I decided to truly get involved with DaVon, Mamma Garrett was certainly one to be wary of.

As the day progressed, I found out that the airports were tentatively slated to open sometime Saturday afternoon, which meant that I indeed had one more night to spend with DaVon. Not surprisingly, Trish had left eight messages for me at the hotel. Because I needed to waste time before returning to the Garrett estate, I decided to call her and give her the scoop. Although I knew that she would be ready and willing to provide me with all types of superficial advice, I needed to talk to someone. And she was the only person I would ever share that kind of juiciness with.

"I cannot believe you spent the night in DaVon Garrett's house!" she screamed, once I told her of my previous night's whereabouts.

"In the guest room," I clarified.

"Whatever! You still slept under his roof!"

"Nothing happened."

"You still have one more night to take care of that. But really, Ny, I don't understand why you just don't stay there until Sunday. Nobody will be looking for your ass until 9 A.M. Monday morning."

"I need to come home, Trish. I have to prepare a draft of this proposal. I'll never get anything done if I stay here for the entire weekend."

"Well, promise me that you'll fuck his brains out tonight—for the both of us." She laughed.

"I can't promise you that!" I exclaimed.

"Why not? Listen, if I wasn't madly in love with my husband, I'd be on the next plane to Houston to snatch that boy away from you. You don't know what to do with him anyway," she teased.

"You couldn't get here if you wanted to. The airports are shut down, remember!" I jokingly replied.

"Hey, Ny. You've been quite active these days. First Lover Boy, then Bill, who's been calling here asking for you by the way, and now fine ass DaVon Garrett. What have you been putting in your bath water, Girlfriend?"

"I don't know. Maybe you're finally rubbing off on me." I giggled.

"Well, I'll have you know that as much as I love my husband and my babies, I'm quite envious of all the fun you've been having lately."

Oh, if she only knew!

"Don't be. It hasn't all been fun. Mr. Bill Peterson was certainly no fun at all. In fact, he was quite the opposite," I said, remembering New Year's Eve and trying to shake the memory from my mind.

"I still can't believe that a big strong-looking man like William Peterson could only last two minutes in bed. And I can't believe he's on Viagra!" Trish cackled.

"Well, believe it, Girl. And even on Viagra he only lasted one minute—not two," I corrected.

"Damn. He sure had me fooled! That's why I think you should redeem yourself by sexin' DaVon Garrett all night long. You deserve it after what Bill did to you. And make sure you come home with all the juicy details."

"I'm playing it by ear. It depends on how the evening flows. If we naturally end up in bed, then so be it, but I'm not going to force anything. It's not like I'm planning on seducing him."

"I think that you should! Seduce that boy! Do you really think a 21-year-old kid is gonna resist a beautiful, intelligent, older and more experienced woman like yourself?"

"That's the problem. If I think about it, the age difference makes me very uncomfortable."

"Then don't think about it."

"It's so hard not to!"

"Look, Ny. You're an older woman—not an old woman! And it's not like you're gonna go falling in love with the brother or anything like that. You're just out for a good time, right?"

I was unable to answer without hesitation. Unfortunately, whenever I thought of having sex with a man, love was always lurking in the back of my mind, as well as in my heart. It wasn't as if I was in love with every guy I ever went to bed with. But in order for me to even consider engaging in sex, I had to at least feel that the guy was someone I would be able to eventually love. I guess that was why after sex I was usually completely infatuated or totally repulsed. That's simply how I was. To me, sex and love were either subsequent or simultaneous.

"Nyagra? I said it's not like you're gonna go falling in love or anything like that, right?" she repeated.

"Of course not," I finally responded.

"You're lying. Don't tell me you've fallen for this guy already. Have you?"

"No, no . . . " She knew me all too well.

"Nyagra, when are you going to stop being a hopeless romantic and stop confusing sex with love? Ever since we were teenagers, you've always fallen in love so damn easy! That's your damn problem! Trust me. I can tell from DaVon's interviews that he's a skilled and experienced ladies' man who's not even thinking about a serious relationship—never mind marriage. Do not go getting your heart all broken up!" Trish warned.

"Just relax. I am not in love with DaVon Garrett. And I'm not thinking about getting serious or marriage right now either. Plus, I've only known him twenty-four hours. He's just a really nice guy. And surprisingly, we happen to have a lot in common," I defensively informed her.

"I can hear it in your voice that it's more than just like, Nyagra Ensley. I don't know what it is, but it sure sounds like something's going on inside that unrealistically romantic head of yours. So maybe you shouldn't have sex with him. If he winds up being as good as I think he'll be in bed, you'll be totally whipped and strung-out, which will only lead to trouble."

"Oh, come on, Trish! You and I both know that I'm not the whipped and strung out type. He's just a nice guy. Anyway, this conversation is probably unnecessary because his mamma is a serious cock blocker."

"Oh, really?"

"Yeah. She's an insecure tyrant and control freak. I even had to put her in her place."

I proceeded to tell Trish all about the conversation I'd shared with Madge Garrett, and we laughed hysterically as I repeated each word of our heated dialogue. My conversation with Trish made me feel a bit more at ease with my situation with DaVon, but it also made me feel more cautious and alert. She was right; I shouldn't go falling for him. Even if it worked out for a moment, it could never last. If I decided to have sex with him, I would have to be very careful not to put my heart into it. But would I be able to remain completely emotionless as I lay in bed with DaVon Garrett? I was not one hundred percent sure I could. I decided not to think about it, especially since I didn't think it would actually happen with Madge lurking around. But on the other hand, Trish didn't know everything. DaVon was so different from the image he portrayed. He was nothing like his interviews, which was all that Trish had to go on. Still I knew I had to be very careful.

I checked out of the Ritz Carlton, but dreaded going back to the house where I might be cornered by Madge Garrett again. Unfortunately, I felt guilty keeping DaVon's driver, Koby, waiting so long. But since he was patient and appeared not to mind waiting for me, I requested that he take me to a department store where I could purchase an outfit. He took me to Lord & Taylor where I bought a red Ellen Tracy gabardine pantsuit that could be worn in either an upscale casual or semi-dressy setting. Since I had no idea what DaVon had planned for the evening, I also threw in a little black dress from Prada, a pair of Manalo Blatnik black satin pumps, red Adrienne Vittadini mules and a little red Christian Dior negligee—just in case.

After my mini shopping spree, Koby and I headed back to the house at 3:30 P.M. When we got there, thank goodness it was empty with the exception of the cleaning woman. I waited in the room where I'd slept for DaVon to return from practice. With great anticipation, I changed into my new outfit as I eagerly awaited his arrival. I was so anxious for him to return that I found it quite difficult to concentrate on the show I was watching on television. In fact, every little noise I heard, I hoped it was him coming up the stairs. Finally I felt someone's presence in the doorway. I turned around to see a young heavy set woman standing there looking at me like she had just sucked on a terribly sour lemon.

"May I help you?" she asked.

"Hi. I'm Nyagra Ensley, a friend of DaVon's," I replied, getting up from the chair and going over to the door where she stood. I reached out my hand to shake hers and she looked me up and down, choosing not to oblige me in any way. Since she looked a little familiar, I assumed she was one of his sisters who had inherited her mamma's shitty attitude and unfriendly mannerism.

"I'm Daphne, DaVon's sister. Does my brother know you're up here?" she abruptly questioned.

"Of course, he does. He invited me here," I replied, in my defense.

"Well, he obviously didn't feel that it was necessary to tell anyone else. DaVon is not the only one who lives here, ya know!"

I really didn't like the fact that not only was DaVon's mamma lurking around, but so was his evil ass sister. And God only knew who the hell else. However, not wanting to start off on the wrong foot with Daphne, I really tried to be nice by replying in a friendly tone. "Oh, well, I'm sure he was planning on telling you. He's just at practice right now." Maybe I could kill her with kindness.

"I know where the hell my brother is," she rudely said.

For the life of me I simply couldn't understand why the women in his family felt the need to be so damn nasty to me. Did I pose that much of a threat? Or did DaVon have so many females coming in and out of the house that his sister and mamma were just plain sick of it? I didn't know, but I was very determined to find out.

Lucky for me, I didn't look my age or else they surely would've tried to run me clear out of the city of Houston. Oh, if they only knew how much older I was than DaVon, they would've really tried to eat me alive! Determined not to be talked to and disrespected any further, I turned my back on Daphne and retreated back to the chair I'd been sitting in before she appeared. I opted not to say anything, since I had nothing nice to say. I heard her huff and walk down the winding staircase as I walked across the room. This sure is a possessive and unfriendly household, I thought to myself.

Feeling more uncomfortable than ever before, I was ecstatic when DaVon finally arrived back from practice at nearly 4:30.

"Sorry I'm a little late. There was an accident on the highway and traffic was backed up for miles." Licking his lips and looking me up and down, he smiled, "You look great! I thought you said you hadn't brought anything to wear?"

"Yeah, Koby was kind enough to take me to Lord & Taylor. He's a very nice guy."

"Yeah, he's my ace." DaVon smiled.

"Well, he's about the only one," I mumbled. "Well, am I dressed appropriately for whatever it is that you've planned for this evening?"

"Oh, yeah. Like I said, you look great. Not that I think you could look anything but," he complimented.

"Um, DaVon, did you happen to see your sister, Daphne?"

"No. Did you get to meet her?"

"Yeah, to say the least. And she didn't seem too happy that I was here."

"Who cares? I pay the bills in this house and I can have whoever I want to in it. She still doesn't get it."

"Still? If you don't mind me asking, how many women do you bring home, DaVon? And how often?"

"Oh, come on, Nyagra. I don't bring home a lot of women. My sisters and my mamma are just very overprotective, that's all. Don't pay them any mind."

He laughed. However, I didn't see anything funny in the day's events. After all, I had been rudely disrespected not once, but two times in one day. Furthermore, I obviously didn't expect him to tell me that he actually brought three to five women home each week; just like I did not expect Victor Reece to tell me that he was still married.

"DaVon, I'm just curious. Who lives in this house with you?" I sternly asked.

"Ma lives in the guest cottage and Daphne, Connie and Daphne's son, Sidney, live over in the west wing. That's all."

That was enough! And much more than I wanted to hear.

"I think I'm going to check back into the Ritz, DaVon. I'm not too keen on staying here with your family. If you lived here alone, it might be a different story."

"Oh, come on! They won't be in our way. They'll be all the way on the other side of the house."

"Thanks, but no thanks, DaVon. Besides, I'm going to try to get the earliest flight out of here in the morning. The airports should be up and running by then."

"Nyagra, I really want you to be a guest in my home. Please accept my invitation," he pleaded.

"I appreciate the hospitality you're trying to display and I'm certainly looking forward to the evening we're about to spend together. But I would really be a lot more comfortable in my own hotel room."

"Is there anything I can say or do to make you change your mind?"

I shrugged as I shook my head. "No."

He shook his head in disgust. "I'm sorry."

"It's OK, really it is. I'm just ready to get out of this house. What do you have planned for us?" I asked, trying to display a more pleasant attitude.

"Well, are you hungry?"

"Yeah," I replied, realizing that I had only eaten fresh fruit earlier that day.

"Great! I made reservations for us at Américas. It's a really fun place. I'm sure you'll like it!"

"Let's go!"

"After you."

DaVon packed all my belongings into the trunk of his silver metallic Porsche so that I wouldn't have to return to the Garrett estate at the end of the evening. He drove like a madman behind the wheel of that car and, although I was a little afraid for my life, it sure was fun as hell! We arrived at the restaurant in little time. DaVon was right; I did like it. Again DaVon was the center of attention as soon as we walked in the place with everyone either knowing him or wanting to. Kids and adults came up to us asking for autographs, and I could tell that DaVon loved every minute of it.

Watching him once again in public reinforced my initial idea that our endorsement would do wonders for his career as well as for StarzSports. Even prior to us walking through the door, I could tell that Américas was definitely a jumping place and we certainly had a great time. In fact, I came to realize that just being with DaVon was a lot of fun. He was simply a fun person. Over a table full of appetizers and drinks, we laughed and talked about everything from our past relationships to our New Year's resolutions.

"I wanna settle down this year," he told me, taking a sip of his Diet Coke.

"Oh, DaVon, you're only 21! You haven't even begun to explore the opposite sex!"

"In this day of AIDS and groupies with their lawsuits, I can't be doin' too much explorin'. My boy got that shit two years and is on his deathbed at 24 years old. That shit is scary."

"Well, you don't have to have sex with everyone you date. Look at us! Here we are in this restaurant just having a good time, laughing and talking. We're getting to know each other as people. That's the way it should always be." I smiled as I shoved a piece of calamari into my mouth.

"Yeah, well." He leaned over into my ear. "I'd much rather be makin' love to you."

He caught me completely off guard with that statement. I didn't think he was bold enough to come right out and say such a thing. Up until that moment, he had seemed to evade the subject of really developing a romance with me. I could tell he was attracted to me and the chemistry between us was undeniable. But with the exception of our passionate embrace the previous night, neither of us wanted to openly consider the other more than just a friend or business associate. That was until he made that comment, of course. Figuring that since he was bold and adventurous enough to make such a statement, I decided to run with it and explore the issue a little further.

"You could've made love to me last night, if you'd wanted to," I said coyly.

"You said that you couldn't, or I would have. I'm a gentleman."

"Yeah, I did say that, didn't I?" I laughed. He shook his head in agreement. "Well, I'm glad we didn't. People need to get to know each other better before they go hopping into bed. Like we're doing now. I like this," I continued.

He shrugged. "You're probably right."

The rest of the evening flowed superbly. After enjoying a delicious meal at Américas, DaVon and I enjoyed a special post-New Year's Alvin Ailey performance. All of Houston's elite attended the incredibly spectacular production, which paid homage to many great African-American legends including the Nicholas Brothers, Billie Holiday, and the fabulous Dorothy Dandridge. Of course, we had magnificent seats and went backstage after the show to meet the dancers, some of which DaVon already knew. It was an absolutely wonderful way to complete the evening and my visit to Houston.

It was almost eleven o'clock by the time I was handed the key to my room at the Ritz. Although it was relatively early, I explained to DaVon that I needed to get a good night's sleep in preparation for my flight back to New York City. Besides, I was quite tired from my recent surge of activities. As DaVon walked me to my room, I realized that I still wasn't sure if I was ready to engage in a sexual relationship with him. And up until the moment I stepped across the room's threshold, I was still confused. Sensing my obvious uncertainty, DaVon didn't force the issue. Being the gentleman he was, DaVon simply thanked me for a wonderful forty-eight hours and asked me if we could perhaps develop a relationship beyond the StarzSports endorsement. We exchanged telephone numbers, assured each other that we would keep in touch, and tightly embraced before saying goodbye. That was it. No lip locking. No tongue waltzing. Just a tight embrace.

As I entered room number 1407 all alone, I couldn't help but wonder if I should run and catch him before he drove off, drag him back to my room, and make love to him until the sun came up. I couldn't deny the fact that he aroused me tremendously—not only sexually, but intellectually. And this was quite scary to me. As I slipped the slacks from my suit down my legs and onto the floor, a million thoughts tossed inside my brain all at once, almost causing a dizziness to take over my body. How could a 21-year-old kid have such an effect on me? How could I be so attracted to him? Did he really find me desirable—a woman eleven years his senior? Why did he have to be so handsome and cute all at the same time? Why did his dimples have to turn me on so much? What was it about his full lips and dark eyes that turned me on so?

Although I was alone, I decided to sleep in the little red negligee I bought so that maybe I would at least feel sexy and perhaps dream of what might have been had I made love to DaVon Garrett. Just as I was about to go into the bathroom to brush my teeth, there was a knock at the door. I assumed that it was the concierge leaving an early check-out slip for me, but looked through the peephole to see DaVon standing there with a very worried look on his face. I assumed something was wrong and immediately opened the door, poking my head out, but hiding my scantily clad body behind it.

"Is everything OK? Did you forget something? Is your car all right?" I asked, worried that from the look on his face, something terrible had happened.

"Yeah, sort of," he replied, nudging the door of the room. "I've been trying to be cool for the past two nights. But I can't anymore. I need to show you how much I want you," he continued as he totally burst into the room, swooped me up in his arms and gently placed me on the edge of the queen-sized bed while he passionately kissed my entire body. As I disappeared beneath his robust physique, I was completely helpless in his arms and totally unable to resist.

He'd caught me so off guard that it actually took me a few seconds to truly digest what was really happening. The scene played like the magnificently choreographed show we had viewed earlier that evening. I suddenly felt like one of those fabulously graceful dancers being caressed in his strongly developed arms. It didn't seem real. But it was. And catching me off guard made me powerless. I was so stunned that I almost couldn't move. However, once I became coherent, I began to return the passion built up inside of me for him with full force. Despite the heat of our desire, we somehow managed to shut off the lights, allowing us to view each other only by the romantic light of the moon. Passion engulfed the atmosphere and in a matter of mere moments, both of us were undressed and ready to receive each other in a way that only two people who shared our colossal chemistry could. The warmth of his soft, moist tongue tickled my nose, my lips, and ultimately, my breasts. He fondled every nook and cranny of my body as if he were strategically glazing melted butter over a lightly toasted Thomas' English muffin. I could tell he wanted to be absolutely one hundred percent certain that I was good and ready before we plunged into paradise together. And by the time he was finished with his careful preparation, I definitely was.

Although I was concentrating on DaVon and what was about to happen, I couldn't help but quickly think of Victor Reece and how there had been so little foreplay between us. It absolutely amazed me how a man half Victor's age could seem so skilled and aware of a woman's sexual needs—physically as well as emotionally. In spite of the fact that Victor had appeared to be a good lover, as I felt the warmth of DaVon's splendidly perfect physique, I suddenly realized that Victor actually hadn't had a clue.

The moonlight glared through the sheerly-draped, hotel-room window, and I could see his flawlessly-sculpted brawny shadow as we placed the condom on together. I couldn't believe how comfortable I felt with him and how happy I was that he understood the importance of safe sex. The air conditioner cooled the room, but perspiration ran down our naked bodies as if we were on the hot sands of Jamaica at high noon. When he finally penetrated my flesh, I felt a burst of heat and energy flowing throughout the veins and cells of my body almost like a plastic syringe filled with some new type of magical heroin. By the time we simultaneously arrived at our pinnacle, I felt completely stupefied. Like a paralyzed junkie, I laid there with the ultimate high.

I awoke to the sound of a cell phone ringing furiously. I rolled over to see DaVon still sleeping peacefully and looking like a cuddly, oversized toddler. It was 8:50 a.m., which meant I was running behind schedule. I wanted to be at the airport by nine to standby for any aircraft heading to New York. However, after the prior evening's events, it would've taken little persuasion to get me to stay in Texas for another night. It's funny how good sex can make a girl change her mind about a lot of things.

The cell phone continued to ring and after searching for mine, I realized that it was DaVon's that was chiming out of control. With my naked body still wrapped in the queen-sized sheet from the bed, I picked up his slacks from the floor and removed the phone to see an entire row of "MAMMAs" flashing across the screen. Concerned that she might be in trouble, I quickly woke him to let him know that she was frantically searching for him.

"It's Mamma!" he exclaimed, jumping out of the bed and tossing on his pants. He ran over to the phone, obviously still a bit disoriented. "Mamma? Ma, is everything all right?" I heard him ask. "I'm sorry, Mamma. I'm fine. I didn't mean to make you worry," he continued in the same childlike manner he had displayed that morning in his kitchen. "I was just out with a friend, Mamma. Yes, yes, Mamma, I'm with a girl. Yes, the girl you met yesterday. No, she's not like that, Mamma. Yes, I know I'm supposed to take you shopping every Saturday, Mamma. I'm sorry, Mamma. I know I should have called. It won't happen again, Mamma. Mamma, don't cry. OK, Mamma. I'm on my way."

I could not believe my goddamn ears! DaVon quickly hung up the phone. And as he hastily threw on his clothes, he turned to me and said, "I'm so sorry, Nyagra. I had a magnificent time, but I gotta go."

"DaVon, is something wrong with your mamma?" I asked, knowing that she was perfectly fine and that this was simply her tactic to get him out of my presence.

"No, she's OK. Just a little worried, that's all. But I did forget that I have to take her shopping," he replied, buttoning his shirt.

"Shopping? DaVon, it's only nine am. Why would you want to go shopping at 9 a.m.?"

"She likes to get an early start."

"Oh."

I found it hard to digest that the man who had meticulously made love to me all night long like a skilled practitioner was a mamma's boy who was unbelievably easily manipulated. I watched him hastily dress as if the hotel fire alarm were sounding for him to be at his mamma's beck and call. It nauseated me almost as much as Bill Peterson had on that dreadful New Year's Eve. If this was the kind of control his mamma had on him, I knew there would never be a chance for us. But subconsciously I pretty much knew there would never be a chance for us anyway. I don't even know why I decided to indulge myself. I knew from the start how difficult it was for me to emotionally separate love from lust. I've simply never been able to do it. And now I was beginning to think my romantic escapades were starting to take a toll on my physical well-being. I literally felt sick. Just as I had vomited my brains out on New Year's Eve after experiencing Bill Peterson's sexual insult, I knew that if this sexual interlude turned out to be a mere one-night stand (because his mamma was "cock blocking" and he was too stupid to realize it), I was sure that there would be an ulcer brewing somewhere inside my stomach.

"You will stay one more night, won't you, Nyagra?" he asked, with his hand on the doorknob.

"I don't think so, DaVon," I said, turning my back to him and looking out the window over the city of Houston. I realized that I surely couldn't bring myself to stay now that he had clearly displayed his mamma's boy tendencies. I kept my eyes on the swiftly moving cars below. Thanks to the incident in his kitchen with his mamma, her phone call and his sister's attitude, I was so turned off that I didn't even want to look at him.

"Why not? I'll come back after I take Mamma shopping," he assured me.

"I've stayed in your city long enough. I have to get back to New York," I softly answered.

"Well, at least let me drive you to the airport," he pleaded. Figuring that it would be harmless to allow him to drive me, I agreed.

"I have to take a shower. Do you think your mamma can wait?" I sarcastically asked.

"Well," he said, looking at his watch, "how long will that take?"

"DaVon, go ahead. I'll take a taxi." I huffed as I walked to the bathroom like a Chinese geisha, still tightly wrapped in the sheet. I gently kicked the door closed behind me and heard him call before he left the room,

"OK, Nyagra. Have a safe flight! I'll call you!"

I let the water beat down my spine at a temperature hotter than usual, almost as if I wanted to wash DaVon off my skin.

Maybe I shouldn't take this personally, I told myself. He probably just really loves his mamma. Who doesn't?

As I stood there in the shower stall thinking about DaVon, I resolved myself to the understanding that there could never be any more to my relationship with him than great sex and conversation. Of course, part of me was fine with that, and part of me—my more idyllic, fairy tale side—wasn't. Still, I reminded myself that I had known any long-term romantic connection with DaVon was an impossibility. I had already known that his age, his popularity and our business connection would be a hindrance to any relationship we might want to develop. But now, I also saw that I couldn't even attempt to compete with his mamma for his affections. I knew that the early feelings I felt for him were way too good to be true. I had been well aware of the fact that getting emotionally involved with him could lead and would lead to nothing but pure disappointment. Thus, once again I had no one to blame but myself. And with those thoughts in mind, right then and there as I stood in the shower lathering up my body with Ivory soap, I decided that the next time I saw DaVon Garrett would be to film that StarzSports commercial and nothing more.

Eleven

Thank goodness I was able to catch an 11 A.M. flight back to New York City and arrive home by three. There was at least two feet of untouched snow on my lawn, but I was so happy to be home that I actually welcomed the idea of shoveling. As I stuck the key in my front door, I experienced an incredible feeling of relief. Unsurprisingly, I had a million messages on my answering machine, including Trish, DaVon and even that lying ass Victor. I just couldn't understand why he chose to continue to pursue me when I'd made it quite clear that I had absolutely no intention of communicating with him.

Tired and weary from the flight as well as from my recent activities, I chose not to return any calls. I needed to lie down in my own bed, and I needed to do it right then. I wanted to rest up before I began working on the proposal I had to prepare for the StarzSports account. Although I had the standard Newman & Stein proposal on my computer, I had to clear my mind in order to alter the document to fit DaVon's particular circumstances. I momentarily put the proposal out of my head, tossed myself across my fluffy comforter, closed my eyes and imagined that I was sailing on a velvety, white cloud. It felt so damn good to be back home in my own bed, for it seemed as though I had been away for ages.

On Monday morning, Newman & Stein was finally up, running, and business was usual. I walked into my office to see another bouquet of flowers sent from Bill Peterson. I hoped it wouldn't be too long before he finally got the hint that I wasn't interested. I thought about calling and trying to let him down easy. I'd tell him that we could still be friends. But remembering his New Year's Eve performance, I decided against it. He wasn't even worth my burp, never mind a full-fledged conversation.

The holidays were indeed over, and everyone was back in the office chatting about their festivities and vacations. Once again, our busy office moved about like the stock market with everyone discussing the prospects of new clients and closing old deals. I must admit, I had missed the hustle and fast-paced environment of my office, as well as the exhilarating feeling of accomplishment.

Becoming fully engrossed in my work as if I'd never been away, I checked my planner and attempted to strategize a manner in which I would fit every important issue into my hectic day. It was Newman & Stein policy to alert all employees of any new business details. It was our way of making everyone feel involved. So I had Judy send out a company-wide e-mail announcing that my trip went extremely well, and if everything continued at the momentum, DaVon Garrett would be the star of our StarzSports commercial. Needless to say, it was one hundred percent unanimous that DaVon was the perfect athlete for the ad.

Later that morning I had a conference call with Mortimer Stein, who was still on vacation in the Swiss Alps with his wife, Maria. I told him every (well, maybe not every) detail of my meeting with DaVon Garrett and he was quite excited. I also informed him that I was certain DaVon would be fair regarding his fee. That all he was truly interested in was his own shoe. Of course, I would have to discuss it further with StarzSports. I had briefly tossed the idea around with Marcia Keller, who thought it was a good idea, but ultimately I knew the final decision would be made by Victor Reece. And that was a conversation I was definitely not looking forward to.

"I leave it in your hands, Nyagra," Stein said. "I have faith in you and know that you will make sure this deal is extremely profitable for Newman & Stein. As I'm sure you already know, your next step should be to go to Atlanta and sit down with StarzSports' people once again. Get an idea of what they are and are not willing to agree to before you send this kid that proposal." He stated the words I dreaded hearing. I was hoping to discuss these matters over the telephone with StarzSports—specifically Victor.

"Mr. Stein, don't you think a conference call would suffice? I'm so swamped here; getting away now would be almost impossible," I stated, hoping he would agree. Unfortunately, he didn't.

"Usually it would. However, with a company the magnitude of StarzSports, I think it would show good client relations and would demonstrate that we have them in our highest regard if we discussed the matter face-to-face. Plus, let's not forget that we are extremely interested in establishing a very personable relationship with them. Don't worry about your other commitments, Nyagra. They'll all be there when you return." Little did he know that unfortunately, I already had established this so called "personal" relationship—maybe a little too personal. "We want to make them feel as though they're doing business with a friend," he continued.

The day zoomed by faster than I thought it would. The new version of Tré Donquio's Nabisco commercial arrived with perfect lighting. I knew he could adjust the brightness if he tried. With the new cookie advertisement copy in hand, the perfect athlete ninety-nine percent secured for StarzSports, and a big boost of confidence, I was ready to take on the world and everyone in it—with the exception of Victor.

Trish was so proud of me when I told her of my rendezvous with DaVon. I deliberately downplayed my true feelings for him by telling her that I wasn't getting all caught up emotionally. I was simply taking the relationship for what it was worth. The truth was that DaVon and I had talked nearly every day since my departure from Houston, and I felt uncommonly good about it. During each conversation, he always stressed his tremendous desire to see me again. Surely, I was flattered that DaVon Garrett wanted to be with me. In fact, it was a huge boost for my recently bruised ego. He seemed to make it his business to speak with me regularly, so I actually started to believe that DaVon and I might have some potential, despite his overbearing mamma. However, I still refused to totally let myself go. Since we had only been communicating over the phone, it was rather easy to remain a bit detached.

The next couple of weeks were hectic. Upon departing for Atlanta to meet with StarzSports reps, I had a terrible case of diarrhea, no doubt caused by my nerves, which were completely on edge from the mere thought of having to sit across from Victor. Upon my arrival at the modern gray skyscraper that housed the StarzSports offices, I tried to keep my composure while my armpits poured out at least a gallon of water as I rode the mirrored elevator up to the twenty-second floor. I was greeted by Marcia Keller and to my surprise (and delight), a gentleman by the name of John Burke.

When I was informed that Victor had an emergency meeting in Philadelphia with Allen Iverson, I did a thousand mental cartwheels and was transformed into my regular confident, unintimidated self again. Without Victor there to make me feel uncomfortable, I was able to easily get through the meeting and convince Ms. Keller and Mr. Burke of everything I felt to be true. The proposal had been faxed to StarzSports prior to my arrival, so they were already privy to its contents, which permitted the dialogue to proceed at a rather fast pace. They informed me that Victor had also read the proposal and had actually been pleased with what I suggested they offer DaVon. Thus, Marcia and John agreed to everything in the proposal, including fee, running dates, and even the sneaker issue. Evidently Victor was in favor of giving DaVon Garrett his own shoe, which I knew would make DaVon ecstatic. The meeting flowed with unusual ease. It seemed as though Victor was making a conscious effort to ensure that this would be easy for me. Perhaps it was his way of apologizing. Whatever the reason for their compliance, I left the corporate headquarters of StarzSports as one happy camper.

"We're coming to New York to play the Jets. Why don't we hook up and celebrate?" DaVon suggested during one of our late-night phone chat sessions. DaVon had signed the StarzSports contracts, and everyone was looking forward to creating a profitable DaVon Garrett advertising campaign. The Cowboys had made it to the Super Bowl, and DaVon's popularity looked as if it was about to skyrocket. The negotiations went well, and I must say, rather swiftly. It had been my goal (and strategy) to get DaVon's signature on the contracts before the Cowboys played in the Super Bowl, and definitely prior to winning it. I knew the cost of a Super Bowl winner was far more than what StarzSports desired to pay. If DaVon's people had been truly smart, they would've advised him to hold out for a little while longer, but they didn't. So, thanks to accurate timing on my part and ignorance on theirs, StarzSports would be able to have a Super Bowl player for far less than the true cost of one. This tactic gained me plenty of points with StarzSports and Newman & Stein. Though I'm sure that my concealed relationship with DaVon helped the situation immensely; his people were quite easygoing and simply eager to close. Not to mention the fact that DaVon was hungry and I couldn't have felt more accomplished.

"I'd like that," I replied. Perhaps this time we could completely get into each other, since his mamma would be a thousand miles away in Houston.

"The game is Sunday, but I'll fly in after practice on Friday so that we'll be able to spend some time together. I've really missed you."

Talking to him and hearing him say such nice things gave me a great feeling inside. It had been a long time since I had felt like I was in the process of really developing a relationship with someone. And once again, I found myself eagerly awaiting the arrival of my handsome, rich suitor. My only hope was that it would turn out a lot better than the last time.

After what felt like the busiest week of my life, it was finally Friday. I left the office early to drive home and shower before meeting DaVon. After such a productive week, I figured I deserved a one o'clock departure. Stuck in bumper-to-bumper traffic and bored out of my mind, I decided to call Trish on my cell.

"You've gotta just let me meet him!" Trish begged. I suddenly had a flashback of the conversation we'd shared prior to my leaving for Houston.

"OK. If you and Rodney aren't busy, why don't we meet for brunch tomorrow? I really want him all to myself tonight," I said. DaVon's flight would be touching down in exactly one hour and I was to meet him at the Hyatt Regency at six.

"Oh, I'm catering an anniversary party tomorrow night. It's my first job but it's not until seven, so I should have enough time to meet you guys in the early part of the afternoon."

"Trish, you've got a catering job? I'm so happy for you! Why didn't you tell me?!"

"Oh, with all the talk about DaVon Garrett, I totally forgot!"

"You totally forgot? You can't meet us! You've got to cook! Are you crazy? How big is the job?"

"About thirty."

"You're bananas if you think you can come all the way to the city to eat with us and still be able to prepare food for thirty people! You'd better not blow it this time, Trish. Rodney will kill you if lose any more of his money. Plus, he made me promise that I would be your financial adviser. We need to sit down and go over the figures. I can't believe you didn't even discuss this with me!"

"It's not that big of a deal, Ny. But maybe you're right. I guess it wouldn't be too smart to come all the way to Manhattan when I have to roast and stuff thirty-five Cornish hens. Why don't you bring him by the house?"

"Trish, keep your mind on your hens."

"Oh, come on. I really wanna meet him!"

"I'll call you tomorrow if, and only if, we're in the neighborhood. I may decide to bring him by my house anyway."

"All right." She sighed.

"In any event, I'll call you so that we can go over the expenses for this catering job. You did keep receipts for everything you bought, didn't you?"

"Yeah, I think so . . . "

"You think so? Don't start this unprofessional shit again, Trish."

"I'm not. I said I kept them, didn't I?"

"You said you thought you did."

"I did." She huffed.

"Whatever. I have to go. We'll talk later."

"OK. Good luck tonight."

"Thanks." I smiled as I wondered if I would need it.

The crowd in the lobby of the Hyatt Regency was absolutely horrendous! At 6:20 p.m., there still was no sign of DaVon. I figured the traffic from the airport was heavy and that he would arrive any moment.

To make sure that we didn't miss each other, I stood at the front desk, figuring that he would have to stop to check in. Finally, at nearly 6:45, I saw DaVon enter the lobby of the hotel. To his left was a bellhop carrying two large pieces of Gucci luggage. To his right, wearing a full-length, black mink swing coat with her hair in an upswept do, was none other than his mamma, Madge Garrett. I nearly fainted! My jaw dropped and I was speechless as he walked toward the desk. He saw me, and with a colossal smile, gave me a soft peck on the cheek.

"Hi," I stuttered, barely able to get the word out.

"Hi! You look great!" he complimented. "Nyagra, you remember Mamma, don't you?" I barely nodded my head as if to say, "Yeah, I remember this heffa."

Without even acknowledging me, this woman said to her son, "Come, come. Let's check into our rooms. It's terribly crowded down here and I must freshen up before we go to the play."

I could not believe that this man had brought his mamma with him on our special weekend celebration! I had spent almost $200 at Victoria's Secret for his ass! Were they sharing a room, too? And what the hell was this I was hearing? Did he plan to take her to a Broadway play tonight and if so, what the hell was I supposed to do? Join them? I think not! I really tried to keep my cool. It was probably the hardest thing I ever had to do, but I was determined not to allow this woman to manipulate me into blowing my stack. Then she would surely have something tangible against me to complain about. I could hear her saying, "Oh, DayDay, this girl has such a bad temper! She's trying to come between us, DayDay!" Hell no! I would not allow this old battle-ax to beat me. Every game I play, I win. So as we stood there at the front desk of the Hyatt Regency, I knew it was on . . .

The woman behind the counter began to type in DaVon's credit card information. We all stood there silently until he began, "Mamma's never been to New York. So when I told her that I was comin', she asked if she could join me. Of course, I'd never say 'no' to my Mamma."

I flashed a fake smile, ready to slap him.

"Oh, DayDay, isn't she a pretty girl? Now that's the type of girl Mamma would want you to marry. Your children would be absolutely gorgeous!" Madge exclaimed, referring to the young lady behind the counter. She was attractive, but I didn't think she had anything on me. The girl blushed, but little did she know that if she were in my shoes, she'd be receiving the very same treatment! It obviously was just Madge's way of trying to be disrespectful and make me feel uncomfortable. She was successful, for I could feel my body temperature rise beneath the collar of my Harve Bernard velvet pantsuit, but I refused to let her know it. But aside from her behavior, what really pissed me off was that DaVon said nothing to his mamma about her rude behavior. Nor did he apologize to me for her obvious disrespectful conduct. She hadn't even said "hello" to me, for goodness sake! Still, he simply grinned like a wide-eyed puppy dog who'd just been tossed his favorite ball. And my fury only increased as I stood quietly beside this "boy" and his overbearing, manipulative mamma. I was so completely enraged that I felt like making a quick and quiet exit. But that's exactly what Madge wanted me to do, and I refused to give her the satisfaction. Be that as it may, I couldn't have left if I'd wanted to, for I seemed to be completely paralyzed by my insurmountable anger.

While I stood at the front desk of the Hyatt Regency, a little bitty voice in my head instructed me to stay put and play the scene out. Perhaps DaVon's mamma would be meeting a friend here in New York, and my hostility was unnecessary. Maybe I would get to be alone with DaVon after all.

I took it as a good sign when the reservations clerk handed them two separate keys. The rooms were on the same floor, but separate nonetheless. At least we would be able to shut her ass out at the end of the evening. It had been over two weeks since I had seen DaVon and experienced the warm embrace of his strong, masculine arms. No matter what, I was determined to get Madge Garrett out of our way so that DaVon and I could pick up where we'd left off in Houston.

The thickness in the air could've been cut with a carving knife as we parted in the hallway, and DaVon and I headed toward his quarters. Thank God Madge chose to go to her room to freshen up, for I felt it was necessary to speak to him in private. It was evident that she didn't want to leave me alone with her 'baby boy', but it would've been too obvious if she had followed us to his room.

"I won't be long, Son," she said snidely, as she walked away. For my benefit, I was sure.

DaVon's room was picture-perfect and romantic. There were fresh-cut flowers in every corner and the lavender bedspread seemed to be begging us to make love on it. We had barely crossed the threshold before DaVon embraced me tightly and smothered me with affection. Of course, I was quite receptive to his advances. But I needed to express my feelings regarding his mamma's presence.

"DaVon." I gently pushed him away. "Couldn't your mamma have visited New York another time? This was supposed to be our time."

"Oh, she won't be in our way. After we go see The Lion King, we'll tuck her in and it'll just be me and you."

"DaVon, you didn't mention anything about going to a long-ass Broadway show when we spoke last night—even if it is The Lion King. Nor did you mention the fact that she was coming. I don't want to spend the evening with you and your mamma. Can't you find someone else to take her?"

"Mamma doesn't know anybody in New York! We can't just desert her! I know I didn't tell you, but she just asked me this morning. Come on, Nyagra, be a good sport."

"What time is the show?" I agitatedly questioned.

"Eight, so we'd better get ready. But I'm sure it'll be over by ten and I'll be all yours after that."

"Well, you'd better be. And no interruptions. Just you and me." I pouted.

He kissed me gently on my forehead with those soft, luscious lips of his and smiled. "Just you and me."

That goddamn play ran past 11 o'clock! It was good as hell, but long never the less and by the time we returned to the hotel, I was completely exhausted. The week's events were finally catching up with me, and all I wanted to do was lie down and go to sleep. In order to salvage what was left of the evening, DaVon suggested that we all order room service and eat in our own rooms. I was proud that he'd made the suggestion. Maybe he's not such a mamma's boy after all, I thought. After hearing such an idea, Mamma Garrett nearly had a fit. You would have thought DaVon had committed a mortal sin.

"I cannot believe you would suggest that your own mamma, the woman who carried you in her body for nine long, uncomfortable months, the woman who wiped your snotty little nose and changed your dirty, smelly diapers, the woman who still has the scar on her stomach where they cut her open after twenty-six hours of labor so that you could come into this world! I cannot believe you would suggest that your own mamma order room service and dine alone in her room! How disrespectful can you get? This cannot be my son talking!" she raved, glaring at me. "Oh, your daddy must be turning over in his grave!"

"Ma, it's the same food as the restaurant downstairs!" he whined like a scolded child.

"That is not the point! How could you even suggest that I eat all alone in my room? Are you trying to get rid of me?"

"No, Ma. Of course not."

"Then you eat with me in the restaurant! How dare you suggest such a thing to your mamma! I'm surprised at you and utterly disappointed!"

If I thought I could've gotten away with it, I would've choked the shit out of her and left her on the hotel floor for dead. But once again, I controlled myself and looked up at the ceiling as she continued to go on and on about the shame and embarrassment his father must be feeling "up there in heaven." I absolutely couldn't believe my eyes or my ears.

Despite my head pounding from exhaustion and from the irritating sound of her voice, we ultimately ate at The Olive Garden across the street from the hotel. I was too angry to express myself. I did not utter one word during the entire meal. I simply watched DaVon's mamma—who now appeared happier than a hog in a pile of shit—manipulate him into granting her every wish. It was absolutely pathetic.

After the long-ass play and the annoying (not to mention boring) dinner conversation, I was way too tired to drive home. So I had no choice but to stay in DaVon's room overnight. I wasn't in the mood to be touched and resolved myself to the fact that DaVon and I would not amount to anything. Not to mention the fact that the emotional roller coaster I was riding was really making me dizzy. I realized that I would never be able to get beyond or compete with the control his mamma had on him.

As soon as I stepped across the threshold, I walked directly to the beautiful king-sized bed and silently laid across its fluffy covers. I refused to change into the skimpy little negligee I had in my overnight bag since I didn't want to give him the wrong idea. After that evening, there would be no hanky-panky up in that room. So I simply laid there, completely clothed.

In an attempt to break the ice, DaVon tried to make small talk but clearly recognized my aggravation.

"I know Mamma can be a little overbearing sometimes, but she means well. Really, she does," he began as he sat beside me on the lavender comforter. "I apologize for her behavior. And I thank you for being so understanding."

Call me a sucker, or desperate to be loved, but his words actually made me feel better. Missing him so much took over my emotions, and I reached over and gave him a hug.

Maybe I shouldn't let that cute little satin outfit go to waste, I thought. Just as I batted my eyes, the sparks began to fly between us again. I was totally submerged by the chemistry we shared. My mind told me I should run as far away from that hotel room as I could. That I shouldn't look back. That I should keep my relationship with DaVon purely professional. DaVon was the biggest mamma's boy I had ever met. I knew I could never deal with that. But I'd also known that in Houston, and it hadn't stopped me from being with him there. I realized that if I didn't think about the true details of what I was doing, I would be able to enjoy my moment with DaVon.

Take this for what it's worth, I told myself. As DaVon sent me into a sensual world filled with ultimate ecstasy, I decided that I should only deal with the present, not the future.

In spite of my fatigue, DaVon and I made love all night long. Nothing seemed to matter as we experienced new sensual heights over and over again. It was as if we were the only two people on the planet.

As we enjoyed each other, I couldn't help but to be interrupted by the telephone, which rang several times. Certain that it was his mamma, we ignored it and continued to enjoy and share our sweaty passion. In all my thirty-two years on earth, I had never experienced such excitement. This 21-year-old "kid" had me swinging from the chandelier, and there wasn't even one in the room! Just as I was about to reach my third pinnacle, to my immeasurable surprise, I heard the door and I opened my eyes to see Madge Garrett in the doorway screaming, "DaVon, what on earth are you doing?!!!"

DaVon, his naked black ass still in the air, came to a complete halt, looked me in my eyes, and uttered, "Mamma?"

"I was calling you on the phone but I can see you're busy!" she blurted.

All in one motion, I slipped my body from beneath DaVon, tightly gripped the sheet around me and screamed at the top of my lungs, "GET THE HELL OUTTA HERE, YOU GODDAMN PAIN IN THE ASS! GET A LIFE! CAN'T YOU SEE WE'RE HAVING SEX?!!!! YES YOUR BABY BOY, YOUR DAYDAY AND I ARE FUCKING! DO YOU KNOW WHAT THE HELL THAT IS?!!! SO WHY DON'T YOU GO BACK TO YOUR FUCKIN' ROOM AND STAY THERE, GODDAMN IT, YOU CRAZY CONTROLLING BITCH!"

Mamma Garrett let out a hefty cry and ran from the room as fast as her feet could carry her as if her life depended on it. And it did. I'd had enough and was surely ready to give her a beat-down she'd never forget—even if she was almost twice my age. At that moment I didn't give a damn who she'd given birth to.

"Nyagra, how could you disrespect Mamma like that? You made her cry!" DaVon scolded, getting up and tossing on his pants. He was evidently going to comfort her. I wasn't surprised but said nothing to him. I immediately got dressed, grabbed my bag, and made the exit I should've made hours earlier. I was a bit amazed at myself because I wasn't that angry. It was damn near funny to me. I guess I should've seen it coming. I surely wasn't as upset as I had been on Christmas Eve. I wasn't even as disgusted as I had been on New Year's Eve. And I definitely didn't feel like shedding a tear. I had no remorse for screaming at that cock-blocking busybody bitch. She had it coming, and really, so did he. At that moment, I didn't give a damn how good the sex had been. This was the absolute last draw! I'd had it with DaVon Garrett, his manipulative mamma and the whole male species in general!

Twelve

The days following the incident with DaVon were extremely difficult for me. I fell into an intensely deep depression. Although I had recently made several professional accomplishments, I still felt like a total failure. I also felt like a cheap whore. In fact, my self-esteem was at an all-time low. If it hadn't been for work, I wouldn't have left my bed. Moreover, all I did do was go to and from the office. I talked to no one about anything other than work, and each day I could not wait for the clock to strike five. Feeling as though everything was closing in around me, I knew I had to get away to clear my head, my heart and my mind. I needed to go someplace where I could hear myself think, and I simply couldn't seem to do it at home or at the office.

I truly needed to take command of my life and regain control of my emotions, so I decided to take a weekend trip. I had to be alone, by choice—not because I ran out on someone, was stranded, let down or dumped. I had to make the conscious decision to go somewhere before I lost myself any further. It was really a matter of emotional life or death. So, without a clue as to where I was heading, I frantically called my travel agent.

"OK, Nyagra, where do you want to go?" she asked.

"I don't know, Donna. Someplace serene."

"Someplace serene? Nyagra, are you all right? You sound a little weird."

"No, everything is fine. I just need to get away. Somewhere that's quiet. Not a lot of people," I answered as I sat at the breakfast bar in my kitchen and held back the tears of depression that so desperately wanted to fall.

"Are you going alone?"

"Yes."

"Someplace warm or cold?"

"It doesn't matter."

"Well, if you're only going for the weekend, you don't want to go too far, do you?"

"It doesn't matter."

"Hold on. Let me pull up a couple of suggestions on the computer."

As I silently held the receiver to my ear waiting for her to return, I suddenly got an idea of exactly where I needed to be in order to fully experience my emotional retreat. It suddenly seemed so clear and I wondered why I had not thought of it before. It was obvious that there was only one place where I could go to truly find myself. At that moment, for the first time in so long, I was actually sure about something.

"The Caribbean is a short plane ride and absolutely beautiful at this time of the year," Donna began once she arrived back on the phone.

"No, Donna. I need to go to Niagara Falls," I interjected.

"Niagara Falls?"

"Yes. My namesake."

"Nyagra, that sounds good and all that, but the weather conditions up by Canada are horrendous at this time of the year. I mean, just look at all the snow we've been getting. It's twenty times worse up there!"

"I don't care. That's where I want to go. That's where I have to go."

"OK. So Niagara Falls, here you come . . . "

Thirteen

It was impossible to get a flight to Canada and after numerous attempts, Donna and I decided that I should just hop in my Range Rover and drive to my hiding place. I was a little hesitant about taking the voyage alone, but it was something that I knew I had to do in order to regain my sanity and to keep what little I had left. I knew that if I hung around the city any longer, I would snap.

So at 4 A.M. Saturday morning I jumped in my truck armed with plenty of reading material, my very favorite CDs, a Thermos filled with Swiss Miss instant cocoa, and my brain that was spinning a mile a minute. With almost no one on the road but me, I did damn near 80 trying to get to my destination.

Despite the fresh snowfall, the roads were clear and dry, obviously recently plowed. Still, I wanted to slow down, really I did. Thank God, I didn't get pulled over by a state trooper. But it was as if I could hear the Park Place Bed & Breakfast softly whispering my name and pulling me toward its doors.

So anxious to arrive, I drove non-stop until 8 A.M. I don't know how I did it, but I didn't even stop to pee. I just wanted to get there and after four hours of driving, I was still only a little bit more than halfway there. In any event, I knew that with my lead foot on the gas, I would be at my namesake as soon as it was earthly possible.

As I drove up north, I couldn't help but notice the winter wonderland. The bare trees layered with clean white snow resembled a perfect picture from a postcard. In spite of all the emotional drama, I suddenly realized that I actually had a lot to be thankful for—that there was so much more to me and the world than my man troubles. Nature sure has a way of letting you know that your existence is just a small entity in a very grand picture.

"God will send me my mate when He's good and ready," I said aloud as I swayed my head to the smooth and soulful sounds of Faith Evans.

It was almost noon by the time I checked into my room at the Park Place Bed & Breakfast. The large cozy, tranquil cottage was the perfect place for me to get my think on. It was countrified but also modern, and the people were extremely friendly and accommodating. My room, which was decorated in soft pastel colors, had an inviting queen-sized, wicker-framed bed in its center. The accompanying furniture blended right in with the room's wicker accents, making the room come fully together. I had a corner room with a view of the inn's garden, which was beautifully sprinkled with fresh fallen snow. Needless to say, I was more than pleased by Donna's recommendation of the getaway with its warm and soothing atmosphere. I couldn't have chosen a better place to spend my weekend of thought and revelation.

After driving for such a long time, I was pretty surprised that I wasn't totally exhausted. In fact, for some reason I had this burst of energy and was compelled to quickly get to the falls. Although it was quite chilly, the sun was shining particularly bright, which I believed was God's way of sending me a little bit of hope.

After putting my things away, of course I had to take a hot shower. Sitting for so many hours had made my body feel grimy and sweaty, creating a desperate need to feel the hot trickle of water running down the fold of my back. But I didn't savor the sensation for long. I was there for a reason and was hell- bent on making sure that I did exactly what I'd come to do. I quickly jumped in and out, only allowing the steaming water to beat down on my spine for a few short moments. Once completely dried off, I hopped into a thick DKNY velour sweat-suit and sneakers. It wasn't the time to be fashionable, although I had paid $140 for that outfit (old habits die hard.) But I really just wanted to be warm and comfortable. I knew that the temperature would prob-ably be lower by the water.

Once ready, I went down to the inn's lobby and spoke to the front desk attendant who gave me directions to the falls, which were only ten minutes away. For some reason, as I drove along the narrow streets, my heart pounded with excitement. It was almost as if I were going to meet Prince Charming instead of fifty billion gallons of water.

I parked my truck at the site and nervously walked toward the observation area. The desk clerk had told me that because of the cold, this was their slowest season. Of course, this pleased me since the last thing I wanted was to be surrounded by a crowd. And to my ultimate delight, it was pretty desolate. I could hear the falls before I could see them, but once I laid my eyes upon the enormous body of flowing water, I was completely in awe.

This is what I was named for? Do I have that much depth? I asked myself. As I looked down over God's creation, I realized that I did not do such a name justice. Niagara Falls was a vision of depth, magnificence, and danger. As I stood above its natural splendor, I couldn't help knowing that although extraordinarily beautiful, its forcefully flowing current could effortlessly kill the most skilled Olympic swimmer. Was that representative of me? Did I deserve to be named for such a phenomenal creation? I really didn't so. I could never live up to what those falls represented. Just watching all that water fall so quickly gave me such an amazing rush. I had seen pictures, but seeing it with my own eyes absolutely took my breath away. If I'd ever questioned the existence of a higher being before, I knew right then and there that God was definitely working overtime.

"God's the bomb!" I shook my head as I said out loud. As I looked down at the water pouring relentlessly from the falls' invisible mouth, I closed my eyes and visualized all of my life's recent events.

I saw the sparkling smile of Victor Reece and then the innocent faces of his wife and daughter not having a clue of what type of man he truly was. Thinking about him made the pain resurface. Not because he had lied to me and not even because I had fallen for him. It was because, once again, I had made a poor choice by becoming intimate with someone I really didn't know. I felt more terrible about my actions than I did about his. I felt used but I had no one to blame but myself. It was a mystery why I couldn't seem to resist men that I knew were bad for me. It was something I truly needed to understand in order to stop making the same choices. The worst part was despite the fact that Victor had lied and deceived me, part of me still wanted to be with him. Though I knew he was an asshole, a little part of me still craved him. And it was that little part of me that I wanted to choke and drown in those waterfalls.

As I stood over the body of water for which I was named, I kept my eyes tightly closed while the hypnotic melody of the flow carried me like a symphonic orchestra.

What are you going through, Nyagra? Why are you so unhappy? I heard my own voice ask inside my head. I was ashamed of my behavior and still felt as though I couldn't share my embarrassment with anyone. As much as I adored Trish and her presence in my life, right then I knew I had to be my own best friend. Just as I had kept the incident with Victor Reece a secret, I thought about how I also couldn't bring myself to tell her what had happened between me and DaVon. As far as she knew, we simply had a brief, meaningless fling, which was definitely over. She didn't know how hard I'd actually fallen for him. I didn't know how hard I'd actually fallen for him. But I then realized that each time I exposed myself emotionally and intimately—which seemed to be one in the same to me—to a man, I was giving him a little bit of my heart and soul.

It was at that point when I began to understand that I'd given away so much of myself lately that there was barely any of me left. And because I was so ashamed, I couldn't help but to isolate myself. I couldn't bear to be around anyone who really knew me because I felt like I was wearing my insecurities on my chest like the most expensive French-laced bra. I couldn't look into anyone's eyes for fear of what they might see behind my own.

As I stood paralyzed above a body of water that flowed eternally, I realized that despite all of my incredibly high standards, I had ultimately cheapened and reduced myself to an immoral, shallow being in search of some sort of "perfect" man who simply didn't exist. In my mind, "Mr. Right" should've been an intelligent, wealthy, educated, black businessman who treated me like a queen and for whom I was the center of the universe. He should've met all the requirements I deemed necessary for the man in my life to possess. But in all my years of searching, I hadn't even come close. Not even once. Probably because there was frankly no such being. Probably because this man I had created was nothing more than an unrealistic entity that no human being could ever measure up to—especially not a mere male mortal.

As difficult as it was for me to admit to myself, I was living in a fantasy world and I knew I had to toss that notion over the shiny black iron divider that separated the world from those beautifully intriguing dangerous falls. And it was so hard for me to do. After all, I'd had that ideal since puberty. But it was that train of thought that was destroying me and my ability to have healthy relationships with men. Until I had completely abandoned it, I vowed to keep my distance from any man I might find the least bit attractive or whom I believed met even one of my so-called requirements.

I had proven to myself for the very last time that I didn't have good judgment when it came to the opposite sex. And the act of mixing business with pleasure was beginning to take a toll on my career. Because of the personal relationships I had foolishly developed with DaVon and Victor, the entire StarzSports account, one in which I had worked so incredibly long and hard to gain, was now my most dreaded project. I didn't care to have any communication with either of them regarding business or otherwise. The incident with DaVon's mamma had humiliated me so profusely that I couldn't even bear to look at him. He had attempted to reach me after the incident, but I kept my answering machine on at home and at my office. I had Judy continuously tell him that I would call him back, which of course, I never did or had any intention of doing. The embarrassment was simply too much for me to bear. How would I ever be able to entertain the thought of accompanying him on a promotional tour for his sneaker?

Eventually, I had to come to grips that I could no longer unemotionally handle the project. So I despondently handed the responsibility over to my associate, Rachel Altman. Of course, she was ecstatic, but everyone questioned why I would hand "my baby" over to someone else to raise. I justified my actions by claiming to be in charge of too many high-profile projects. I explained that the Wendy's account was taking up so much of my time, and I didn't want to spread myself too thin.

Not to mention everyone knew that I was also concentrating on gaining Gateway computers as a client. All of these reasons, of course, seemed valid and understandable. However, if it hadn't been for my personal relationships with Victor and DaVon, I would've been able to handle everything on my plate just fine. I simply couldn't deal with them, and I blamed these feelings on the fact that I thought these two men somehow possessed the desired characteristics of this fictional man I had created. Subconsciously, I knew he did not and could not exist. God just hadn't created men that way.

I must have stood above those falls for a full two hours before I could budge. I was oblivious to everything around me except for the water, which flowed endlessly below. I was physically paralyzed and in a deep trance. I felt like my spirit had elevated itself from my body and I was staring down at myself. In my mind, I jumped over the edge and soared into the river as it rapidly gushed southward, and my imagination whirled as I stood one hundred eighty feet above the never-ending stream. With my eyes still tightly closed and my mind outside my head, I could see and feel my body as it plunged into the foaming, icy blue water-sinking deeper and deeper until I was almost at the ocean's floor. When I finally lifted my eyelids, I felt a little bit freer, a little bit lighter . . . a little bit better . . .

I enjoyed a wonderful dinner in my room that night. A light meal of lemon grilled chicken, angel hair pasta and a fresh green salad with vinaigrette dressing hit all the right places in my tummy. As I sat silently consuming my food while the sounds of Billie Holiday played softly in the background, I knew that I had left a few of my woes at the falls. I felt about twenty pounds lighter with most of the weight being lost off my head now that my mind was a little clearer. I could think a little straighter and actually allowed myself to enjoy a moment alone without letting stress bombard my every thought. With every swallow of my food, I simply enjoyed its flavor. Through my window I calmly observed the stillness of the snow-covered garden and I started to feel like I could face the world again, hopefully as a better woman; mentally, emotionally, and spiritually. I prayed that God would help me lose the notion of this "perfect" man and just go with my life's purpose instead of holding on to so many requirements for everyone who entered my life. I knew I wasn't going to change one hundred percent overnight, but as I sat there deeply and peacefully in thought, I believed that I was certainly on my way.

I hadn't seen as much snow in my whole life as I'd seen in the past few months. It was only the second week in February, and the city of New York was starting to feel like some Antarctic Peninsula. Every other day it seemed as though a foot of snow would fall, causing all types of transportation difficulties and aggravation and it seemed as though the stress of New York residents was at its highest level ever.

Surprisingly, I felt pretty good inside—not one hundred percent but a hell of a lot better than I did before I'd left. My trip to Niagara Falls had given me the little extra boost I seriously needed. It was my recent escape that had wiped my slate and prepared me for new challenges and conquests. Yet, despite my new disposition, I was becoming increasingly introverted. My search to find myself had only begun at the falls. I knew that it would be an ongoing daily process that I was going to face before I would fully arrive at my emotional and spiritual destination.

As far as the outside world was concerned, I was still in my emotional shell. I discussed only work-related matters with my co-workers, and came straight home after work, only doing overtime when it was absolutely necessary.

I spent a lot of my spare time helping out the financial matters of Trish's catering business which, thanks to her lack of professionalism, was failing miserably once again. Her problem with punctuality and unenthusiastic attitude about the actual running of the business had her clients complaining and ultimately taking their business elsewhere, despite the wonderful taste of her cuisine. I was one hundred percent convinced, as was Trish, that she just didn't have it in her. As long as she was cooking for fun, she was all right. But the moment she attached the words "work" or "business" to it, she just fell apart. As much as I loved my best friend and wanted her to succeed, we finally gave up. Funny, though, but I think I was more upset about it than she was.

Other than helping Trish and going to work, I spent more time than ever on the telephone locked behind my townhouse doors. For some strange reason, I was beginning to feel the desire to become closer to my own family. I spoke with Mamma and Juanita more frequently. I even chatted with my brothers and sisters on a couple of occasions. The initial conversations felt a bit awkward, but as they continued, I began to feel more comfortable. David had now completed his twelve-step program and was trying to stay on the right track. I didn't like to rub in someone's mistakes, so I never brought up that incident in Mamma's house again.

After my recent personal experiences and because I would soon be turning 33, I believed it was time to acquire a new degree of maturity. I wanted to stop behaving like a spoiled, self-centered child and start accepting people as they were—not as I desired them to be. I also knew that before I could do that with strangers, I had to begin within my own family. Subconsciously, I believed that although I would never develop the closeness with my siblings that I had with Trish, I hoped that with a little work and tolerance, we might all find some way to be cordial and friendly, at least for our mamma's sake.

I came to the conclusion that the reason why I continuously sought financial security and unconditional acceptance from men who appeared powerful was probably because I had felt such a lack within my immediate family. I told myself that if only I could love my family more and feel love from them, then perhaps I could be more in love with myself, thus not needing any man to love me. I honestly believed that if I changed my attitude and aura, eventually the right man would come along. However, romance was the last thing on my mind.

As time passed, I began to feel a lot better. I wasn't as depressed as I had been, but my mood was still considerably melancholy. In addition, Michael had finally agreed to give up his half of the townhouse, which shocked the hell out of me! He didn't even want to sell it to me. He simply signed over his fifty percent share and promised not to continue to make my life miserable. Of course, this made me extremely happy. Much to my surprise (and pleasure) it was an effortless procedure which took less than ten minutes at my lawyer's office to complete. Needless to say, I walked out of there feeling as though the Empire State Building had been lifted off my back. Initially, the new year was pretty shaky, but it seemed not to be turning out too badly after all.

It was the third blizzard in February, and the roads were hazardous and slick. I decided it would be best to wait for the weather to let up before venturing onto the expressway. But by 6:30 it was still coming down profusely. I needed to prepare a new business pitch for Gateway, but after a busy day filled with meetings and conference calls, I didn't want to spend another moment in my office. I wanted to ease my mind, so I decided to go to a nearby TGI Friday's restaurant for dinner while I worked on my campaign.

Despite the weather, the restaurant's atmosphere was lively and animated. I think most people had the same idea as I did and wanted to give the snow a chance to subside before heading to their destinations.

The majority of the crowd was at the bar, so it was relatively easy to get a table. As I munched on Cajun chicken fingers and French fries, I became proud of the campaign I was preparing for Gateway. I added, deleted, and edited until I came up with what I felt was the perfect pitch. Just as I placed the final period on the last sentence, I felt someone tap me on my shoulder from behind. To my surprise, it was Will, the Federal Express delivery guy.

"Hey," I uttered, shocked to see him there.

"Hey! Are you here all alone?"

Not really wanting to admit that I was, I hesitantly replied, "Yeah, but I'm working."

He smiled. "Oh, don't worry. I won't bother you. I just wanted to say hello. See ya around."

He was still in his FedEx uniform and as he walked away, for some reason, I felt a little cast aside. Not that I wanted him to join me, but I think my ego wanted him to ask if he could so that I could turn him down. Nevertheless, he didn't. He merely said "hello" and continued on his merry way.

After seeing him, I found it sort of hard to concentrate on my work. In fact I began to wonder why he hadn't tried to sit with me—especially since he asked me out to lunch almost every time we saw each other. Did I look ugly that night? Did he find a girlfriend? Maybe he was just trying to game me all along by asking me out to lunch knowing he was already involved with someone. I have to admit that his behavior sparked my curiosity and I wondered what the deal was with him.

As I looked around the establishment, I saw that he was actually sitting at a nearby table alone. I watched him as he read a book and stuffed his face with cheese fries. It was obvious that he was totally into whatever it was that he was reading and not even thinking about me. Feeling devilish and overlooked, a little bit of Trish slipped out of me and I decided that I would not be ignored. I walked over to Will's table, stood above him and in my most feminine voice, lied. "My pen has seemed to run out of ink, and I'm in the middle of writing a proposal. Would you happen to have an extra?"

"You're actually hand writing a proposal? Where's your laptop?" he questioned, catching me out there in my devilment because I actually was using my laptop. He was smarter than I had given him credit for.

"Oh, I always hand write a rough draft first, then I type it in. I'm old school," I lied.

"Oh," he replied, digging in his pocket and handing me a sterling-silver Tiffany ink pen with eighteen-karat gold detailing. For a moment, the superficial, judgmental personality that I'd been working so diligently to destroy suddenly resurfaced. What is a Federal Express delivery guy doing with a $250 writing utensil? I thought to myself. But I didn't say anything nor did I act as surprised as I was that he had it in his possession.

"Thanks a lot. I'll bring it right back," I assured him. I sauntered back to my table and said lowly to myself, "Now what, stupid?" I surely hadn't expected Will to hand me a pen from Tiffany's. So I figured that there was probably more to Will than met the eye. But despite my initial curiosity, I didn't really want to know what it was. Well, I did but I didn't. I was surely not in the mood for a game of cat and mouse. My unrealistic romantic notions had gotten me into enough trouble already. Plus, Will and I were worlds apart. Not even in the same league.

After a few moments of trying to act like I was actually using the pen I had borrowed, Will finally made his way over to my booth.

"What are you working on?" he asked as he approached.

"A new business pitch."

He sat down beside me and glanced over my shoulder. "Mind if I take a look?"

"Oh, OK," I hesitantly answered. I figured he was harmless. After all, it wasn't like he was the president of Compaq or IBM, or anything like that. As he quickly skimmed over my scribbled papers, I waited to hear his opinion.

"This is very interesting. It seems like it will be a fair and convincing pitch," said Will. "If I worked for Gateway, you'd have my business."

I laughed. "Oh, I would, would I?"

"Definitely!"

After a moment of silence and a wee bit of awkwardness, Will and I tried to make small talk. I must admit it felt weird to be talking to him outside of my office reception area or lobby. We were both the same people, but the encounter just felt different.

"So, what are you doing in here all by yourself, Nyagra?"

"Well, I needed to get out of the office, but the weather is too bad for me to be on those roads. I came here to unwind until the snow slows up. How about you?"

"Same here. I wanted to give the weather a chance to let up before I head home."

"Where do you live?"

"In the Bronx."

"Oh," I replied, not wanting to get too familiar by letting him know my place of residence.

"So . . . ," he began. "Why do you always turn me down when I ask you out to lunch? Are you involved with someone?"

"I do my share of dating, but there's no one special in my life. In fact, I'm somewhat of an idiot magnet." I laughed.

"Oh, I don't believe that at all."

"Believe it," I assured him.

"You just haven't met the right guy. He's been trying, but you refuse to give him a chance."

"Excuse me?" I smirked.

"Why do you always decline my offer?"

"Well, my job just takes up so much of my time. I don't have many free opportunities to socialize," I lied. What was I supposed to say? I'd rather not go out with a delivery guy?

"But I thought you just said that you do your share of dating," Will stated, once again catching me up in my own words. He knew he had me, too, but I tried to get out of it by saying, "Well, yes . . . I do, but whenever you ask, it's just always a bad time. I mean, lunch is bad for me. I don't take lunch that often and when I do, it's usually with a client."

"Yeah, tell me anything." He laughed, displaying the deepest dimples I'd ever laid eyes on. I could tell he had a good sense of humor as he attempted to make light of a rather uncomfortable situation. And although he seemed like a pretty easygoing type of guy, I still wanted to hold back.

"Well, you don't have to try to make me feel good. I know that an advertising executive like yourself might feel a bit uneasy going out with a FedEx delivery guy." He shrugged. He was a lot smarter and more perceptive than I had given him credit to be. But I wasn't about to admit to him that he was indeed correct. In fact, I didn't even want to admit it to myself.

"That is not true!" I lied. "I date all types of interesting men. It doesn't matter what they do for a living!"

"OK, prove it! Since lunch is so inconvenient for you, let me take you out to dinner." He was really putting me on the spot. If I didn't want to look like a superficial liar, I would have to accept his offer. I hesitated as I thought of a reply to his request, but before I could answer, he playfully huffed. "I didn't think so."

"Oh, come on! Give me a break! What makes you think that we'd have fun on a date anyway?!"

"What makes you think we wouldn't?"

I didn't really have an answer.

"Well . . . " I thought a moment. "What if we don't have anything in common? I've had enough bad dates to last me a lifetime!"

"What if we do have things in common?"

I didn't know what to say. As much as I didn't want to go out with him, I felt that if I truly desired to be the better person I claimed I wanted to be, my reason for not wanting to go on a date with him really wasn't good enough. If he had been CEO or some big-time attorney, I would've jumped at the chance to go out with him. In my heart I knew that it was wrong for me to turn him down purely on the basis of his job. So, in order for my conscious to sleep easy, I had to find another reason.

"How old are you, Will? You look a little young," I asked, hoping he was too young for me.

"Thirty-three," he proudly replied.

He didn't look a day over 25. "Really? Are you sure?" I questioned. "Lemme see some ID!"

Will whipped out a dark brown leather Coach wallet and showed me his New York State driver's license which clearly indicated that he was telling the truth.

With a raised eyebrow, I proceeded to ask him, "Well, do you live with your mamma?" I was hoping he had an acute case of DaVon Garrett's mamma's boy syndrome, which would give me an out.

"Nope. I live alone."

"Kids?"

"No."

"Married, engaged, living, sleeping with or seeing someone?"

"Nope, nope, no, no, and nope." He laughed.

"You're lying." I glared at him.

"I'm serious! You can call my house anytime or stop by unexpectedly and see for yourself! I have nothing to hide. I'm a simple guy. I have an economical Toyota Corolla and a modest one-bedroom apartment not too far from Yankee Stadium. On a clear day, I can watch the game from the roof of my building! I'm not in a relationship and I'm not just getting out of one! I've been single and unattached for over three years now."

"Why, what's the matter with you?" I asked suspiciously.

"I'm busy and picky." He nonchalantly shrugged.

"You're busy?" I asked, wondering how demanding the life of a Federal Express delivery guy could be.

"Yes, I am. And you'll just have to join me for dinner to find out about all the things that keep me occupied," he jokingly snapped. I laughed at his evasiveness, but liked his style. "Now is it a date or not?"

"When?"

"You name it."

"Saturday night."

"See you then!"

We casually exchanged personal information as I wondered what I was getting myself into. Then I figured he couldn't be any worse than the recent peons I'd been with. And even though he was cute with a sparkle of charm, in my mind, he still wasn't my type. He simply seemed fun and harmless, especially for my heart—and that's exactly what I needed.

Fourteen

I didn't experience my usual anxiety as I got ready for my date with Will. I didn't get dressed up nor did I feel the apprehension I usually felt when a man came to my home for the first time. I actually felt like I was just going to hang out with a friend. I hadn't spent hours on my hair, clothes, or makeup. I didn't expect him to take me anyplace fancy, so I threw on black jeans and a red mock-neck shirt. I was simply in "comfortable" mode while I relaxed and patiently awaited his arrival. I hadn't even told Trish that I was going out with him. I wasn't sure if I was ashamed or not. I guess I just chose not to discuss it. After all, it really wasn't that big of a deal to me.

Although I had been a little skeptical about letting him pick me up from my home, I ended up telling him to be there at seven. The clock read 6:57 when the doorbell rang. I peeked out the window to see Will with a bouquet of long-stemmed red roses. How sweet, I thought to myself as I opened the door.

"Hi!" I smiled.

"Hi. These are for you. And it's only a half-dozen, 'cause I didn't wanna scare you away." Will grinned, handing me the flowers. He looked youthful in his red and blue ski jacket, dark blue jeans and Timberland boots. He was cute, but in a "little brother" kind of way. There was no physical contact between us. We didn't hug, kiss or touch in any way.

"They're lovely, but you really didn't have to."

"Of course, I did. This is supposed to be a date, isn't it?"

I took the flowers to the kitchen and quickly returned with them in a vase.

"You have a very nice home," he complimented, as he gave the place a once-over.

"Thanks." I didn't ask to take his coat since I had no intention of entertaining him in my house, not even for one moment. As I walked over to the closet to grab my own jacket, I asked, "So, where are we going tonight?"

"I figured we'd have a night of fun. Nothing too intimate or romantic. Like I said, I don't wanna scare you off." He chuckled.

"Oh, I'm not that easy to scare," I fibbed, allowing him to help me with my jacket.

Will smirked. "I'm not so sure about that."

"You're harmless," I nonchalantly remarked as we closed the front door behind us.

We got into his cute little black Corolla and took off. He was more familiar with the area than I thought. The conversation in the car was general. We discussed what we'd done that day and how our week had gone. We both complained about the frigid and stormy weather. We got on the highway and eventually exited at Westchester Avenue where we headed to Red Lobster in Scarsdale. The wait for a table was thirty minutes but we decided to stay anyway. I figured the wait would give us an opportunity to learn a little more about each other. Since I had agreed to go out with him, the very least I could do was find out where he'd gotten that Tiffany pen.

"So, how is it working for Federal Express?" I asked.

"Do you really wanna know?" he sarcastically asked.

"Of course, I do. I asked you, didn't I?" I laughed.

"Yes, you did. Well, it sucks. It's just something to pass the time and pay the bills while I'm in school."

"Oh, you're in school? You didn't tell me that," I stated. I knew still waters ran deep.

He shrugged. "There's nothing to tell."

"What are you studying and where?" I probed.

"Enough about me . . . I wanna know all about you. Where did you go to school? You did go to school, didn't you?" he asked.

I didn't want to talk about me. I wanted to know what he had going on in his life, but yet I answered. "Of course, I went to school! Do you really think I could be the vice president of a company like Newman & Stein without going to college? In fact I have a master's in business and advertising," I defensively and cockily stated.

"I'm impressed, but you never know. Every single person who holds a big-time position doesn't necessarily go to college."

"Well, I did. I had to work my ass off to get to where I am. Maybe every white person in such a position doesn't have to go to school, but you better believe that as a black female, I had to be educated to even get the time of day!" I arrogantly huffed. Will just shrugged his shoulders. The distraction of his statement made me forget that the conversation was supposed to be about him!

"So where'd you go?" he questioned.

"Undergrad at Cornell, grad at Fordham," I proudly answered.

"Like I said, I'm impressed."

"And you?"

"Um, City College—nowhere nearly as prestigious as you," he casually uttered.

Oh . . . , I thought.

"Not as fancy as Cornell and Fordham, but it's an education nonetheless."

"Oh, definitely! You should be proud of whatever institution you attend," I stated in the phoniest way. As I listened to my own words, I asked myself if I could really get rid of personality traits I'd had for so long. It sure was going to be hard! If this was my first test, I was failing miserably.

Dinner went well. I ordered the broiled king crab legs and he selected the salmon and shrimp combination. Surprisingly, the conversation was far more intriguing than I had expected. Will was an interesting person who had done a lot of things in his life. The only child of Sara and Charles Jones, Will (short for Willis) was born and raised in Poughkeepsie, New York. He had served a stint in the United States Army to which I attributed the great physique all the girls at the office loved. He'd also traveled to many places and experienced various cultures. He was even fluent in French, Spanish and Japanese! He knew so much about politics, social issues and current events. Needless to say, there wasn't a moment of silence during the entire meal.

I found him more and more intriguing as we exchanged stories and experiences. And by the time we finished our meal, he'd made me laugh so hard I had a terrible pain in my side. He had an extraordinarily animated personality, which kept my undivided attention as I awaited the details and outcome of each of his stories. As much as I hated to admit, Willis Jones was a lot of fun and I was happy that I had accepted his invitation.

After dinner, the evening was still young and we were definitely not ready to call it a night. In ten-below-zero weather, we decided to go bowling. I couldn't remember the last time I had been to the lanes. I think my parents might have taken me and my brothers and sisters once when I was little, and although I knew I wasn't too good at it, I was game. But I felt comfortable with him and eager to be myself. I didn't feel as though I had to be on my best behavior or like I had to make an impression. I didn't have to check my makeup every five minutes, or suck my stomach in so that he wouldn't be able to see the couple of pounds I'd put on over the holiday season. I was just into having a really good time, and I knew that we'd have a ball at the bowling alley.

We drove to the Happy Lanes in White Plains, which seemed to be filled to capacity. I had no idea that bowling was such a popular pastime! The place was packed, but after a forty-minute wait, we were finally able to get a lane. And even though I was a terrible bowler, Will was fantastic and we really had a good time! It was the first time I had lost at something and was still able to walk away with a smile. Of course, I would rather have bowled his ass under the table, but I had such fun, it didn't matter that I didn't walk away the winner.

The night eventually came to a close and as we came down off our laughter and excitement high, I felt satisfied, relaxed and better than I'd felt in years. On the ride home from the alley, I couldn't remember when I'd had so much fun. I was glad I finally made the right decision about something. Going out with Will was probably the best choice I'd made for my personal life in ages.

As he walked me to my doorway, I didn't feel the usual "what happens now" anxiety. I felt as though I was just about to say goodbye to a good friend. There was no lust or stupidity running through my veins. For once, my head was screwed on completely straight, and it felt incredibly good.

In spite of the cold, we stood in front of my door and talked. Because we had such a great time together, I didn't want to ruin it by inviting him in. The simple evening we'd shared turned out to be one of the best dates I'd ever had. Still, I wasn't sure if I wanted us to ever be any more than friends. Although we might not have come from such different worlds, I truly believed that we belonged to opposite universes now. He was unquestionably a great guy, but something inside me prevented my eyes from viewing him in a romantic way. In fact, I really kind of saw him like a brother—the type I'd always wanted. However, whatever my feelings were, I knew that I didn't have to decide right then, as I could tell he wasn't about to make any type of advance toward me that I'd have to reject. Will Jones was a perfect gentleman.

"I hope you had as good a time as I did," he began.

"I most certainly did." I smiled.

"Are you glad you said yes?"

"Very much so." I blushed.

"Can I call you?"

"Please do."

"Goodnight, Nyagra. Thanks for a great evening," said Will, placing a tender kiss on my cheek.

"Thank you," I softly replied. I opened the door, gave him a hug and said, "Drive safely."

"I will," he answered as he walked toward his car and got in. I waved to him as he pulled out of my driveway and down the street.

"I'll call you soon!" Will yelled from the driver's side window. As he drove out of sight and I went inside the house, I felt content and at peace—two feelings I hadn't really experienced in a long while. At that moment, I didn't know if Willis Jones and I would become the best of friends or the best of lovers. I was just convinced that I definitely wanted to spend another fun-filled evening with him.

Fifteen

Between the office being so hectic and Will and I spending time together, time just seemed to fly. Before I knew it, it was two weeks before Easter. I sure was glad to see the winter weather finally tapering off and spring gradually approaching. The brutal winter season had frequently chilled my bones, but the friendship I'd developed with Will warmed my heart. It wasn't quite a romantic relationship. And it definitely wasn't sexual. In fact, the issue of sex never even came up.

I often wondered how Will viewed our companionship. But I was having such a good time with him that I was afraid to approach the topic. I feared that I would open a can of worms that I was unprepared to deal with. Still, we enjoyed going to the movies together, eating at fancy as well as casual restaurants, and just plain old hanging out. My favorite times were the nights we would rent movies, order take out and just relax at my house or his. I took a lot of pleasure in spending hours at his rather surprisingly spacious but cozy apartment. I hadn't expected it to be quite so enchanting. It had a great deal of character and charm.

On top of his many talents, Will was also an excellent artist and interior decorator. Carefully mounted on every wall was some sort of brilliantly created abstract painting with deep, lively colors and a thousand-and-one interpretations. He particularly liked purples and golds, and the colors were repeated throughout his apartment. I was quite dazzled by his talent and taste. The apartment, which was located on the sixteenth floor of an old pre-war building, had thirteen-foot-high ceilings and impeccable hardwood floors. Will and I spent a lot of nights sitting on each other's couch just laughing and talking. However, at the end of the evening, whoever was the visitor, went home. It was a pure and honest relationship. And I felt as though I was 16 years old again, when my dating game was innocent and sweet. I really didn't want to put a label on our interaction because I liked us just as we were.

As exhilarated as I felt during that time, I chose to keep my bliss a private affair. Trish complained about never seeing me anymore, but I simply told her that work was overwhelming and apologized for not having any time to spend with her. The truth of the matter, of course, was that I was spending less time at the office than ever and sharing all my free moments with Will.

Unfortunately, I just wasn't ready to tell Trish, or anyone, about him. It wasn't that I was ashamed of him or anything like that. After all, we were only friends. But I didn't want Trish to pick him apart nor did I want him to feel uncomfortable around all of her money and shallowness. Will was simple and pure and I didn't want him to feel out of place. And since I didn't feel ready to share our friendship with anyone, I kept Will from my friends and my family. No one at my office knew either. If I happened to bump into him when he came during his FedEx rounds, we acted as we always did toward one another. In that atmosphere, there was little contact and even less dialogue between us. I definitely didn't want my co-workers to know that we had developed such a friendship. In my mind, it was clearly none of their business.

Will and I walked up and down the aisles of Blockbuster in search of the perfect movie to watch on a rainy, chilly Friday night. The weather was bad and we were both beat from a long and busy week. We opted to rent a movie, pick up some Chinese food and relax. We arranged to meet at Blockbuster around seven and then grab the food before going to my house. Unfortunately, all the good movies were checked out, and we were having a hard time finding any that we both wanted to see. He was easier to please than I was, as I just couldn't seem to find a movie I was in the mood to watch. So, after keeping him waiting for what must have felt like forever, Will finally said, "I'm going to look in the classics section. I'll be back in five minutes and you had better pick at least one movie!" He laughed as he walked away, leaving me to continue my hunt. My eyes searched every video on the wall, but I still couldn't decide. As I continued to look up and down the shelves, I felt a powerful tug on my shoulder bag. Thinking someone was trying to snatch my purse, I quickly and defensively turned around. It was Trish. I could've died! The very last thing I wanted to do at that moment was introduce her to Will.

"Funny how my best friend is too busy to hang out with me but not too busy to rent a movie from Blockbuster!" she stated sarcastically.

"What's up, Girl?!" I said hesitantly. Though I was relieved that I wasn't being robbed, I was completely uncomfortable about letting her in on my secret. Trish never would've been able to understand why I hadn't told her about Will and would've held it against me for life. Irregardless, I was not ready to tell her and I didn't know when or if I would be.

"And what are you renting?" she questioned in that same sarcastic voice.

"I don't know. I'm really just looking," I lied as I discreetly looked around for Will's whereabouts. When I didn't see him, my heart began to pound profusely as I hoped that he would not come back anytime soon. However, I knew that after running into me, Trish would surely want us to leave the store together. It was weird, but I almost felt like I'd just gotten busted cheating by my husband or like a sneaky teenage girl, snagged by her mamma. The agony of being caught doing something I didn't want anyone to know made me dizzy.

"Why don't you come over and hang out with me and Rodney? I'm getting three blaxploitation flicks! I got Superfly, Uptown Saturday Night and Let's Do It Again. I'll put the twins to bed, we'll order Japanese and it'll be so much fun!" She tried to coax me as she grinned from ear-to-ear and placed the videos damn near on the tip of my nose.

I pushed the tapes out of my face. "Thanks, Girl, but I'm really tired. In fact, I don't think I'm going to get anything after all. I think I'm just going to go straight home and crash. Yeah, that's exactly what I'm going to do." I let out a phony yawn and attempted to look completely exhausted.

"Oh, come on, Ny. We never see you anymore! We miss you! The kids miss you. Come over and chill out with us. You could sleep in one of the guest rooms or I'll have Rodney drive you back if you're too tired," she pleaded.

"Thanks so much for the invitation, Trish, but I really just need to get some rest in my own bed. I promise I'll come over to visit on Sunday. But tonight—oh, it's cold and it's raining! I really just need to get home."

"Oh, all right. Well, come on. At least wait with me in line while I pay for this. We'll walk out together."

Just as I was trying to think of some excuse to get away, Will walked up to us.

"There you are! I was looking all over for you! How about the Raiders of the Lost Ark trilogy?" he asked, shaking the video case gently with both hands.

I absolutely wished I could've disappeared into thin air! Trish looked at him with a puzzled expression, then at me and back at him.

"Thanks, but I decided not to get anything after all. Thanks for your help." I tried to smile as I walked away and left him. Trish and I marched toward the front of the store to the cash registers. I didn't want to turn around and look at Will who I knew probably stood motionless and absolutely dumbfounded in the center of the aisle. I couldn't believe what I'd just done! I was actually treating one of the best friends I'd ever had like he was some Blockbuster video stock boy that I didn't even know. I felt more ashamed than ever, but I kept going with it. For some reason, I felt like I had to.

"For a moment, I thought you knew that guy." Trish laughed. I didn't attempt to say anything because there was a lump in my throat the size of a cantaloupe. "Too bad you don't. He was cute. Did you see those dimples?"

I remained silent. Out of the corner of my eye, I saw Will exit the store and watched him as he got into his car and drove away. I wanted to run after him but couldn't. I wanted to cry but wouldn't. Ultimately, I walked Trish to her car, promised her once again that I'd stop by on Sunday and said goodbye. Dangerously doing 80 on the highway, I couldn't get to my house fast enough. I hoped with all my might that

Will's car would be sitting in my driveway when I got there, but it wasn't. Although it was difficult, I tried not to get upset when I called his house until midnight and continued to get his answering machine. Something told me to drive over there, but I decided against it. I felt like shit because I knew he was probably angry and he refused to pick up the phone so I could at least explain. It pissed me the hell off. After a while, I decided to stop calling and figured he'd get over it in a day or so and call me when he got ready. I knew I'd been wrong and wanted to apologize. But I still wasn't about to start stressing out over a man. After all, we were just friends.

Sixteen

Almost a week had passed without a word from Will. I hadn't thought that what I'd done was so terrible that he would never want to speak to me again. I called his house practically every day, but continued to get the answering machine. I also didn't bump into him at the office and since I didn't want to seem like I was looking for him, I asked no one of his whereabouts. However, I did keep my eyes and ears open. Unfortunately, to no avail. It seemed as if Willis Jones had disappeared off the face of the earth.

Thursday came and not only had my curiosity reached its peak, but I was also a little worried. Not to mention the fact that it was quite difficult to concentrate on my work at the office. Had he gotten so angry that night at Blockbuster that he'd gotten into an accident on the way home? Maybe he was hurt and needed my help. I had to at least try to find out.

When the clock struck five, I hauled my ass out of there and drove to Will's house to check out the situation. Afraid that he wouldn't want to let me in, I didn't want to ring the buzzer, so I was pretty relieved when an elderly woman exited the lobby just as I approached the door. With the ease of a snake in the grass, I effortlessly slipped into the building and with my heart pounding a mile a minute, rode the elevator to the sixteenth floor. I slowly walked down the corridor to Will's apartment. As I reached the door, I closed my eyes, took a deep breath, and with little expectation of him being home, gently rang the bell.

"Will!" I heard a woman's voice call from inside. "Someone's at the door!"

Footsteps got closer and closer, until the door opened. Will, standing barefoot in a navy sweatsuit, stared into my face with a look of astonishment. For a moment, neither of us said a word. We just looked at each other in pure awe. I wasn't sure if it was because he was so surprised to see me there, or if it was because he had a woman with him. I also wasn't sure if I was shocked because he was home or because of the woman. Whatever the case was, we were both speechless. After a moment of silence, a pretty young woman appeared in the doorway beside him.

"Will, who's this?" she asked.

"A friend of mine," he replied, without taking his eyes off of me.

I suddenly felt my blood boil as it rushed through my body to the tips of my fingers and toes. My initial reaction was to choke him, but I decided against that. My second was sheer disbelief that even a simple, broke ass guy like Will Jones was full of shit! At that precise second, I honestly believed that every single man on the planet was a liar and a cheat. I also suddenly realized that the feelings I'd had for Will were more than simple feelings of friendship. If I had truly viewed him as just my "buddy," I wouldn't have suddenly felt so angry and jealous.

"I just came to see if you were still alive," I said before turning around and marching down the hallway.

"Nyagra!" he called from the threshold.

I refused to turn around. I wasn't about to go back there and talk to him when he had some female in his apartment. I quickly walked down that corridor with no intention of ever laying eyes on him again. I'd only gone there to see if he was OK anyway and, as I could see, he was just fine. As far as I was concerned, Willis Jones was just another guy I could flush down my bad-relationship toilet bowl.

"Will! Come on! We have to finish! You have to be ready for those boards, ya know!" I heard the woman tell him.

Boards? I asked myself. But I couldn't think straight and I rode the elevator to the ground floor as I felt the sensation of warm water swelling up in the corner of my eyes.

Don't you dare cry, Nyagra Ensley! I told myself. Don't you dare!

I cuddled up in my bed all alone, extremely sad and definitely mad. But it angered me that I felt any emotions whatsoever. I thought that

I'd left all that sentimental romantic shit at those waterfalls. Obviously, I hadn't. I had experienced soured relationships so often. They seemed to be a way of life for me, and I was forced to wonder when and if I'd ever become immune to such occurrences.

Although I was angry with Will for having a woman at his apartment, I nevertheless believed that this particular situation was somehow different from all the other incidents. I knew that Will wasn't a bad guy and part of me was convinced that I was partially responsible for the outcome. After all, I was the one who had been ashamed to admit I was dating a FedEx delivery guy. Maybe Will had known deep down that I didn't really think he was good enough for me. Oh, he was good enough to hang out with—in private. But I had treated him like he wasn't good enough to introduce to my friends, or to develop a romantic relationship with. In fact, I felt absolutely terrible about the way I'd behaved.

As I snuggled beneath my comforter, a million thoughts of Will ran through my mind. I couldn't help but think of him. I genuinely didn't want to lose him in my life, and it wasn't because he was a great lover, because we hadn't made love. And it wasn't because he represented financial security, because I made more money than he did. It was simply because I realized that I truly didn't have any real reason to be angry with him. It had never even been established that we were indeed a couple. How could I fault him for spending an evening with a beautiful woman when I couldn't even acknowledge that we were in Blockbuster together? Because of what I felt to be his lack of financial and social status, and despite the fact that he'd treated me like a queen, I hadn't wanted to admit the way I really felt about him. I wasn't even certain if I truly realized it until I saw him with that woman. I wanted to blame him for my rage, but I couldn't. As much as I hated to admit it, I knew that it was really my fault and I had to bear the consequences of my own actions.

During the time we shared, Will had been everything I'd been searching for for such a long time—a gentle, loving, honest man, who respected and accepted me for who I was. I was myself with him. No facades, airs, or acts. He admired me, Nyagra Marie Ensley, the girl from Harlem with all of her flaws, family problems and insecurities; not

Ms. Ensley, vice president of Newman & Stein Enterprises. None of my accounts or high-profile clients mattered to him.

In fact, Will had been the first man to actually make me feel like my job wasn't the only important and gratifying thing in my life. I wanted to run and tell him how I truly felt, but I couldn't help thinking about him and that other woman. I wondered how serious their relationship was and figured that she probably adored him. What girl in her right mind wouldn't? We might not ever be a real couple, but I knew I still had to let him know my feelings. My only hope was that if nothing more, he'd allow me to at least still be his friend.

As I tossed and turned in my bed, I tried to put myself to sleep so I wouldn't have to think about the situation. But I just felt worse and worse. I buried my face in my pillow, and I did something I hadn't done since my daddy passed. I cried a stream of tears that wouldn't stop. No matter how hard I tried, the flow of sadness continued like a broken faucet. Realizing that my sorrow was beyond my control, I just let the tears roll. As I was taken over by my emotions, I realized that they were determined to fall.

Seventeen

Hours passed and I thought I'd feel better, but I didn't. I was still distraught. I just couldn't seem to drum up the nerve to call Will. I promised myself every sixty minutes that I'd call him within the next hour, but never did. I refused to leave the house the entire weekend, secretly wishing that he'd make the first step and call, but I guess he was as stubborn as I was. For two whole days, I drove myself absolutely crazy hoping, contemplating, and thinking about Will. Finally, I began to accept that perhaps he really hadn't wanted any more than what he was getting from me after all.

It was seven o'clock Sunday evening and I began to prepare for the upcoming week. Still afraid to call Will's house, I decided to wash my hair to take my mind off the situation. As I let the deep conditioner penetrate the curly locks I had been recently neglecting, I prepared a grilled chicken salad and watched 60 Minutes.

Just as the show went into an interesting story about an outbreak of the deadly e-coli bacteria in nearby restaurants, the doorbell rang. I was totally engrossed in the story, and had to pull myself away from the set to see who it was. I wasn't expecting anyone and figured it was just Trish. I looked through the peephole and nearly fainted when I saw Will on my townhouse steps. I wanted to see him, hug him and just blurt out my every emotion. But I didn't want him to see me looking like the battered housewife from hell in my frumpiest, faded yellow terrycloth robe and Tweety Bird slippers with a plastic heating cap on my head.

"Yes?" I nervously asked.

"Nyagra, open the door. We need to talk," he replied.

We certainly do, I thought, but said, "I'm not decent."

"I don't care. Open the door," Will ordered. I slowly unlocked the door and opened it. He stepped inside and stated with a smile, "You weren't kidding."

"Oh, shut up!" I jokingly said. I couldn't believe how happy I was to see him. I just wanted to wrap my arms around him and give him the biggest hug and kiss known to mankind. But I didn't know if I should so I stood still.

"The other night," he began. "It wasn't what it looked like."

"Well, what was it?" I softly asked, lowering my eyes to the floor and tightening the belt on my dowdy housecoat.

"Lyla and I are, well, we're study partners," he began.

I smirked. "Oh, I don't know about that, Will. You guys appeared to be a bit more than study partners."

"Well, that's all there is to us. But you know what, Nyagra? So what if it wasn't? What difference would it make if I fucked her brains out the moment you left?" Will said with a venomous tone. I'd never heard him speak like that before. I didn't even know he could speak like that!

"What?"

"You shouldn't care what the hell I do or who I do it with! You obviously don't want a relationship with me!"

"Will . . ." I sighed.

"No. Don't say a word. Listen, for a change. I care a lot about you, Nyagra. In fact, I'm definitely in love with you. But you just wanna be friends. Or should I say, you just want me the way you want me. Or you don't want me, but you don't want anybody else to want me. Your pompous, shallow ass doesn't think that I'm good enough for you. You think that just because you see me delivering FedEx packages that you're better than I am. Because you thought I was just some little delivery guy, it took me ages to get you to even agree to let me take you out. And you only did because you didn't want to look like the materialistic, superficial prejudiced female you really are! Plus, you never thought your ass would actually like me. But you did. And I knew that you would. That's why I chose not to tell you certain details of my life. And you're so full of yourself, you never even thought to ask!"

"That's not true! You told me lots of things about yourself! You're not being a hundred percent fair!" I interjected.

"You know what I told you, but did you ever ask me anything about myself?! What am I studying in school, Nyagra? Huh? Do you know? Or was it simply not important enough for you to inquire about, because after all, I'm only going to City College!"

"That's not true," I replied in my defense. Although he was right, I felt his manner was a bit harsh. And his insults about my personality kind of pissed me off, too.

"You're right, it's not. It's not right that I felt in order for you to get to know me and like me for my true self, I had to leave out real aspects of my life. I could tell that you're so damn superficial and easily impressed by nothing, I knew that if I told you that I'm actually getting ready to graduate from Columbia University medical school, you'd like me no matter what! Not because you really thought I was a nice guy. I wanted to prove that you could actually be intrigued by a man you didn't think was rich or successful by your bullshit standards! And you did like me—admit it, but because you didn't think a Federal Express guy could have any type of prosperous future, you didn't even want to think about going to the next level with me. And you didn't wanna introduce me to your stuck-up friends or co-workers. You really messed my head up that day in Blockbuster. But the crazy thing is that despite all of this, I still love you. But where's it gonna get me? Medical school or no medical school, I'm not rich! And I won't be for a long time—if ever! In fact, I wanna help sick people in inner cities—the ones who can't pay for good medical treatment. And you know there's no pot of gold at the end of that rainbow! But if I was some wealthy banker or CEO, we'd practically be married by now. You're a real fucked-up individual, Ms. Ensley, and you need to check yourself!" he sternly preached.

I was absolutely speechless. Will attacked the situation and my personality head-on, making me realize that he had me totally figured out. His words pierced through my psyche like a machete dipped in salt, and the embarrassment and shame was unbearable. I instantly realized how much of an amazing man Will definitely was. I couldn't believe that while holding down a full-time job, he was actually getting ready to graduate from medical school—Columbia Medical School! From the first moment I talked to him in TGI Friday's, I'd known that there was much more to Willis Jones than met the eye, and I believed that there was more to be seen. But to be honest, I had fallen in love with him no matter what. The truth was that I would still have been in love with him if he'd never entered the door of any university. After such an intense revelation and accurate character assassination, all I could bring myself to say was, "I'm sorry . . . "

"Don't apologize to me; apologize to yourself. You're missing out on a lot of good things and people being the way you are. Not only doctors, lawyers and businessmen are good people, Nyagra. Besides, you act like you were born a Trump-like you've never been poor or struggled! Don't forget where you came from, Nyagra, or else there'll be no place for you to go."

I stood there looking ridiculous, still in my heating cap and bathrobe. There was simply nothing I could say. The words that spewed from Will's mouth were one hundred percent right, and I didn't want to live the rest of my life being that type of person. Despite my bogus attempt to be a so-called "better" person over the past few months, it wasn't until Will vividly described the ugly aspects of my personality that I realized I hadn't really tried at all.

"I love you, too," I uttered. It wasn't even something I said consciously. I obviously caught Will off guard with my statement. He immediately changed his intonation and bewilderedly asked, "You do?"

"Yes, I do . . . ," I said as I walked over and tightly wrapped my arms around him. It was the first time in all our encounters that we actually shared more than a "buddy"-like hug. This particular embrace, which was filled with love and adoration, sent an indescribable sensation of unconditional devotion throughout my body, and for the first time in my whole life, my mind. Our display of affection slowly graduated from a tight embrace to tender and passionate kisses, starting small but with increasing intensity as we climbed the delicate scale of passion. As the softness of Will's lips met mine, I began to feel like I was spinning on top of an incredibly large wheel.

While in his arms, I recognized and admitted how truly wounded I had been in the past as I searched for love in all the wrong places. Large, salty tears began to flow from my eyes when I finally opened up my heart and permitted the grieving process to begin. I realized how much Michael's mental abuse and infidelity had hurt me. I admitted the sub-conscious insecurities I had experienced by not being desired over Victor's wife or chosen over DaVon's mamma. But it wasn't that I grieved for not having been given their love. To the contrary. I grieved for myself, for my desire of things not good for me and for the time I had wasted on unworthy individuals. I had never acknowledged my true sadness each time my romantic experiences became disappointing. Sure, I got mad and upset, but I never cried or really let out any of my emotions. I never even talked about the incidents. I simply buried them above my heart, which I now understood had blocked my ability to accept true love when it finally came along. As Will gently kissed my face and neck, I believed that this was the way I was supposed to feel with the man in my life. It was a feeling of ultimate and eternal love and sensuality, with no lust in sight. Of course, I wanted to eventually become one with him. But I knew that we would go there when the time was right. I knew that neither of us had any intention to separate. We had all the time in the world to make love. I honestly believed that the feelings Will and I shared were not just frivolous, passing emotions. They were real. And reality never fades away, thus making my desire to feel this way forever so intense that it penetrated every cell in my body.

Six Months Later

"I now pronounce you man and wife." Reverend Parker smiled.

The loud cheers from our guests thundered throughout the elo-quently decorated church as Will and I embraced and shared the most beautiful kiss we had within our souls to give. When we finally came up for air, I was delighted as I looked around at the joyful faces of our fam-ilies and friends. I saw tears in Trish's eyes as she stood to my right in her cinnamon-colored, tea-length taffeta dress, seeming happier for me than anyone in the room other than my mamma.

We had opted not to have attendants with the exception of Trish as my matron of honor and Will's cousin as his best man. We really wanted to keep the event moderately-sized and simple, but as much as I tried to prevent it, the guest list uncontrollably soared past two hun-dred! Notwithstanding the fact that he was an only child, my new husband had far too many relatives to count. And though they were an absolutely delightful group of people, it seemed like he had over a hundred aunts, uncles and cousins alone!

His parents, the Honorable Judge Richard Jones and Mrs. Sara Jones, were especially wonderful and supportive of our union, instantly making me feel welcome and comfortable as a new member of their family. To my relief, the Joneses highly approved of their son's choice of spouse; although I was sure it wouldn't have mattered to Will if they hadn't. My husband was his own man, not to be browbeaten by anyone. This was one of the many reasons I adored him so.

Will was a strong and intelligent man who had chosen to put himself through medical school although his parents could have effortlessly sent him. His family was very proud of him and I surely couldn't blame them, as he was definitely someone to be revered.

Everyone was in a joyous frame of mind, and Will and I fed off the positive energy that filled the sanctuary. My family was even on their best behavior. However, Juanita was furious with me for not asking her to be my right-hand girl. But no one was closer to me than Trish, and she was better suited for the position of matron of honor. She was even hosting our reception at her home where she had willfully, diligently and enthusiastically prepared a feast fit for the royal family. Despite all the champagne, beauty and rapture in the atmosphere, all Will and I really wanted to do was leave for our honeymoon. Ironically, in spite of all the pre-marital sexual indulging I'd done in the past, Will and I had decided to wait until we were married. But I knew that the moment we entered our honeymoon suite in Hawaii, it would be on! And boy, was I ready!

I never thought that dreams actually come true, but they do. Falling in love with my husband made me realize that anything in life is possible if you allow yourself to be open to new experiences. Who would have thought that the man I would spend the rest of my life with was the same one who had delivered my signed StarzSports contracts, my executed proposals, and everything else with my name on it? The power of love felt so amazing. And I thanked God every moment for sending Willis Alexander Jones into my life and for blessing me with the desire to alter my personality just enough to make a big difference in my life. I was so happy and I wanted to shout it out to the whole world!

As I changed out of my lacy white gown in Trish and Rodney's bedroom and prepared to leave for our long-awaited voyage, my best friend knocked on the large oak door that separated us.

"Can I come in?" she asked, poking her head through the door.

"Of course." I smiled.

"Hi, Mrs. Jones . . . I just wanted to tell you one-on-one how happy I am for you. Will is really a great guy and you two truly deserve each other. I know I drive you crazy sometimes, but that's only because you're my sister and I love you, Girl," she sincerely told me as we hugged tightly and cried tears of happiness on each other's shoulder.

For someone who had refused to shed a tear for so many years, I sure was crying a lot these days! I guess I was finally becoming in tune with my true feelings. Thus, for the first time since my teenage years, I was looking forward to the future. I always had known that professionally I would be successful, but for the first time in my life, I truly felt that my personal forecast also looked promising. I anticipated growing old with Will and entering middle-aged womanhood with my other best friend by my side. I knew that as the mamma of twins, Trish surely would be able to answer most any question I had about pregnancy, childbirth and parenthood-even about being a wife. Of course, my mamma had mounds of expert advice, but times had changed a little since she'd been a newlywed. Still, I knew she would be there if and when I needed her. It sure felt good to have people I knew I could depend on no matter what—people who truly loved me for no reason other than because I am me. I reminded myself of DaVon in that respect—a person who never felt loved just because. It felt even better to be genuinely in love, to be sincerely loved, and to be able to unconditionally love. Through all my experiences, I guess one of the best lessons I could have learned was that love without fear is the very best kind of love of all!

As I looked at Trish's face, which approved so much of the path I was on, I couldn't help feeling guilty about leaving certain details of my life out of our recent conversations. Before I left that moment behind and allowed it to pass into an eternity never to be regained, I had to come clean with my very best friend.

"Trish." I turned to her. She was quiet, but I knew she was all ears. "I haven't been as honest with you as I could have, or rather should have been over the past few weeks—months even." My closest girlfriend on the planet still stood silent as she patiently awaited the cautious words that flowed from my lips.

"I didn't exactly get tired of Victor Reece. On Christmas Eve, I flew down to his house and was greeted by his wife and daughter . . . You were right."

I closed my eyes and waited for the verbal bashing of "I told you sos" and "that's what you gets." But Trish remained silent as she looked me dead in the eye with nothing but compassion and peace. A moment passed before I opted to break the silence.

"Go ahead—say it . . . "

"Say what?" she asked.

"You know what! I told you so! You should've listened to my instinct! Never underestimate my vibes! Go ahead! I know you want to!" I laughed.

"Why should I say anything? You just said it all," she replied with the calmness and gentleness of a new mother with her little baby.

"Well, I know you're thinking it . . . ," I playfully said.

"No. What I'm wondering is why you didn't feel like you could trust me enough to let me know because I'm sorry that you had to go through all of that alone. You should've let me be there for you. We've always been there for each other."

"Yeah, yeah, I know . . . But I was ashamed. Embarrassed." I shrugged.

"You should never be ashamed or embarrassed where I'm concerned. I'm your sister."

"Yeah, I know. But . . . "

"Listen. That's all behind us now. So what, that asshole was still married?! You didn't need a liar and a cheat like that anyway. You got over it, and over that juvenile ass DaVon Garrett. And we won't even mention Bill Peterson . . . " My friend laughed. I couldn't help but follow. "All that matters now is that you have a happy and prosperous life with Will. That's all that's important—and that you never keep anything like that from me again, OK?"

"OK." I hugged my friend tightly, almost as if I was moving to another country and would never see her again. It was at that moment when I truly understood and realized why I'd chosen her to be my best friend and confidante forever. She knew what it meant to be a friend. And more importantly, she knew what it meant to be a sister.

The party downstairs was going strong. I could hear the laughter and stirring of our guests as I walked down the spiral stairs and entered the grand ballroom. Anxious to make our exit, Will tossed the garter and I the bouquet—right to Juanita! As if she needed another husband!

As the color of the sky turned from light azure to deep sapphire and the stars brilliantly began to appear above our heads, we were finally able to pull ourselves away and drive off into the sunset in our white Rolls Royce. Sitting beside the man of my dreams, I could do nothing but let out the biggest sigh ever. It was finally my time to exhale and as I got ready to spend three weeks on the glorious beaches of Hawaii with my Prince Charming, I hoped and prayed that my fairy tale would have a happy ending. But for the first time in my life, I refused to worry about the future. All I cared about was that I could honestly say I was finally at peace, and it felt so damn good . . .

About the Author

Born and raised in New York City, Michelle Valentine has been a part of the entertainment industry for most of her life. A former Sesame Street kid, catalog model, and pageant winner, Michelle spent much of her early years in recording and rehearsal studios with her mom who introduced her to the world of entertainment. Naturally, her childhood experiences cultivated her love for writing poems, short stories, plays and songs at a very early age. Thus, surrounded by so much creativity, Michelle seemed destined to navigate toward the arts and ultimately obtained formal training in dance, creative writing, acting, and music theory.

A cum laude graduate of Marymount Manhattan College, Michelle wears many hats including recording artist, actress, songwriter, and most recently, Mommy. In addition to her already hectic schedule, she is also the co-host of a nationally syndicated weekly radio show called The Coast to Coast Hip Hop Count Down while simultaneously holding the position of Editor-in-Chief for a new e-zine for young women of color called Epitome. Needless to say, her vast experiences have helped cultivate her writing style, which is considered by many to be contemporary, urban, and witty with characters that are truly universal.

When her busy day is done, Michelle goes home to Baychester, New York where she resides with her daughter, Morgan.